BOOK OF LIFE:
Marlena

HEATHER O'BRIEN

Copyright © 2024 by Heather O'Brien

All rights reserved.

No part of this publication may be reproduced, stored or transmitted in any form or by any means, electronic, mechanical, photocopying, recording, scanning, or otherwise without written permission from the publisher. It is illegal to copy this book, post it to a website, or distribute it by any other means without permission.

This novel is entirely a work of fiction. The names, characters and incidents portrayed in it are the work of the author's imagination. Any resemblance to actual persons, living or dead, events or localities is entirely coincidental.

First edition

Cover art by GetCovers.com

For George, Simon, & Gumbee

Author's Note

Book of Life: Marlena includes adult content that will not be suitable for some readers. I've included a list of these elements at the end of the book (marked "Content Warning"). If you have concerns, please check it out so you can decide whether to continue reading.

"The past held many doors that should have been locked, and now it was too late to close any of them."
    Aaron Callahan

Table of Contents

1………   3
2………   6
3………   12
4………   19
5………   25
6………   32
7………   38
8………   46
9………   53
10………   60
11………   66
12………   75
13………   84
14………   92
15………   99
16………   107
17………   117
18………   128
19………   137
20………   146
21………   152
22………   160
23………   169
24………   177
25………   185
26………   195
27………   201
28………   206
29………   216
30………   226
31………   233

32	241
33	251
34	257
35	266
36	277
37	286
38	294
39	306
40	316
41	327
42	336
43	344
44	352
Book of Life: The Series	359
Author Profile	361
Acknowledgments	359
Content Warning	360

1

Philadelphia: July 9, 1985

The mechanic's shop was a dim cave. Flickering lights cast eerie shadows on the grease-stained concrete floor. The air reeked of motor oil, gasoline, and sweat; the noxious mix clung to every surface. Old car parts littered the space, a graveyard of rusting metal and twisted wires.

Big Mike, a towering giant, stood in the shop's open center. His oil-splattered shirt molded to his rippling muscles, and a single bulb faintly lit his stern face. His six gang members flanked him. Their faces were hard and etched; their eyes glinted with malice. They had seen too much and done much worse. They stood with crossed arms, radiating menace.

At the back of the shop, a man shrank against a rusting sedan. His eyes were wide with fear, and he raised his hands in a futile defense. Big Mike's gang closed in around him, their voices as low and threatening as the ominous rumble of a storm. A muscular man with a snake tattoo etched along his neck stepped forward, brandishing a heavy wrench.

"Please," the cornered man begged, his voice fragile glass in a hailstorm. "I wasn't serious, Mike, I swear. It's stupid talk, something I thought you might be into." His words dripped with desperation, trying to calm the giant before him.

Big Mike took a slow, deliberate step forward to cast a long shadow. His massive frame was a dark specter, hovering over the frightened man. "Bullshit," he thundered, his voice a caged beast straining to break free. "You think you can do that shit and walk away from it?" His anger was a palpable force, a living entity that filled the room with intensity. "We've got rules around here, Scott… standards."

Outside, the night was a tranquil blanket, the city lights a distant glow on the horizon. Only the occasional passing car and chirping crickets broke the silence. Their gentle harmony clashed with the brewing turmoil in the garage. Big Mike's wife approached the shop, her steps quickening each second as she worried about her husband's absence. She pushed the heavy metal door open and stepped through, her heart skipping as she took in the scene before her.

Her dark eyes widened at the sight of her husband, towering and menacing, his face contorted in a grotesque mask of anger. She looked around the circle of gang members, their faces cold and unfeeling, like icicles that would never thaw. And then she caught sight of the man, cowering in terror, his gaze fixed on the abyss of death that loomed before him.

"Mike!" she called out, her voice trembling and nervous. "What's going on?" Her question hung in the air, a gauntlet thrown down into the darkness that closed in from all sides.

Time froze in the room; the gang members paused; they were stone statues, though the tension darting between them was electric. Marlena's eyes darted around, taking in the scene, the fear, and the impending violence that hung like a sword of Damocles.

The cornered man leaped forward, using the distraction to try for freedom. The man with the tattoo lunged forward to grab him, slamming him to the ground with brutal force. Big Mike spun and leaped forward. His massive fist flew at the prone figure, making a sickening sound against his flesh.

Marlena choked back a cry, her hands flying to her mouth as if to stifle a scream. She stared at the man on the floor, a dark puddle of blood spreading around him like a macabre halo. Her dark eyes looked as if she knew that this moment would forever change the trajectory of their lives.

Big Mike's face was a mask of fury and regret as he turned back to his wife, his eyes blazing with anger and guilt. "Get out of here, Marlena. You don't need to see this." His voice was a command, a pronouncement that sealed the downed man's fate.

But it was too late. She had already seen everything. The darkness around Big Mike had now touched her. It left a stain that would never wash away, a scar that would forever mar their lives.

2

Aaron did not know how it worked. Months ago, his mother, Marlena, mentioned a company that could download someone's memories and turn them into a book. She'd talked about it: a random commercial she'd seen during one of her evening shows… nothing special. The company compiled all this data and delivered a book to a designated person after the individual passed away. The bulky rectangular package in his hand proved she had gone through with it. Its thick wrapper was brown paper, with his address in the center. The left corner had an embossed stamp: "Legacy Manuscripts."

He tossed it onto the couch with the rest of the mail: bills, a handwritten card, and some papers. The pile tumbled across the worn cushions, but he did not spare a glance at it. Aaron sighed and shrugged off his coat and gloves, setting them aside. His stomach grumbled, and his mind screamed for whiskey. The mail—and whatever memories his mother had left behind—could wait.

In the kitchen, a crusty plate sat on the counter, egg dried at the edges. A greasy frying pan tipped sideways; its contents were a lone shriveled strip of bacon. Aaron's jaw clenched. "Which one of you assholes can't wash a dish after breakfast?"

"Dude, I cook, you clean. That's the deal," Alex called from the table, stretching as he winked at Aaron. "Dishes aren't my thing—Jared can handle them."

"Handle what?" Jared's voice came from the other room. "Nah,

Alex, you eat; you clean. Stop passing the buck."

"See, Aaron? We need a woman around here." Alex laughed, winking at him again.

Aaron rubbed his temples, tired of their bickering. He'd known these two forever, but sometimes the banter wore thin. "I don't care who does it, but it won't be me. Not today. I've got enough on my mind."

"Aye, chief, say no more," Alex mock-saluted, rising to his feet. "I'll get it done."

Aaron collapsed into a chair at the kitchen table, staring out the window into the yard. The dull throb of a migraine lurked behind his eyes, and his thoughts refused to settle. A new work project was starting this week. He had the broken fence that needed fixing—and that damned package: the book of memories.

He pressed his palms against his eyes, frustration bubbling up. *Why couldn't she tell me whatever she wanted me to know?*

The thought echoed. She might have if she'd had more time. His mother hadn't been sick long enough for any of it to make sense. It started with a cough and tightness in her chest. It was a cold or flu; she assured the family. Then came the hospital, pneumonia, and a tumor they found far too late. Three weeks later, she was gone, leaving him with unfinished business and unspoken words.

Aaron swallowed hard, blinking back the sting of hot tears that threatened to spill over. *Why didn't I cry back then?* He had sat by her bedside, unable to feel anything but a gnawing emptiness. The arguments over politics, the anger: none of it mattered when she slipped away. Now the tears came too often, for everything and nothing. The anger remained directionless.

The kitchen was silent now. Alex had finished the dishes and slipped out without a word. A single glass of whiskey sat by Aaron, the ice melting with the moments. He reached for it, grateful for the quiet. He downed half the glass in a swallow as he wandered into the living room.

The pile of mail drew his attention. He sat on the couch, moving the package from Legacy Manuscripts to the coffee table. Later. First, he would check the rest of the mail. The bills went into one pile: water, gas, electric, and car insurance. He paid these bills online, but never remembered to turn on electronic delivery. This stack would go into the shredder before it landed in the recycling bin. He sifted through the sales fliers: a new mattress company opening downtown and a car dealership with "rock-bottom prices" joined the stack bound for recycling.

He picked up the card next: a lacy floral pattern edged the corners of the envelope next to his hand-written name and address. It smelled faintly of roses. *Who is this from?* He didn't have many friends outside of work. He rarely dated, and never for any length of time. *Maybe a thank you note from a satisfied homeowner—but that would come to work, right?* He tore the side of the envelope off, not sure what to expect from the contents.

The card inside was delicate, with a basket of embossed flowers on its face. He flipped it open, realizing he was anxiously holding his breath. The printed text read: "Reminder that you are due for your annual check-up at Boyertown Dental. Call today to make your appointment. We can't wait to make your smile bright!"

Exasperated, he rolled his eyes and tossed the card into the recycle pile before downing the rest of his whiskey. He looked at the brown paper package, then decided it wasn't time yet. Gathering the mail, he set his glass on the sideboard before dropping the bills into the shredder in his office and the fliers directly into the recycle bin.

He flipped on the television in the office, settling into his leather armchair to flip channels. Nothing would hold his focus though—the package in the living room dominated his mind. "Goddamnit, Mom," he muttered, echoing his earlier thoughts. "Why didn't you tell me?"

He sighed, walking with heavy feet back to the living room. The urge to leave the package unopened pulled at him, but he couldn't avoid it forever. He sat on the edge of the couch, lifting the package into his lap. His finger traced the edge of the brown paper and his heart hammered in his chest. Steeling himself, he tore the paper away, revealing a thick leather-bound book. The cover was simple, embossed in gold with three words: *Memories of Marlena*.

His hands trembled as he opened the cover. The first page held a handwritten note in his mother's familiar script.

> My dearest Aaron,
>   If you're reading this, I'm no longer here. There's so much I wanted to tell you, but

time was not on our side. I won't lie—creating this book was scary for me, but you need to know who I was, from beginning to end. I hope these memories will bring you some peace.

With all my love,
Mom

Aaron's chest felt constricted. The promise of untold stories, the secrets she'd kept, all seemed to pour from the book. He flipped through the pages, knowing what he would look for first.

He wanted to understand. His father's past, Big Mike's time in prison—he had looked it up once and found out the man went away for second-degree murder. *But who did he kill? Why did we leave Philadelphia so fast, never to return? Why wouldn't Mom ever talk about it?*

With trembling hands, Aaron turned the page. He was ready to confront his past. This was his only chance to unravel the mysteries that haunted him.

July 10, 1985: Marlena

Something was off about Mike, I could tell. He'd been on edge for days, speaking to me in one-word answers, and waving off my questions with nonsense about a "business meeting." Another one of his late-night meetings at the shop. I'm not dumb; I know what goes on there. But most nights, he'd come home before midnight. When it got late, I was worried.

I put the boys to bed and left my sister with them while I checked on him. He would be in a decent mood when the meeting finished; I thought so, anyway. We would walk home together like old times, with his arm around my waist. Looking back, I don't know how I was so naïve. What was I thinking?

I pushed open that heavy door, and the moment I stepped inside… I felt it. This was not a regular meeting… this was something worse.

The entire crew stood there—Turbo Sal, Hammer, Slick Leo, Beans, even the Kosta kid, and Rudy. Mike—my Mike—stood there, his face set in anger. He did not soften when he saw me.

The man in the suit—the skinny guy I'd noticed earlier near the butcher shop—shook like a leaf, looking at me like I would save him. Before I registered what was happening, he made a run for it. Slick got to him first and slammed him to the ground, and that's when Mike… snapped. The wrench arced through the air, over and over. The sound of his skull cracking against the concrete—I'll never forget it. Blood, thick and dark, pooled around the back tire.

Mike looked at me, eyes cold, and said one word: "Go."

I ran.

Aaron stared at the book in his lap. His mother's neat, looping handwriting stared back at him, recounting the night Big Mike killed a man. The truth he had wanted for years now lay bare before him, but instead of clarity, a storm of emotions crashed over him.

He dragged a hand through his hair, gripping it tight, trying to balance the chaos in his mind. The man he feared and resented as a child was a murderer—reading the first-hand account felt different from reading it in a court file. The nightmare was real, and his brain struggled to absorb the brutal facts.

Anger flared hot and fast. He slammed the book shut; the pages flapping closed like a final, cruel punctuation. All those years, his mother refused to speak about that night, leaving him to fill in the gaps with wild guesses. None of them came close to the raw, violent truth. He ground his teeth as frustration swelled inside him. The silence, the secrets—it was all a betrayal.

But beneath the anger was a hollowness: a numb, sinking emptiness. The truth hit like a truck, leaving him breathless. He rubbed his eyes, trying to blink away the disbelief. More questions crowded his mind, relentless and tormenting. *Why did my father do it? What pushed him over the edge? Who was that man Mike killed? And why did Mom keep it hidden for so long, burying the truth under layers of silence?*

The book slipped from his hands, thudding to the floor. He leaned back, staring at the ceiling, his breath shallow. The room spun around him. His heart was a chipped stone lodged in his chest; his mind a tangled mess of confusion and pain. The answers he craved now were a loose piece of yarn unraveling.

His gaze drifted to the mantel, landing on a photo of his mother holding him as a baby. He picked it up, tracing its worn edges with his thumb. The memory of her warmth and love clashed with the cold, hard truth he had read in her book. He drowned in the conflicting emotions, unsure how to process the emotions that raged inside him.

With a shaky hand, he placed the photo back. The intensity was too much, and he felt paralyzed. The idea of confronting the past and piecing together the fragments of his family's history was overwhelming. Not to mention making peace with whatever he uncovered. *I need a drink.*

3

Aaron Michael Callahan was born on the north side of Philadelphia in the fading light of a hot summer day in mid-June 1982. It was a hard-pressed neighborhood where generations of families knew the weight of hardship and the resilience it demanded. By day, men labored tirelessly to support their families, and by night, they packed the bars, drinking away their worries. Factory workers, mechanics, and construction workers of every sort gathered at The Red Baron after dark. All were ready to drown their sorrows and, often, any surplus pay they might have earned. At home, their wives pulled double duty, juggling jobs in factories, as servers, retail clerks, or hotel maids. After long shifts, they came home to cook, clean, and manage their households, all while keeping an occasionally watchful eye on their children.

The homes in North Philadelphia were typically rowhomes, sharing walls with neighboring properties and creating a continuous street front. Their facades were reddish brick, and the yards were small, sometimes barely more than a stoop. Aaron's home featured a wrought-iron railing along its tiny porch and front steps. The streets were lively, with neighbors chatting and sometimes shouting at one another throughout the day and night. Children rode bicycles, played kick the can, or roamed in small groups, looking for empty lots to explore or stray cats to chase.

The local market sat on the corner, offering basic groceries and cigarettes to weary adults and shrewd teenagers alike. A fish market sat half a block further, its glass-front freezers packed with cod, flounder, haddock, and whiting, their lifeless eyes still lolling as they waited to be chosen for tonight's dinner by tired wives. The pungent smell from the open front door wafted across the entire block, drawing enterprising cats to line up by the overflowing trash cans in the side alley. Bakker Butchers was a block to the northwest, with chickens hanging by their feet in the front window and the rhythmic clang of Mr. Bakker's giant knife on the butcher block counter ringing through the open door.

The Red Baron bar, owned and operated by Rudy Muller, had proudly stood on its alcohol-soaked foundation since before Prohibition came and, gratefully, went in 1933. It was one year before Rudy, known as The Baron to those who mattered, was born. The Red Baron was a dimly lit, no-frills establishment. Its front door, made of heavy wood with a glass panel, creaked on its hinges as patrons entered. The interior was a patchwork of worn wooden booths and a long, scarred bar lined with mismatched stools that had seen better days. The wall decorations were a mix of vintage advertisements, old photographs of local heroes, and faded memorabilia from a bygone era.

The bar, polished to a dull sheen from years of use, contained a modest selection of beers and well-worn liquor bottles. Above it, dusty glasses scattered across the shelf in a cluttered array. A jukebox in one corner offered popular tunes from the era.

The air inside was thick with the mingling aromas of spilled beer, cigarette smoke, and the faint scent of cheap, greasy food from the bar's small kitchen. A lone pool table in the back corner was a popular draw, often surrounded by men taking a break from their daily grind. The sound of clinking glasses, low conversation, the occasional burst of laughter, and the less occasional scuffle filled the room. It created a warm, albeit smoky, atmosphere where the troubles of the outside world seemed momentarily forgotten.

The Baron reigned as king within these walls, and his presence was commanding. His booming voice and laugh startled the unprepared. He knew everyone in the neighborhood. If you needed a job done discreetly, he was the man to arrange the details with an unerring blend of charm and authority.

Just around the corner from Bakker Butchers stood Big Mike's Auto Shop, owned by Aaron's father, Big Mike Callahan. The shop was a North Philadelphia landmark, a rough-hewn symbol of working-class resilience. The weather-beaten brick building bore a faded sign, the bold letters chipped but still defiant above the entrance.

Inside, the air wept with motor oil, gasoline, and grease. Tools and auto parts littered the floor, each coated in a stubborn layer of grime. Worn hydraulic lifts occupied one corner, hoisting vehicles in various states of disrepair. The rhythmic clatter of tools and hum of machinery filled the space with a mechanical rhythm. Grease-stained mechanics moved with purpose, their hands deftly twisting and turning through engines and exhaust systems like second nature.

Big Mike's wasn't only a repair shop—it was a hub for the community's working class, a place to fix cars, share stories, and escape the grind for a few moments. It was also where Rudy Muller often stopped by to arrange the finer details of his under-the-table dealings.

The neighborhood featured many abandoned lots, where tall grasses swayed among shards of broken bottles, cigarette butts, and the occasional wildflower that pushed through the cracks. These resilient blooms nodded in the tangy breeze, carrying the gritty scent of the inner city. Wandering food carts, selling hot dogs and pretzels, added to the lively, makeshift vibe, their clattering wheels and sizzling grills a constant presence.

In the early 1980s, politics barely grazed the lives of North Philly's residents. The Democratic machine dominated the area; its grip on local politics strengthening through patronage and party loyalty. Political leaders used their clout to dole out jobs, contracts, and favors, cementing their control. Corruption—bribery, kickbacks, backroom deals—was rampant, breeding deep distrust and cynicism among the people.

For the neighborhood's blue-collar workers, labor unions were their strongest advocates, deeply entwined with local political campaigns and movements. Conversations about urban renewal and gentrification often sparked resentment, with residents suspicious of outsiders trying to "improve" their turf. They preferred to stay in their corner of the city, resisting changes that might threaten their way of life. North Philly's politics in the early 1980s was a volatile mix of entrenched machine power, grassroots community activism, and a simmering struggle over the future of their streets.

Aaron had been unaware of the complexities of life when he was young, catching only bits of his parent's whispered conversations and loud arguments. But he remembered vividly the corner by his front stoop, where a tiny yard and thin trees fought to grow through cracks in the concrete—small, stubborn signs of life amid the urban decay. He recalled the woman in the house across the street who owned two Capuchin monkeys. The beasts would hurl rocks at passing cars and pedestrians from her window. And the boy with the red wagon, piled high with buttery, salted pretzels, shouting, "Fresh pretzels, get 'em while they're hot!" as he wove through the streets.

Closing his eyes now, the images of his boyhood home came back in flashes, hazy but distinct. He remembered tumbling down the steep stairs and splitting his chin open, his mother rushing him to the doctor's office in a taxicab. The ride was thrilling, full of unfamiliar sights, but the excitement vanished when the doctor stitched the gash. The tiny scar stayed with him, a small piece of North Philly etched into his skin forever.

He shared the upstairs bedroom with his baby brother, Sean Patrick. Everyone called the baby Patty, though, never Sean. A worn blue quilt covered his twin bed, its surface dotted with old stains. A thin pillow in a Chicago Bulls case rested on it—his favorite team, thanks to cousin Jack, who had declared them the best. Aaron, eager to follow, agreed without question. Beside his bed stood a rickety bookshelf, home to his most cherished possessions: Hot Wheels cars, a firetruck with a working siren, books handed down from cousins, and his prized Grand Prix pajamas.

Patty's crib sat by the window, lined with a blue bumper pad, stuffed animals, and scattered cloth diapers. Overhead, a colorful mobile spun—red puppy, blue bunny, yellow sheep, white horse—twirling to Brahms' Lullaby. Aaron watched it turn as he fell asleep at night, though he would never admit it. His father had scolded him for playing with Patty's stuffed bunny once, and he wasn't keen on earning another spanking.

A heavy wooden dresser stood on the far wall, its drawers too stubborn for Aaron to manage. He despised it, a loathing that started in the winter of 1984 when he tried to climb it to reach his pajamas. The dresser toppled forward, pinning him to the floor. The solid piece of furniture crushed the air from his lungs, and he thought for a moment he might die there. His father had stood over him, a cold smirk on his angular face. It wasn't until his mother burst in, screaming at Big Mike to lift the dresser, that Aaron could take a breath. After that day, she let him keep his pajamas on the bookshelf by his bed. The memory of that incident, like the scar on his chin, would never leave him.

Aaron pulled himself from the memory and glanced at the book on the floor. He picked it up and flipped through the pages, skipping around until he found the entry he was looking for.

February 17, 1984: Marlena

I was standing at the sink, scrubbing the last dish, wondering if I'd gone overboard with the salt in the chicken pot pie. The laundry pile waited to be folded, and I was mentally going through my chore list when I heard Aaron's cry. It wasn't his usual fuss—it was sharp and cut through my thoughts. I turned off the water and listened, straining to hear up the stairs. "Did Big Mike go up after him?" I wondered, already feeling the tension creeping up my spine.

Then I heard that low, mean laugh echoing from the boys' room. My heart dropped. I knew that laugh—it meant someone was being humiliated. It always came before something ugly.

I flew up the stairs, and there he was—my Aaron, my baby— pinned under that heavy dresser, his face flushed and purple, struggling to breathe. "Mike! Get him up! Help him!" I screamed, panic rushing through me. Big Mike stood over him, giving me this hard, sharp look before he finally bent down and lifted the dresser like it was nothing. "Maybe if he wasn't so damn stupid! This wouldn't have happened! Did you even think about that before you started nagging me?" He slurred, the stench of beer still fresh from dinner.

He stomped out of the room, boots thudding down the stairs, leaving me with a sobbing Aaron. I gathered him into my lap, calming his tears, and rocking him like I did when he was smaller. He was shaking, nearly inconsolable, and it tore at me, but there was no time. I still had to feed the baby, finish the dishes, and fold the laundry. If Big Mike came home to a mess, there would be hell to pay.

Aaron will be fine. He's tough. He'll be okay. But my heart ached knowing that I couldn't stop everything to protect him.

The memory of being pinned under the dresser, his small chest straining for air, always clung to Aaron on sleepless nights. Reading the words on the page now brought it all roaring back. His father's distant laughter cut through the silence with cruel precision. He could almost hear his mother's frantic voice, her footsteps pounding up the stairs, and feel her panic as she rushed to save him. His hands trembled as he turned the page, each word pulling the knot in his chest tighter. What he had seen as a painful but singular memory of childhood now came alive with layers of terror, filtered through his mother's eyes.

It hit him—his father was drunk that night. This wasn't a one-off; it was who the man was. Rage bubbled inside him. He had not grasped the full depth of what his family endured. His mother, balancing her chores, shielding her children, navigating his father's fury—it all crashed down on him, the burden she had carried in silence.

He closed the book with a sharp breath; truth settling in his gut like ice. The same rage that filled their home, that scarred him and his mother, was the same fury that pushed Big Mike to murder. The brutality of it all, the undeniable link between past and present, overwhelmed him.

Aaron stood by the window, his mind flashing between the sunlit days of his childhood and the ugly truths they concealed. He never understood the fractures forming behind the scenes, or the arguments his mother tried to hide. The image of his father committing murder replayed in his head, gnawing at him with questions. *Why did she stay silent? Why did Mike choose violence, leaving behind nothing but scars and pain?*

Anger sparked within his gut—anger at his father for the damage, his mother for shielding him from the truth, and himself for still wanting to understand and forgive. The answers were hollow now, crushed under the brutal reality. The search for closure was only beginning.

4

On the Fourth of July in 1985, the rowhomes of North Philadelphia gleamed under the bright summer sun. Their red brick facades hung with fluttering American flags and patriotic bunting. The entire neighborhood came together to transform their block into a festive celebration of Independence Day: the air buzzed with excitement and the promise of fireworks later that evening.

The street, now closed to traffic, was an ocean of red, white, and blue. Long tables lined with checkered red and white tablecloths stretched the length of the block, heaped with an abundance of homemade dishes. Bowls of coleslaw, trays of barbecued ribs, platters of fried chicken, and plates of deviled eggs competed for space with baskets of corn on the cob and baked apple pies. Succulent grilled meats mingled with the sweetness of summer fruits, creating an irresistible aroma that wafted through the air.

Neighbors exchanged smiles and laughter, their voices carrying above the cheerful din. Mrs. Ricci, her silver hair shining in the sunlight, presided over a massive pot of her famous meatballs, dishing them out to eager partygoers. Johnny "Hammer" O'Connor, one of Big Mike's closest friends, flipped burgers and hot dogs at the large charcoal grill. The sizzle and pop of the grill punctuated his jovial banter with friends.

A boombox on a stoop sang classic rock anthems that had everyone tapping their feet and swaying to the beat. The familiar strains of Springsteen's "Glory Days" blared through the speakers, and neighbors joined in, their voices merging in a spirited chorus that echoed off the rowhomes.

Children darted through the crowd, faces painted with stars and stripes, clutching sparklers and waving miniature flags. Aaron Callahan, now three years old, clasped his mother Marlena's hand, his eyes wide with wonder at the colorful spectacle around him. Marlena, a festive ribbon pinned in her short dark hair, chatted with neighbors, glancing to be sure Aaron and his younger brother, 22-month-old Patty, were close.

Big Mike Callahan stood on the periphery, his usual stern demeanor softened by the day's festivities. He exchanged nods and brief conversations with familiar faces, his presence a stern influence amid the revelry. The neighborhood knew his menacing side well— but today he was a father.

As the sun set, casting a warm glow over the scene, strings of fairy lights hung between the rowhomes flickered to life, adding a magical touch to the gathering. The smell of fresh cannoli and funnel cakes floated through the air, drawing everyone to the dessert tables for a sweet treat to cap off their meals.

The highlight of the evening was the much-anticipated fireworks display. As darkness fell, the crowd gathered in anticipation, their faces lit by the glow of sparklers and lanterns. The first firework shot into the sky with a loud bang, exploding in a shower of red, white, and blue sparks that drew gasps of delight from the onlookers. Aaron and Patty, sitting on a blanket with their mother, watched the bursts of color in awe.

The Fourth of July block party was not only a celebration of independence; it was a testament to the close-knit people of North Philadelphia. Neighbors stood shoulder to shoulder, united in their pride and joy, creating memories to cherish for years. Laughter, love, and patriotism: a perfect snapshot of Americana.

July 4, 1985: Marlena

The day was beautiful—sunny and warm. The block smelled of grilled meats and magnesium. Laughter echoed as children chased each other with sparklers, their giggles mingling with the crackle of fireworks in the distance. Even Big Mike seemed content, which is a rarity these days. He gave me that old look—the little grin that crinkled his eyes at the corners—like he always used to. I hadn't seen that look in so long, and for a moment, I dared to hope for a perfect night.

Alas, he ended up at The Red Baron with Hammer and Slick. By the time he stumbled home, that old look was gone, replaced by the all-too-familiar sight of him drunk, reeking of booze and cocaine. He knows I never want him to come home like this.

At least the boys were already in bed when he came crashing through the front door. Aaron and Patty had a wonderful day—they deserve more days like today. Patty fell asleep in my arms, his chubby little hand resting on my chest, while Aaron's head rested on my knee. I watched Turbo Sal swing sparklers around, his laughter echoing through the air as he chased after the girls. It was a fine day. I wished it could have lasted.

When Mike came home tonight, we argued, as we always do. No matter how hard I try to keep my mouth shut, my face always betrays my feelings; it is unavoidable. If Mike wanted to fight, he found something to fight about. Tonight, it was the food at the barbecue, of all things.

He glared at me, frustration etched across his face. "You should've made more potato salad, Marlena! There wasn't enough for me to have seconds!"

I swallowed, trying to keep my voice quiet and neutral, before reminding him. "I made two enormous bowls, Mike. But with the whole neighborhood eating, it's no wonder there wasn't enough left for seconds."

His stare made my heart sink—I wished I could shrink into the floorboards.

"So there would not be enough, huh? You knew you didn't make enough and didn't make enough on purpose! I guess I'm an idiot to think that I should be able to have seconds of the food my wife made.

Is that it? Am I an idiot? Is that what you're saying here, wife?" His voice dripped with venom, and I could feel the tension crackling between us.

I tried to keep my voice even, but it trembled anyway. "No, I didn't say that, Mike. It's... I thought..."

"Thought what?" he interrupted, his voice rising. "That you could serve me scraps and I'd be grateful? Do you think I'm some charity case? You think I won't notice when you shortchange me?"

I held my breath, fearing where this was heading. I needed to be careful: I could see the rage bubbling beneath the surface.

"Please..."

"Please what?" he shouted, stepping closer, his breath hot against my face. "You think you can stand there and make excuses? Talk your way out of this?"

I took a step back, but he was faster. He grabbed my wrist, squeezing hard enough to make me wince. "You will not deflect this, Marlena. You will answer me."

Tears threatened to spill from my eyes as I fought to keep my composure. "I'm sorry, Mike. Don't be upset, please. I wanted everyone to have a good time."

He released my wrist as if realizing what he was doing. The fire in his eyes flickered, replaced by a momentary look of confusion. But the damage was done, and I could see the shadows of his anger still lurking below the surface.

"Whatever," he mumbled, turning away from me. "You always do this, don't you? Make excuses. Play the victim." He flopped onto the couch, the old springs creaking under his weight. I could see the tension in his shoulders, a silent battle between his anger and the remnants of that earlier fleeting happiness.

I pushed down the fear in my belly. "Let's not fight, Mike. I want things to be okay between us."

"Yeah, well, you've got a funny way of showing it," he muttered, eyes closed, face turned away.

I moved to the kitchen, trying to breathe and calm myself. I wanted to scream, to lash out, but I knew it wouldn't change anything. Instead, I busied myself with washing the few dishes left in the sink, my mind racing. I thought of the boys—their joy today—and how easily it unraveled in moments like these.

The thought of Mike and his anger loomed over me like a dark cloud. I wished I could keep my family safe from it. As I finished the dishes, he called, "You think I'm an idiot?"

I took a deep breath, steeling myself for what came next. "No, Mike. I don't think you're an idiot."

"Then what do you think?"

"I think you need to cool off."

His laugh was harsh. "You think you can tell me to cool off? You don't get to make that call, Marlena. Not anymore."

A shiver ran down my spine, and I gripped the edge of the sink, feeling its coldness seep into me. I had to keep it together for the boys.

"Leave me alone," I whispered, but my voice lacked strength.

Aaron's eyes scanned the page, his mind drifting to the Fourth of July block party when he was three. He could picture the scorching sun and hear the distant crackle of fireworks, even though the memory was hazy. It seemed like a day filled with joy for everyone, but what stuck in his mind was his mother's description of his father's simmering anger. Big Mike had raged over something as trivial as potato salad, furious that Marlena hadn't made enough. That fury hung over the day like it had over so much of Aaron's childhood.

His phone buzzed, pulling him from the memory. *Lucas.*

"Hey, man," Aaron said, answering.

Lucas was his easygoing brother: six years younger than Aaron, and the second of three children from his mother's second marriage. He was married now, with two kids, balancing his life between work and family. Aaron and Lucas were close, and he felt guilt for keeping Lucas in the dark about everything he'd been reading. He wasn't ready to share it yet, though.

"Checking in," Lucas said. "How's your week going?"

Aaron leaned back, pushing the book aside. "It's been... alright. I'm thinking about some stuff. My biological father: Big Mike."

Lucas's tone shifted. "Man, that guy was bad news, wasn't he?"

Aaron stared at the book. "Yeah, he was."

"Be careful," Lucas warned, his tone gentle. "Don't go too far down that rabbit hole. The past can mess with your head."

Aaron nodded, even though Lucas couldn't see him. "How's Renee and the kids?"

"Renee's always busy. The kids are great. They keep us hopping, that's for sure!"

Aaron smiled, the thought of his niece and nephew pulling him back to the present. "Sounds like you've got your hands full."

"Always," Lucas laughed. There was a pause before he added, "You sure you're okay?"

Aaron hesitated. "Yeah, I'm good. Just... thinking."

"Alright. Don't let it get to you, okay? No need to dig up old ghosts."

"I hear you." Aaron kept his voice light, though his thoughts lingered on Big Mike. He wasn't ready to let those ghosts go yet.

He glanced at the clock. 1:42 a.m. "It's late for you, bud. Don't you have work tomorrow?"

"Yeah, I do," Lucas said with a laugh, "but I woke up feeling like I needed to check in on you. Besides, you're awake too, so you can't say much."

Aaron chuckled. "Fair enough. I need to sleep. I've got a new project starting. Broke ground yesterday on a new building at the county park."

They chatted for a few more minutes before they called it a night. "Alright, man, get some sleep," Aaron said.

"You too," Lucas replied. "Don't stay up too late with those thoughts."

After they hung up, Aaron grabbed the book and headed upstairs. He flipped through the pages, skimming sections he had already read, but his eyes grew heavier with each turn. The words blurred together as exhaustion finally won out. The book slipped from his hands, falling to the floor as Aaron drifted into a fitful sleep, the echoes of old memories dwelling beneath the surface.

5

Aaron's alarm rang for a third time, dragging him from the half-remembered fragments of a restless sleep. He shuffled out of bed. He was groggy but driven by the need to start the day. Sitting at the kitchen table with a strong cup of coffee, his mind buzzed with mixed emotions.

Determined not to let the memories in his mother's book cloud his focus, Aaron prepared for work. He would have liked to stay home but pushed himself to go to the work site. *The owner of Callahan Construction Company has to show up on time. How can I expect the crew to, if I don't?* He dressed, shifting gears to the demands of the construction site. His routine was methodical, his movements efficient—he couldn't afford to let his thoughts drift during the day's tasks.

At the construction site, the physical demands of the job grounded him. He threw himself into overseeing the crew, measuring, and coordinating tasks with practiced efficiency. The clamor of machinery and the heat of the day gave a welcome distraction from his inner turmoil. Between the noise and the tasks, snippets of his mother's words lingered at the back of his mind.

Lunch was a brief respite. Aaron sat on the edge of the site, eating his sandwich, while his mind wandered. The contrast between his mother's depiction of that idyllic day in July and the reality of his father's apparent turmoil was stark. He pondered, as he felt sure his mother had, how things might have been different if the happiness of that day had endured.

The afternoon dragged on; the heat intensifying and his focus wavering. He found himself lost in thought: the quiet moments between tasks becoming opportunities for his mind to wander back to the book. He wrestled with the bittersweet emotions it stirred.

Aaron ended the workday feeling drained. He packed up his tools, said a quick goodbye to his crew, and headed home. The drive home was fast, and the house was quiet. Alex and Jared were out, offering him a rare moment of solitude.

He sank into the living room couch, the day's reflections pressing on him. Memories of the block party, the fleeting joy of his childhood, and the tangled threads of his family life all swirled together. He knew he needed to focus on the present and not get too swept up in reliving the past. The book made that very difficult, though.

Aaron closed his eyes and pictured his mother the last time he'd seen her. Her face was slack in death, touched up the way funeral homes do. Her hands folded over her heart. She wore a dark blue dress purchased for a wedding years ago. It felt strange, a harsh contrast to her usual t-shirt and jeans—one more reminder of how much she had changed, how far from the woman he had known.

The dress, with its simple lines and soft fabric, complemented her complexion, but it couldn't mask the stillness that surrounded her. At that moment, he felt an overwhelming mix of sorrow and nostalgia, a longing for the sound of her laughter. He remembered the way she had always encouraged him to embrace life, to face challenges head-on, and her sharp advice that he did not always want to take.

Standing before her then, he grappled with the finality of it all. He wished for one more moment to feel the comfort of her presence: to hear her voice and see her smile. Instead, he had only memories, each one more precious than the last, and the lingering ache of loss that seemed to seep into every corner of his heart.

Marlena and Aaron had a close but rocky relationship. Their political differences led to heated, frustrating arguments. Before she was sick, they fought often, with raised voices and stubborn tempers, both refusing to back down.

In the end, Aaron and his mother made peace. He sat at her bedside for days. Their arguments gave way to mutual appreciation. His other siblings gathered, too. They shared stories, laughter, and tears. Now Aaron replayed those precious days in his mind. He longed to hold on to the sense of peace they had found. It had been a rare opportunity to express the love that always existed beneath the surface, even during their most heated disagreements.

May 7, 2015: Marlena

I can feel the end creeping closer. The pain never lets up. Lying here, surrounded by the people I love most, I'm overwhelmed with gratitude—and regret. My children—Aaron, Patty, Nico, Lucas, and Elise—are here. I look at their faces, marked by worry and sorrow, and I'm both comforted and haunted. These moments are precious, but they remind me of all the things left undone, the words I never said.

Aaron sits by my side, holding my hand. I see the worry in his eyes. He's always been my strong and independent rock, but I know he's struggling with losing me. I worry about how he'll cope without me, how he'll navigate life. He's been through so much. I never forgave Rob for how he treated him all these years. Aaron deserved better than being labeled "Big Mike's son." I hope he finds peace.

Patty stands by the window, staring out but not seeing anything. He's always tried hard to win Rob's approval, always looking for something that has never been there. My heart breaks for him—always striving, always falling short in Rob's eyes. I hope he finds his happiness and steps out of that shadow.

Then there's Nico. My sweet, brave Nicolaus. He's sitting, thinking. His relationship with Rob has been strained since he came out, and it hurts me. I wish Rob could see how wonderful he is, beyond his narrow views. Nico has always been true to himself. I'm so proud of him. I hope he knows that.

Lucas, my unshakable one, stands beside Nico. He's grown into such a fine man. But I worry about him too—how he and Rob will manage without me. Lucas is always trying to hold everything together. I hope he doesn't lose himself.

Elise, my princess, hovers at the foot of the bed. Her eyes look wide and scared. Rob's always doted on her. She's his favorite. But now, I see the fear and uncertainty. She's been through a lot. Yet, she's so full of life. I hope she remembers the love and laughter and finds strength in those memories.

I can't help but think of Harrison and Lydia. My oldest kids. I lost so much time with them, and never made peace with either of them, and that regret weighs on me. I loved them—I wish I could have been there for them.

And Robert—my husband for all these long years. He's supported us, but I've always known he's not a good man. His dealings, his favoritism—it's been hard. But he saved us from what we were before. I stayed with him, even though my heart was always with Mike. My first love, my greatest passion, and the man I feared most. I never stopped loving him, and that's a secret I'll take to my grave.

The fear of leaving my children behind grips me more than the illness. But I see their faces, and I know they're strong. They'll find their way.

My grandchildren—how I wish I had more time with them. Drew: so talented and dedicated to hockey. Julian and his boundless energy. John and Lily, Elise's little ones, are so full of light and promise. Samuel and Elisabeth, Lucas's pride and joy. I hope they remember me. And I think of Aaron's son, Oliver, the one we never got to hold. I never met Rose and Chloe, either. Lydia's girls. Strangers to me, yet a part of me. It's a loss I'll never get back.

I hope my grandchildren know their heritage and the strength of this family. I hope they carry the best of us forward. And I hope they always feel my love.

Aaron's chest ached as he read his mother's words, her expressions of love and regret resting on him like a stone tied to his heart. Her vivid descriptions of his siblings and himself, each etched with her deep understanding and concern, touched him to the core. She knew their weaknesses and strengths well; her fears and hopes for their futures reflected that.

Seeing his name, Aaron felt a rush of sorrow and pride. He remembered his mother as his rock, and she saw him the same way.

Her acknowledgment of his hardships, especially her unspoken resentment towards Robert's favoritism, felt like a bittersweet validation of his pain. Yet, her wish for him to find peace and strength stirred a determination in him to honor her hope.

But as he read on, confusion crept in; there were names he didn't recognize—Harrison, Lydia, Rose, Chloe. *Who were these people?* His mother's regret over losing time with Harrison and Lydia: her oldest kids? The mention of Rose and Chloe, and her sorrow over never meeting them, added another layer of mystery.

His mind raced with questions. *What happened between Mom and them? And why did she never talk about them?* The answers seemed forever out of reach, buried with her.

Harrison and Lydia. His older brother and sister—it felt weird to think about. What happened that his mother decided not to mention their names to anyone? He had always been the oldest child; he thought. He felt a sudden shudder of loss for these people he had never met. *I would have liked to have a big brother to look out for me.* His mouth formed a sad smile as he imagined it.

Her lingering feelings for Big Mike were another blow. Aaron had always sensed there was more to his mother, but this secret love painted a picture of a woman torn between duty and passion, a woman who had stayed committed to a man she didn't love. It explained so much about her loyalty and suffering, yet it also deepened his sadness for the life she might have wanted but never lived.

Her tender words about his son—and her other grandchildren—brought tears to his eyes. Love for them shone through every word. Her hopes and dreams for their future were a testament to her enduring spirit. He felt a pang of regret that she didn't have more time with them, but a fierce resolve to keep her memory alive for them.

As Aaron closed the book, he felt overwhelmed by sadness. The book revealed new layers of his mother's life and the family's hidden history. He knew he needed to piece together these fragments and carry her legacy onward.

His thoughts shifted to her funeral, only eight months ago. He remembered the quiet and the last goodbye. Marlena's funeral felt peaceful. The local funeral home in Harrisonburg, Virginia, filled the room with sunflowers, daisies, and lavender—flowers she had loved.

The Shenandoah Valley had been her home and favorite place for nineteen years, and she would rest here forever.

Family and close friends gathered to share stories and memories, focusing on celebrating Marlena's life. There were no religious ceremonies, as she had never been fond of them. Instead, the room buzzed with heartfelt conversations, laughter, and tears as people recounted her strength, humor, and love.

A table in the corner displayed photos of Marlena's life: her children, grandchildren, and cherished moments. Attendees passed around a memory book, jotting down their favorite memories of her.

After the service, the family met at the Blue Ridge Diner for a casual meal. The initial reunion radiated warmth; it shifted into a cool distance by the time the server took their orders. Elise and Tom arrived late, and Elise's dramatic grief seemed more like a performance. Tom looked overwhelmed by her display.

Patty and his son, Drew, sat next to Elise. Patty, who had always been close to Elise, did not like Tom, and the feeling was mutual. Their tension was clear in the way they regarded one another.

Nico and Andy sat far from Rob, speaking only to each other and their son. Rob's disapproval of Nico's sexuality had strained their relationship, and the distance between them was obvious. Lucas and Renee, the only warm presence at the table, chatted with everyone. Yet, Aaron noticed Elise's smirks at Renee and Renee's returned eye rolls.

Robert, Aaron's stepfather, sat to his left. Aaron wished he could be at the other end of the table. Rob's resentment toward Aaron, rooted in his resemblance to Big Mike, had always been plain. Aaron felt Rob had never forgiven him for the love his mother showed him.

Aaron scanned the room, noticing Patty: a blond, tanned version of himself. Patty had excused himself to the restroom multiple times and seemed distant. Elise, looking polished and stylish, maintained a composed appearance, as if she were handling her mother's loss with relative ease, in stark contrast to the dramatic show she had put on earlier. Nico's haggard, red-eyed look said he wasn't handling things nearly as well. Nico's husband, Andy, touched his cheek in concern; Aaron was the only witness to Rob's disapproving snort.

Lucas, Aaron's favorite sibling, chatted with pride about his children. Sam and Elisabeth were active in various activities, and

Lucas and Renee attended them all. Aaron admired Lucas's dedication and felt a pang of regret that his family couldn't be closer.

Patty wiped his nose as he returned from the restroom; Elise linked arms with him again. The question of Patty using drugs again crossed Aaron's mind—his brother struggled with cocaine addiction—but he focused on Nico, realizing how little he knew about Julian. With Marlena gone, Aaron feared he would see even less of Nico's family.

Rob sat across from Tom, looking lost and defeated. For a moment, Aaron almost felt sympathy for him. The man who had once been a figure of authority now seemed diminished. Rob's gaze frequently landed on Elise, who dominated the conversation.

Aaron asked Rob if he was okay. His stepfather grunted a reply and left to talk to the server about the check. When he returned, Patty had ordered drinks for everyone. The family raised their glasses in a solemn toast to Marlena, honoring her memory.

Aaron stayed with Lucas and his family that night, sleeping on their basement couch. The next day, he drove three hours back to his quiet home. Meanwhile, Robert spent the following eight months distancing himself from all but two of his children, as though he hoped they would never be all together again.

The dinner had marked the end of his mother's life, and now, faced with her revelations, Aaron felt her absence more deeply. He had to honor her memory by exploring the secrets she left behind and ensuring her hopes for the family lived on.

6

Aaron's mind wandered back to that family meal at the Blue Ridge Diner less than a year ago. His mother's absence had been glaring, leaving a hole no conversation or laughter could fill. He remembered Rob, stiff at the head of the table, while the siblings tried to keep things normal. The air had been thick with awkward small talk and forced smiles.

His mother's words echoed in his head, and Aaron felt anger and sadness rising. She had tried so hard to get Rob to accept Nico, pleading with him to look beyond his prejudices. But Rob had stayed shut off, refusing to accept the son who needed him most.

Aaron thought of Nico at that dinner, sitting, eyes down, avoiding Rob's gaze—nothing like the lively, confident man who lived outside his father's shadow. Aaron admired his brother's courage for being true to himself, even in the face of Rob's disapproval. He wondered how different things might have been if Rob had listened to their mother and seen Nico for who he was—a brave, kind person deserving of his father's love.

Lucas had tried to keep the peace, making jokes and steering the conversation away from tension. Elise had been clingy and chatty, seeking approval from everyone. Patty had been the worst, trying to win Rob's approval with every word, every gesture. The meal had been a painful reminder of how deeply Rob's favoritism had scarred them all.

His mother's last words colored the memory. Aaron felt grief for his siblings, for the love and acceptance they had all missed. He wished he could step back in time. He would tell his mother how much he appreciated her efforts and understood what she had been trying to do.

He opened her book again, flipping through pages and scanning various entries, looking for the Christmas after Nico had come out to the family as homosexual. Rob had been an unrelenting jerk—refusing to speak to Nico for months. He wouldn't discuss Nico with any of the family either. Aaron had tried once and been shut down instantly. He knew Lucas had tried to open up the conversation with Rob a few times, but gotten nowhere.

Their mother had cried many tears over the phone with him: distraught at Rob's censure of Nico in their lives, but unwilling to consider leaving him to move in with Aaron. Her drinking, which had started when he was a child and gotten progressively worse before he moved out, had increased considerably during this period. Marlena always said, "I don't want you to see me like this, Aaron. I'll figure it out."

He scanned past days of mundane activities—shopping, chats with the neighbor lady, ordering entire cases of Grey Goose and Kahlua—until he found the entry he was looking for. This was the last Christmas Nico had come to their family dinner.

December 26, 2010: Marlena

I woke this morning with a heavy blanket of yesterday's events weighing on my chest. Christmas is supposed to be a time of joy and warmth, but this year was different. I can still hear the echoes of angry words and hurtful exchanges ringing in my ears.

The kids had come home, and I hoped things would go well. I wanted nothing more than for our family to enjoy each other's company. But as soon as Nico walked through the door, I felt the tension, like a live electrical wire hanging over the room. Rob was already on edge, and it took only a short while before their differences boiled over.

Christmas dinner started well enough—lively jokes and stories, Nat King Cole playing in the background—but as the night wore on, the undercurrents of resentment surfaced. Nico brought up an innocent memory from his childhood, something that struck a nerve with Rob, and the atmosphere shifted. Rob's jaw-flexing told me everything I needed to know.

"You beat me at tennis. Once! What's so funny about it?" Rob snapped, his voice icy and cutting across the room. "You act like you can waltz back here and pretend nothing has changed?"

Nico's face turned red, frustration and hurt flashing in his eyes. "I'm not pretending anything! I'm trying to connect with you again, Dad."

Aaron and Lucas joined in, and the argument escalated. I tried to intervene, to calm the storm, but the chaos drowned out my voice. "Can we enjoy the holiday?" I pleaded, my heart aching for my family. But they were too far gone, all unwilling to back down.

The moment the words "dead to me" left Rob's lips, my heart shattered. I believed I could mend the tears, but those words were a dagger. I watched Nico's heart break before my eyes, and the pain in his expression was unbearable. Aaron jumped up from his chair and yelled at Rob, who is never one to back down from a fight.

As they continued to shout at each other, the warmth of Christmas faded, replaced by a chill that wrapped around us all. I envisioned a night filled with love and laughter, and instead, my family disintegrated before me. Elise was sobbing and Patty tried to comfort her, but his wife Ashley was suddenly screaming too— they've had issues for a while now, but this was not the time or the place. My Christmas dinner is not supposed to be a free-for-all for family fighting.

Patty and Ashley left with little Drew, and shortly after, Elise's boyfriend came to pick her up. Aaron, Lucas, and Renee stayed the longest, but I was glad when they left with baby Elisabeth. It was all too much.

After the fight, I made a White Russian and sat alone in the living room, the decorations still twinkling around me. They did nothing to fill the hole in my chest. I listened to Nico crying in the bathroom, and it broke me. I wanted to comfort him and tell him I loved him, and that it would work out in the end. But my love can't shield him from Rob's anger.

Rob had stormed off to our bedroom while the kids were leaving. With a strong drink under my belt, I followed him, desperate to understand. "You can't keep pushing him away like this, Rob! He's our son!" I said, my voice rising in desperation.

He turned to me, the hurt in his eyes mingling with anger. "You don't understand! He made his choice! He's the one who turned his back on us!"

I shook my head, tears stinging my eyes. "No, he's still our son, Rob. We need to show him we love him despite everything. That's what family is."

Rob looked away as if trying to block out my words. "I will not have a queer for a son. I didn't raise him to be like that, and I will not have it. It's... unnatural."

His words tore at my nerves— that's my son he's talking about. How dare he? I knew we couldn't go on like this. "He's the same person he's always been. Who he loves doesn't have anything to do with us, nor should it. We can't let anger tear us apart. Not now. Not when we need each other the most."

He refused to look at me, so I left him to his thoughts. I returned to the living room, where Nico sat. He looked up at me with red, puffy eyes as I wrapped my arms around him, wishing I could erase the pain of the evening. "Sweetheart," I whispered, "I'm so sorry. I thought this Christmas would be different."

"Thought it would be better than this. I thought I could be part of the family again, Mom," he said, his voice trembling.

If only my arms could protect him from the hurt. "We'll find a way, I promise. We'll figure this out together."

But as I sit here today, the shadows of yesterday's arguments linger around me, and I can't shake the feeling that our family is hanging by a thread, fraying with every harsh word. Christmas is a time of hope and renewal, yet this year, it's a reminder of how fragile our connections are. I can only hope we can recover from this—that I can hold my family together, even as the pieces threaten to scatter.

* * *

She described it just like he remembered it. The anger and Rob's intense refusal to accept Nico's sexuality had pissed him off then, and it pissed him off now. Nico didn't deserve it, and the rest of the family had paid the price when he pulled away from them and moved to Maryland. He didn't come to family events anymore and only texted briefly here and there. Aaron's conversations with Nico were simple and brief updates on life and family. Lucas filled him in on Patty, Elise, and Rob—they had stopped talking to Aaron and Nico without a word after Marlena died.

Now he sent Lucas and Nico texts, asking about their weekend plans. He thought about messaging Patty—he decided against it when he saw his previous fourteen messages, marked "Unread". Reaching out to Elise wasn't an option either; they'd never been close. Scrolling through his contacts, he paused at his ex-wife's name—Rachel. They hadn't spoken in months; every conversation since the divorce had been strained. After seven years, he wasn't even sure why her number was still on his phone. Sighing, he closed the contact list.

The clarity of his mother's revelations settled over him. He had always wondered why Rob kept a wall between them. Now he knew, but it brought no comfort—only loss. His mother had tried to shield him, but she couldn't change who Rob was or undo the damage.

Aaron picked up his phone and scrolled to Lucas's name. Maybe talking to him would help clear his head.

"Hey, bro," Lucas answered after a few rings. "What's up?"

"I didn't tell you last night, but I got something in the mail yesterday," Aaron said, trying to keep his voice even. "A book from this company called Legacy Manuscripts. It's like a diary of Mom's memories."

"What do you mean, her memories?" Lucas sounded confused.

"I don't know. They use some tech or something to record a person's memories. Mom must have signed up for it."

"That sounds… unbelievable," Lucas said, skeptical. "Are you sure it's legit?"

"I think so. It's detailed. Her last entry talks about all of us, and it's brought up a lot."

"Like what?"

"Like how hard she tried to get Dad to accept Nico," Aaron said. "She pleaded with him, but he wouldn't budge."

Lucas sighed. "That's Dad for you. Stubborn as ever."

Aaron nodded. "I keep thinking about that last meal. Now it makes so much more sense why it was so awkward."

"I remember," his brother said. "It was tough for all of us, but we've got to move forward."

"I want us to be closer," Aaron said. "I want Nico to know he's loved, that we're all connected still."

"We can do that," Lucas replied. "We're adults now, so we can choose to be there for each other."

Aaron hesitated. "But it's not that simple. Patty, Elise, and Dad have cut us off. Elise only talks to you when she needs something. They've sided with Dad, and I don't understand why. None of it makes sense."

Lucas sighed again. "Yeah, it's a mess. After Mom died, Dad's control over their finances became even more clear. Elise and Patty stick close to him. Because of that, I'm sure. But we can't let it stop us. We can stay connected, even if it's only you, me, and Nico."

Aaron felt a small wave of relief. "Thanks, Luke. That means a lot."

They talked a few minutes longer, making plans to get together soon. When Aaron hung up, he felt lighter. Sharing the existence of his mother's book made it feel less like a burden. As he glanced at the book on the coffee table, he considered looking into the Legacy Manuscripts company to understand more. He headed to bed, feeling a renewed sense of purpose.

7

A lightning storm swept through the next morning, closing Aaron's building site. They could handle snow and rain, but lightning made the site too dangerous for laying long steel rebar beams. Leaving early on a Friday meant a long weekend for the whole crew. One of his foremen, Jeff, suggested that Aaron join the guys for a celebratory drink to kick off the weekend. After a few halfhearted attempts to decline, Aaron gave in.

As he stepped into the bar, the familiar buzz of chatter enveloped him. The dim lighting and rustic decor created a warm, inviting atmosphere. He spotted Jeff and a few other crew members gathered around a large wooden table, drinks in hand, discussing the latest football game.

"Hey, look who joined us!" Jeff called out, raising his beer in salute. The others turned to greet him, some lifting their glasses in unison while a couple of guys shouted playful insults about him taking too long.

Aaron couldn't help but grin as he made his way over. The week's stress melted away, replaced by the camaraderie that always seemed to thrive in this bar. He sat next to Jeff, who slid a cold beer in his direction.

"Here's to you, boss!" Jeff announced, raising his glass. The others followed suit, laughter mingling with the sound of clinking glasses.

"Anyone got any plans?" Frank asked, taking a long swig of his drink.

"Not much," Aaron replied, taking a sip. "Catching up on some much-needed rest."

"Rest? Where's the fun in that?" Jeff laughed. "You need to get out, live a little. You know, find some trouble to get into."

The table erupted into a chorus of suggestions for weekend activities. They ranged from hiking to bar hopping to playing video games. Aaron enjoyed the excitement. Work and personal issues slipped further from his mind with each passing moment.

As the drinks flowed, the banter became livelier. They shared stories from the job site: ridiculous mishaps that left everyone in stitches. Aaron laughed along; the sound was foreign yet liberating after the long week.

But as the clock inched closer to midnight, the atmosphere shifted into more subdued conversations—it had been a hard week of work. Aaron could see it in Jeff's eyes and the tired expression on his face.

"Hey," Aaron said, over the hum of conversation. "Let's raise a glass for the long weekend. We earned it!"

The group nodded in agreement, and Jeff stood up once again. "To a well-deserved break!"

They all raised their glasses, the clinking sound echoing in the now-quieter bar. "To the weekend!" they echoed, and for a moment, the worries of work and life slipped away.

After the toast, laughter filled the air, their spirits buoyed by the fellowship. At the last call, Aaron found himself ten beers deep. He stumbled to his car, knowing he couldn't risk driving. He sank into the driver's seat and squinted at his cell phone, ordering an Uber to take him home. Twenty minutes later, he thanked the driver, who seemed relieved that Aaron hadn't vomited in his backseat.

Wobbling up the steps to his front door, Aaron fumbled for his house key. His roommate Alex saved him the trouble by flinging the door open so hard that Aaron saw double for a moment.

"Welcome home, you drunk bastard!"

"Back off, I need to sit." He propelled himself toward the living room, struggling to maintain balance, and collapsed into the armchair.

"You look like hell, my good man. But I'm glad you look like hell because it means you went out and did something besides brood for a change."

"Yep. Went out. Drank too much. Might puke. Need to sleep."

"Me Tarzan, you Jane, got it," his sarcastic buddy laughed. "Want help to get up the stairs?"

The only response was snoring; Aaron would sleep in the armchair tonight.

The sharp sun pierced Aaron's eyes a few hours later. He stretched, his joints rumbling in protest. His mouth felt and tasted like it was full of mothballs. Alex and Jared's voices drifted from upstairs, sounding distant and muffled, as if through a static-filled radio. Aaron loosened his bootlaces, pushing the heel of one boot into the rug to slide his foot free, then used the toes of that foot to ease off the other boot.

The cheap beer still sloshed around in his belly as he pulled himself upright. At the staircase, he gripped the oak railing hard. Yesterday's work shirt hit the upstairs hall floor, and he slammed the bathroom door shut harder than he meant to, pivoting to slip off his jeans and boxers. The hot water filled the room with steam, and he stepped in, turning his back to the water. He did not like having water on his face. He felt his sore muscles loosen as the spray swept over his body. It had been several months since he had last ventured to the bar, and this crappy after-morning feeling kept him away in the meantime.

When the scalding water turned cool, he shut it off and reached for a towel. Wrapping it around his waist, he glimpsed his face in the foggy mirror. His deep chestnut hair, short and tousled, had a few strands of silver hinting at his age. His green eyes stared back at him from under his brow, which often furrowed in concentration. High cheekbones framed his angular face, a cleft in his chin, and a strong jawline, shadowed by stubble that seemed to appear mere minutes after he shaved. He flexed his hands, calloused and strong from the hard work he put into his job every day, and noted that he was developing a little belly, despite his overall lean and muscular build from the years of physical labor. *Too much whiskey.*

He flipped off the bathroom light and headed to his room to get dressed. Alex was sitting on his bed, with Jared lounging in his armchair. "What the hell, guys? Here to watch me get dressed?"

Alex grinned, unfazed. "Nah, we're here to make sure you don't fall flat on your ass."

Jared chuckled from the armchair. "Yeah, we're your sobriety check."

Aaron rolled his eyes and grabbed a pair of jeans from his dresser. "You two are relentless."

"Only because we care," Alex said, leaning back on the bed. "How are you feeling, chief? That was some serious drinking last night."

Aaron shrugged, pulling on his jeans. "I've had better mornings. But I'll live."

Jared tilted his head, studying Aaron. "You've been working non-stop for months. Maybe it's time to take a break, man."

Aaron grabbed a shirt and slipped it on. "I can't afford to slow down. There's too much to do."

Alex stood up, stretching. "You're not doing anyone any favors by burning out. Take a day, get your head straight."

Aaron sighed, running a hand through his hair. "I hear you. But the work won't wait."

"Neither will life," Jared said in a low tone. "Just think about it, okay?"

He nodded, appreciating their concern despite his stubbornness. "Yeah, I will. Thanks, man."

Alex clapped him on the shoulder. "Good. Now, let's get some breakfast. You'll need it."

Aaron followed Alex and Jared downstairs, the smell of coffee wafting through the air.

"Who's on breakfast duty?" Aaron asked, filling a mug with coffee.

"Alex," Jared replied, pouring himself a glass of orange juice. "I did it yesterday. You're next, buddy."

"Fine by me," Aaron said, sipping his coffee. "Anything but oatmeal again, please."

Alex turned from the stove, spatula in hand. "Hey, oatmeal's a classic. But don't worry, today it's bacon and eggs."

He settled at the kitchen table, watching as Alex flipped the bacon. "Smells good. Do you guys have any plans today?"

"Not really," Jared said, sitting down across from him. "Maybe hit the gym later. What about you? Going to bury yourself in work again?"

Aaron shrugged. "Got some projects to finish. But I might take a break later."

Alex set a plate of bacon and scrambled eggs in front of him. "Good. You need to relax a bit, man. Maybe even go out and meet someone. It's been a while since you brought a girl home."

Aaron chuckled, shaking his head. "I've been busy. Besides, it's not like you two are bringing anyone home either."

"Touché," Jared laughed. "But you've got to balance work with life. And I hear there's a new book you've been obsessed with. What's it about?"

Aaron took a bite of bacon, savoring the crispy salty goodness. "It's a… history book I found. It's made me think a lot about my family and the past. You know how little I know about it."

Alex raised an eyebrow. "Sounds like heavy stuff. Anything interesting in it?"

"Yeah, some pretty surprising things," Aaron said. "Stuff that makes me question a lot about my family. It's like opening a door to a room you didn't know existed."

Jared nodded. "Sounds intense. Maybe that's why you need to balance things out. Dive into the past, but don't forget to live in the present."

He smiled, appreciating their concern. "You guys are right. Maybe I'll take it easy today. For a change."

Alex grinned, joining them at the table with his plate. "That's the spirit. Now, let's enjoy this breakfast. And later, we'll see about dragging you out of the house."

They continued to eat; the conversation shifting to lighter topics. Aaron felt thankful for his friends and the normalcy they brought into his life. He had known Alex and Jared since they were kids. Growing up together had forged a bond that weathered time and distance, making mornings like this feel like a cherished routine.

June 23, 1986: Marlena

As I step into our small apartment in Kirby, a wave of relief and nervous energy washes over me. The air here is fresh—clean—so different from the heavy, smog-laden atmosphere of North Philly. I pause, letting the quiet envelop me. It is so unlike the chaos I left behind. There are sounds of nature outside, instead of the constant sirens and honking horns. It's rural and peaceful, with wide-open spaces and a sky that stretches endlessly above us.

I glance over at Rob, unpacking boxes with Aaron and Patty. The boys giggle as they explore their new surroundings, their laughter filling the room. It's surreal being here, after such a hard year since Big Mike got arrested. I remember the judge's words when he handed down that fifteen-year sentence. I kissed Mike before the bailiff took him away—the whole situation still hangs over me like a dark cloud. Rob's recent divorce has shaken things up too, but he stepped in to help us when we needed it most, and for that, I'm grateful.

My mind drifts back to the drive here. The sun rose above the horizon, casting a warm golden glow over the landscape, as we packed up our life in Philadelphia and set out for Kansas. Our car was cramped with luggage, pillows, bags, and toys. Aaron and little Patty were squeezed into the backseat, giggling and shoving each other at every bump in the road. Rob adjusted the rearview mirror, glancing back at the boys with a smile. "Ready for our journey?" he asked, his voice full of enthusiasm.

Aaron nodded, his imagination running wild with visions of vast fields, mountains, and mysterious forests. Every twist and turn of the road felt like an adventure. Patty, bouncing in his car seat, kept asking, "Are we there yet?" with all the innocence of a toddler. Rob chuckled and replied, "Not yet, buddy. But the best part is that we're on our way," as he pulled onto the highway. The open road stretched out before us like a promise.

I watched the world outside the window blur into a tapestry of color and movement, fueling our collective excitement and hope. I had agreed to leave Philadelphia, to leave everything familiar behind, in search of a new beginning for me and my children. But as we drove further from the city's bustling streets, a mix of emotions tugged at my heart. I was excited, yes, but also anxious about what lay ahead.

Would Aaron and Patty find the same joy and comfort in Kansas that they had back home? Would we find the peace I so desperately sought?

"Look at the fields, Aaron!" Patty had exclaimed at one point, pointing out the window with his chubby little hand. Aaron's eyes lit up as he took in the endless expanse of farmland, golden wheat swaying in the breeze. "Wow! It's so big!" he shouted, his voice full of wonder. I smiled, hoping this new world would hold the happiness we searched for.

Rob turned on the radio, filling the car with soft rock music, and we kept driving, mile after mile. We stopped for gas and snacks, so the boys could stretch their legs and explore. Aaron ran around one small store, eyes wide with excitement at the colorful candy displays. "Can I have Cow Tales, Mom?" he asked, his voice hopeful. I chuckled and told him, "Alright, but you have to share with your brother." With his candy clutched in his hand, Aaron seemed braver, more ready to face whatever lay ahead.

Standing in this little apartment, I can't shake the worry that creeps into my mind. Will Big Mike contest my request for a divorce? The thought tightens my chest. Facing him in court after everything we've been through, fills me with dread. He's a dangerous felon. Maybe I won't have to look him in the eye and hear him ask why I won't wait for him. But for now, I push those thoughts aside.

I take a deep breath, trying to shake off my worries. For now, we have safety. This little apartment is our refuge, a chance to rebuild. Maybe here, in this quiet corner of Kansas, we can find the peace we desperately need.

In 1988, Kirby, Kansas, was a small rural town with the simplicity and close-knit community spirit typical of the American Midwest. Main Street bisected the neighborhoods, and here, residents ran their errands, caught up with neighbors, and attended to their daily needs.

There was one gas station, a vital stop for travelers passing through and for locals. It was a place where you could fill up your tank, grab a cold soda and a pack of smokes, and chat with the attendant, Oscar, who knew the local customers by name. Across the street was the town's small grocery store, a cornerstone of daily life. Stocked with all the basics, it provided everything from fresh produce to pantry staples.

The local library was a cherished institution. It offered a quiet place for reading and learning, with select books that catered to both young and old. Next door, the public pool was a popular spot, especially during the hot summer months. Past the pool from the library was Kirby Park. The park and playground offered open green spaces for picnics and sports. It was a place where the community came together, whether for a casual baseball game or a family outing.

The video rental store was a popular destination on weekends. Two doors down: the hardware store, built in 1884, when the railroad first came through, offered everything needed for home repairs and projects.

Modest homes, fields of grain, and cattle farms dotted the town. Kirby was a perfect example of rural American life during the late 20th century.

8

Aaron could remember little about Kansas. His family had lived there from 1986 to 1990, but he had only snippets of memories to look back on. He could recall making friends with the neighbor's old horse, who hung out by the fence along the road. He and Patty would take him bananas and apples from the fruit bowl on the kitchen counter.

The old horse, who they named Herman, would approach the fence tentatively, his large nostrils flaring slightly as he sniffed the offering. Aaron could recall exactly what it felt like when Herman's warm breath tickled his palm. The horse's soft, velvety lips would reach out to carefully grasp the fruit, curling around to get a secure hold without using its teeth. Once Herman had a good grip, he would lift the fruit from his hand, and with a slight toss of his head, he would begin to chew. His strong jaws worked methodically as he savored the treat, and when he was done, he would come back to snuffle at their outstretched hands again, looking for more snacks.

One day, the old horse had not been at the fence when they went to feed him, and the man in the yard said he had died. Aaron couldn't remember if Patty had been sad, but he remembered crying hard into his pillow when they got home. He had loved Herman.

He remembered the large tortoise who lived in their neighbor's yard. He didn't have a name that Aaron could recall, but his mother said that spring had arrived when the yard turtle came out of his hole in the ground. "Like a Kansan groundhog," she had said.

He had spent a lot of time outside in those days. Despite his early performance, his new stepfather wasn't a kind man, and Aaron and Patty had learned quickly to stay out of Rob's path. Mostly he had played with his friends Liam and Joey, whose fathers worked at the meat-packing plant with Rob. Alex had been around too—he couldn't remember when Alex wasn't around. In between these flickering memories though, there were dark spots of time that he couldn't conjure any memory for. He knew that Nico, Lucas, and Elise had been born in Kansas, but he couldn't bring up any image in his head of them as babies.

Bright spots and dark shadows—that's all Kansas was for him, looking back.

June 12, 1988: Marlena

Today was one of the happiest days of my life. Aaron's sixth birthday—he's a little man now. His eyes lit up when he saw the bicycle. It was shiny black with metallic red details like he had dreamed. He hugged me hard, saying, "Thank you, Mommy!" Seeing him so happy, I felt like the best mother in the world.

Little Patty, almost five, was thrilled, though his excitement was more for the cake and balloons than the new bike. Nicolaus, two years old, stumbled around, trying to keep up with his older brothers, while baby Lucas, only a month old, slept in his crib, oblivious to the commotion.

Aaron chose Centurions: Power Xtreme for his party theme. I had to drive to Dodge City to find the decorations, but seeing his little face light up made it worthwhile. Decorations filled the room with images of Max Ray (his favorite), Jake Rockwell, and Ace McCloud, bringing vibrant colors and action-packed energy to the dining room. The cake was a masterpiece, featuring a detailed image of Max Ray in an action pose, surrounded by green and yellow icing. I don't know how Mrs. Pasquale pulled that out of her hat, but she did a beautiful job.

His friends from the neighborhood, Liam and Joey, were here, joining in the festivities with boundless energy. They played games inspired by the Centurions' missions, racing around the yard in makeshift power suits crafted from cardboard and foil. They searched for hidden "power modules" to complete their suits in a scavenger hunt, and each find met with cheers and laughter.

The relay race was the highlight of the party. The kids split into teams, pretending to be their favorite Centurion, and completed tasks that mimicked the show's adventures. Aaron led his team, dressed as Max Ray. His enthusiasm and determination shone through every challenge.

As the day wound down, the kids gathered around the dining room table for pizza and cake. Aaron's eyes sparkled as he made a wish and blew out the candles, surrounded by his brothers and friends. The party favors, small action figures, and stickers of the Centurions were a hit, and the boys played in the driveway until long after the party ended.

I hope I never forget this day, filled with laughter, joy, and my sweet boy's smiling face. I wish Rob could have been here, but he had that fishing trip planned with his buddies from work. It's for the best; he's so short-tempered with Aaron over the smallest things. The noise and racing kids would have only irritated him.

Aaron sat in the old armchair by the window. The soft sunlight filtered through the curtains, casting a warm glow on the pages. His eyes moved, taking in each word, each memory. He chuckled, imagining his younger self's excitement over the bicycle and the Centurions-themed party.

Reading about the shiny black bike with metallic red details made a smile spread across his face, remembering how much he had loved that bike. He hadn't thought about that bike, or that party, in years. He could not remember himself or his brothers ever being that young.

As he continued reading, he felt a pang of longing mixed with gratitude. The detailed description of the party, the decorations, the games, and the cake showed how much effort his mother had put into making that day special for him. Remembering the relay race and his friends Liam and Joey felt like watching an old home movie.

Aaron paused for a moment, a thoughtful look crossing his face. "I think Alex was there too," he murmured to himself. He could almost picture Alex running around the yard, joining in the games with the other kids. It was such a vivid memory that he was certain Alex had been there, even if the book didn't mention him. He would have to ask him later.

He continued reflecting on that day, remembering how Alex had fit in with Liam, Joey, and the other kids. They must have played together, sharing the same excitement and joy, their laughter filling the air. Aaron smiled, feeling a warm connection to his childhood friend, grateful for the memories that included his family, and the close friends who had been like family to him.

He paused when he read about his mother's wish to remember the day. He closed the book, holding it in his lap for a moment, lost in thought. Marlena wrote about Rob's absence: his stepfather had gone fishing on his birthday. He went fishing a lot with his friends from work back then.

His two friends would come to the house, walking in through the kitchen door without knocking as if they lived there. The shorter one, Kevin, would stand around the kitchen, snacking on whatever Marlena was preparing for dinner. He would lean against the washing machine with his legs stretched way out. The other, taller man, would park himself on the couch in the living room, grabbing whichever child was closest and plopping them into his lap, restraining them there until they cried out or Marlena came into the room.

Aaron remembered how he and Patty would try to get their toys out of the living room and into their bedroom before Knobby Chin (as they called him privately) grabbed them. They were too young back then to know words like "creepy" and "sketchy", but those words certainly slammed into his mind now at the memory. There was always a sigh of relief when Rob would emerge from his study to collect his friends and leave the house.

A wash of uneasiness swept over him. The birthday memories faded into the backdrop of his father's friends. He remembered the way Knobby Chin would laugh. It was unsettling, evoking a sense of discomfort he couldn't quite articulate as a child.

The image of Patty and him stashing their toys away from the man lingered in his mind: a response born from a child's desire to protect their space. They had been too young to voice their fears, and too innocent to understand why their father's friends made them uncomfortable. The tension in the air had been like a shroud that seemed to settle over the house when the men were around.

Aaron couldn't help but see those visits through a different lens now, as an adult. The thought of the short man with the thick neck leaning against the washing machine, snacking carelessly while Marlena bustled about, was disturbing. The pressure of expectation surrounded them; unwritten rules that dictated how to behave and what to ignore. His mother was not exempt from those rules.

The relief that came when Rob ushered his friends out of the house was stark in contrast to the anxiety that lingered when they were there. Aaron had craved the return of peace and the comfort of being a kid again.

He set the book down beside him, feeling the ribbons of memories intertwine with his present. Aaron took a deep breath, reminding himself that he had grown up and moved on from those days, yet the echoes of his childhood still shaped his understanding of family and friendship. As he glanced back at the pages, he felt a quiet determination to create a safe and joyful environment for his nieces and nephews, far removed from the shadows of the past.

As Aaron sat in reflective silence, the door creaked open, and Alex and Jared stepped into the room, their energy filling the space.

"Hey, we got your car from the bar," Alex said, grinning. "Hope you didn't miss it too much."

"Thanks, guys. I appreciate it."

"Anytime," Jared chimed in, leaning against the door frame.

After a moment of hesitation, Aaron asked, "Hey, Alex, do you remember the Centurions birthday party in Kirby?"

Alex's expression brightened. "Of course! How could I forget? That was such a fun party! Your mom went all out."

"Right? I read about it in this book she had made," Aaron said. "It was such a big deal for me."

"I remember that shiny black bike," Alex continued, his excitement contagious. "And there was that gigantic cake with Max Ray on it. We were all so into the Centurions back then!"

"I can't believe you remember that," Aaron exclaimed. "We had all those games and the scavenger hunt. I remember how we raced around trying to find the 'power modules.'"

"Yeah! And the relay race!" Alex laughed, his eyes dancing. "You were leading your team as Max Ray, and we were all trying to keep up. It was hilarious!"

Aaron shook his head. "Man, that was one of my best birthdays. Can't believe you were there to witness it."

"Yeah, well, I had to be. The day wouldn't have been as cool without me," Alex teased. "Plus, that cake alone was worth showing up for!"

"Damn straight! The best cake ever. Honestly, how did we survive those birthdays without diabetes?" Aaron shot back at his oldest friend.

"None of Rob's weird friends around either," Alex said, shaking his head. "Can you imagine the creep factor they'd have brought?"

Aaron blinked in surprise. He couldn't remember them ever talking about Knobby Chin or Kevin. "Right? Do you remember them too? That guy with the mustache was asking for a restraining order. Mom had some serious patience to deal with those clowns."

"She didn't even argue with Rob about fishing that day. I think she was glad to have him out of the house," Alex said. "I mean, who wouldn't be?" They both laughed in solidarity.

Jared, who had been listening, raised an eyebrow. "Sounds like a solid party, my bros. I guess that was before my time, eh?" he said, trying to sound nonchalant. "I'm about to fix the broken back fence before it falls in. Not all of us can sit around reminiscing about birthday parties." He shot them a teasing grin before heading for the door.

Aaron shook his head with a smirk. "Good luck with that, man. Don't let it fall on you."

"Yeah, yeah," Jared called back over his shoulder. "I'll send you a postcard from the other side of the fence."

Once the door clicked shut, Aaron turned back to Alex, his expression warm. "You know, it's funny how the past can sneak up on you like that."

"Yeah," Alex replied, leaning back in his chair. "It's not always pretty, but it's ours. And it's good to remember the good stuff, too."

Aaron nodded, comfortable in the company of his friend. Their banter had transformed what once felt like a burden into a shared experience. They had built something lasting together—a bond forged through years of friendship and understanding. With Alex by his side, Aaron felt he could face whatever came next.

9

Robert Bakker had worked in the meatpacking industry his entire life. He inherited his father's butcher shop in North Philadelphia and sold it to a large company, Luca Meat Distribution. After moving to New Jersey, he married the daughter of someone important in the company and had a few kids, though Aaron wasn't sure how many or what had happened to them. He had only heard them mentioned in passing, in low tones not intended for his ears. The marriage ended around the same time Big Mike went to prison, and only a few months later, Rob drove their family away from North Philly.

In Kirby, Rob served as the manager for one of the Luca Meat Distribution plants. In that role, he oversaw all aspects of butchering, processing, and packaging various meat products. He often boasted that he was "the only one who does shit," a sentiment he expressed about every job he ever held.

Busy though he might have been, he always made time for two things: going on long fishing trips with his friends and harassing Aaron. If this harassment sometimes escalated from verbal to physical abuse, well, that was Aaron's fault, if you asked Rob.

Aaron recalled one such occasion when he was eight years old. It was July—sweltering hot and so humid that his shirt clung to his skin within seconds of stepping outside. Tasked with pulling the weeds along the side of the driveway, he hesitated and asked his mother if he could wait until it cooled off. She told him to ask Rob, who had assigned the chore. He had dragged his feet the whole way down the hall to the study. As soon as he mumbled the question, he wished he could pull the words back into his mouth.

Rob spun in his chair, his hateful glare sending chills down Aaron's spine. "No, you may not wait until it's cooler. Get your lazy ass outside and weed that goddamn driveway!" He stood up, looming over Aaron. "I'll come help you."

Aaron's heart sank. He hustled outside, desperate to get it done. Rob followed him with the riding lawnmower, dismounting to hand Aaron a bucket of golf balls. "Toss these out into the yard."

Toss golf balls into the yard you're about to mow? He was confused but did as he was told, hurling the balls into the long grass. Rob climbed back onto the mower, and after two passes, he hit a golf ball that flew across the yard toward Aaron. He jumped out of the way in time, but the next ball struck his thin arm, sending pain shooting through him. Rob laughed. "Weed that goddamn driveway, you lazy bastard."

More balls flew at him, hitting his leg and the side of his head. Panic surged through Aaron as his mother rushed out of the kitchen, shouting, "Rob, stop! What the hell are you doing?"

"Teaching the boy a lesson, Marlena. If you won't do it, someone has to. Get your ass back in the house or figure out how to manage all of this shit on your own." His voice bellowed over the roar of the mower. She retreated, a look of distress on her face that haunted Aaron.

The mowing resumed, and the golf balls flew at him again and again. He had cried and pulled those weeds as fast as he could, the green stains smearing in the sweat on his dirty hands. When Rob finished, he put the mower away without a word and went inside. Aaron stayed outside until long after dark, desperate to pull every weed along the driveway's edge. By the time he finished, it hurt to stand, his arms and legs covered in bruises and blood—Rob's lesson.

His mother cleaned his wounds and reheated a dinner plate, hugging him as she set a glass of milk in front of him. But she never spoke of what had happened. That was only one instance. Aaron could recall countless others, punishments that always exceeded the perceived crime.

He had both hated Rob and wanted his approval since he was a small boy. In those days, when they lived in Kirby, Rob had showered all the little affection he had to spare on Nico and little Lucas. He had called the little ones "my boys" and referred to Aaron and Patty as "Marlena's boys".

When Rob had decided one weekend that Marlena's boys would go fishing with the men, Aaron had been excited. He was a big boy, seven years old now, old enough to be included. Picturing that day now, he remembered his determination to catch a big fish and impress his new dad, and how he had agreed without hesitation when Knobby Chin offered to show him how to cast his fishing pole. The tall man instructed Aaron to stand between his knees, then wrapped his long arms around the boy's body. Together, they cast the line, and Knobby Chin had scooted forward until he pressed against Aaron's back, one hand dropping to rest on the boy's belly, then lower, and… the day went blank.

The next thing he could recall was the next day: he woke up in his bed to hear Rob crowing to Marlena about what a good job Patty had done catching his first fish. "Aaron? Your boy couldn't seem to figure it out, of course. Roger showed him how to do it, even took him off to the small pond for one-on-one lessons, but the boy's an idiot, Marlena, you know that." It was one of his clearest memories of Kansas, and half of it was a blank. From then on, Patty was one of Rob's boys, and he alone was "Marlena's boy".

Aaron was no fool. He could guess what had happened in those "one-on-one lessons" with the tall man and his groping hands, but he couldn't remember it. Whenever it would pop into his head, he would try to recall, but the blank part was as immovable as the ink stain on his floral couch.

Those men had continued to be in their lives for years. Moving away didn't change the bond between Knobby Chin Roger, Creepy Kevin, and Rob. Though the family moved from Kansas to California, to Canada, back to California, and then to the East Coast, the two men had always shown up.

Aaron went on three fishing trips with the men before his attendance was never required again. Patty continued to go with them for years: in every state they lived in, well into his teenage years. When their baby sister Elise was six years old, she became a fixture on the fishing trips as well, though she begged to stay home. Rob wanted her to go—"father-daughter bonding time"—so she had no choice.

Aaron wondered what his mother thought about those men. Rob always said they were part of the family, and Marlena would press her lips together and nod in agreement. Regardless, Aaron had spent his childhood trying to stay away from all three of the men.

August 2, 1989: Marlena

They pulled into the driveway at a quarter after four this morning. I was nursing Nicolaus when I heard them come in through the kitchen. Roger passed the door to our bedroom carrying Aaron in his arms, and Kevin came behind with Patty asleep on his shoulder. Rob came last, straight into the room to kiss the baby's forehead and then my lips.

"Boys fell asleep. Aaron took a fall, but he's fine. The guys will get 'em tucked in."

I moved to put the baby down, wanting to check on the boys. He stopped me.

"They're fine, Marlena. Let them sleep."

"I need to see—"

"No. Put the baby to bed and go to sleep."

His voice was firm, and I did not dare to argue further. He left the room; I could hear their voices in the boys' room and moving to the living room. It was an hour before I heard the kitchen door slam shut, and then Rob came in, kicking his clothes across the carpet and settling in behind me. As soon as his breathing became regular, I crept from the bed to check on my boys.

Patty was fast asleep with his stuffed bunny in the crook of his elbow, his thumb planted in his mouth. I bent to kiss him and he let out a quiet sigh and snuggled into his blankets. Aaron was curled in a tight ball on his side under his blue quilt, both of his thin arms wrapped around his face. When I stroked his hair, he uncovered his face enough that I could see the fresh bruise on his cheek and around one of his wrists.

"What happened, baby?" I whispered, sitting down on the side of his bed. He shrugged, his wide eyes confused and dark. "How did you get hurt? Was it Robert?"

He shook his head and covered his face again. I could hear the muffled answer: "Don't know, I fell." I kissed his head and told him I loved him, but he would not look at me again. I tucked the quilt around his shoulder and closed the door, slipping back to bed without a sound.

When the baby woke me up a few hours later, I asked Rob what had happened. He said that Aaron fell, that he was running towards the old dock at a small pond and Roger had to grab him to keep him from falling into the water. He said he fell on the dock and hit his face, bruising up his backside as well. I don't know. It makes sense. Aaron gets so excited. I'm sure he didn't think that a dock is slippery and dangerous. It's a good thing Roger was there with him, or who knows what could have happened.

Several days later, Aaron's phone rang while he was driving home from work. Lucas had learned about creating a "Legacy Manuscript". The company's website was not very clear. He had read through their descriptions but did not understand. He had contacted customer service, and a sales rep explained the compiling of memories.

"Hey, Aaron," Lucas' animated voice crackled through the speaker. "I found out about Mom's book. It's pretty wild how they put it all together."

"Yeah?" Aaron replied, trying to focus on the road and the conversation. "What did you find out?"

"They use photos and letters, digital files and audio recordings," Lucas explained. "The customer submits those. But they also use advanced neural chips. They capture brain waves—like something out of a sci-fi movie."

Aaron raised his eyebrows, intrigued. "Neural chips? Like, they record thoughts and stuff?"

"Something like that," Lucas continued. "They implant these chips that tap into your neural network and record memories directly from your brain. It's all voluntary and safe, according to the rep I talked to. They take handwriting samples and generate the text from that, so it looks real. Mom must have gone through the whole process to get those detailed memories."

Aaron felt a mix of awe and disbelief. "That's wild. No wonder the book feels so vivid."

"Yeah," Lucas agreed. "They do interviews and compile data from the neural chips—they create a complete story. The goal is to capture the essence of someone's life."

"She wanted us to have something tangible to remember her by," Aaron mumbled.

"She did," Lucas responded, his tone softening. "It's her way of staying with us, I guess."

"Thanks for looking into it, Lucas."

"Of course," Lucas said. "I figured you'd want to know. And hey, I'd love to read it one day. It sounds like it's full of incredible memories."

"Sure thing, bro. When I'm finished reading it, it's your turn," Aaron replied, a small smile forming.

Ending the call, Aaron drove the rest of the way home in deep thought. The innovative technology his mother had embraced to preserve her memories was not insignificant. It surprised him—Marlena had not been a progressive woman. Yet, she went to great lengths to create this book for her children. For Aaron.

He had been so busy with work for the last few days that he hadn't had time to dwell much on the book's contents. The crew had wrapped up a job today, though. There was one more to finish next week, and then a couple of minor projects going on until the beginning of next month. Turning onto his street, he toyed with driving down to Philly this weekend. *Kick some old rocks over.*

The idea stirred a mix of nostalgia and apprehension within him. *Would I even recognize the place where I spent my early years?* Four years old was too young for any lasting memories, yet the thought of retracing his steps felt oddly compelling.

As Aaron approached his driveway, he imagined the streets of North Philly: the sights, sounds, and smells that might still linger there, buried beneath layers of time. So many of the memories were vague, flickering like shadows in the back of his mind. He could see glimpses of familiar corners, and hear the echo of laughter and yelling, but the specifics were unclear.

He parked the car, taking a moment to gather his thoughts. The idea of exploring the past—his past—filled him with a sense of purpose. Maybe he'd discover something about himself. Maybe there were pieces of the puzzle that still needed to be found. Before he left town, though, there was something else he had to do. His son Oliver's birthday was on Friday; he needed to visit his son. The visit was always a bittersweet reminder of what he had lost.

10

Early Friday morning, Aaron parked his Jeep Trailhawk along the curb and stepped out into the snowy grass of Boyertown Cemetery. He pulled the small bouquet of daisies and a plastic bag from his back seat. He only visited this place a few times a year, but he had been coming here for so many years that his feet knew where to go. His son's headstone was small, with a carved lamb under the words "Oliver Nathan Callahan" and the date "February 25, 2005".

"Happy birthday, Ollie." His voice cracked as he knelt, placing the flowers at the base of the stone with care. Today, his son would be 11 years old, a milestone filled with what-ifs. He imagined Ollie going to middle school, having buddies who'd come over to play video games and eat him out of house and home. Maybe his home would be a happy place, and he would still be married to Ollie's mother, Rachel. But none of that would ever happen now.

Aaron thought back to when he met Rachel in college. The couple was inseparable. Both were passionate about their futures—he in construction management, she in education. When Rachel got pregnant at the end of their senior year, they celebrated. They married three months after graduation.

But when their son was born still and silent, everything changed. They grieved together at first, sharing tears as they held their tiny son just once before the funeral home came to collect him. They held each other close on the night they went home from the hospital empty-handed. The closeness did not last, though. Aaron, feeling a deep drive to provide for their future children, threw himself into his work. He took on more hours, never satisfied with his internal goalposts. Rachel's grief, however, became obsessed with having another baby, and with each negative pregnancy test, her sorrow would unravel them further.

They moved to Boyertown, Pennsylvania, in 2007. On Ollie's second birthday, they interred his cremated ashes in the spot where Aaron knelt today. Rachel designed the memorial stone herself, engraving their names on the back: "Beloved son of Aaron and Rachel Callahan." She was ready to be pregnant again, wanting four or five children. But Aaron was starting a new business and felt they should wait until it grew more.

When they cut the ribbon on the front door of his new construction company downtown, Rachel was home, painting the nursery—the only room she cared about decorating. They fought that night, their growing distance becoming clear. He bought her a new dark green Subaru Outback for her birthday, a family vehicle for the children they would have. His wife laughed and told him it was too late. Rachel was pregnant, but the child was not his. The next week, she moved out, and by January 2009, he was a divorced man.

The big house he had bought for his future family now housed only himself, his roommates, and his regrets. The Subaru sat in the garage, never driven—a monument to the family he and Rachel would never grow.

He laid the daisies on the fresh snow, the cold seeping through his jeans as he knelt. Fishing a few packs of Hot Wheels cars out of the plastic bag, he opened the packages with careful fingers. Setting the cars on the front of the memorial, he lined them up under the silent stone lamb.

"If you were here, you'd have a favorite one of these, eh?" He chuckled, a sound that felt foreign in the cemetery's stillness. "I'd tell you to focus more on your studies than cars. Wish you were here so I could scold you, Ollie."

His voice trembled as he whispered, "I wish you were here." Tears spilled over, warming his cheeks against the chill of the winter air, and he wiped them away with the back of his hand. "Your mama will come by later. She's working, if I had to guess. Or with your... little brothers and sister. She loves you, Ollie. I love you too. I miss you, son."

He stood and straightened his coat, the crispness of the snow crunching beneath his boots. "I miss you." Reaching down to touch the headstone once more, he lingered a moment longer, feeling the cool stone beneath his fingers before stepping backward, and then turning back to his jeep.

Once inside, he sat and let the heat warm him through, allowing memories of that fateful day to wash over him, the ache in his heart familiar and heavy. As he pulled away from the curb, he glimpsed Rachel's car passing the guardhouse.

"See, son, I told you she'd be here soon," he murmured, the words heavy with regret. He thought of what might have been, and the life they could have shared if only fate had been kinder. The ache in his chest deepened as he drove away, the ghost of his lost son lingering at every turn.

February 25, 2005: Marlena

Aaron called this evening and gave me the horrible news. My poor sweet boy. My poor little grandson. How could this have happened? They did everything right, didn't they? Rachel went to all those doctor appointments, more than I ever had to when I had my babies. All those tests and ultrasounds; they didn't even offer all of that when I was pregnant. Only to be told the baby didn't make it and that "sometimes these things happen"? It's not fair. It's just not fair.

I hope my boy is okay. I'll go to the hospital in the morning if they don't mind my company. It will be best if I go alone; Rob is never sensitive to this kind of situation, and I doubt he will try, since it's Aaron. I can only imagine how hard my boy is taking this, or how he will react. He has always compartmentalized his pain and soldiered on through the hardest of things. Everything Mike did, then everything Rob threw at him, and all the moving, his dog dying in Alberta—I wasn't sure if he would ever get past that—and now this? I hope he and Rachel can get through this.

Just thinking about Aaron losing little Oliver has me remembering Harrison and Lydia. Roy Walker took my first babies because I didn't want to marry him. I was too young to be married, only 22 when Harrison came along and 25 with Lydia. I wanted to fall in love, not marry an old man who only came through town every couple of months. Roy would rumble up in that shiny big rig. At first, he was so exciting and exotic, but that lasted for a lot less time than I'd hoped it would. He became a chore, a tether that kept me from my friends, from dating the men who would ask me out, from my job at the grocery store (and I loved that job). If I'm honest, the babies were a tether too, but I wasn't ready to see them as anything more than that. And when I told Roy I wouldn't marry him, he got ugly.

Roy played dirty. He got his parents to pony up money for that fancy lawyer and they took my babies away to South Georgia. I saw their little faces in the back of the car, driving away from me, for years. Now I can barely remember what they looked like, and almost no one knows they ever existed. Harrison is gone now, dead at 23 years old from a heroin overdose. The last time I laid eyes on him, he was only three years old. In his obituary picture, he looked so much like my father.

Lydia is still out there. The last time I looked her up, she was in south Georgia, a little place called Vidalia. She's married and has babies of her own: Rose and Chloe. They're seven and nine... their mama is 27. My oldest living child and she does not know who I am or that I never forgot about her. Sometimes I think I should write to her, but what good would that do? I abandoned her and her brother. I didn't fight for them. Couldn't fight for them. Should have fought for them and didn't. I was trying to keep my head above water, and tethers would only make that harder.

Now it's too late. Too much time has passed. I don't want to disrupt their lives. I have my other kids to think about—what would they think about having siblings they never knew existed? It's better to keep all of that separate. I need to focus on my boys and Elise. She's in her first year of high school and brings home plenty of drama every day. Imagine how she would feel to find out she's not the only daughter.

I can't do that to her. For that matter, I would upset Aaron right when he's grappling with his loss. It would be cruel. I did the right thing by keeping everyone apart. Dwelling on what could have been only leads to heartbreak. Moving forward and doing better is the only way. I'll tell Aaron that if he'll listen. I don't want him to get caught up in thinking that his life is over because Oliver died. He can focus on work and future children. Things can always get better.

Aaron walked into his bedroom, grabbing his suitcase from the top shelf of his closet. He laid it open on the bed and began packing for his weekend trip to Philadelphia. The routine task of folding clothes and organizing his toiletries soothed the turmoil in his mind.

He had read the entry in his mother's book when he returned from his trip to the cemetery, and now he struggled to make sense of it. Harrison and Lydia: the siblings he had never known existed, taken from his mother before he was born. He read the entry three times, absorbing the details of his mother's pain, the loss she had buried, now laid bare in her own words. The mention of his older sister, living in Georgia with her children—Rose and Chloe—and Harrison, who had died from a heroin overdose at only 23 was a lot to take in.

This new knowledge was almost too much to bear. He zipped up his suitcase with a heavy sigh and sat on the edge of his bed, running his hands through his hair. He felt the familiar pull of the past, the unresolved pain of losing Oliver, now compounded by the discovery of a brother he would never meet and a sister who was a stranger. *How am I supposed to process all of this?*

Aaron picked up his phone and tapped out a text message to his brother: *Headed to North Philly for the weekend. Found out more about Mom's past… need to process. I'll fill you in when I get back.*

He stared at the screen before hitting send, hoping Lucas would understand. Aaron's heart ached with the same raw pain as when he thought of Oliver. But alongside the pain was a new, burning determination.

This trip to Philadelphia was about revisiting the place where he was born, where his father, Big Mike, committed murder, and the places and people his mother had run from. He needed to see those places, walk those streets, and understand the shadows that had shaped his family's history.

With his suitcase packed and his mind made up, Aaron stood and looked around his room. He found Alex and Jared in the living room, absorbed in their activities.

"Hey, guys, I'm heading to Philadelphia for the weekend," Aaron said, trying to keep his voice calm. "I need to deal with some family stuff."

Alex looked up from his phone, concern etched on his face. "You okay, bro?"

"Yeah… a lot on my mind. I'll be back in a few days."

Jared nodded, giving him a reassuring smile. "Take care of yourself, man. We'll hold down the fort here."

Aaron grabbed his keys and headed out the door. He was ready to face whatever the weekend might bring. This journey was about confronting the past, about piecing together the fragments of his family's story.

11

Aaron had lived in Boyertown, only two hours northwest of the city where he was born for nine years, and never once had he ventured into his old neighborhood. He hadn't had a reason to go to Philadelphia, and only thought of the big city on rare occasions, outside seeing it on the news. It was a place his mother had feared and never spoken of. The knowledge only fueled his anxiety as he headed down the Schuylkill Expressway toward his past.

The radio seemed determined to mess with his head today. Kid Laroi singing about how he had promised to change, knowing he would not—he thought of Rachel; turning the channel, Adele crooned about stubborn people who allow no room for change—more regret. He punched the scan button again: Bieber swearing that the ghost of a person was enough when they can't be near, prompted him to drive the rest of the way in silence.

After a long wait for traffic to move, he took the Girard Avenue exit by the Philadelphia Zoo and turned his jeep towards his old neighborhood. He had an aunt who still lived on the same street as the old rowhome. She had not answered his message on Facebook, but he hoped she might answer the door. A quick search informed him that there were no hotels in his old neighborhood, not even one, so he found one on the Delaware River near Fishtown.

The hotel was nicer than he expected, and he laid down on the king-size bed overlooking the river for long enough that he almost dozed off. Shaking himself awake, he unpacked and headed downstairs to find a bite to eat. The busy streets had come alight with bright neon signs advertising funky beer gardens and hip music venues. He stopped at one, a few blocks from his hotel: indie music every night, craft beer, American fare. *Sounds good to me.*

As Aaron walked into the bustling restaurant, the lively sounds of laughter and music enveloped him. The warm, inviting atmosphere made him forget his worries and stress, if only for now. He approached the host stand and requested a table for one.

"Right this way," the hostess said with a friendly smile, leading him to a cozy corner table. Aaron sat, looking through the menu, which offered a tempting array of American classics with a modern twist.

After ordering a burger with sweet potato fries and a craft beer, he settled back into the rhythm of the restaurant, observing the surrounding crowd. Young couples chatted, groups of friends laughed over shared plates, and a solo guitarist strummed soft melodies in the corner.

While he waited, Aaron's eyes wandered around the room until they landed on a woman at the bar. She had strawberry-blond curls framing her face, bright blue eyes sparkling in the dim light, and long, tan legs that highlighted her confident posture. She looked like Rachel for a moment, and his heart skipped a beat.

To his surprise, she caught his gaze and smiled, a playful glint in her eyes. She picked up her drink and walked to his table, exuding an effortless charm.

"Mind if I join you?" she asked, her voice warm and inviting.

"Sure," Aaron replied, intrigued, but focused on his thoughts.

"I'm Bethany," she introduced herself, settling into the chair across from him. "What brings you to this side of town?"

"Just visiting," he said, trying to keep the conversation light. "Thought I'd check out some old memories."

"Sounds mysterious," she teased, leaning in. "Maybe I can help you create some new ones."

Aaron smiled. "I appreciate the offer, but I'm not looking for anything right now."

"Fair enough," she replied, still playful. "But if you change your mind, I'll be at the bar."

She stood up, giving him one last lingering smile before returning to the bar. As he watched her go, he felt no regret in his decision—only a sense of clarity about where his mind was today.

His food arrived, and he took a bite of his burger, savoring the rich flavors. The night was still young, but company was the last thing he wanted. He needed time alone to process everything in his mind.

After finishing his meal, Aaron paid and stepped out into the crisp night air. The streets were alive with activity, but he sought a quieter spot. He wandered down to the riverfront, where the Delaware River reflected the city lights in a mesmerizing dance of colors.

He leaned against the railing, staring out at the water and the lights of New Jersey in the distance. The rhythmic flow of the river was soothing, and he let his thoughts drift. His mother's book, his family's past, and this morning's visit to Oliver's grave all melded together in a complex tapestry of emotion.

Fishing his phone out of his pocket, he checked for messages. None from his aunt. He considered calling Lucas but decided against it. Some things were better processed alone, at least for now.

Aaron took a deep breath of chilly night air into his lungs. He thought about the places he planned to visit over the weekend—his old neighborhood, the house he grew up in, the streets where his father had once walked. It was a journey into the heart of his past, and he needed the solitude to brace himself for it.

He stayed by the river for a while before walking to the hotel. The walk was calming, the quiet of the night giving him the space he needed. Once back in his room, he kicked off his shoes and lay on the bed, staring at the ceiling.

The day had been long and emotionally draining, but he felt a sense of resolve building within him. This trip was necessary, a step towards understanding and possibly healing. He set his alarm for the morning, determined to face whatever the next day would bring.

The city's distant hum provided a strange comfort as he closed his eyes. Aaron knew he was on the cusp of something significant.

September 4, 1989: Marlena

My little sister is getting married today. Our baby sister Cassandra called me last Thursday to give me the news. I guess Daphne is too busy organizing her wedding to call me herself. It doesn't matter. We have not spoken since the boys and I left Philly. She didn't want me to go, but that's no surprise: she never liked Rob — always said he was odd, too familiar. I remember she said he flirted with her once... when Rob and I were in high school and she was only 11 or 12. As if a grown man of 20, working hard delivering for the butcher shop all day, would have time or inclination to stop and flirt with an 11-year-old girl. It's ridiculous, as it was when she told me then.

I thought about going to the wedding; I did. Daphne's marrying Turbo Sal, that skin-dirty mechanic that used to run with Big Mike. He was there that night. The rest of them will be at the ceremony too. Rob says they blame me for Mike being in prison, and it would be dangerous to go anywhere near that neighborhood, that city. I'm sure he's right. I don't want to end up dead under a sedan because Slick Leo wants payback, or Hammer thinks I'm the one who put Mike away — I didn't tell anybody anything. Never will.

It's not worth chancing it; those men never would listen to reason. Dangerous criminals, Rob calls them. I don't know what Daphne's thinking. Turbo won't stay loyal to her. He always thought he was hot shit, strutting around the neighborhood like Freddie Mercury himself in those tight pants. Ridiculous.

I can't go, anyway. Aaron's been so quiet since he fell on the fishing trip - he barely talks to anyone, not even Patty. I don't want to leave him when he's not better yet. He's been coming home late after school—he says he's playing with his friends Alex and Jared, but I don't know. At seven years old, he's old enough that I don't worry too much. This is a safe place to live, not like Philly.

Aaron woke up to the gray light of dawn filtering through the hotel curtains. He checked his phone but had no message from his aunt. He sighed, got dressed, and headed out, determined to visit his old neighborhood, regardless.

The drive was short, but the journey back in time felt long. As he navigated the narrow streets, the sights and sounds of his childhood flooded back. The rowhomes stood shoulder-to-shoulder, a continuous line of brick facades stretching for miles. Cigarette butts littered the sidewalks, and overturned garbage cans spilled their contents into the street. People milled about, some with a purpose that was hard to discern. Many rowhomes stood abandoned, their windows boarded up and their facades bearing the scars of neglect.

Aaron's heart sank as he turned onto his old street. It was a shadow of the place he remembered. The once-vibrant neighborhood was now a tapestry of decay and desolation. He pulled up in front of his childhood home and killed the engine, sitting still as he took in the sight.

The rowhome bore the marks of abandonment. Broken windows with jagged edges of glass framed the plywood nailed over them. The gate leading to the narrow alley that separated the house from its neighbor hung from one hinge, threatening to collapse. The front door sported the marks of violence, its surface dented and splintered as if someone had taken a baseball bat to it in a fit of rage.

Aaron stepped out of the jeep and approached the house, his footsteps echoing in the eerie quiet of the morning. He reached to touch the gate, feeling the rusted metal beneath his fingers. It creaked as he pushed it open; the sound cutting through the stillness. He walked down the narrow alley, memories of playing there as a child flashing through his mind.

He returned to the front of the house and stood on the cracked, weed-choked steps leading to the front door. The house loomed before him, a ghost of the place he had once called home. He thought about knocking, but there was no one to answer. Instead, he placed his hand on the weathered wood of the door, feeling the rough texture beneath his palm.

This was where it all began. The fights, the fear, the running. His mother's desperate attempts to shield him from the harsh realities of their life. And now, standing here, it all felt so distant and yet close.

Aaron took a deep breath and stepped back, taking in the entire scene. He pulled out his phone and snapped a picture, unsure why but feeling the need to capture this moment. Perhaps it was a way to document his journey: to mark the starting point of whatever understanding he was seeking.

He looked up and down the street, recognizing a few familiar landmarks amid the ruin. The corner store had long since closed down, its barred windows now dark. Aaron walked further down the street, his feet carrying him toward the park where he used to play as a child. The sight that greeted him was both familiar and foreign. The park where his cousin Jack had taught him how to shoot hoops was overgrown. Weeds and tall grass reclaimed the space that had once hosted laughter and games.

A group of boys played basketball on the neglected asphalt. The battered hoop they aimed for sported a mesh basket that hung by only a few chains; they made a clinking sound with each shot. The kids played with an intensity and focus that reminded Aaron of his younger days, their laughter echoing in the still morning air.

He stood there, watching them, a bittersweet smile on his lips. The place had changed, but the stubborn resilience of the residents had not. It was a small glimmer of hope among the decay. He turned back toward his street, looking for his aunt's house. Her rowhome was across the street from his own, four down on the left. As he approached, he noticed it looked better maintained than most others on the block, with a few flower pots on the front steps.

He knocked and waited. It took a long time before he heard shuffling footsteps approaching from inside. When the door opened, his Aunt Daphne stood there, a look of confusion on her face. She squinted at him, her eyes narrowing as if trying to place him.

"Can I help you?" she asked, her voice tinged with suspicion and confusion. "What are you doing here, Mike? I told you, I don't want you here, and Sal's at the shop."

Aaron wrinkled his brow in confusion. "Mike? No, Aunt Daphne, it's Aaron Callahan. Marlena's son."

She stared at him for a few more moments, her brow furrowing deeper. "Aaron? Little Aaron?" Her eyes widened, but she still seemed unsure.

"Yes, Aunt Daphne. It's been a long time." He tried to offer a reassuring smile, but he could see she was struggling to connect the man standing before her with the memories of the past.

Daphne blinked a few times, then her expression softened as

recognition dawned. "Oh my goodness, Aaron! I didn't recognize you at first. You've grown up so much. You look so much like your father, it's unsettling."

Aaron nodded, feeling a mix of relief and sadness. "Yeah, it's been a long time. Can I come in?"

She hesitated, then opened the door wider and stepped aside. "Of course, come in."

He stepped inside, feeling a rush of mixed emotions. The house smelled of fresh coffee and a hint of lavender. The living room was cozy, filled with old photographs and knick-knacks collected over her lifetime. It was like stepping back in time.

"Have a seat," Daphne said, gesturing to the worn but comfortable-looking couch. "Can I get you something to drink? Coffee, tea?"

"Coffee would be great, thanks," Aaron replied, taking a seat and looking around. He spotted a photo of himself as a child on one shelf, standing by his mother. "I'm sorry to surprise you like this. I sent a Facebook message, but I don't know if you saw it."

Daphne returned with two steaming cups of coffee and sat across from him. "Facebook? No, I never remember to look at that. No matter. What brings you back to this old neighborhood after all these years?"

Aaron took a deep breath, bracing himself for the conversation. "I found some things in Mom's old stuff... things about Harrison and Lydia. Things about my father. I needed to see this place again and understand more about our past."

Daphne nodded. "I wondered if you'd ever come back, especially after everything that happened. It's not a simple place to revisit, I know. But sometimes, we need to face the past to move forward."

Aaron took a sip of his coffee, gathering his thoughts. "Mom never talked about this place, or you. She passed away last year, and I found her book. That's how I learned about Harrison and Lydia."

Daphne's eyes widened with shock and sadness. "Marlena... she's gone?" She put a hand to her mouth, tears welling in her eyes. "I didn't know. We lost touch after... after everything."

Aaron nodded, his own emotions raw. "Yeah, she passed away from cancer last year. It happened fast."

His aunt stood up and walked to the window by her front door.

Bracing one hand against the door frame, she covered her face with the other. She paused there for a few moments, then returned to the couch, reaching to place her hand on his. "I'm so sorry, Aaron, for everything. Your mom had her reasons, and I'm sure they were good ones, but I'm here now. Whatever you need to know. If I can, I'll help you."

They sat in silence for a moment. Aaron felt a minor relief at confronting this part of his history. He had come looking for answers, and while he didn't know what he would find, he felt like this was a step in the right direction.

She stood again, wringing her hands before gathering her coffee cup and carrying it into the kitchen. Aaron followed, not wanting to seem rude but eager for her to talk about his mother. Daphne washed and dried her cup before leaning on her Formica counter and looking at him. She looked so much like his mother right then that Aaron took a deep breath.

"Aaron," she began, "your mother was always so strong. She went through more than anyone should have to bear."

He nodded, feeling a lump form in his throat. "I know she did. But she never talked about it, not really. I learned about Harrison and Lydia from her book—she never mentioned them."

Daphne sighed, her eyes misting with memories. "Harrison and Lydia... she lost them, you know. She never got over that. It broke her heart."

Aaron leaned against the doorway, his mother's hidden pain pressing down on him. "Why didn't she ever tell us? Why did she keep all of this a secret?"

"She thought she was protecting you," Daphne whispered. "Marlena didn't want you to carry the same burdens she did; she wanted you to have a chance at a normal life."

"But how could she think keeping it all inside was better?" Aaron's voice cracked with emotion. "It only made things more confusing, more painful."

Daphne walked over and placed a hand on his shoulder. "Your mom did what she thought was best. She was trying to shield you from the darkness of the past. But I agree, it might have been better if she had shared some of it with you. Maybe it would have helped you understand her better."

Aaron took a deep breath. "I feel like there's so much I don't know about her, about our family. I don't even know where to start."

Daphne gave him a sad smile. "You're starting now, Aaron. By being here, by asking questions. It's time for the truth to come out."

Aaron nodded. "I want to know everything, Aunt Daphne. About Harrison, Lydia, Mom, and what she went through. I need to understand."

She squeezed his shoulder reassuringly. "Then let's sit and talk. I don't have all the answers, but I will tell you what I know."

12

As they talked, the sunlight pouring through the front window intensified and waned as the hours passed. Aaron listened as Daphne recounted memories of his mother. She spoke of how Marlena had been a bright, spirited girl, and how losing her kids had been shattering.

"She was so strong, you know," Daphne said, her voice softening. "After everything with Harrison and Lydia, she put on a brave face, but you could see the cracks. She loved those kids, Aaron. I remember how she would talk about them—she wished she could have kept them close."

He nodded, absorbing how much his mother had gone through before he came into the world. He had never known the full extent of his mother's pain, and hearing it from his aunt made him realize how deeply it had affected her.

"And then, after that… well, that's when Big Mike came into her life," Daphne continued, with a hint of nostalgia in her eyes. "Mike scooped up the pieces of her broken heart like candy from a baby. He was so handsome—he looked just like you. Such a charming smile, you know? I think he thought he could make her happy again, and for a while, he did."

"What was he like?" Aaron asked, his curiosity piqued.

"Mike? Oh, he could be funny and sweet when he wanted to be. But he also had a darker side—things he was involved with that

Marlena didn't approve of. He could be scary; the neighborhood saw it plenty of times. But Marlena was smitten. She thought he was quite the catch."

Aaron listened, trying to reconcile the charming man who had stolen his mother's heart with the man who had left a trail of destruction in his wake. The true story of their family history had so many layers of pain and love, and they had shaped them all.

The afternoon sun dipped lower, casting shadows across the kitchen. Aaron asked about Big Mike's imprisonment. Daphne, who had been chopping potatoes for dinner, paused before saying, "Well, what did your mama tell you about it?"

Aaron swallowed hard, choosing his words carefully. "Only that he… killed someone at the shop. I know it was bad, but I don't know the details."

Daphne glanced at him, her expression shifting. "Yeah, it was a tough time. It shook everyone up, especially in the neighborhood. We all knew Mike had a temper, but… I don't think anyone expected him to go that far." She set the knife down, wiping her hands on a dish towel. "It was a night like any other, but things just… escalated."

He watched her, trying to gauge how much she knew. "Do you know what happened? I mean, was it self-defense or something? Did he have a reason?"

His aunt shook her head, her eyes distant, as if recalling something painful. "All I know is that there was an argument. I wasn't there that night, but Sal said it got out of hand. Someone pushed the wrong button, and the next thing you know… well, it was all over. Mike went to prison for it, and we all tried to move on."

Aaron felt a mix of anger and sadness swirl within him. "And Mom? What was it like for her after?"

Her expression softened. "Your mother was heartbroken. She was trying to raise you and take care of everything alone. I know she loved Mike, despite everything. It was hard on her. I think she felt so alone."

"Did she ever talk about it?" Aaron asked.

"A little here and there," Daphne replied, leaning against the counter. "She'd talk about how much she wanted things to be different, how she wished Mike would change. But you know how it is. Love can blind you to a lot."

Aaron's stomach churned as he listened. He had always felt the shadow of Big Mike looming over him, but hearing the details made it even more real. "Did Mom ever visit him?" he asked, fearing the answer.

She shook her head, a sorrowful look crossing her face. "She couldn't bring herself to. She thought it was better for you kids to stay away from that world. And after a while, it became easier to forget." She was filling a Dutch oven with water and raised her voice so he could hear her.

"And then, of course, Robert showed up again. He always swept back in—took every chance he could to charm Marlena again. He flitted in and out of her life since their high school days. I never liked Rob—believe me, I have my reasons—but she always listened to him. She moved from one awful man to another. My poor sister."

Daphne sighed, her eyes reflecting a deep-seated pain. "It's a cycle, isn't it? She deserved so much better, yet she never seemed to realize it. I often wish I could have done more for her. Maybe if I had been there, things would have turned out differently."

Aaron nodded, feeling a deep ache for his mother, the choices she had made, and the pain she had carried alone. It was as if he were peeling back layers of their family's history, revealing the scars that had shaped them all.

His aunt leaned against the counter, her expression turning thoughtful. "You know, it wasn't only Marlena. All of us seemed caught in the same cycle. Susanna, your cousin Jack's mother, never settled down with one man for long. She was always chasing something, but it never seemed to last. She died alone over a dozen years ago now. It's sad to think about how many chances she had, but she never found the right one."

Aaron listened, his heart heavy with the weight of his family's history.

"And then there's Cassandra, our baby sister," she continued, her voice trembling. "She married Nikos—everyone called him Greenie. He was one of Big Mike's crew, and when he caught her with another man back in '91, he killed both of them. It shattered our family even more. We thought Marlena had it tough, but Cassandra's death... left a mark on all of us. I still can't believe she's gone."

Aaron's stomach turned at the thought of the violence that had stained his family's history. "It's hard to hear all of this," he admitted.

"I knew there were struggles, but I never understood… I didn't understand how much."

Daphne nodded, her eyes glistening with tears. "It's been a long road for all of us, Aaron. We always hoped things would get better, but sometimes it feels like the past keeps coming back to haunt us. At least Marlena ended up in a happy marriage, right? I guess maybe I was wrong about Rob. Or he changed."

Aaron felt his stomach tighten. He wanted to comfort her, to reassure her that things had worked out for his mother, but he couldn't bring himself to speak well of Rob. "I… I hope that's true," he replied cautiously. "It's hard to see everything from the outside. People change, and sometimes it's for the better."

Daphne seemed to take solace in his words, her expression softening. "Yes, that's true. I guess I worried that the cycle would continue. I never wanted that for her, for any of us. But maybe she found the happiness we all wished for."

"Maybe she did," Aaron said, forcing a small smile. It was a complicated truth. He wasn't ready to unpack with her yet. Instead, he focused on the warmth of the moment, grateful for the connection he was rebuilding with his aunt, even among the painful memories.

As they settled back into a more comfortable rhythm, Daphne leaned against the counter, glancing out the window as if searching for something out of sight. "You know, Big Mike lives close to here. I don't know exactly where he is now, but the guys at the shop would know. They still all hang out together. Thick as thieves, 15 years of prison be damned."

Aaron's heart raced at the mention of his father. The idea of coming face-to-face with Big Mike sent a jolt of anxiety through him. "Yeah? I guess it makes sense he'd still be around," he replied. "But I'm not sure I'm ready to see him."

His aunt turned to him, concern etched on her face. "You should consider it, Aaron. He's your daddy. Maybe it would help you get some closure or answers."

He shook his head gently. "I appreciate your concern, Aunt Daphne, but today has already been a lot to process. I need some time."

She sighed, a touch of disappointment in her eyes. "Well, I was hoping you'd stay for dinner. Sal would love to talk to you. He might have some insights on Mike. He'll never believe what a carbon copy of your daddy you are."

Aaron forced a smile, wishing he could accommodate her request. "I appreciate it but I've already got dinner plans. It's just too much in one day."

"Of course, I understand," she said. "But promise me you'll come to see me before you leave town?"

"I promise," he replied. "I'll be back to visit you, I swear."

As he stepped toward the door, Daphne squeezed his arm. "Take care of yourself, Aaron. And remember, we're family. We're here for you."

"Thanks, Aunt Daphne," he said, her words lingering in his mind as he walked back into the bustling streets of his past.

December 4, 1985: Marlena

The courtroom was a cold, unforgiving place. I sat in the gallery, my hands clasped in my lap, trying to control my breathing. My boys, Aaron and Patty, are too young to understand what is happening and haven't even asked for their father these past few months. They were with their Aunt Daphne today. She has been doing her best to keep all three of us occupied and shielded from the chaos.

Big Mike stood at the defendant's table, his broad shoulders slumped, looking smaller than I had ever seen him. He didn't even fight the charges against him, even though his lawyer had been pushing him in that direction for months. The judge's voice was a distant echo, words of condemnation and judgment hanging from the air like a heavy fog.

The judge handed down the sentence—fifteen years—and Mike didn't even flinch. He turned to look at me, and in that moment, I saw both the man I love and the monster he has become. His eyes were dark, filled with pain and resignation, devoid of the warmth and charm that drew me to him all those years ago.

I left the courthouse with my baby sister Cassandra, feeling the weight of the world on my shoulders, and that weight has not lifted in the hours since I got back home. I know our lives will never be the same. The man who has been both protector and tormentor is gone, and it is up to me to pick up the pieces.

Mike has called me from jail twice a week since his arrest, insisting that he won't be in for long and that I should wait for him. He swears every time we talk, his crew will take care of me and the kids. Hammer dropped by and brought me almost $6000 two weeks ago. I don't even want to think about where he got that much money. He wouldn't answer questions either, just stuffed the envelope in my hand and walked away with his hands in his pockets. Slick stopped me in the grocery store the other morning and promised he would take care of Christmas for the kids. Still, their attention makes me nervous. The boys are so little and my sisters are busy with their lives. I can't lean on them forever.

An old friend, Robert, has been calling to check on me. I haven't seen him since July, the day of the murder, when I ran into him outside his father's old butcher shop. I guess he lives out in New Jersey now, in a much better place than here. He has been an angel, checking up on me and the kids, offering a lifeline in this sea of uncertainty. I can't help but hope he calls me again tonight.

The auto shop looked the same as in Aaron's hazy memory, although it had seemed much larger in 1985. The painted words on the dirty front window had changed: Slick Leo's Auto Shop. "Not a name that inspires confidence in workmanship," he thought, but the moniker did not appear to impede the business.

The garage was busy, with the sound of clanking tools and the hum of engines filling the air. Mechanics moved around with purpose, appearing far more professional than the outer facade of their workplace. Aaron stood at the bay door, taking in the familiar but altered scene, and then walked inside.

The interior smelled of motor oil and rubber, a mixture of scents that brought a flood of buried memories. He approached the front desk, where a middle-aged man with graying hair and a thick mustache looked up from a clipboard.

"Can I help you?" the man asked, his tone gruff but not unfriendly.

"I'm looking for Sal," Aaron replied.

The man eyed him for a moment before nodding. "Sal's in the back. Head on through."

Aaron nodded his thanks and made his way through the cluttered garage, weaving between cars in various states of repair. In the back, he spotted Sal—a wiry man with a bald head and a well-worn face talking with another mechanic.

When Sal looked up and saw Aaron approaching, his expression shifted to surprise and curiosity. "Hey, can I help you?"

"Sal, it's me, Aaron Callahan. Marlena's son."

Recognition flickered in Sal's eyes, and he nodded. "Aaron. It's been a long time. You were a little kid the last time I saw you. What brings you here?"

"I'm looking for some information. About my father, Big Mike."

Sal's expression hardened, but he nodded. "Yeah, I figured this day might come. Let's step outside where it's quieter."

They moved to the side of the building, away from the noise of the shop. Sal lit a cigarette and took a long drag before speaking. "So, what do you want to know?"

Aaron took a deep breath. "I need to know where he is. And I need to know what happened back then."

Sal exhaled a plume of smoke, studying Aaron with caution and pity. "Your old man... he's been lying low. He's got a place not too far from here. But, Aaron, are you sure you want to dig into this? Some things are better left buried."

"I need to know," Aaron insisted. "I need to understand."

Sal took another drag on his cigarette and gave Aaron a once-over. "You know, you look just like him. Spitting image. It's almost eerie."

Aaron felt a shiver run down his spine at the comment, but kept his resolve firm. "I've heard that before. I'm ready, Sal. Tell me everything."

Sal took another drag from his cigarette, the smoke curling around his face before dissipating into the air. "Alright, kid. Your old man, Big Mike... he's been keeping a low profile ever since he got out. He's got a place out in Doylestown. It's up north, a couple of hours, not bad. It's not the sort of neighborhood you'd want to stroll through after dark."

Aaron nodded, absorbing the information. "Doylestown. Got it. What about... what happened that night? The night he... killed a guy?"

"You gotta be more specific, kid," Sal chuckled, triggering a cough that sounded like a dying seal. Aaron kept his face still, hiding his annoyance.

When he recovered from the paroxysmal cough, Sal's expression darkened. "I know which night you mean, kid. That night was a mess. It was supposed to be a simple meeting, but things went sideways fast. Your mom was there. She saw everything."

Aaron clenched his fists, feeling a surge of anger and sorrow. "I know. She never talked about it, but I know she was there."

Sal nodded. "Yeah, she was. And she wasn't supposed to be. Big Mike didn't want her involved, but sometimes you can't control how things unfold."

"The guy at the meeting... who was he? I know this name—Edward Scott. That was in the news, the court documents. But who was he? What went sideways? What was he even doing there?"

Sal took another drag, letting the silence hang between them. "Look, Aaron, what happened that night... it changed everything for all of us. Some of us moved on and tried to build new lives. Others, like your dad, couldn't. They got stuck in that moment, in that place. Those questions of yours... I ain't got those answers. You'll have to ask your old man."

Aaron looked at Sal, his gaze unwavering. "I need to see him. I need to talk to him."

Sal sighed, flicking the cigarette butt to the ground and crushing it under his boot. "Alright. I'll give you the address. But be careful, kid. The past has a way of biting back."

They stepped back inside, and Aaron followed the old man into an office in the back corner. Sal scribbled an address on a scrap of paper and handed it to Aaron. "Here. Don't be stupid, alright?"

Aaron nodded, taking the paper. "Thanks, Sal. I appreciate it."

Sal gave him a long, hard look before turning to the garage. "Take care, Aaron. And remember, some things are better left in the past."

As Aaron walked back to his jeep, he felt a mix of anticipation and dread. Seeing his old neighborhood, reconnecting with his family, and now the prospect of confronting his father—this was a lot to process. But he knew he couldn't turn back now, not when the answers were so close.

He climbed into his jeep and took a moment to compose himself before starting the engine. He glanced at the scrap of paper with the address, then tucked it into his pocket. Doylestown could wait for tomorrow.

13

Aaron felt a tight knot of anxiety coiling in his stomach as he drove back to the restaurant from the night before. The thought of meeting his father loomed over him, a dark cloud hanging in the corners of his mind. He needed a break from it, a chance to breathe and think about something else.

He pulled into the restaurant's parking lot. The neon lights flickered like an escape sign. The sounds of laughter and clinking glasses spilled into the evening air, promising a reprieve. He stepped into the cozy ambiance and the faint strumming of an acoustic guitar filtering through the crowd.

He settled onto a bar stool, the polished wood cool beneath him, and signaled for a drink. "What can I get ya, pal?" the bartender asked, raising an eyebrow.

"Whiskey, neat," Aaron replied, leaning back against the bar. As the bartender poured the amber liquid into a glass, he let his eyes wander over the room, hoping to see Bethany. She had left an impression on him—her confidence, her amiable smile. He wondered if fate would bring her back around tonight.

The bartender slid the glass in front of him, and Aaron took a sip, savoring the warmth that spread through him. He closed his eyes, letting the music wash over him. It was a soothing mix of familiar tunes and new melodies, and he let himself get lost in the rhythm.

The beautiful woman from last night danced in his mind again.

Why didn't I ask her to sit down? It had been seven years since his divorce, and in the time since, no one had filled that void. Some one-night stands... a few stuck around for a week or a month... but his heart always hesitated. A commitment was beyond him at this point—even as he wished for it.

As he finished his drink, his phone buzzed on the bar. He glanced down to see a text.

> 02/26/16 9:07 pm
> From Lucas: Hey, man, checking in. How's everything?

Aaron hesitated for a moment, fingers hovering over the screen. He could tell Lucas everything—the anxiety, the impending confrontation with Big Mike, the overwhelming need for answers. But he opted for a simple reply.

> 02/26/16 9:12 pm
> To Lucas: All good. Grabbing a drink. You?

> 02/26/16 9:13 pm
> From Lucas: Hustling kids off to bed, maybe watch a movie after. You need to come up soon. It's been a minute since I saw your ugly mug.

> 02/26/16 9:15 pm
> To Lucas: I might do that.

He took another sip of his whiskey; the alcohol dulling the edges of his anxiety. With each passing moment, he felt a little lighter, the worries about tomorrow fading, if only for a while.

The door swung open, and in walked Bethany. She looked around for a moment, her gaze landing on him. A smile broke across her face, and she made her way over, a vision in her fitted jeans and a flowing top that swung around her as she moved.

"Fancy seeing you here again," she said, sliding onto the stool by him.

"Yeah, I needed a drink," Aaron admitted, a grin tugging at his lips. "How about you?"

"Same. The music here is too good to resist," she replied, glancing toward the stage where the next band was setting up.

They talked, the conversation flowing as easily as the liquor. Aaron felt the tension in his shoulders ease as they spoke. With each sip of whiskey and each word exchanged with Bethany, he remembered that not all moments had to be weighed down by the past. Her eyes never left his face, and the way they sparkled when her wide grin lifted them was captivating.

Even as he enjoyed her company, the meeting with his father remained in his mind. He couldn't shake the feeling that he stood on the cusp of something monumental; a turning point that could either set him free or pull him deeper into the shadows of his family's history. For now, though, he let the music and the warmth of the bar envelop him, grateful for this fleeting distraction before the reality of tomorrow set in.

February 3, 1981: Marlena

Today I had a date with Big Mike Callahan. I think it's the first time I've thought about anything besides working at the grocery store or helping with my sister Susanna's new baby, little Jack. Holding the baby makes me feel useful in a way I haven't felt since I last held my babies, almost three years ago. I hope my babies are okay.

When Big Mike walked into the store, I almost didn't see him—so lost in my thoughts. Every time he comes in, he flirts with me. His smile is contagious, and that dimple in his chin draws me in. His funny, charismatic charm makes me feel like I'm the only one in the room. My heart races a little every time he walks through the door.

I was stocking shelves this morning when he leaned over the counter, his eyes sparkling with mischief. "Hey Marlena, how about we grab a bite sometime?"

I couldn't believe it. "Sure," I replied, trying to sound cool but feeling butterflies in my stomach. "I'm off work an hour after noon."

"I'll be here, pretty lady." He winked and my knees buckled. It's a wonder I didn't mix up every bit of canned goods I stocked today, because he was all I could think about from then on.

He was at the end of the alley when I left the store right on time. We walked to the corner diner, and he led us to a back booth. He ordered fried chicken and macaroni and cheese—his favorite. I watched him talk, his excitement about some sporty car they were working on up at the shop radiating from him, and I couldn't help but smile.

When we left, the cold air was nipping at my cheeks. He noticed my hat slipping over my ears and adjusted it for me, and my heart skipped a beat. It was such a sweet gesture, and it made me feel special. No one has noticed me in a long time; most of the time, I almost don't notice myself.

Walking to my house, our fingers brushed together, sending shivers down my spine. When we reached my front door, he leaned in, and I closed my eyes, anticipation buzzing through me. His lips touched mine, and everything else faded away.

It was only a few hours ago, and I can't wait to see him again. Maybe he'll come into the store tomorrow. I can't help but think this is the beginning of something amazing. Who knows where this path will lead? It could be a beautiful journey with a man who might change my life forever.

Aaron woke up to the warm glow of the hotel room. He blinked, trying to orient himself, and then turned to see Bethany lying beside him, her strawberry blond curls spilling across the pillow. She looked peaceful; her face relaxed in sleep, and he couldn't help but smile at the memory of the night before.

They left the bar—the connection between them developing into a magnetic pull. They walked along the river. The cool night air whipped around them, and flirtatious glances and casual touches punctuated their conversation.

"So, you said you work in construction?" she had asked, her

fingers brushing against his as they strolled.

"Yeah," Aaron answered, "residential homes and commercial buildings. Keeps me busy and out of trouble."

Bethany's laugh was melodic and made him want to keep her smiling. "That's important. I work with troubled kids, so I know a thing or two about staying out of trouble."

"A social worker, huh? That's a tough job," Aaron said, impressed.

"It can be," she admitted, "but it's rewarding. I moved up here from South Carolina to get my master's. Fell in love with the city and stayed."

"Philly has that effect on people," Aaron said. "I'm from here, but I live in Boyertown now. It's not too far from here. It's a quiet place, but I like it."

As they walked, their hands found each other, the contact electrifying. They talked about their favorite places in the city, the quirks of their jobs, and the little things that made them who they were. But it was all surface-level, a dance of getting to know each other without delving too deeply.

The moon was high in the sky when they reached his hotel. She had accepted his invitation to come upstairs; the invitation had been impossible to resist, she said. They had spent the night wrapped up in each other, the physical connection mirroring the easy rapport they had shared earlier.

As the morning light grew brighter, Aaron replayed their conversations and how she looked at him. He had felt a sense of calm he hadn't experienced in a while, a respite from the anxiety that had been gnawing at him since his decision to confront his father. *How long will this last—one night? One week? A month? Or maybe… it's too soon.*

Now, Aaron could feel that anxiety was creeping back in, and his mind wouldn't let him rest. He slipped out of bed, careful not to wake Bethany, and reached for the book he had brought—his mother's memoir. Sitting in a chair by the window, he flipped through the pages until he found the story of how his parents had met.

The memory of that day in 1981, though filtered through his mother's perspective, served as a vivid reminder that even the most hopeful beginnings can lead to unforeseen outcomes. He rubbed his eyes, trying to clear his mind, and glanced back at the bed.

Bethany stirred, her eyes fluttering open. She smiled when she saw him. "Morning," she murmured, her voice husky with sleep.

"Morning," Aaron replied, putting the book aside. He climbed in beside her, wrapping an arm around her shoulders. "Sleep well?"

"Better than I have in a long time," she admitted, stretching and then snuggling closer to him. "How about you?"

"Same," he said, feeling the truth of it. "Last night was…nice."

"Yeah, it was," she agreed, her eyes twinkling with mischief. "We should do it again sometime."

"I'd like that," Aaron said, surprised by how much he meant it. He wanted to see where this could go, even though his immediate future was uncertain.

For now, though, he pushed those thoughts aside and focused on the woman beside him. This morning, this moment, was something good in the middle of the chaos, and he was determined to savor it.

They lingered in bed; the morning stretching out before them as if it were theirs alone. The warmth of her body next to his was inviting, and as their eyes met, the connection between them deepened. Without words, they drew closer, the intimacy from the night before rekindling with a new intensity.

He ran his fingers through her strawberry blond curls, tracing the curve of her neck and the line of her shoulder. Bethany responded by leaning into him, her touch soft but sure as she explored his body. They moved together, the rhythm of their breaths aligning as they surrendered to the moment.

For a while, the outside world disappeared. It was only them, wrapped up in each other, the concerns of the day slipping away. Aaron felt a fleeting sense of peace… as if they were the only two people who mattered. This was a brief escape, a sanctuary they had created together, and he was reluctant to let it end.

The moment passed, and they settled back into the pillows, the silence between them comfortable and content. Aaron held her close, kissing her forehead as she nestled against his chest.

"What time is it?" Bethany asked.

"Close to breakfast," Aaron replied, glancing at the clock. He didn't want to think about what came next—about the day that awaited him once he left this room.

She smiled, tilting her head to look up at him. "I could eat."

"Me too," he said, tracing patterns on her back. He hesitated, then added, "I'll order us something."

He reached for the phone to call room service, and Bethany propped herself up on one elbow. "What's on your agenda today?" she asked, her tone casual.

Aaron paused, not wanting to burden the moment with the weight of his plans. "Just wrapping up my trip," he said, his voice light. "Nothing major."

She seemed to sense his reluctance to share more and didn't press him. Instead, she smiled and nodded, accepting his answer without question. "Well, I'm glad we got to spend this time together," she said, kissing him.

"Me too," Aaron replied. They spent the next hour savoring the calm before the day's complications would pull them back into reality.

After breakfast, they lingered at the table, the remnants of their meal scattered between them. Bethany's laughter filled the room as they shared stories from their lives—little anecdotes that felt safe and light, steering clear of anything too deep. Aaron smiled more than he had in a while.

But as the clock ticked closer to noon, reality seeped back in. Bethany glanced at her phone, the screen lighting up with a message. She sighed, setting it back down on the table.

"I should get going soon," she said, her tone a mix of reluctance and resignation. "I have some plans this afternoon that I can't push off."

Aaron nodded, understanding but feeling a twinge of disappointment. "Yeah, I get it," he said. "I've got some things I need to take care of, too."

Bethany smiled, reaching across the table to take his hand. "I'm glad we met," she said, her eyes warm as they locked with his. "Last night was… well, it was exactly what I needed."

"Same here," Aaron replied, squeezing her hand. He meant it. Despite everything weighing on his mind, the time he'd spent with Bethany was a welcome reprieve, a chance to forget his troubles for a little while.

They both stood, and Aaron walked her to the door. She gathered her things, her movements unhurried but purposeful. Before she left, she turned to him one last time, leaning in to kiss him.

"Take care of yourself, Aaron Callahan," she whispered, her voice soft but sincere.

"You too, Bethany," he said, watching as she walked down the hallway, her figure disappearing around the corner.

14

Once she was gone, the quiet of the hotel room was deafening. Aaron took a deep breath, trying to ground himself. He knew what he had to do next, but the thought of it filled him with a sense of dread.

He began packing up his things, going through the motions as his mind raced ahead. There was still the matter of saying goodbye to Aunt Daphne and tying up loose ends here in the city. And then, after that, his father waited for him in Doylestown, the confrontation hovering over this entire trip.

After a quick shower, he packed up the rest of his things, careful not to leave anything behind. The book—his mother's memoir—lay on the nightstand, and he hesitated before tucking it into his bag. It felt like he was carrying more than just a book with him; it was his map of the memories, the history, and the unfinished business that still lingered between him and his father.

As he zipped up his bag, his phone buzzed with a text.

> 02/27/16 12:11 pm
> From Aunt Daphne: Don't forget to say goodbye.

He smiled at the message, grateful for her. Yesterday had been a day of reminiscing and reconnecting, and though they had talked about so much, there were things he had kept to himself. There were things he wasn't sure his mother would want everyone to know.

> 02/27/16 12:16 pm
> To Aunt Daphne: On my way. See you soon.

He grabbed his keys and slung his bag over his shoulder, taking one last look around the hotel room before heading out into the uncertain path ahead.

The drive to Daphne's was short, but it gave him time to think about the conversations they'd had, the way she'd looked at him with concern and understanding, sensing there was more he wasn't saying.

When he arrived at her house, she was waiting on the front stoop, a cup of coffee in hand. She smiled as he approached, her eyes scanning his face as if searching for any sign of what was inside his head.

"Hey, there you are," Daphne greeted him, setting her coffee aside to hug him. "I was thinking you were going to skip out on me."

Aaron chuckled, hugging her back. "Wouldn't dream of it. I just needed some time this morning."

She nodded, pulling back to look at him. "You look like you've got a lot on your mind."

"Yeah, I guess I do," Aaron admitted, running a hand through his hair. "It's been a lot to process, being back here and all."

Daphne studied him for a moment, then gestured towards the stoop. "Why don't we sit for a bit? I've got fresh coffee. You can tell me what's on your mind."

He hesitated but nodded, and sat down by his mother's sister. The afternoon sun cast dappled light through the trees onto the sidewalk. It was peaceful here, nothing like the turmoil he felt inside.

April 4, 1986: Marlena

I've done it: I filed the divorce papers. My hands were shaking when I signed them. My lawyer says it shouldn't take more than a couple of months with Mike in prison. I can only imagine how furious he'll be when he finds out. Thank God he's incarcerated, because I know how unforgiving he can be. I hope his friends leave me alone. They've offered help and money for months, but I've turned them down so many times. I appreciate their intentions, but I don't need their help. I have Robert now to take care of me.

He finalized his divorce over the winter, and he's been back here ever since. He has a couple of kids in New Jersey, but his ex-wife won't let him see them. She tried to take everything from him, even accusing him of doing awful things to the kids. Some people will stop at nothing to get what they want. Rob says she was after his money, but she's doing just fine working for a lawyer. She's beautiful—he showed me a picture once—but he says she doesn't hold a candle to me.

Of course, he has nothing nice to say about Mike. He never knew him like I used to. They were a couple of years apart in school, but miles apart in every other way. Mike was a shop guy even back then: always the tough guy in his leather jacket with a cigarette tucked behind his ear. Rob was an athlete—he played football and baseball, studied hard in school, and worked every evening at the butcher shop.

I tried to explain how sweet and funny Mike used to be, but Rob wouldn't hear a word of it. He called Mike "an idiot, a thug who was going nowhere fast." Why should I come to Mike's defense? He had me and mistreated me. That I wish things had been different doesn't change what's happened. Rob always had a thing for me; I knew that even back then. We dated twice before I met Roy. I guess I've always made the wrong choices—until now.

He's so good with my boys. He bought them toys and took us all to the zoo last weekend. The sun was bright, and the animals came out of their enclosures. Patty loved the big cats—the lions, the tigers, and the cheetahs. Aaron, of course, was all about the turtles. We had snow cones and rode the little train. Big Mike would never have shared a day like that with us. "Too busy," he'd always say. But Robert? He always makes time for the kids.

Aaron paused at his jeep, taking in the familiar row of houses on the street where he had spent his earliest years. The sight again stirred memories—flashes of his childhood before everything changed. He slid into the driver's seat; the engine rumbling to life, a sound that broke through the quiet afternoon. Pulling out his phone, he tapped quick messages to Alex, Jared, and his foreman Jeff, warning that it would be a couple more days before he made it home. He wasn't worried about the work; his crew could handle things without him. He slid his phone into the cup holder and fastened his seatbelt.

As he pulled away, the neighborhood unfolded around him, each house a reminder of a time long past. He passed by the brick house where he and Patty had lived, then the little park where he had learned the game of basketball with his cousin Jack. They'd spent hours there, teaching themselves to dribble the ball on the cracked pavement. The echo of the ball against the asphalt was still vivid in his mind. He hadn't been here in so long, yet the memories were as fresh as if they had happened yesterday.

The familiar sights and sounds of the city faded. The rowhomes gave way to wider roads and open fields, the landscape shifting from urban grit to the greener outskirts. It was a slow transition, but with each passing mile, Aaron felt the tension building within him.

Driving to Doylestown was more than just a journey—it was a step toward confronting a past he had long avoided. As the city fell away, replaced by the calm of the countryside, his thoughts turned inward. The memories he had been trying to escape for so long were now at the forefront of his mind, demanding his attention.

With the road stretched out before him, flanked by tall trees and vast fields, he should have felt calm, but his anxiety intensified—the anticipation growing. The closer he got to Doylestown, the more the reality of what lay ahead weighed on him.

When the town sign came into view, it marked the point of no return. The town was quiet, its streets lined with historic buildings and old trees. The place seemed untouched by time. But for Aaron, time had done nothing to dull the emotions that surged within him now.

His eyes scanned the storefronts, the restaurants with outdoor seating, and the families strolling along the sidewalks. It was peaceful here, the antithesis to the turmoil brewing inside him. As he drove further into the heart of the town, he spotted a place that felt right—a modest, two-story inn with white shutters and a small garden out front. It wasn't flashy, just comfortable.

Aaron pulled into the small parking lot, turned off the engine, and sat, staring at the entrance. *This is it. I'm here.* He'd stay here, gather his thoughts, and prepare his mind. After a deep breath, he grabbed his bag from the backseat and walked inside.

The inn's lobby was cozy, with warm lighting and well-worn furniture that gave it a homey feel. A friendly woman behind the desk greeted him with a smile, and within minutes, he had a key in hand. His room was on the second floor, overlooking the street, and as he stepped inside, he felt a strange mix of calm and unease.

The room featured a bed with a quilted coverlet, a wooden dresser, and a small desk by the window—small but comfortable. Aaron set his bag down and moved to the window, looking at the town below. The sun dipped in the sky, casting long shadows across the street. It was beautiful in a way, but Aaron couldn't appreciate it. His mind was already on what he had to do next.

Confronting his father wouldn't be easy, and he wasn't sure what he hoped to achieve. *Closure? Understanding? A chance to tell him how he's made me feel all these years?* Whatever it was, he had to face it head-on.

But for now, he allowed himself to breathe, to take in the room's quiet and the stillness of the evening. Tomorrow, he would face his father. Tonight, he would try to find some peace, however fleeting.

Aaron slept late the next morning. His anxiety made it hard to pull himself from bed. By the time he was on the road, the sun had climbed high in the sky. He made his way to the address Sal had given him. The location was a few miles outside town, away from the midday traffic of Doylestown. The road grew narrower, flanked by trees that seemed to close in on him as he approached.

When he spotted the rusty, battered mailbox labeled "Callahan," his pulse quickened. He turned onto the gravel driveway. Right away, the loud baying of a hound dog filled the air. Aaron spotted the dog bounding toward the jeep, its deep, resonant bark echoing through the quiet surroundings. The dog, the guardian of this secluded property, followed along, baying at the tires as Aaron drove toward the house.

The manufactured home came into view, its peeling front deck and worn appearance hinting at years of neglect. Aaron's eyes shot to the man who emerged from the shadows of the doorway, stepping onto the deck. Even from a distance, Aaron could tell that this man could only be Big Mike. At sixty-three years old, he still looked every bit the imposing figure Aaron remembered—a towering man with silver hair, not balding but full and thick, and a muscular build that spoke of a lifetime of physical labor. He wore flannel pajama pants and a white tank top that showed off his brawny arms.

Aaron parked and took a deep breath before stepping out. The dog's barking had subsided into a low growl, but its eyes remained fixed on him, ready to pounce at a moment's notice. Before Aaron could say a word, the old man's voice cut through the air, rough and commanding.

"Which one are you? Aaron or Patty?"

The question caught Aaron off guard; the bluntness striking him like a blow. He hadn't expected this kind of reception, and for a moment, he hesitated, searching for his voice. Years of distance and silence between him and this man compressed into this moment.

"Aaron," he replied, meeting his father's steely gaze.

Big Mike studied him for a long moment, his expression unreadable. The silence between them stretched, filled only by the faint rustle of leaves and the occasional huff of the dog at Aaron's feet.

"Come on up," Big Mike said, his tone gruff, but carrying a note of something Aaron couldn't quite place—*was it curiosity? Annoyance? Something else?*

Aaron moved toward the house, the uneasy feeling building with every step. He knew that whatever happened next would be a turning point.

As soon as he stepped into the living room, a mix of stale odors assailed his nose—the musty stench of cigarette smoke and weed mingled with the lingering scent of fried chicken. The worn sofa and an armchair that had seen better days dominated the cramped room. The faded carpet and a large TV sat against one wall, a muted episode of "Wheel of Fortune" playing through static.

Big Mike wasted no time, pointing to the sofa with a brusque gesture. "Have a seat," he said, his tone clarifying that it was more of an order than a suggestion. Aaron hesitated for a split second before he complied, lowering himself onto the sagging cushions. The room felt heavy and oppressive; it had absorbed years of tension and anger.

Without another word, Big Mike settled into his armchair, picking up where he had left off before. He leaned over the coffee table, his large hands working as he rolled a thick marijuana blunt. The casual way he handled the weed suggested that this was a routine activity for him, something that had become as natural as breathing.

Aaron watched in silence, feeling the gap between them widening. It was strange to be here, after avoiding the man's presence for so long, and even more strange to see him engaged in a habit that felt worlds away from the fatherly image Aaron had once tried to conjure.

Big Mike spoke again, his deep voice carrying a rough edge. "I heard about your mother. I saw the obituary online. Goddamn shame it is, goddamn shame."

Aaron nodded, his throat tight. "Yeah, it is."

The old man sighed, his expression softening just a fraction. "She was the best lady I ever knew." His words hung in the air, thick with unspoken memories.

Before Aaron could respond, a voice cut through the room, sharp with protest. "Best lady you ever knew, huh?" A woman emerged from the kitchen, her gaze narrowing at Big Mike. She was in her early 60s, her once-dark hair now streaked with silver. The years had etched deep lines into her face, hinting at a beauty that had long since faded. She wore leopard-print leggings and a faded Harley-Davidson sweatshirt, an odd mix of past glamour and present practicality.

Mike looked over at her, his eyes rolling. "Aaron, this here's Loretta," he said, waving a hand in her direction.

Loretta crossed her arms, standing her ground. "I don't know about all that 'best lady' talk," she muttered, her voice laced with sarcasm and lingering jealousy.

Big Mike shrugged, unbothered by her tone. "You know what I mean, Loretta. Just sayin' what's true."

Their squabble looked like a well-worn routine; Loretta huffed and turned toward the door. "I'm gonna go check on the chickens," she said, her voice carrying a note of finality.

She left the room, the screen door creaking as she stepped outside. The air in the living room seemed to settle a bit in her absence, but the tension between Aaron and his father remained.

15

Mike finished rolling the blunt and reached out, offering it to Aaron with a slight nod. Aaron hesitated for a split second. He was only an occasional weed smoker, but he didn't want to offend—not when he needed answers. Taking the blunt from his father's hand, he scanned the cluttered coffee table until he spotted a lighter wedged between empty beer cans.

He sparked the lighter and brought the blunt to his lips, inhaling. The familiar burn in his lungs was almost comforting in its way. He took another drag, feeling the tension ease before passing it to his father.

Aaron let his eyes wander around the room. The wood paneling was dark, giving the space a cave-like feel. A Harley-Davidson throw lay over the back of the worn sofa. Ashtrays scattered across various surfaces, each one overflowing with cigarette butts and the ends of joints. A record player sat in one corner, with stacks of records lined up beneath it. Wooden shelves adorned the walls, filled with an odd assortment of collectibles—some old sports trophies, a few framed photos, and a shot glass collection from different states.

The blunt came back to him, and he took another hit, letting the smoke curl from his mouth in a lazy fog. Mike's gaze was intense, his face an unreadable expression.

As they passed the blunt back and forth, Mike leaned back in his chair, studying Aaron with curiosity. "So, what do you do for a living?" he asked, his tone casual but laced with an underlying intensity.

"I own a construction company," Aaron answered. He watched the man, trying to gauge his reaction.

"Construction, huh?" Mike replied, his eyes narrowing. "Guess you took after me, then."

Aaron raised an eyebrow. "I didn't know you were in construction."

"Not really," Mike said, shrugging. "Just always knew how to build things—cars, houses, fences, whatever. But you kids moved a lot, huh?"

"Yeah, we did," Aaron replied, keeping his tone even. "Rob's jobs took us all over."

"Mmhm," Mike said, his voice tinged with sarcasm. "That Rob—never trusted him."

Aaron felt a flicker of surprise at Mike's candor. "Why not?"

"Just a gut feeling. You know, he was always too smooth, too charming. I'm not the only one who noticed," Mike replied, taking another drag from the blunt before passing it back.

Aaron studied his father's face, searching for any sign of regret or empathy, but found none. Instead, Mike continued, "What about your brother Sean? Or do you all still call him Patty? Is he working at the meat plant? A regular stepdaddy's boy?"

The words stung, though Aaron wasn't entirely sure why. "Yeah, Patty's working at the plant," he confirmed, his voice flat. He wasn't in the mood to defend his estranged brother, especially not to a man who had barely been part of their lives.

Mike nodded again, taking a moment to let the silence stretch between them. "Ain't seen him in a long time either. I guess that's how it goes, though. Life pulls you apart."

The conversation continued... a strange mix of banter and probing. Through it all, Aaron couldn't shake the feeling that Mike was testing him, trying to see how much he'd inherited from him—not just in terms of looks, but in character too.

"So, you went to UNC-Greensboro, huh?" Mike asked as if the fact was common knowledge.

"Yeah," Aaron replied, surprised again. "How do you know that?"

"I kept track as best I could over the years. Always worried about you boys and your mother," Mike said, his voice lowering. "Like I said, I never trusted that Rob."

Aaron felt an odd mixture of disbelief and curiosity. *Why is this man I have not seen in more than three decades keeping tabs on us?* "Why?" Aaron pressed, wanting to understand this unexpected connection.

"Why what?"

"Why did you keep track of us?"

"Because you're my kids, damn it. And your mother—well, she was something. Too bad I fucked that up, eh?" His laughter sounded forced, as though it was the only other option besides tears.

The admission hung in the air, a strange sincerity that left Aaron speechless.

Mike shifted in his chair, the moment passing. "So what else is new?" he asked, changing the subject to small talk as he took another hit from the blunt.

Aaron found himself drawn into the rhythm of the conversation, feeling uneasy with each exchange. Mike seemed to know so much about their lives, yet there was a distance, a sense that this catching up was more about filling in the gaps than reconnecting. They finished the blunt, the room now thick with smoke, and Aaron couldn't shake the feeling that the actual conversation was yet to begin.

"Alright, now tell me what brought you here today. I don't think you woke up thinking you'd come here and play Twenty Questions with an old man out of the thin blue sky. What is it you want to know?"

Aaron's heart raced, the question hanging in the air with the thick cloud of smoke. He shifted in his seat, aware of the intensity of Mike's gaze. The words felt like a challenge disguised as a curiosity. Aaron took a deep breath, the familiar burn of the blunt still lingering in his lungs, and for a moment, he hesitated. "I came to talk about Mom," he said, his voice steadier than he felt. Memories of her laughter and warmth flooded his mind, clashing with the cold reality of the man before him.

Big Mike's expression shifted; his curiosity mingled with something deeper. *Regret or guilt?* The space between them felt charged, like the years of distance had reached a breaking point.

"Yeah? What about her?" Mike asked, leaning forward, a glimmer of interest igniting in his steely eyes.

Aaron's pulse quickened. "I want to know what you remember," he replied, the words spilling out before he could stop them. "I need to know who she was to you. And I want to know about that night in July, the man you killed."

The room fell silent, the only sound the distant rustling of leaves outside. Mike's eyes darkened, a shadow passing over his features. For a long moment, he said nothing, Aaron's words echoing like thunder before a storm.

He exhaled, a hint of bitterness in his voice. "You think you know everything, don't you?"

Aaron's heart pounded in his chest. "I know nothing; that's the problem. You were there. You know what happened. I need to understand."

Mike leaned back in his chair, crossing his arms. "Some things are better left buried, kid. You don't know what you're asking for."

"But I need to know," Aaron insisted, feeling the urgency rise within him. "Not just for me, but for Mom. She deserved more than to be a footnote in your life."

The old man jumped to his feet, angry. "She was never just a footnote in my life!" His face contorted with anger and hurt, the lines on his forehead deepening as he struggled to contain his emotions. "You think you can come here and demand answers like you know me? Like you know her? You don't know shit about what I went through!"

Aaron felt a swell of frustration. "Then tell me! Make me understand. I can't just walk away not knowing who she was to you. She was my mother!"

Big Mike's fists clenched at his sides, the veins in his neck bulging as he wrestled with the memories. The silence stretched between them, thick with tension, before he sank back into his chair, the anger deflating into something more vulnerable.

"Alright," he said, his voice a low growl. "But you better be ready for the truth. It ain't pretty, and it ain't what you want to hear."

Aaron nodded. "I'm ready."

Mike's gaze shifted to the window, staring into the distance as if the answers lay somewhere in the trees. "She was… a fighter. There was always a fire in her. But she was also lost. I saw that in her, even if I didn't understand it. And that night... it was a turning point. A moment of no return."

Aaron leaned in, every word pulling him deeper into the tangled web of their past. "What happened?"

Just then, Loretta entered the room, balancing a wicker basket filled with freshly gathered eggs. She glanced at Mike and then shot Aaron a quick, assessing look before moving toward the kitchen.

"Mike, can you give me a hand with these?" she asked, her tone practical but tinged with a sense of urgency.

"Yeah, just a second," Mike replied, then turned back to Aaron, his voice lowering. "Listen, I can't talk about this now. Come back tomorrow after five. Loretta will be out, and I'll give you the answers."

Aaron hesitated, the urgency of his questions still gnawing at him. "You're sure you'll talk then? You won't just shut me out again?"

"I said I'd fucking talk, didn't I?" Mike snapped, but a hint of regret tempered the edge in his voice. "Just... come back tomorrow. We can figure it out then."

Aaron nodded, knowing he had little choice. He stood up, feeling light-headed and a little dizzy from the weed he'd smoked. "Alright, I'll be back."

As he made his way toward the door, he called out to the woman in the kitchen, trying to keep the mood light despite the tension in the air. "It was nice to meet you, Loretta."

"Goodbye, darling. It was good to meet you," she replied, her voice warm but distracted as she placed the eggs in a bowl. "Be safe driving out."

At the bottom of the porch steps, Aaron scratched the hound dog behind the ears, the dog leaning into his touch with a grateful huff. Just then, Mike appeared at the door, his expression unreadable. "Come on in, Duke. Tomorrow, son. After five," he said, his tone firm yet soft.

Aaron glanced back at him, a mix of hope and frustration swirling in his chest. He nodded and stepped off the porch, leaving the old house behind.

As he walked away, he could feel Mike's eyes on him; a silent acknowledgment of the uncharted territory they were about to navigate. Aaron's heart raced at what tomorrow might bring, knowing that whatever answers he received would change everything.

August 20, 1983: Marlena

I brought the groceries in and sensed that something was wrong. The sound of running water echoed from upstairs, punctuated by a little cry, followed by a sharp splash. I raced up the stairs to Aaron's room, but his crib was empty.

Panic surged as I dashed back to the hallway. The bathroom door was cracked, and I saw water pooling on the floor.

"Mike!?" I called out, dread coiling in my stomach. What in the world was he doing? He wasn't bathing Aaron, was he? At just 14 months old, my baby needed careful hands, not someone who had never shown an interest in baby care before.

I shoved the door open to find my husband kneeling at the tub's edge, both hands gripping my tiny son under the water.

"No! Mike, no!" I screamed, pounding on his back and shoulders. He released the baby, and as soon as Aaron broke through to the air, he started coughing and sputtering before unleashing a terrified wail.

I shoved Mike aside—he let me, I know that now—and snatched Aaron from the rushing water, fleeing the bathroom.

My sweet boy's terrified expression tore through me. I only had time to wrap him in a towel before Big Mike loomed behind me, his voice fearsome, his eyes hazy. He was high, or drunk, or both.

"He's my son too, and I don't want him anymore, Marlena! I fucking told you, we can't afford babies!"

"So you try to kill him?" I shouted back, my fear transforming into anger. "What about this one in my belly? You want to kill that one, too?"

"Don't fucking tempt me, wife!" He advanced toward me. I stepped back against the crib, placing the still-wailing baby on the mattress before blocking him with my body.

"Stay back, Mike. You stay back!"

He did not. I should have known better. He hit me so hard that I woke up with my face on the floor, crusted blood around the split skin near my eye. Thankfully, he was gone. But Aaron was quiet, and my mind raced to the worst outcome.

Jumping up wasn't an option after the beating I just took, but I rose as fast as I could, cradling my pregnant belly in one arm. Aaron was asleep, naked, but for the towel I'd thrown around him. When I reached into the crib, he startled awake, opening his beautiful eyes and crying.

"My sweet boy, I'm so sorry." I lifted him like broken glass and limped to the rocking chair. He was so hungry that he couldn't get to my breast fast enough. After he had his fill, I dressed him and laid him back down to sleep in the crib.

What if I hadn't come home when I did? Then what would I do? I don't know what to do.

I spent the night in the rocking chair, waking every few minutes to check on my babies: one sleeping in his crib and the other kicking in my belly.

Aaron sat on the edge of the bed in his room at the inn, the force of his mother's memory crashing over him like an endless wave. He clutched the leather book, his heart racing as he replayed the scene in his mind: Big Mike kneeling at the tub, his tiny body submerged, his mother's frantic cries echoing in his ears.

The room felt too small. The walls closed in, and he struggled to breathe as panic bubbled up inside him. A lifelong fear of getting his face wet flooded his mind. It was a fear he had never understood, a ghost that haunted him every time he took a shower—the panic did not kick in unless he was in the shower. Now it made sense. The truth was ugly and raw, tearing at the fabric of who he thought he was.

Anger surged through him as he thought of Big Mike's distorted love, the man who could drown his son without a second thought. "You always loved her? Best lady you ever knew? Something special?" he spat into the emptiness of the room. "What kind of love is that?" The memories of his father's declarations echoed in his mind.

Desperation washed over him, and he buried his face in his hands. His mother had fought for him, had wrapped him in a towel, and held him tight against her chest. But what good was that now? She was gone, leaving him to grapple with the fallout of a life built on secrets and violence.

"What do I do with this?" he whispered, his voice cracking. The impotence felt like a vice squeezing around his chest, squeezing the air from his lungs. He couldn't change the past or erase the damage done. All he could do was sit here, alone with the ghosts of his childhood.

A tear slipped down his cheek, and he swiped it away. He wasn't weak; he wouldn't let them see him break. But the truth was undeniable: others' choices shaped his world. The cycle of pain was inescapable.

With a deep breath, he pulled himself together. He needed to confront this, to understand it better. Tomorrow would bring him back to his father, and he couldn't let Big Mike's shadow hang over him any longer. He had to reclaim his life and break free from the swirling waters of his past.

16

Aaron gave up on sleep after a restless night of tossing and turning. The sheets tangled around his legs, and the pillow felt damp from hours of fitful sweat. He sat up, rubbing his face, the exhaustion clinging to him like a fog. Deciding that a shower might help, he dragged himself into the bathroom.

The hot water eased his tension at first, but as he washed his hair, his chest tightened. The steam thickened around him, and the pressure of the water dripping onto his face felt overwhelming. A panic attack gripped him, his breath coming in short bursts. He fumbled with the faucet, shutting off the water, and stumbled out of the shower, dripping and trembling.

With a towel wrapped around his waist, he collapsed onto the toilet seat, trying to slow his breathing. His heart pounded as if it might break free from his chest. The thought of facing his father later that day twisted the anxiety even tighter. He grabbed his phone and texted Jared desperately, needing the connection to pull him back to some semblance of calm. Seeing Jared's replies helped, if only a little, as he fought to regain control over the storm inside him.

Aaron dressed, the lingering unease from his panic attack making every movement uncertain. Downstairs, the inn's lobby was already bustling with early risers. His hands trembled as he poured coffee from the carafe on the sideboard, and a splash of hot liquid hit his hand. He winced but ignored it, brushing off the concerned inquiry from the attendant. He needed to be outside, away from the confined space.

The downtown street was alive with midweek energy: shoppers and business people. Pennsylvania's long winter was ending, or at least taking a break from the snow and ice; the air was warmer than it had been in months, prompting a much larger crowd than he had expected to see. He turned away from the inn, walking past a deli where tables spilled onto the sidewalk, shaded by colorful umbrellas. The smell of fresh pastries wafted through the air, mingling with the faint hum of conversation. He kept his head down, avoiding the cheerful scene as he continued past a gym, its large windows revealing people on treadmills, their expressions focused as they ran in place.

Aaron's footsteps slowed as he passed an antique shop. Old treasures filled the shop's small window—faded photographs, a tarnished silver tea set, and assorted books. The door seemed to offer an escape from the tangled emotions inside him.

The warm air inside the antique store greeted Aaron like a comforting embrace, carrying the smell of cinnamon and apples. As he stepped inside, a woman, perhaps in her late fifties, was stocking a shelf of old books. She balanced a worn cardboard box on her knee, her movements deliberate and precise. Her short gray hair framed a kind face, and when she noticed Aaron, her eyes lit up with a genuine warmth.

"Oh, hello there!" she greeted him, her voice cheerful and inviting, as if she were welcoming an old friend. "What a lovely day to be treasure hunting, don't you think?" She wiped her hands on the apron she was wearing, adorned with a pattern of tiny sunflowers. "Are you looking for something special? Or just browsing for fun? Either way, feel free to take your time. I'm here if you have any questions."

Her demeanor was so approachable that Aaron couldn't help but feel at ease. She returned to her task, placing each book on the shelf with the care of someone who loved what they did, but her attention remained on him, ready to assist if needed.

As Aaron wandered through the aisles, she called out with a bright smile, "We've just put some new items in the back, if you're into old records or vintage jewelry. And if you're looking for a gift, I might have just the thing for you. You never know what you'll find in here!"

Aaron nodded with a polite smile, appreciating her friendliness. Her upbeat energy was a comforting contrast to the heaviness he felt. As he browsed, her presence in the background, humming as she worked, added to the store's cozy atmosphere, making him feel like he'd stepped into a small pocket of peace amid the chaos of his thoughts.

As he wandered through the cluttered aisles, his eyes drifted over the various relics of a bygone era. There were ceramic salt and pepper shakers shaped like cows and cacti. Near the front, a sturdy old metal Singer sewing machine was built into a wooden table next to toys from the 1960s; stacks of vintage Tupperware sat on the shelf above. A quiet sense of curiosity stirred in him as he moved past shelves lined with dusty records, delicate teapots, and an array of costume jewelry.

Then, something caught his eye—a brilliant emerald-green glass shoe perched on a display shelf, its surface shimmering under the warm light. The shoe was elegant and whimsical, with a small cat peeking from the inside of the heel. It was so striking and unexpected, that Aaron couldn't resist picking it up. The cool, smooth glass felt solid in his hand as he examined the intricate details.

As he stood there, captivated by the delicate piece, the clerk appeared beside him, her smile widening as she saw what had caught his attention. "That's gorgeous, isn't it?" she said, her tone filled with genuine admiration. "That's a Fenton shoe, very collectible. They're quite the treasure for anyone who loves glassware. I've got a few more tucked away if you're interested in seeing them?"

Her enthusiasm was infectious, and for a moment, Aaron found himself almost tempted by the offer, but he shook his head, offering her a polite smile. "It's beautiful, but I'm just looking around today," he replied.

"No worries at all," she said, not missing a beat. "It's always fun to look, even if you take nothing home. Let me know if you change your mind."

Aaron nodded, placing the shoe back on the shelf, the cat's tiny face still peering out at him. He lingered for a moment, feeling a small sense of loss as he let go of the fragile piece, but then continued, his mind already pulling him toward the next item in this cozy labyrinth of memories.

Aaron stopped in front of a glass case of vintage Betty Boop figures. His eyes locked on the iconic character driving a lemon-yellow Beetle car.

Marlena had owned this exact figurine. He pictured it, sitting on a shelf in their living room, a bright spot in a world that often felt dark and uncertain. She had an entire collection of Betty Boop memorabilia, each piece arranged and dusted with utmost care. Betty Boop was more than just a cartoon character to her—she was a connection to her mother, who had passed down many of the figurines to her. Over the years, she had continued to add to the collection, each new piece a small celebration in her life.

Aaron could almost hear his mother's voice, warm and full of affection, as she explained to him as a child why she loved the character so much. "Betty's a fighter," she would say, with that spark in her eye. "She's always smiling, no matter what life throws at her."

His mother had been the same way, finding joy amid their struggles. Seeing the figurine now, in this small antique shop, it was as if a part of her was reaching out to him, reminding him of the love and strength she had always tried to give him.

He closed his eyes as another flash of memory ripped through his mind, vivid and painful. The yellow Beetle, smashed on the floor, half of Betty's head lying by the fireplace, the other half shattered into pieces near the staircase. Big Mike came home in a fury, his voice a thunderclap in the small living room. Aaron had cowered in the corner, small and frightened, hoping not to be noticed.

His mother was sobbing, on her knees, gathering the pieces as though they were diamonds, fragile and precious. "My mama gave me this," she whimpered, her voice breaking under the weight of her grief.

"Hey, you destroy my things, I destroy your things," Mike spat back at her, venom dripping from his words.

"They were just old work boots, Mike! You have new ones—" she tried to reason, her voice shaking with desperation and sorrow, but he cut her off.

"They were MINE!" he bellowed, as if that ownership gave him the right to shatter not just objects, but the very fabric of their lives.

Aaron squeezed his eyes shut, the memory clinging to him like a barnacle to a buoy—a heavy reminder of the chaos and fear that had lived in their home. The warmth of the antique store felt like a distant dream, a stark contrast to the turmoil churning in his chest.

He cleared his throat and got the woman's attention, a surge of determination pushing him forward. "I'd like to buy that," he said, pointing at the Betty Boop figurine. Her eyes lit up with surprise and delight, and she set her cardboard box down.

"Oh, that's fantastic! You have great taste," she exclaimed, her voice bubbling with enthusiasm. "Betty Boop is such a classic! Let me get that for you."

As she lifted the figurine from the display, she chatted animatedly. "You know, these vintage pieces are becoming quite collectible. I can't keep them in stock! It's so nice to see someone appreciate them like you do. How long have you been a Betty Boop fan?"

"Not me, my mother. This was one of her favorites. It broke years ago."

"Oh no, poor Betty! It sounds like it held a lot of sentimental value for both of you. I can see why you'd want to bring it back into your life. If you ever want to share more stories about her collection, I'd love to hear them. These little pieces of nostalgia can connect us to our loved ones."

While she rang up the figurine and prepared to box it for him, she almost couldn't contain her excitement. "I've got some other Betty pieces in the back if you're interested. You won't believe the collection I've built up over the years!"

Aaron nodded, feeling a mix of nostalgia and warmth from her enthusiasm. As she wrapped the figurine with care, he smiled at her passion for the little treasures around them.

He thanked her and collected his bag to leave. As he passed the shelf of books she had been stocking, the title Early Domestic Architecture of Pennsylvania drew his attention. He flipped through the pages, lost in the photographs of historic rowhomes when the woman rushed back through the curtain from the back room.

"Sir! I have another piece you might like!"

The woman held out a figurine of Betty Boop in a pink evening gown, her white-gloved hands raised to the sky in a joyful pose. Aaron blinked, and he was back in Kansas, hiding once more, this time in the hallway. He could hear Robert's enraged voice slicing through the air, screaming as he threw things at Aaron's crying mother. The sight of the broken figurine flashed in his mind—one of Betty's arms lay by the front door, her head near the aquarium, and the other arm clinging to the rest of the figurine in Rob's fist.

"If you don't like the way I treat him, you know where the fucking door is, Marlena!" he roared. His anger reverberated through the house. He hurled the rest of Betty against the far wall with a violent motion, where she exploded into slivers of glazed ceramic.

"Sir? Sir, are you okay?" The concerned shop owner tapped his arm.

"Yeah, yeah, I'm fine," he replied, holding up the architecture book he had been flipping through. Aaron shook his head, trying to focus on the kind face in front of him while shutting out the sobbing woman in his mind. "Sorry, I was just off in my head, thinking about this book."

"Beautiful row houses, aren't they? Of course, those neighborhoods don't look so hot these days, but hey, time does a number on us all, doesn't it?" She laughed, and he joined, hoping his laughter didn't sound as forced as it felt.

"I had this Betty back here," she continued, glancing toward the back room. "The one you bought made me think of it. Did your mother have one of these? She's pretty rare—hard to find, with no cracks or chips."

Aaron felt his eyes watering. "Yeah, I think she did. Hers was pretty beaten up, though." He swallowed the lump in his throat, struggling to maintain composure. "Tell you what, I'll take her, and this book, too."

Her eyes lit up. He followed her to the register, listening to her happy chatter as she wrapped his purchases. He almost didn't want to leave the peaceful ambiance of the antique store, but neither could he shake the memories that had just surfaced. He bid the woman goodbye, promising that he would be back soon.

Aaron made his way back to the inn in a quiet daze. On the way, he stopped at the deli, now buzzing with the lunch crowd as people filled the tables. He ordered an Italian hoagie and chips to go, his mind elsewhere as the server handed him the bag with a polite smile.

Back in his room, Aaron set the food down on the small table by the window and flipped on the TV, more out of habit than interest. The flicker of channels blurred together as he surfed through the options, his mind still half in the antique store, half in memories he wished he could forget. He unwrapped the hoagie and took a bite, the taste barely registering as he chewed, his eyes glued to the screen but not seeing it.

His thoughts drifted back to his mother's cherished Betty Boop collection. He unwrapped the figurines he had just bought and placed each piece on the desk. His fingers lingered on the smooth glass and ceramic surfaces, feeling the connection to the past in their delicate forms. The sight of them brought a wave of sadness; he could almost see his mother's face lighting up as she arranged her collection, each figurine a little piece of joy in her life.

I wonder if her collection is still on the shelf in the living room. Dusty and unappreciated for the first time in decades. The thought made his chest hurt again. That house was no longer welcoming to him. Since her death, it had become a place filled with bitter memories and closed doors. The figurines on the desk seemed almost out of place, as though they belonged to another life—a life where his mother was still there, still smiling at her beloved Betty Boops.

October 20, 1990: Marlena

I tiptoed around the living room, wrapping my Betty Boop figurines in layers of tissue paper and bubble wrap. Each one had to be secured with packing tape before I placed it in the box marked "fragile." I wouldn't take the chance of my collection getting damaged on that moving truck. The sound of cardboard boxes being sealed and the soft rustle of packing materials filled the house, but my mind was elsewhere, lost in memories of the figurines that had smashed over the years.

As I wrapped the next piece, I couldn't help but think of Mike and Rob, and the moments of anger that had shattered not just these delicate figurines, but pieces of my heart. I could still see the fragments of ceramic scattered across the floor and feel the sting of tears as I gathered the remains of what had once brought me so much joy. Some figurines I packed have chips and cracks—scars from the hasty move from Philadelphia to Kirby. I've tried to mend them as best I could, but the imperfections remain, little reminders of the hell we've been through.

One figurine in particular—Betty Boop in a red polka-dot bikini, my mother's favorite—catches my attention. As I wrapped it, I noticed a sliver of ceramic missing right on the front. How did I not see that before? The minor flaw bothered me, an imperfection I couldn't ignore. I set the figurine down and headed to Rob's office, determined to find a red marker to fix it.

In the office, I began rummaging through the drawers, my hands moving aside pens and other detritus as I searched. It was a mess: Rob hadn't even packed his things and we're supposed to move in just a few days. That's when I found a folder marked "The Red Baron." The hair on the back of my neck stood up. The Red Baron is Rudy Muller's bar, back in Philly. He was Mike's friend. I didn't even know he knew Rob, except maybe in passing. I paused, holding the folder and wondering what secrets it held. But before I could look, I heard the front door open. Rob is home. My heart skipped a beat, and I closed the drawer, leaving the folder untouched.

I dashed back to the living room, my hands trembling as I resumed packing. I haven't stopped thinking about that mysterious folder all day since.

The chipped figurine will have to wait. There are other things to worry about now, like making sure we're ready for the move to Fresno. But I wonder how many secrets my husband has, and just what he's up to.

Aaron rubbed his eyes, trying to shake off the exhaustion that clung to him after a restless night. He needed to clear his mind, especially with the evening meeting ahead. The memories stirred up by the Betty Boop figurines had left him feeling even more drained, but he knew sleep was out of the question.

He grabbed his phone to check his emails, hoping to distract himself with something more tangible. Sure enough, a message from his foreman, Jeff, was waiting in his inbox. Jeff had questions about the specifications for the current project. Aaron scanned the email and then dialed Jeff's number.

"Hey, Jeff, it's Aaron," he said when his foreman picked up.

"Hey, boss," Jeff replied. "Got a couple of things I wanted to run by you. About those restrooms at the county park…"

They talked shop for a few minutes, going over the project details. The familiar rhythm of work grounded Aaron, giving him a brief reprieve from the chaos in his mind. They discussed tile choices, plumbing installations, and deadlines. Aaron assured Jeff that everything sounded correct and that he'd be back by Thursday or Friday, though he couldn't say for sure.

"Sounds good, boss," Jeff said. "We've got it under control here. Just let us know when you're back."

"Will do," Aaron replied. "Thanks, Jeff."

He hung up, feeling more centered, but still aware of the tension in his chest. The call had helped, but the thought of the evening meeting still lingered, a dark cloud on the horizon. There was no escaping it, and he knew he had to be prepared. Taking a deep breath, Aaron reached out for support.

First, he tried calling Lucas, but it went to voicemail—not out of the ordinary, considering it was the middle of a workday. He thought about texting Bethany but decided against it. He landed on someone who would understand: Alex.

He dialed the familiar number, and his oldest friend answered on the first ring. The sound of his voice was a comforting presence.

"Hey, what's up?" Alex's tone was light, but Aaron could hear the concern.

"I'm meeting my dad in a few hours," Aaron admitted, the tension clear in his voice. "I'm trying not to freak out, but…"

Alex cut him off with a sarcastic laugh. "So, the usual then? You still doing that deep breathing crap?"

Aaron couldn't help but chuckle. "Yeah, yeah. Trying to keep it together."

"You'll be fine, man. Just remember, he's the one with issues, not you. You've got this." Alex's words, though wrapped in his usual sarcasm, held a reassurance that Aaron needed.

They talked a few minutes more, Alex slipping in a few jokes that had Aaron smiling despite himself. By the time they hung up, Aaron felt a little more ready to face what lay ahead.

The clock read three hours until he had to meet Big Mike. He tried to relax, settling back on the bed to flip through channels on the television again. Within moments, he drifted off, sleeping until the ringing phone jolted him awake. He jumped, disoriented for a moment, before realizing it was Lucas calling him back.

His heart raced as he noticed the time. It was 4:45, and he was supposed to be at Big Mike's in just fifteen minutes. He answered the call, his voice a little breathless.

"Lucas, hey," he said, trying to shake off the grogginess.

"Hey, sorry I missed your call earlier. Everything okay?" Lucas asked, his tone concerned.

"Yeah, everything's fine. I was just checking in," Aaron replied, glancing at the clock again, the minutes ticking by. "I've got to head out now, but I'll call you when I get back to the room in a few hours, okay?"

"Alright, take care," Lucas said, and Aaron could hear the unspoken worry in his voice.

"You too," Aaron replied before hanging up. He took a deep breath, trying to gather himself. The nap had been unexpected, but at least he felt a little more rested. Now it was time to face the evening.

17

Aaron was driving back to his father's place before the clock read five minutes after the hour. Duke, the hound dog, greeted him again, baying at the tires as he rolled down the rutted driveway. Stepping onto the front porch, he heard a large door sliding open on creaking hinges. He turned toward the old shed a short distance to the left, and Big Mike stepped out.

"Over here, son," Big Mike motioned to Aaron.

The weathered building did not look capable of withstanding a strong wind, but Aaron walked through the door into a well-stocked mechanic's garage. The space was lit by rows of fluorescent lights overhead, casting a stark glow on the organized chaos below. A modern automotive lift dominated the center of the room, the only hint of newness in a space filled with well-worn tools and equipment.

Cabinets and counters lined the walls, cluttered with wrenches, screwdrivers, and assorted car parts. Oil-stained rags hung from the edges, and grease-smeared manuals filled the empty spaces. One long side of the garage held steel shelves crammed with plastic jugs of oil, transmission fluid, and other automotive fluids, alongside boxes of spare parts, brake pads, and old carburetors.

In the center stood a 1967 Chevy Camaro, its hood raised like a battle-scarred warrior. The car's once vibrant red paint had faded over the years, now covered in patches of gray primer that marked ongoing repairs. Bondo-filled dents and rust spots were the visible scars of a restoration project that had seen better days.

The air was thick with the familiar smells of motor oil, gasoline, and metal. Aaron felt a strange mix of nostalgia and apprehension. This was his father's realm, a sanctuary for machine repair and story sharing—yet it also felt like a threshold to unresolved issues, waiting to be confronted.

Mike shook Aaron's hand before turning back to the car. "Just gotta finish torquing down the bolts on this intake manifold," he said. He explained the process in a few quick sentences, detailing how it would enhance the car's performance, and the power it could unleash once everything was in place.

After a moment, he stepped back, wiping his oil-smeared hands on a rag. The fabric only polished the accumulated grease, leaving dark streaks across the red material. He looked back at Aaron, a hint of pride in his eyes as he gestured toward the Camaro. "This baby's gonna run like the devil once I'm done with her," he said, an edge of excitement in his voice.

Aaron wasn't much of a car guy, but he couldn't help but admire the Camaro's sleek lines and classic design. "It's a beauty," he said, nodding.

Mike's expression shifted as he replied, "You know this was your mother's favorite car? Never could afford to get her one, but..." His voice trailed off, the unspoken words hanging in the air. He turned away, walking to the back wall and busying himself with a task on the counter, avoiding Aaron's gaze.

"Come here," Mike called, gesturing with one hand. Aaron walked to the back of the car, only to find his father using a razor blade to cut neat lines of cocaine on the dirty counter.

"You can take the first one," the old man said.

Annoyance bubbled up in Aaron. This wasn't why he'd come; he'd waited long enough for a genuine conversation. "No thanks," he replied, his voice even. "I'm not a college kid anymore. Neither are you, last I checked. I came here to talk, not to screw around with this nonsense."

Mike remained unfazed. "I'll take the first one then." He bent over the counter, snorting the first line, then the second. He looked back at Aaron, brushing off the powder residue from his nostrils. "Here's how it works: you have questions, and I have answers. I didn't spend fifteen years in Graterford Prison without learning a thing or two... like not giving away information to someone who's not invested in staying out of prison like I am. So, step down from your high horse, take the straw, and snort a damn line. Then we can talk. Otherwise, I think we're done here."

Aaron could say nothing to that. Leaving without answers was not an option; not after he had come this far. He stared at his father for a long minute, then stepped up to the counter.

"Atta boy, I knew you'd see reason," the old man taunted, a chuckle lacing his voice.

Aaron brought the straw to his nostril. A rush of anticipation and anxiety coursed through him. The powder hit his sinuses, and a sharp, electric sensation surged through his body. It was intense and invigorating. It felt like a jolt of energy igniting every nerve, sharpening his senses, and clearing the fog that had settled in his mind.

The world around him faded, replaced by a euphoric clarity that made everything more vivid. His heartbeat quickened, and the adrenaline flooded his system. The shadows of the garage receded as clarity flooded his mind. He turned his attention back to Mike, who watched him with a calculating gaze, waiting for him to react.

"Now, about those answers," Aaron said. "I need to know what happened. You hurt my mother. You tried to kill me. Why did you keep track of us all those years?"

Mike's expression shifted... a flicker of something—guilt, perhaps —crossing his face. "Aaron, I never meant to hurt your mother. It was the drugs, the lifestyle—it took over. I lost control. I thought I was protecting you both."

"Protecting us?" Aaron stepped closer, the anger bubbling to the surface. "I don't care about your fucking excuses. You went to prison for murder. You tore our family apart, and I need to understand why. Why did you keep tabs on us? What did you want?"

Mike's gaze flickered. "It wasn't just about you or your mother," he said, his voice low. "It was about the choices I made, the life I led. I couldn't just let you go, not after everything. I had to know what was happening with my family."

"Family?" Aaron scoffed. "You don't get to call yourself family when you've done what you did. You think tracking us was protection?"

Mike's face hardened again. "I didn't say it was okay. I didn't say I was proud of it. But you need to understand—my choices didn't come easy. I made mistakes, and I had to live with them."

Aaron clenched his fists, frustration rising. "And what about us? We had to live with those mistakes too. You don't get to hide behind your choices and pretend it didn't affect us."

Mike's eyes narrowed. "I'm not pretending anything. I'm here now, aren't I? I'm trying to explain. But you need to listen."

"Explain what?" Aaron pressed. "How you broke my mother and put us through hell? Just tell me the truth."

Mike walked back to the front of the Camaro, his silence heavy. He leaned against the car, his hands resting on the hood as he stared at the ground. The air between them felt charged, both men standing on opposite sides of a chasm carved by years of pain and betrayal.

"I didn't mean for things to turn out the way they did," Mike said, his voice almost a whisper. "I never wanted to hurt her... or you... or your brother."

Aaron scoffed, disbelief flooding his system. "But you did. You went to prison. You left us with nothing."

"I know," Mike replied, his tone lower now. "I didn't have a choice. It was just supposed to be a meeting. A basic damn meeting, like we'd had a million times before. But that little rat bastard... he said some shit he shouldn't have said, and things went off the rails. I was in charge. I was the leader. I'm Big Mike. So yeah, I went down for it. What else could I do? The buck stops here and all that jazz."

His words made little sense to Aaron. "What does this have to do with... "

"Just listen, dammit. You asked, didn't you? Shut up and fucking listen," the old man interrupted, wringing his hands. "Come on in the house. I need to smoke."

Aaron wasn't sure he had the capacity for more drugs in his system, but he followed his father out of the garage. Big Mike closed the door behind them, and they crunched through the brittle winter grass to the house. Mike threw off his canvas jacket and went straight to the kitchen. He called over his shoulder to ask if Aaron wanted a beer.

"No, I'm good. Water maybe?" Aaron said, shedding his coat and hanging it on the overfilled coat stand behind the door. He reclaimed yesterday's spot on the couch, trying to settle his racing mind and tamp down his frustration with the old man's procrastination.

Mike handed Aaron a glass of water dripping with cold condensation. He accepted it without a word, his eyes fixed on his father, who was already twisting the cap off a beer bottle. The sharp hiss of escaping carbonation seemed to echo in the quiet room, grating on Aaron's nerves.

Mike dropped into the worn armchair opposite Aaron, setting the beer on a nearby table. He leaned back, reaching into his pocket for a small tin, from which he pulled out a dense nugget of marijuana. He broke it apart, the dried leaves crumbling between his calloused fingers.

The old man worked as long minutes passed. Mike's movements were deliberate and slow. Aaron's frustration grew with every passing moment.

"Are you going to get on with it?" Aaron's voice cut through the silence, sharper than he intended.

Mike glanced up, his eyes narrowing, but he didn't pause. "Patience, son," he muttered, licking the edge of the paper and sealing it with practiced ease. "I've got a lot to say, and you'll want to hear all of it."

Aaron clenched his jaw, his fingers drumming against the arm of the couch. "I didn't come here to watch you roll a joint, Mike. I came for answers."

Mike set the blunt down, his eyes locking onto Aaron's with an intensity that hadn't been there before. "And you'll get them," he said, his tone low and measured. He reached for his beer, taking a long, deliberate swig, the silence stretching again.

Aaron's impatience was reaching a boiling point. His mind raced with anger and anxiety. He could feel the questions bubbling up, ready to spill over, but Mike's calm demeanor held him back, forcing him to wait.

After what felt like an eternity, Mike set the empty beer bottle aside and leaned forward, the blunt resting between his fingers. He took a deep breath, his eyes never leaving Aaron's.

"It's time you knew the truth," Mike said, his voice carrying the weight of years gone by. "About that night... and about Robert."

The tension in the room intensified as Mike lit the blunt—the flame flickered before settling into a constant burn. The anticipation eclipsed Aaron's frustration, his breath catching as he braced himself.

Mike took a long drag, then held the blunt toward Aaron, who waved his hand to decline the invitation. Another drag and the old man spoke: "Rudy set up the meeting. It was a cocaine thing, a regular deal. Some guys from New Jersey had been selling up in New York; they wanted to expand their operation into Philly. That was right up our alley, so I assumed this would be routine. Rudy said one guy was from the neighborhood: a punk Hammer and I went to school with. Athlete, his father owned a store down the street until he sold up, moved out, married some rich skirt, and got a job in her daddy's company. I didn't like the guy, but that doesn't mean we can't do business, you know?"

"Robert?" Aaron's voice was confused. "Your meeting was with Rob? For cocaine? You sure you don't have your details—"

Mike's sharp voice cut through his. "My details are perfect, boy. Just listen!" He inhaled again and offered the blunt once more to his son. This time, Aaron accepted his offer, putting the blunt to his lips with a slight tremor in his hand.

"So anyway," he continued, "we're all in the shop. It was a Tuesday, right? Not busy, just a few cars left to finish up before the weekend. Beans had come in to work on the books—you remember Beans?" Aaron shook his head no and handed the blunt back to his father. "Beans was a good man, one of the best. He did the books, you know? For the shop... for whatever. Had an actual job, real life, a wife, and a couple of little girls. He only came in when we needed him, you know?" He raised an eyebrow as if he wanted Aaron to acknowledge his words.

Aaron nodded, annoyed at this long exposition, and he couldn't seem to balance the competing drugs in his system and the unfolding story in front of him.

"Beans was there that night," his father said again. "Turbo, Hammer, Slick, Greenie too. Rudy showed up and said that Rob had called and he wasn't coming, 'something came up', but the other fellow would be there. It was pretty irritating, I remember that. I never minded screwing with that punk, and he couldn't even bother to show."

He stopped, stamped the dying blunt out in the ashtray, and got up to get another beer from the kitchen. Exasperated, Aaron stood and paced the room. *When would he ever get to the fucking point?* Mike returned with three beers this time, already drinking one of them. He set one unopened in front of Aaron's seat and the other on his side. "Sit down, take some deep breaths or something. You're like a racehorse at the starting gate, kid."

Aaron turned to snap at his father, then decided against it. He collapsed once more on the sofa and twisted the top off his beer. It tasted cheap and abrasive, nothing like the craft brews he was used to. It was cold though, and the carbonation felt good on his dry throat. He drank half of the bottle in the second gulp.

"Robert chickened out on the meeting, but his buddy showed up. Eddie. Another punk in a business suit." Disgust colored the old man's features. "We said hey, did the meet and greet shit, talked about cars for a minute, then Greenie shut the door, and we got down to brass tacks." His face contorted a little, a mixture of dread at reliving the next few minutes, and anger at what had transpired there.

"I mean, it all went fine. We made the deal: moving bricks from New Jersey over to Philly, then on to guys Eddie knew in Virginia, Kansas, California, Texas, whatever. It was exciting, right? We weren't a minor operation anymore. Big Mike's gang was going to make some real coin." His tone was sarcastic, the edges curled and coarse. "So we're wrapping up, back to talking about stupid stuff, who's girl looks the best—stupid guy shit, you know?"

Aaron nodded, swigging the rest of his beer in one swallow and placing it back on the table without looking away from the older man.

"Hammer joked my girl was the prettiest. The guys always told me this, just always giving me a hard time about how pretty Marlena was, how I didn't deserve her." He chuckled at the memory. "And this guy... Eddie. He's laughing along, then he says 'Your girl's a foxy one, yeah, but what about his girls' and when he says this, he points at Beans." Mike's hands are shaking now, though he tries to disguise it by rolling the fingers between one another. "We all freeze, kinda looking at each other like 'what the hell?' cause A. Beans' girls are 14 and 6 years old. And B. how does he know what they look like? And C. who thinks a little girl is foxy or whatever word he used?" He stands up, his face as angry as it was that night in July 1985. "And D. why would you tell their Pops that shit?"

"We all stood there for a minute before Beans was like 'the fuck do you mean?' and this little worm starts back-peddling, trying to walk back that mess that just came out of his mouth. He goes with 'sorry, I was just kidding' like that makes it any better. We all look at Beans for what direction he's feeling like going in, you know? He stares at this chump for a second and then says 'You watch yourself, buddy', and it could have just stopped there, you know? But this Eddie. he's a moron of the highest order, and he babbles about how he doesn't like his skirts that young, but some guys do, and how there's a lot of money to be made… just fucked-up, right?"

He stands now, pacing along the same path Aaron had taken a few minutes before. "Hammer hit him first, knocked him back against the sedan we'd been working on. He mumbles some apology: says he was out of line and misread the situation, and Hammer hits him again. He gets up and says he's leaving, and we might have let him go, except he looks right at Beans and says 'Just you watch those little girls, friend, they're worth a fortune to the right person'. It all just went to shit then. Beans rushed him—and Beans is not a fighter, you know? He's an accountant, a wiry guy in a tie. Slick and I tried to stop him, and then the door opened. Greenie didn't lock the damn door."

He sank into his chair again, one hand on each arm, his fingers tapping against the ends. "Marlena was standing there, looking at us all like a deer in the headlights, right? I told her to 'go, get out' and this measly little piece of shit takes that moment, when we're all looking at the door, to run. Beans jumped past me, I lunged to hit the worthless chump, and just like that," he snapped his fingers. "It was done. He was fucking down, his head bleeding all over my goddamn concrete like a stuck pig. Stupid motherfucker."

He leaned forward at the end of his speech, burying his head in his gnarled, oil-stained hands. Aaron stared at the top of his head, trying to process all that he had just heard. It was overwhelming… information overload. He slammed his hands on the coffee table, knocking the empty beer bottles to the floor in a crash. His father did not move from his hunched position, even when Aaron jumped up and ran outside.

Aaron was furious. He was confused and frustrated. He wanted to scream, but also to cry. Walking fast across the field to the garage, he slammed his fist into the clapboard siding. From there, he moved toward the road, his feet moving without consulting his brain, his mind racing.

"Come back, Aaron," his father's voice carried over the dusky yard. "I know what you're thinking."

White-hot rage seared through Aaron's head. "You don't know SHIT, old man! You don't know me, you know nothing about me but insignificant facts, little trivia you've collected from the internet or your rat friends or wherever." His feet were now taking him back to the porch, where he stood below the man, yelling up at him. "WHY? I want to know why!"

"Why what?"

"Why?! You could have told the cops that the guy was a pedophile. Or told them you had a good reason to kill him? Self-defense? Defense of others? That's a thing, Pops!"

"Stop, son. Just stop. Come inside. It's cold out here." The older man turned back through the door, letting the screen slam behind him. Aaron stared up at the darkening sky for what felt like an hour before trudging up the steps to follow.

Mike was rolling another blunt, his fingers breaking up the weed. Aaron went to the kitchen, helping himself to another beer, hesitating a second before grabbing one for his father. He stood at the edge of the couch, not yet ready to let go of the rage. "Tell me. Talk."

The old man chuckled. "Why didn't I tell the cops I had a good reason to kill a man? Are you listening to yourself, boy? Even in this brave new world, that wouldn't fly, and it sure wouldn't have in '85 Philly. I was a criminal. Do you understand that? We were criminals who ran drugs and stole cars and chopped them into parts. We were dirty, rotten criminals, and we had a businessman with his head bashed in on the ground of my shop. What options do you think we had?"

"Was it even you that killed him? Or was it—"

"Don't do that. Don't even go there. I went to prison for that crime because I was responsible. Period. Due process of the law, justice was served, all that jazz." He went back to rolling the blunt, shaking his head. Under his breath, he said, "like I'd let my boys go down for that shit."

"So it wasn't you then," Aaron said. The thought brought him no comfort. *What difference would it make if my father was the one to bash the man's brains in? He disappeared from my life as surely as if he had been the one who died.*

A spark and the blunt roared to life. "Beans had little girls to protect, Aaron. Hammer had a baby girl. They needed to be there to protect their girls."

"Never mind protecting your kids, right?" Aaron spat the words at the man. Images of Rob and his friends Kevin and Knobby Chin flooded his mind: a rapid slideshow of the fishing pond, the van they drove around, his bedroom in Kirby, and the golf ball bruises he'd worn for a week.

"Boys can protect themselves! You didn't need a jerk like me around to do it. You went to college; it's not like you sell dope and screw around in a garage all day, right? What do you have to complain about? Your daddy wasn't there?" His voice was bitter. "I did you a favor, just like I did my guys. I took one for the team, as they say. You're here, ain't you?"

"Boys can protect themselves? God, are you as big a moron as Rob always said you were?"

The words caught Mike off guard. "What do you mean?" He exhaled, the smoke billowing around his head.

Aaron extended his hand to reach for the blunt and his father handed it over, his eyes now glued to his son. He inhaled, trying to put all the pieces together.

"That bastard was trying to set up some child trafficking shit, right?"

Mike nodded, his expression unchanging.

"So he's some kind of pedophile, into kids or whatever."

Again, a nod, though Mike's face twitched a little.

"And Rob was supposed to be at that meeting?"

"What's your point?" Mike took the blunt back, taking a long drag.

"And then you went to prison and left us with the guy who was supposed to be at the child trafficking cocaine smuggling meeting. No warning to Mom. No letter from prison saying 'Yo, your man might be into some weird pedo shit' — not one of your buds thought that might be relevant information for Mom to have when she was moving us all across the fucking country with the guy?"

The color drained from the old man's face and he set the blunt in the ashtray with shaking hands. The veins in his neck looked ready to burst, and his eyes burned like cold, hard steel set in a furnace.

"Are you fucking kidding me?"

18

Aaron's heart pounded in his chest as the echo of his father's roar reverberated through the room. Mike was on his feet now, his eyes wild, fists clenched as if ready to punch the truth out of the air.

"What the hell do you mean, Aaron? What did that bastard do to you?"

Aaron stepped back, feeling his father's fury pressing against him. He hadn't meant to blurt it out like that, but watching Mike's attempt to justify leaving him and Patty to the fate of Rob, choosing the daughters of his crew over his sons had touched a nerve. And now it hung between them like a live wire, sparking and dangerous.

Mike's voice dropped, rough and jagged as gravel. "You better talk, boy. Right now."

The words sat in Aaron's throat, bitter and rough, unwilling to come out. He swallowed hard, his eyes narrowing as he weighed the anger boiling in his father's eyes against the years of silence that had strangled him.

A beat passed. Mike's expression hardened, his jaw clenched as he crossed the room in two furious strides. He grabbed Aaron's shoulder, not harshly, but with a grip firm enough to demand attention. "Tell me, Aaron. What the hell did that son of a bitch do?"

Aaron shoved his father's hand off, fire blazing in his eyes now. "What do you think, old man? You leave us with a psychopath, and you're surprised something happened?" His voice cracked, the years of rage and helplessness flooding back at once. "It wasn't just Mom who took the hits! You weren't there. You can't imagine what he did to us, the things he did to Patty."

Mike's face went slack, and he staggered back as though he had received a punch to the gut. His hand trembled as it sought the arm of the chair for support. "Patty? That bastard—?"

Aaron cut him off, his voice trembling with restrained fury. "Yeah, Pops. Patty. You think I'm the only one who's pissed at you? You have no idea, do you?"

Something broke in his father's eyes, a crack in the hard shell that Mike had worn for decades. The old man slumped into the chair, his hands falling into his lap. He looked smaller now, diminished by the weight of what he was hearing.

A long silence hung between them, broken only by a ticking clock somewhere in the house. When Mike spoke, his voice was hoarse, thick with regret. "I never... I didn't know. Goddamn it, Aaron. I didn't know."

Aaron's anger was still there, but beneath it, something else was bubbling up—something raw and aching that he hadn't let himself feel for a long time. He sank onto the edge of the couch, his head in his hands, the fight draining out of him as quickly as it had flared up.

"I know," Aaron whispered. "But it changes nothing."

Mike stared at him, his expression haunted, as if he were seeing his son for the first time. "Maybe it changes everything."

He held his gaze for what felt like an eternity. His face was full of anguish and regret. Then, without a word, he pivoted and walked down the narrow hallway toward the bathroom. Aaron heard the door close and the faint sound of running water.

Left alone in the dim living room, Aaron sank back into the worn couch, his mind swirling with the conversation that had just torn open old wounds. It all felt crushing. He glanced toward the kitchen, debating whether to grab another beer. The taste of the last one still lingered in his mouth, but the thought of sitting here, sober, with all these memories, was unbearable. He pushed himself up and walked to the fridge, pulling out another cold bottle, then hesitated before grabbing one more for his father. It wasn't an olive branch, but it was something.

He returned to the living room and stared out the window into the darkness. The glass was cold against his forehead. Beyond it, the yard was nothing but shadow. His eyes drifted to the ceiling, where a spider plant hung in a basket, its long green tendrils spilling over the sides like a cascade of memories. His mother had always loved these plants. Every time they moved — every time Rob forced them to pack up and leave — she would always take a cutting, or a "spider baby," as she referred to it, and give them as gifts to their neighbors and any friends she had made during their brief stays. It was her way of holding on, of keeping a piece of herself alive in all those strange places.

Aaron reached up and touched one of the plant's dangling leaves. *How many of these had she given away over the years? How many times had she tried to plant roots in soil that was never stable?* He could almost see her now, pinching off a piece with a smile and handing it to a neighbor she knew, telling them how easy it was to grow, how resilient it was. *How much like her.*

The sound of the bathroom door creaking open pulled Aaron out of his thoughts. He turned to see Mike shuffling back into the room, his face a little more composed, though his eyes were red-rimmed. Without a word, Aaron handed him the beer. Mike accepted it with a nod and took a slow drink. Then he looked at Aaron, a strange determination in his gaze.

"Come on," Mike said, his voice rough. "Let's head back to the garage. I've got something to show you."

Aaron followed his father to the front door, where they both shrugged into their coats. It was early March, and though there was no snow, the night air was biting cold. Mike led the way across the yard, their boots crunching on the frost-covered grass. The garage loomed ahead, its door creaking as Mike pulled it open. It stuck — Mike said it always did when the temperature dropped — but he gave it a hard tug and it gave way with a groan.

He flipped the switch and the fluorescent lights flickered to life, taking a moment to reach their full power. Mike headed straight to a set of shelves in the back: chock full of worn cardboard boxes and car manuals. He began moving things aside, muttering to himself as he searched.

"It's here somewhere," Mike grumbled, shifting a stack of manuals. He wrestled open the cardboard flaps of one box and then another, peering inside, then shoving them away unsatisfied. "I know it's here..."

Aaron stood by, the cold seeping through his coat as he watched his father dig through the past. There was something comforting about the way Mike was so intent on finding what he was looking for as if this was his way of making amends. The sound of shuffling boxes filled the room.

At last, Mike stopped, his hand resting on one of the old, battered cardboard boxes. He looked back at Aaron, his expression unreadable.

"Here," he whispered, taking the box from the shelf and placing it on the workbench to open it with some struggle. "I think you need to see this."

Aaron stepped closer, his breath misting in the cold air. Whatever was inside, he knew it would change things—maybe not for the better, but it was something. He watched as Mike lifted the lid and pulled a dust-choked black leather-bound ledger from its depths.

Mike flipped the front cover open and rifled through the pages. Hundreds of pages covered in long rows of numbers and letters filled the thick volume. "Shop ledger. Not the cars, you know? The other stuff. There's a few in here... from when we opened in 1964 until he died in 1997. I was in the pen for the back half, but it didn't stop business. Nothing stops business." He walked away again, fiddling around with the cocaine still spread on the workbench before leaning in to take a long sniff of the drug.

"Beans is dead?" Aaron asked. He couldn't remember the man his father had gone to prison for, but he could see how much he had meant to Mike. He looked down into the cardboard box: six thick ledgers like the first, a handful of papers, and a few cheap composition notebooks: the complete contents of a crooked accountant's desk, gathered upon his death and deposited with his old friend to keep safe from the eyes of his wife and children.

"What?" Mike turned from the workbench, looking down at a framed photograph. "Yeah, died in '97. Heart attack. He was older than me, you know? He was almost 50 when he died. Still too damn young, though."

Aaron stepped forward to look at the photograph in his father's gnarled hands. It was an actual photograph, as Marlena would have said, meaning that a photographer who wasn't a family member took the photo. Its Kodachrome reddish tint belied its period: the early 1980s. Three men stood on either side of the central couple, who faced one another, gazing at the camera with their cheeks pressed together and brilliant smiles on their youthful faces. The men framing the couple joined in with their smiles. They embraced each other, throwing their arms around their shoulders. They posed before a shiny 1967 black Lincoln Continental, looking for all the world like a group of college kids, rather than the ragtag gang of criminals they were.

"Our wedding," the older man said in a hoarse voice. "Your mom and me." His shaking finger pointed to the center couple. Marlena wore a long white gown covered in embroidered flowers. Her neck and chest peeked through the sheer lace material, which continued down the sleeves to the embroidered cuffs. Big Mike wore a vest and a bowler hat with his suit pants. His shirt sleeves bulged over his impressive biceps. He looked imposing, formidable, and happy.

Now he pointed to the other figures in the photograph: The Baron, Hammer, and Slick on one side, Beans, Turbo, and Greenie on the other. "More than half of these guys are dead now. Beans: heart attack in '97, like I said. The Baron: The damn flu got him in 2014. 81 years old, still lived above the bar. He gave The Red Baron to his son Dave to run. Ain't like the old times there anymore. Hammer had a car accident and lost his head back in 2008. Drinking. And Greenie... you know about him, right?"

Aaron nodded, thinking of what his Aunt Daphne had shared. "He killed Aunt Cassandra?"

"Yep, sure did." He shook his head. "Her and her boyfriend. She shouldn't have messed around, but that's no way to handle the situation. Greenie could've left her, ran the guy out of town, or I don't know, something. He didn't have to beat them to death like a maniac. Marlena's sister didn't have to go down like that." He glanced at Aaron, who was watching his father's face. Mike seemed to hear his hypocrisy and had the sense to look embarrassed. "Anyway, he's gone now too. Ran into him out in Graterford in '91. He didn't last very long there. An unfortunate accident during rec one day. Fucked around, found out."

Mike leaned over the workbench, cutting two more lines of cocaine. Aaron's gaze lingered on the photograph. The ghosts of those men stared back at him—some long gone, some lost in ways that made them as good as dead. In the middle, his beautiful mother stared back at him, unaware of all that would come.

He should have felt something, Aaron thought. Anger, sadness, maybe even nostalgia. But all he felt was numb — Mike's voice, rough and low, cut through his thoughts.

"Jackass should have locked that shop door."

Aaron didn't ask which door Mike meant: the prison shop door, or the one in the garage in 1985. In the end, it didn't matter. The past held many doors that should have been locked, and now it was too late to close any of them.

Mike straightened up from the workbench, wiping his nose with the back of his hand. "Want a taste?" Mike asked, his tone casual. There was an intensity behind his eyes that made Aaron hesitate. It had been such a roller coaster of a night already—drugs he hadn't done in years, confessions and revelations he didn't expect to hear or say. Not to mention the several bottles of beer. Then again, he'd come this far. *I might as well embrace the journey.*

He nodded, swallowing hard as Mike stepped out of the way. He moved forward and inhaled the powder. The familiar burn hit his nostrils, sending a rush of warmth through him. The world around him sharpened again, the edges of reality crystallizing in crisp focus.

"Good, huh?" Mike said, a smirk creeping onto his face. "Just like old times."

Aaron forced laughter but felt a tinge of regret. He looked back at the ledger lying closed on the other workbench. *Why did you show me this?*

He opened the leather-bound account book, flipping through the pages. The numbers danced—long rows of amounts, dates, initials—each column felt like a riddle he couldn't decipher. He scanned the pages, feeling a mix of curiosity and confusion.

"What am I looking for?" he murmured. Mike's presence loomed behind him, heavy and expectant.

"Just look. It's all there," Mike urged, his voice low, thick with something resembling pride. "It's the history. Our history. You need to understand where we came from."

Aaron frowned, feeling lost in the deluge of numbers. "What do these initials even mean? I don't get it, Pops."

"Those are names, son. They were my guys—some still around, some not—and the guys we did deals with. Each line matches a deal, a job, or something bigger. See the totals? That's what we were moving, the profits."

A wave of nausea washed over Aaron. "And you expect me to just... understand this?" Frustration bubbled up, hot and unyielding.

"Not just understand it. I want you to know what you're connected to." Mike's tone shifted, seriousness creeping in. "You can't wipe away the past because it stings. Face it." He paused, his gaze steady. "Robert Bakker is in that ledger. He's in more than one. You can see the connection to that Eddie chump."

Aaron's heart raced, the adrenaline mixed with the cocaine heightening every emotion. He looked down at the ledger, then at the stack of ledgers still in the box. These books contained evidence of choices made long before him.

The air felt charged, thick with unresolved tension as he tried to piece together the father he had known and the man he was still trying to figure out.

He was intent on deciphering the ledger pages when his father's voice snapped him back into the garage. "Tell me what he did to you, son."

"I don't want to talk about that," Aaron said, glancing sideways at Mike, trying to gauge the storm behind his father's calm facade.

"Was he a kiddie diddler? A fucking pedophile? Did he touch you and Patty?" Mike's voice trembled with rage, a raw edge to his words.

Aaron swallowed hard, his pulse quickening. He forced himself to look at the ledger; the pages blurring with his tears. "Rob never molested me. I think he is a pedophile. But I wasn't his type." He drew a deep breath. "I can't remember everything. But I'm pretty sure my baby sister was his type."

"Your baby sister? What a piece of... goddamn..." Mike's pacing intensified, fists clenched, searching for something to hit. He paused, turning to Aaron, anguish painted on his face. "So he didn't touch you? Didn't screw with you and Patty?"

He took another deep breath, bracing himself against the weight of Mike's anger. "Oh no, I didn't say that. I said he didn't molest me. I looked too much like you for him to do anything but beat me every chance he could."

"That bastard—"

"Every single chance he could."

"A kid! My kid! My fucking kid! Who the hell did he think he was? Touching Big Mike Callahan's son?! He's lucky I was in prison, I tell you, goddamn lucky. If I'd known…" His voice trailed off into the fog of unspoken regrets between them. "So you weren't… molested? What do they call that, a ray of fucking sunshine? What about Patty?"

"Not by Rob, no. He didn't mess with either of us that way."

"But…" Mike's face was apoplectic, confusion mixing with fury.

"He had friends. Everywhere we moved, he had old friends. And he made new ones."

"I'll fucking kill him."

Mike's anger filled the garage, and the room felt as hot as if they'd wandered into a boiler room mid-winter. *In a way, we did.*

Aaron felt a deep ache in his chest. The intensity of the confessions, admissions, and pain of the past two weeks felt like he was on the edge of a precipice, and if he fell, there would be no one to catch him. He couldn't take it anymore.

"Can I take the box of Beans' ledgers with me?" Aaron asked, his voice breaking through the silence.

Mike blinked, surprised by the change of subject. "What? Why?"

"I need to see it all—like you said, understand what you were involved in. See the connection to Rob. I can't do that here, not with you pacing like a caged animal." He gestured toward the cardboard box still on the workbench. "I need to go through this away from all… this."

Mike's jaw clenched, and for a moment, Aaron feared he'd refuse. But then he let out a slow breath, his shoulders sagging as he considered the request. "You think you're ready for that?"

"I haven't been ready for about ninety percent of what's happened in my entire life, Pops," Aaron replied, meeting his father's gaze. "There was no choice on any of that, and I don't think I have a choice now. I have to understand what it all means, for all our sake's." He spoke not just of himself and Big Mike, but of Marlena, Nico, Lucas, Elise, and Patty.

Mike studied him for a long moment, the fire in his eyes cooling. "Fine. Just… don't let it swallow you whole."

Aaron nodded, a sense of relief washing over him as he reached for the box. He could feel the history contained within it, the echoes of other people's choices. "I won't. I promise."

As he lifted the box, he felt a sense of purpose ignite within him. The tension between them still lingered, but now there was also a thread of understanding, however fragile. He glanced back at Mike, who was watching him.

"Maybe this is a start," Aaron whispered.

Mike gave a slight nod. Although the heaviness of their conversation remained, taking the ledgers felt like a stride toward something different. Aaron turned to leave the garage, the box cradled in his arms, a tangible connection to their past and a potential path forward.

As he stepped into the frosty night air, he took a deep breath, feeling the crispness of the moment wash over him. The past would always be there, but now he had the tools to confront it—one ledger at a time.

19

Aaron woke with a groan, his head pounding like a bass drum. His nose was running, a persistent sniffle punctuating the silence of the hotel room. Every muscle in his body ached as if he'd run a marathon in his sleep. His right hand throbbed: three knuckles shone with dark purple bruises, reminding him he'd taken his frustration out on the wall of Mike's garage last night. He stretched, wincing as his joints protested the movement, and then sank back into the bed, staring up at the ceiling as yesterday's events replayed in his mind.

The visit with his father felt like a fever dream, a hazy wash of old wounds and fresh revelations. It was hard to piece together everything that had happened—the confrontation, the anger, the ledgers—but the weight of it all still sat on his chest.

His gaze drifted around the room, landing on the two Betty Boop figurines perched on the desk. The playful, wide-eyed characters seemed so out of place in the stark reality of his current situation, yet they were a constant in this temporary refuge. He blinked against the bright midday sun streaming through the window, his eyes burning from the light. He'd forgotten to close the curtains last night. It was a wonder he even stripped off his clothes before collapsing into bed.

The clock on the nightstand read just after noon. He'd gotten maybe eight hours of sleep, but it felt like minutes. The lingering effects of the beer and drugs, combined with the emotional toll of the night before, left him feeling more drained than ever.

He shifted under the covers, pulling them tighter around his aching body, but no warmth could ease the chill that settled in his bones. The inn's bed, though soft, offered little comfort today. All he could think about was what lay ahead—sorting through the ledgers, facing the truth of his father's life, and dealing with the mess of emotions that followed him everywhere.

But for now, he allowed himself a few more minutes of quiet, lying in bed with his thoughts. The day was already half gone, but he wasn't ready to face it yet. First, he needed to push the memories of last night into some distant corner of his mind, where they could haunt him later.

He took a deep, shaky breath, rubbing his temples to ward off the headache that throbbed behind his eyes. Today was another chance to untangle the mess of his past, but it would have to wait until he could stand without feeling like the world was spinning around him.

It was three in the morning when he got back to the hotel. He didn't know how he managed the drive, let alone getting the box of ledgers inside. Today would be long, but there was no escaping it—no more hiding from the ghosts that had found him once again.

Aaron groaned as he forced himself to sit up in bed, the pounding in his head making every movement feel like a chore. He couldn't take the bright sunlight any longer. With a huff, he swung his legs over the side of the bed, wincing at the stiffness in his muscles, and yanked the curtains closed, plunging the room into a dim light.

He stumbled toward the bathroom, each step clumsy, and fumbled with the doorknob before opening it. Once inside, he headed straight for the toilet, relieving himself with a sigh. The cool tiles under his feet were a harsh reminder of how disconnected he felt from his body.

Afterward, he shuffled to the sink, splashing cold water on his face to wake up, to feel somewhat human again. He grabbed his toothbrush and scrubbed at his teeth, trying to erase the lingering taste of last night's excesses—beer, cocaine, weed, and the bitter remnants of regret. The familiar routine grounded him, pulling him back into the present.

He wiped his face with a towel, glancing at his reflection in the mirror. The man staring back at him looked exhausted, his eyes bloodshot and shadowed with dark circles. But at least he felt a bit more ready to face the day.

He returned to the main room and picked up the phone to dial room service. His voice was hoarse as he placed his order: eggs, toast, bacon, and sausage, with two glasses of orange juice and a coffee. He hung up and glanced at the clock. It would be a little while before the food arrived.

With a sigh, Aaron stepped into the shower. The hot water cascaded over him, soothing his aching muscles and washing away the remnants of yesterday's turmoil. He stood under the stream for a long moment, careful not to let the hot water cover his face. There was no time for a panic attack today—too much to do to be side-tracked. He stood with his back to the water, letting the heat work its magic before reaching for the soap. As he scrubbed himself clean, he tried to clear his mind.

As Aaron dried off and dressed, he couldn't help but glance at the box of ledgers sitting on the floor by the TV stand. It loomed there like a reminder of the burden he now carried—the secrets, the pain, the complicated legacy his father had thrust upon him. He sighed, rubbing the back of his neck as he tried to shake off the growing dread.

The call of "room service" at the door interrupted his thoughts. The smell of fresh coffee and bacon filled the room, and his stomach growled in response. He set the tray on the small table by the window, and pushed everything else aside, focusing on nourishing his body.

The sunlight filtered through the curtains he'd drawn earlier, casting a soft glow across the room. He would take it one step at a time—eat, regroup, and then tackle the ledgers. But not yet. He would allow himself this small moment of peace for a little longer before diving back into the chaos.

April 6, 1991: Marlena

The evening has rolled around, and I'm still thinking about that trip to Mexico City. It bothered me all day, even though I tried my best to push it out of my mind. I remember standing by the kitchen window this morning, watching Rob's car disappear down the road, feeling that familiar tug of unease in my gut.

Rob's been on plenty of trips before, always with Kevin and Roger. It's for fishing most of the time—the three of them packed into a van with coolers full of beer and gear, off to some lake or river for a weekend. But this time, it was different. "Business," he said. To Mexico City, of all places. For a meat distribution company in Fresno, California? I was surprised when he told me. It made little sense. He goes on trips all the time, of course: Detroit, Philadelphia, New York, Dodge City, Los Angeles, but he goes alone, to represent the plant as its manager. I could see him and his buddies heading off to some conference in Omaha, or maybe a factory visit in Chicago, but Mexico City? Is that something you would send a plant manager from Fresno and his pals from Kirby, Kansas to? It seems like a trip for the suits upstairs, not the guys who work on the floor. But what do I know?

I could've asked him about it. I wanted to. But I didn't. I know better than to question Rob about his work. It never ends well. He either shuts me down with a look or gets angry and wants to fight, or he changes the subject so fast it leaves me spinning. So I kept my mouth shut like always, nodded along like I understood, and let it go.

But I didn't let it go, not really. All day, it's been there in the back of my mind, nagging at me while I went about my routine. When I cleaned up after breakfast, when I watered the plants out front, when I folded the laundry, the thought kept creeping back in. Why did all three of them go to Mexico this time? It's not like I will get answers by wondering, but that didn't stop me from thinking about it.

As the sun dips below the horizon, I stare out the window again, lost in thought. Rob won't be back for a few days. By then, maybe I'll have put these feelings to rest, to tuck them away like I do with so many other things. Or maybe not. I may have more questions and more doubts. But for now, I'm here alone with my thoughts, waiting, as always, for the other shoe to drop.

Aaron ate like a starving man, the salty crunch of the bacon grounding him as his mind raced through the tangled web of thoughts. He'd ignored his decision to enjoy breakfast and grabbed his mother's book for a little morning reading. *A business trip to Mexico? She's right, that makes no sense. What the hell was a meat distribution plant manager doing in Mexico City? And with those creepy guys from Kansas, no less?* He couldn't shake the feeling that there was more to this trip than simple business.

The questions swirled in his mind like smoke he couldn't clear. *Was it a legitimate business trip, or was something darker at play?* His stepfather had never been someone he could trust or understand. But now, the puzzle pieces were coming together in a way that made his skin crawl.

His thoughts circled back to the conversation with Big Mike that had left him reeling. His father's revelation that Rob was supposed to be at that fateful meeting with Eddie Scott gnawed at him. *Why didn't Rob end up going? Was he part of Eddie's proposed child trafficking scheme, or is it just a sick coincidence that they were both twisted pervs?*

Aaron took a swig of orange juice, trying to wash down the bitterness that rose in his throat. The thought of Rob being involved in something as vile as child trafficking made his blood run cold, but it also made terrible sense.

The way Rob had hurt him, the way he'd manipulated Patty and Elise's lives... it all pointed to a darkness Aaron had always felt but never understood. He pushed the empty plate away, his appetite gone. The possibilities churned in his mind, each one more sickening than the last.

Leaning back in his chair, he stared at the ceiling as if it might offer answers. But all he could see were more questions, more shadows lurking in the corners of his past. Aaron knew he needed to dig deeper, to uncover the truth, no matter how much it hurt. But right now, all he could do was sit with what he'd learned, the reality of his stepfather's potential involvement pressing down on him like a stone.

This wasn't just about the ledgers or the trip to Mexico. It was about unearthing the truth, no matter how ugly it might be. Aaron wasn't sure he was ready for what he might find, but he had to know. He had to understand what kind of man his stepfather was.

The phone rang, its sharp chime jolting Aaron from his spiraling thoughts. Glancing at the Caller ID, he felt a pang of guilt when he saw

Lucas's name. He had promised to call his brother back last night, but by the time he'd stumbled back into his room, the last thing on his mind had been making phone calls.

With a sigh, Aaron answered the call. "Hey, Lucas."

"Aaron, man, I was getting worried. You didn't call me back last night," Lucas sounded concerned. "What's going on? How's the trip going?"

Aaron's head pounded, hearing the rapid-fire questions. He wasn't ready to get into everything with Lucas—not now. He hadn't even updated his brother about the trip to Doylestown—Lucas still thought he was in Philly. Trying to keep his tone light, he rubbed his temples, answering, "Yeah, sorry about that. I got back late and was pretty wiped. I didn't want to wake you."

"Late? What were you doing? I thought you were checking some stuff out." Lucas wasn't letting it go, his worry clear in his voice.

Aaron hesitated, searching for the right words. He didn't want to lie to Lucas, but he didn't want to unload everything on him right now. "It's been… complicated. There's a lot to sort through. But it's fine. I'm handling it."

His brother was silent for a moment, not satisfied with the vague response. "Are you sure? Because you don't sound fine. You sound… I don't know, off. What's going on, Aaron?"

Aaron forced a small laugh, hoping to ease the tension. "I promise, Lucas. I'm okay. Just a lot of old stuff coming up, you know? It's been a long time since I've been to Philly, and it's bringing up some memories. But I'm good. I'll head back home in the morning."

Lucas's sigh was heavy with skepticism. "If you say so. But listen, if you need to talk, I'm here, okay? I don't want you dealing with all this alone."

"Thanks, Lucas. I appreciate it." Aaron's voice softened, grateful for his brother's concern even if he wasn't ready to share everything. "I'll call you when I'm on the road tomorrow and let you know how it all went."

"Okay," Lucas replied, his tone displeased. "Just… take care of yourself, Aaron. Don't push yourself too hard."

"I won't. Talk to you tomorrow." He hung up, staring at the phone for a moment longer. The conversation had left him feeling like he was walking across ever-shifting sands in an endless desert. He knew he wasn't giving his brother the full story, but it was too much to unpack over the phone. Especially with everything still so raw.

His eyes drifted to the box of ledgers sitting on the floor by the desk. With a resigned sigh, he leaned over and pulled one out, flipping it open. Cramped handwriting—initials, dates, amounts scrawled in ink that had faded over time—filled the pages. He squinted at the columns, trying to make sense of them, but the numbers and symbols felt like a foreign language.

It was like trying to decipher Greek. The entries seemed random and disconnected, and he couldn't guess what any of them meant. Now and then, he recognized a name or a date, but he had no context for them.

Frustration gnawed at him as he scanned the pages, flipping through them, hoping something would jump out at him, something that would make it all click. But it was no use. The ledgers were a puzzle, and he was missing too many pieces.

Closing the book with a thud, he ran a hand through his hair. He wasn't an accountant or a financial whiz; he barely kept his own finances in order. Figuring out decades-old business dealings was beyond him. But then a thought struck him—maybe he didn't have to do it alone.

Jim, his business accountant back home, was sharp, detail-oriented, and someone Aaron trusted. *Jim: my version of Beans.* Aaron chuckled at the thought. If anyone could help him make sense of this mess, it was him. Aaron made a mental note to call him when he got back. Maybe he could look at the ledgers and provide some insight. There might be something in these pages that he needed to understand —some link between his father, Rob, and everything else that had been haunting him.

But for now, he was at a dead end. He shoved the ledger back into the box and pushed it away. There was still so much he didn't know, but at least he had a plan, a next step. And that was better than nothing.

Aaron's phone rang again as he pushed the box of ledgers further under the desk. The sound made him tense, and his mind raced with the worry of what could be wrong. When he glanced at the screen, he saw it was his foreman.

Unease settled in his stomach as he answered the call. "Yeah, what's up?"

"Aaron, it's Jeff. We've got a situation here at the site." His foreman's voice was tight, laced with concern.

He sat up straighter, every muscle in his body on alert. "What happened?"

"It's Frank. Something happened with his shoulder—he was working on the lower framework, and the next thing we knew, he was on the ground, screaming in pain. He can't move his arm. We called an ambulance, and they're taking him to the hospital now, but... man, it was bad. Everyone's pretty freaked out."

Aaron's heart sank. Frank was his rebar guy, one of the most reliable guys on his crew. Hearing of his injury made Aaron's mind race with worry and guilt for not being there.

"Did anyone see what happened?" Aaron asked, trying to gather his thoughts.

"No one's sure. It all happened so fast. One minute he was fine, the next... it was chaos. We've secured the area; I wasn't sure what to do next."

Aaron took a deep breath, forcing himself to stay calm. "Okay, listen to me. Close the site for the day. Secure everything and keep everyone away from the area. I don't want anyone else getting injured. After that, send everyone home. I'll deal with the rest when I get back."

"Got it, boss," Jeff said, his voice shaking.

"And Jeff," Aaron added, trying to sound as reassuring as possible, "Don't worry. I'm heading home today. I'll be there soon to take care of everything."

"Thanks, Aaron. We'll handle things here until you get back."

He ended the call, staring at the phone. The ledgers, his father, and everything that had consumed him over the past day took a backseat now. His crew needed him.

He needed to get home.

He shoved his belongings into his bag with quick, efficient movements. The urgent situation back home left no room for hesitation or second-guessing. Zipping the bag shut and slinging it over his shoulder, he grabbed the box of ledgers and tucked it under his arm. His mind was already on the drive ahead as he headed out of the room and down the hallway to the front desk.

The check-out process was a blur. He nodded along with the clerk's polite small talk as he handed over his room key and signed the final paperwork. His thoughts were on Frank and the crew, and the road ahead. Everything else felt like background noise.

Loading the last of his things into the jeep, Aaron glanced at the time on his phone. Almost three in the afternoon. He could make good time if he left now, and be at home before it got too late. But as he stood there, keys in hand, another thought crept into his mind.

Big Mike.

Their talk the night before lingered in his thoughts. He had not planned to see his father again before leaving town, but now he felt a tug of obligation. He didn't have Big Mike's phone number, and leaving with no goodbye felt wrong, like leaving a door half-open.

But he was already behind schedule, and Frank needed him. The crew needed him.

Aaron drummed his fingers against the steering wheel, caught between the past's pull and the present's demands. It was tempting to leave the complications of his father behind for now. After all, he had more than enough to deal with at home.

He decided on a quick goodbye to acknowledge the old man, and then he would be on his way. It wouldn't take long. He started the engine and pulled out of the inn's parking lot toward Big Mike's place. He'd make it brief, say what he needed to say, and then get back on the road.

The sooner he did this, the sooner he could get to the things that mattered.

20

Aaron drove toward his father's house, his mind still racing with the pressing need to get home. He tapped his fingers against the steering wheel, planning the quickest route and wondering how bad the situation was with Frank. But as he approached the first intersection, he slowed to wait for a family to cross the street.

His eyes drifted to the antique shop on the corner. Sitting there, the memory of a particular item in the store tugged at him. Without understanding why, he felt an impulse to stop. *There's something I need to do before leaving this place.*

Aaron pulled up to the curb and stepped out of his jeep. He hurried into the store, not giving himself time to second-guess the decision. The item he had in mind sat on the shelf, waiting for him. He didn't take long to purchase it—it felt important, like a small token of the time he'd spent here, or maybe just something to anchor him to the present amidst all the chaos of the past few days.

He set his purchase in the passenger seat, not bothering to unwrap it, and started the jeep again. The errand had taken only a few minutes, but it felt like it had given him a moment to breathe, to center himself. He drove the rest of the way to Big Mike's house, the road familiar yet crowded with the memories of their last conversation.

When he pulled to the end of the driveway, he found his father in the garage, tinkering with the Camaro again. The car seemed to be a constant in Big Mike's life, something he could rely on when everything else was falling apart. Aaron walked over to the garage, his footsteps crunching on the gravel.

"Hey," he called out as he approached. "I've got to get going. One of my guys got hurt on the job, so I'm heading back."

Big Mike looked up from under the Camaro's hood, his expression unreadable. "That so?" He wiped his hands on a rag, nodding. "Well, you're a good leader for looking out for your crew like that. Shows you've got your priorities straight."

Aaron shifted on his feet. "Yeah, well... I didn't want to leave without saying goodbye. Just didn't seem right."

Big Mike's eyes flickered with something Aaron couldn't quite place, but he covered it with a nod. "I appreciate that. More than you know."

There was a brief, awkward silence, the kind that always seemed to stretch between them. Big Mike cleared his throat, looking like he wanted to say something, but couldn't.

"You, uh... Have you looked at those ledgers yet?" Big Mike asked, almost casually, but there was a tension in his voice.

Aaron shook his head. "Not yet. But I will."

"Good." Mike's voice softened. "Keep them safe. They're... important."

"I will," Aaron promised, though he wasn't sure what his father meant by 'important.' It felt like there was still so much he didn't understand.

The older man nodded, then hesitated, glancing at the ground before clapping Aaron on the shoulder. It was a stiff, hesitant gesture, that spoke more of the distance between them than any words could. Aaron could tell his father wanted to say more, but the old man wasn't the type for sentimental goodbyes.

"Take care of yourself, Aaron," Big Mike said, the words sounding forced, like they were being dragged out of him.

"You too," Aaron replied.

On impulse, he extended his hand. Big Mike looked at it, then reached out and grasped Aaron's hand, the grip firm. It was an old-fashioned gesture but seemed fitting—an unspoken acknowledgment between them.

Aaron nodded, then turned and walked to his jeep, the strange mixture of relief and sadness swirling inside him. As Aaron backed out of the driveway, he glanced toward the house and saw Big Mike's wife, Loretta, stepping onto the front porch. She stood there with a small smile and raised her hand in a gentle wave. Her presence was a marker of the softer side of the life his father had built in this small corner of the world.

Aaron hesitated before returning the wave. Loretta's smile widened, and for a moment, Aaron felt a warmth that cut through the chill of the past few days. It was a minor comfort, but one he held onto as he pulled away from the house, heading down the road that would take him back to his life and the responsibilities waiting for him.

As the house disappeared from his view, Aaron couldn't help but think that Loretta's wave was more than just a goodbye. It was a reminder that there were still connections worth holding onto, no matter how complicated or strained they might be.

The drive home was uneventful, the miles passing in a blur as Aaron's mind wandered. As he neared Boyertown, he hit the inevitable five o'clock traffic, a slow crawl that tested his patience but didn't last long. He kept his hands tight on the wheel, his thoughts drifting back to the bizarre fact that had struck him earlier—the realization that his father had been living just an hour away from him all these years, and he hadn't known until this week. The combination of the proximity and the decades of estrangement felt like some cosmic joke.

He called for an update on Frank, and the phone rang twice before Jeff picked up.

"Hey, Aaron," Jeff's voice came through.

"Hey, I'm on my way back. How's Frank?" Aaron asked.

"They took him to urgent care," Jeff explained. "The doctor there wasn't sure what was going on with his shoulder, so they called for transport to the hospital in Pottstown. Said it might be something serious."

"Alright, thanks for the update, man. I'm headed to Pottstown now. I'll check in with you later."

"Got it, boss. Be safe. Let me know what's up."

Aaron hung up and took the next exit, his GPS recalculating the route toward Pottstown. The detour didn't bother him—nothing else mattered except making sure Frank was alright. The ledgers, his father, the weight of the past few days—all of it could wait. He focused on getting to the hospital and being there for his crewman.

Aaron parked his jeep in the hospital emergency room's parking garage and hurried inside. The sterile antiseptic smell hit him as he stepped through the sliding doors. His boots echoed on the polished floors. He made his way to the emergency desk; his eyes scanning the area for any familiar faces.

"Hi, I'm looking for Frank Wesley," Aaron asked the young woman behind the counter.

"Frank Wesley, the construction worker?" she confirmed.

"Yeah, that's him," Aaron replied with a nod.

She scanned the screen for a moment before meeting Aaron's gaze again. "He's assigned to a room, but they've just taken him back for an assessment."

"Do you know how long it might be before he's back?"

"It's hard to say, but it might take a little while," she replied, offering a sympathetic look.

"Can I wait for him in his room?" he asked, hoping he could be there as soon as Frank was out.

The receptionist shook her head gently. "I'm sorry, but only family members can wait in the patient's room. You'll have to wait in the main waiting area."

Aaron sighed with frustration. "Okay, thanks."

He turned away from the desk and found a seat in the waiting area, trying to push down his anxiety. All he could do now was wait, his mind filled with thoughts of what could be wrong and how Frank was holding up. The hours ahead seemed daunting, filled with uncertainty, but he knew he needed to be there for Frank—no matter how long it took.

Aaron decided he needed some fresh air after a few minutes in the waiting area. Stepping outside, he headed to his jeep, feeling the cool breeze hit his face as he unlocked the driver's door. It was a relief to be away from the sterile atmosphere of the hospital, but the worry for Frank lingered in the back of his mind.

Aaron flipped through the ledger again to distract himself. His brow furrowed as he tried to make sense of the cryptic entries. It all blurred together in a frustrating jumble. He tossed the ledger back into the box and reached for his bag instead.

Pulling out his mother's book, he hoped for some light reading to help pass the time. He flipped it open, scanning the familiar handwriting. As he read, the words provided a brief escape from the anxiety of the day. It was a small reprieve, a way to connect with a piece of his past as he waited for news about Frank.

But even as he read, his mind drifted back to the ledgers and the troubling implications of what he had discovered. He couldn't shake the feeling that within those pages were the answers he sought, waiting for him to uncover the truth.

August 11, 1992: Marlena

It's been a long day. Rob left this morning for another one of his business trips—this time to Guatemala. I can't quite wrap my head around it. Why take his friends Kevin and Roger along? His trips to Los Angeles and Charlotte made some sense; those cities are hubs for the meatpacking industry. But Guatemala? I must not understand how this industry works.

The baby, Elise, has been sleeping since I put her down, but the boys are like little tornadoes. Aaron's ten now, and he thinks he's the boss of everyone. Patty is following his lead, while Nico and little Lucas are just trying to keep up. It's exhausting.

After I settled them, I checked on Elise again before closing the boys' door. Their laughter faded to whispers, and I felt a moment of relief fall around me. But as I stood there, staring at Rob's closed office door, a familiar stab of curiosity formed in my mind.

I can't shake the memory of that Red Baron folder I stumbled upon last year. What could be in there? I've tried not to pry too much into Rob's affairs—he always says he'll fill me in later—but I'm wondering if there's more going on than he's let on.

I took a few cautious steps toward the door, my heart racing, but when I tried the knob, it wouldn't budge. Locked. Of course. Rob always keeps his office locked. I'm not surprised.

I walked away, a mix of frustration and concern gnawing at me. Maybe I'm just being paranoid. Maybe it's the fatigue of motherhood talking. But something feels off, and I can't quite put my finger on it. I took a deep breath, shook off the unease, and headed back to the living room. It's going to be a long weekend, and I need to be ready for whatever chaos tomorrow brings.

As Aaron left the hospital, he reflected on the past hour. He had closed his mother's book, his mind still tangled with thoughts of those cryptic journal entries. The questions about his stepfather's mysterious international business trips lingered, but he'd forced himself to push them aside as he headed back into the hospital to check on Frank.

Once inside, he'd been relieved that he could see Frank. When he walked into the room, his crewman had been lying there, his eyes glazed over from the pain medicine. His wife, Lisa, sitting beside him, looked exhausted and worried. She'd explained that the doctors suspected a torn rotator cuff with impingement and that Frank might need to see an orthopedic surgeon. The uncertainty had taken a toll on her.

Aaron had done his best to reassure her that worker's compensation would cover Frank's injury and that they would still get paid, even if it took some time to process the paperwork. He'd promised they would get Frank back on his feet, easing Lisa's fears at least a little.

Frank, groggy but grateful, had thanked him, and Aaron had given him a gentle pat on the leg, telling him to focus on getting better. After a few more minutes of reassurances, he'd said his goodbyes and left the hospital.

Now, as he headed toward the parking lot, Aaron felt a small measure of relief. At least, for the moment, things were under control. But as he started the engine, the thoughts of his stepfather, the trips, the ledgers, and the questions they raised crept back into his mind.

21

Aaron spent all morning on the phone with the insurance company. Before construction could resume on the work site, there were reports and inspections to be done. The work was time-consuming, but he didn't mind. Around noon, he decided it was time for a break. "Nicole," he called, "can you order sandwiches for everyone in the office? Let's make it a working lunch."

He turned to his accountant. "Hey Jim, you got a minute? I've got something I'd like you to look at."

Jim looked up from his desk, intrigued. "Sure thing, boss. What's up?"

Aaron handed the ledger to Jim, who opened it with a curious expression. "This is from my father's old auto shop," Aaron explained. "I need you to show me how to read it."

Jim flipped through the pages, his interest piqued. "Every accountant has a unique system, but I'm pretty sure this isn't just for an auto shop," he said, eyebrows furrowing as he examined the entries. "These amounts seem too large for just car repairs or parts. And look here," he pointed, "these initials appear to be recurring on specific dates. It's like some regular payments are happening."

Aaron leaned in, paying close attention. He hadn't noticed the pattern before, and Jim's observation made him even more curious. "You think this could be something else?"

Jim chuckled, but his eyes betrayed a hint of worry. "I don't want to jump to conclusions, but... yeah, it's possible. Maybe something not... legal? These entries don't scream 'legit business' to me. Are you sure you want to be digging into this?"

Aaron could sense Jim's unease, and he reassured him. "This has nothing to do with our current business. It's just an old relic from decades ago. I'm just trying to understand what I'm looking at."

Jim nodded, still flipping through the pages. "Alright, if you say so. But just be careful, Aaron. Sometimes old skeletons are better left buried."

Aaron thanked Jim for his insight. The recurring dates and payments were a new clue to dig into. As they wrapped up their conversation, the sandwiches arrived, and Aaron set the ledger aside, ready to dive back into the rest of his day.

By the time the workday was over, he was more than ready to escape the confines of his office. The hours had dragged on, filled with the monotony of phone calls, paperwork, and discussions about Frank's injury. It was necessary, but after days of emotional upheaval and the discovery of the old ledgers, he was desperate for something more normal.

He sent a quick message to Alex, asking if he needed to pick up anything for dinner. The reply was almost instant.

3/3/16 5:07 pm
From Alex: Jared ordered Chinese—
should be at the house around the
same time as you.

Aaron smiled at the thought of a low-key evening with his friends. They knew him well enough to sense when he needed to unwind with no fuss. He left the office, feeling lighter as he headed to his jeep.

The drive home was uneventful, giving him time to shift gears from work to the evening ahead. The smell of takeout was wafting through the air when he pulled into the driveway. He could see the bags on the kitchen counter through the window, and his stomach growled in response.

"Hey, man," Alex greeted him as he walked in, handing him a pair of chopsticks. "Perfect timing."

"Smells amazing," Aaron said, shrugging off his jacket and grabbing a beer from the fridge. He could feel the tension dissipating as they settled into the comfortable familiarity of their routine.

Jared was already at the table, dishing out portions of General Tso's chicken and fried rice. "Hope you're hungry. I might have gone a little overboard."

Aaron chuckled as he sat down. "I'm never going to complain about too much food."

They focused on eating, but as the plates emptied and the beer bottles clinked, the discussion shifted to more serious topics.

"So, how'd the trip go?" Alex asked, leaning back in his chair. "You find out what you needed to?"

Aaron took a sip of his beer, choosing his words carefully. "Yeah, I did. Found out more than I expected."

Jared raised an eyebrow. "Good or bad?"

"A little of both," Aaron admitted. "Mike gave me some old ledgers—they have to do with his side business."

The room went quiet for a moment. Alex broke the silence. "You mean… the drug trafficking?"

Aaron nodded. "Yeah. Jim looked at one ledger today. They kept track of payments and shipments—not just for the auto shop."

Jared let out a low whistle. "Damn. So what are you going to do with them?"

Aaron rubbed the back of his neck. "I need to figure out where the ties to Rob are in all of this. He was involved, but I need to know how deep. I've been thinking about what it all means, trying to piece it together. Jim noticed some patterns—recurring payments from the same initials on regular dates. He thinks it's a setup for something bigger than just a small-time operation."

Alex gave him a serious look. "Sounds like you're dealing with some dangerous stuff. You sure you want to dig into this?"

"I have to," Aaron mumbled. "I can't just let it sit there. But it's unsettling, seeing it all laid out. It makes everything feel more real."

Jared, ever the pragmatist, shifted the conversation. "What about Bethany? Did you talk to her after you got back?"

Aaron shook his head, a hint of regret in his expression. "No, I haven't. We said goodbye before I left, and I've thought about texting her, but I haven't reached out yet."

Alex nodded. "You've got a lot on your plate. But maybe it wouldn't hurt to send her a message. See how she's doing."

"Yeah, maybe," Aaron replied, considering. It was tempting after the past few days.

"Do it," Jared encouraged. "You don't have to dive into anything serious. Just let her know you're thinking about her."

The conversation moved on after that, circling back to more mundane topics. They debated the best takeout spots in town and caught up on the latest local gossip. By the time the beer was gone, Aaron felt a sense of relief. Sharing his worries with Alex and Jared made them feel more manageable.

As they cleaned up and settled in for a movie, Aaron felt a quiet gratitude for the normalcy of the evening. It wasn't just the food or the laughter; it was the comfort of being with people who knew him, flaws and all, and who had his back no matter what.

Before the opening credits rolled, Aaron pulled out his phone and tapped out a quick text message.

> 3/3/16 8:27 pm
> To Bethany: I've been thinking about you all week. I hope you had a good one!

> 3/3/16 8:35 pm
> From Bethany: I've been thinking about you too, Aaron! I hope you let me know the next time you're in my neighborhood.

> 3/3/16 8:39 pm
> To Bethany: Of course! I hope to see you again soon.

He slid his phone back into his pocket; the smile lingering on his face. He might not have all the answers yet, but at least he didn't have to face them alone.

February 10, 1993: Marlena

The house was quiet, save for the rhythmic hum of the washing machine. Rob left for a business convention in Atlanta this morning. The boys were at school, and baby Elise was down for her afternoon nap. She is such a fussy baby and always wants to be held. I got her settled and had a moment to breathe and think.

I had been cleaning all day, trying to keep busy, but my mind drifted back to the folder I saw two years ago in Rob's desk drawer — the Red Baron. I still can't figure out why he would have anything to do with it. He never worked there. He never mentioned Rudy or anyone involved. And now, with him out of town, the curiosity was eating at me. His office door called to me.

I expected a locked door, but that didn't stop me this time. Using a kitchen butter knife, I jimmied the lock open within seconds. My heart was pounding, but I told myself it was because I was nervous about what I might find.

I went straight to the desk drawer. It was empty—no folders or papers. Oh, the disappointment that washed over me. But then I saw the safe, tucked away in the closet. Rob's guns are in there, I know that much. But maybe his paperwork is too? I can't shake this pressing need to know what's inside.

The keypad blinked up at me from the safe. I tried Rob's birthday first, then mine. Nothing. I tried Nico's, Lucas's, and Elise's birthdays, but the red light kept flashing, taunting me.

I sat back on my heels, thinking. Then it hit me—the day we got married. Not the actual date, but the one Rob always tells people, the one that makes it seem like we've been together longer than we have: January 14, 1987. I punched it in, holding my breath.

The red light flashed, and the lock clicked open. My hand hovered over the handle; I couldn't convince myself to turn it. Something in my gut told me that if I did, Rob would know. I can already feel his eyes on me, cold and accusing. A shiver ran down my spine, and just thinking about it now sends ice water running through my veins.

I slammed the door closed, my heart racing. I wiped the handle with my sleeve as if my fingerprints would glow under his scrutiny. He couldn't find out I was in there. I flipped the thumb latch on the doorknob, closing the door behind me as I rushed out. My hands were shaking, but I forced myself to calm down. I had to act as if I'd been cleaning all along—like my curiosity didn't just lead me down a path to things I don't have any business thinking about.

As I pick up the laundry basket and head back down the hall, I feel like I've dodged a bullet. But the questions still thrum in my head. What is my husband hiding? And why do I feel like I'm in over my head?

Aaron rubbed his temples to ease the dull throbbing headache as he went to bed. The intense action-adventure movie he'd watched with Alex and Jared earlier had marked its start. Alex loved those kinds of movies, and while Aaron found them entertaining, tonight the relentless gunfire and explosions had only added to the mental clutter he was trying to push through.

He hesitated before reaching for his mother's book. The leather cover felt like a touchstone to a past he was still trying to understand. Aaron flipped it open, reading through the entry she'd written in early 1993.

The words transported him to that day when his mother had given in to her curiosity about Rob's mysterious Red Baron folder. He could picture her standing in Rob's silent office. He could imagine the tension she must have felt as she picked the lock to Rob's office door with a butter knife, only to find the drawer empty of the folder she sought. The discovery of the safe, and her panic when she cracked the code, must have been a moment of intense fear and hesitation.

Aaron's mind replayed the entry as he lay in bed, his mother's fear settling on him. *What had been in that folder? And why was Rob so secretive about it?* The safe, that locked vault of secrets, might hold the answers he needed. But now it was his turn to decide if he would be the one to pry it open.

Sleep didn't come, his thoughts circling the possibilities and what-ifs. He kept thinking about the indecipherable ledger. And now, on top of that, the safe his mother hadn't opened because of the terror of what she might find—or what might happen if Rob found out.

He needed answers. But could he get them?

He decided almost before he realized it. In the morning, Aaron reached for his phone. Lucas was the first person he needed to talk to.

The phone rang several times before Lucas picked up. His voice sounded as if he'd just woken up.

"Aaron? What's up?" Lucas's voice was groggy.

"Morning, Lucas," Aaron said, trying to keep his tone light. "Sorry to call so early. I didn't wake you, did I?"

"Nah, I was just… getting up," Lucas replied, the lie clear in his voice.

"Listen," Aaron began, sitting on the edge of his bed, "I was thinking about coming over for a visit. Maybe this weekend? There's something I need to check on."

"Uh, yeah, sure," Lucas said, his tone cautious. "You know you're always welcome. But what's going on?"

Aaron chose his words with care. "I was hoping you could arrange a visit with Dad. There are some things I need to ask him about, stuff I've thought about since Mom died."

There was a long pause on the other end of the line. Aaron could almost hear the gears turning in Lucas's head as he processed the request.

"Aaron, I don't know…" Lucas said, uncertainty coloring his voice. "Dad doesn't pick up when I call, you know? It's been… strained. Not even sure he'd agree to see me, much less you."

"I get it," Aaron said, not wanting to push too hard. "It's a long shot, but it's important, Lucas. If you can get him to take your call, or try to set something up. I'd appreciate it."

Lucas sighed, a heavy sound that conveyed just how difficult this request was for him. "Okay, I'll try. No promises, though. If he's in one of his moods, there's not much I can do."

"That's all I'm asking," Aaron said gratefully. "I owe you one."

"Yeah, you do," Lucas replied, a hint of a smile in his voice. "But don't expect me to work miracles."

Aaron chuckled. "I won't. Do what you can."

They ended the call, and Aaron stared at the phone in his hand. Talking with Lucas had not filled him with confidence, but at least the wheels were in motion. He had to start somewhere, and confronting Rob was as good a place as any.

The morning was a blur of phone calls and paperwork. Aaron buried himself in the daily operations of his business. He met with the city inspector and signed paperwork and checks—these tasks kept his mind occupied.

But now and then, his thoughts would drift back to that safe, the ledgers, and Rob's shadowy connections. The questions refused to be ignored.

By the time lunch rolled around, Aaron felt like he'd run a mental marathon. When Nicole came by to tell him the sandwiches had arrived, he was more than ready for a break. But even as he joined the rest of the office staff for a quick meal, his mind was still on what he might find if Lucas could get Rob to agree to a meeting.

He felt sure that whatever was locked away in Rob's safe might blow everything wide open.

The future felt uncertain, but Aaron had a path forward. He hoped that he'd be ready to face whatever answers he uncovered.

22

Early Saturday morning, Aaron set out for Virginia. The sun was coming up as he loaded his jeep, but he hoped to beat the traffic and give himself time to prepare for a tense day. The three-hour drive stretched before him, and though the highway was familiar, his mind was anything but settled.

The visit to Rob's house consumed Aaron's thoughts. On the surface, this trip was about trying to mend the fractures within the family. The distance that had grown between himself, his siblings, and Rob was undeniable, and Aaron knew they needed to address it if there was any hope of moving forward as a family.

But beneath that facade, Aaron had a different agenda. He needed to get into Rob's safe—there was no other way to put it. The contents might hold the key to deciphering the entries in the ledgers. They could reveal how deeply involved Rob was in whatever illegal activities had occurred.

He replayed his phone call to Lucas over in his head, considering how he would approach the day. He knew he couldn't tip his hand too early. Rob was intuitive, and Aaron knew he would pick up on any inconsistencies in his behavior. The challenge was finding the right moment to gain access without arousing suspicion. He knew Lucas did not know what he was after, but his brother had kept his questions to a minimum anyway, which Aaron appreciated.

As he entered Virginia, Aaron felt his phone buzz in his pocket. He pulled it out and saw that it was Lucas calling.

"Hey, I'm almost there," Aaron said, answering on the second ring.

"Good timing," Lucas replied, his voice a little tight. "Look, I have to tell you something... Dad's expecting me around noon, but I didn't mention that you'd be with me."

"You didn't tell him I was coming?"

"I'm sorry, man," Lucas said. "If I told him, he'd refuse to see me, and neither of us would get through the door. You know how he is."

Aaron let out a slow breath, trying to keep his irritation in check. Lucas was right; Rob had a stubborn streak a mile wide, and if he knew Aaron was coming, he might have shut the whole thing down. "I get it," Aaron said after a moment. "I just wish we had a better plan."

"Yeah, me too," Lucas admitted. "But this was the only way I could think of to make sure we got in the same room with him. Hopefully, he'll be cool about it."

"I hope," Aaron echoed, though he could only imagine the look on Rob's face when he saw Aaron standing in his doorway unannounced.

"I'll be there in about ten minutes," he said, glancing at the GPS. "We'll figure it out."

"Okay," Lucas replied. "We'll figure it out."

They ended the call, and Aaron's mind continued to churn as he navigated the last few turns to Lucas's place. This would not be easy, but nothing with Rob ever was. He needed to balance keeping the peace with his determination to uncover the truth.

When Aaron pulled into Lucas's driveway, he steadied himself before he stood. He grabbed his bag from the passenger seat, slung it over his shoulder, and walked to the front door. Lucas was already waiting, his expression a mix of nerves and determination.

"Ready?" Lucas asked as he opened the door for him.

"As I'll ever be," Aaron replied, stepping inside.

They didn't linger long at Lucas's house. The drive to Rob's place was short, but it felt like a much longer journey as they headed toward what Aaron knew could be a pivotal moment for them all. Pulling up to the last house where their mother had lived, Aaron's heart rate picked up. The house looked the same as it always had—

modest, well-kept, with a trimmed lawn and a car parked in the driveway—but today, it felt like it held secrets Aaron wasn't sure he was ready to uncover.

Aaron parked, and they both sat for a moment, neither of them making a move to get out.

"You sure about this?" Lucas asked, breaking the silence.

Aaron looked at the house, then back at his brother. "We have to do this. For all of us."

Lucas nodded, though his expression remained troubled. "Let's go, then."

They walked up the path to the front door. Lucas knocked, and they waited in tense silence until they heard footsteps approaching. The door opened, and there stood Rob, his face as unreadable as ever.

"Lucas," he said, giving his son a brief nod. His eyes flickered to Aaron, and there was a moment of hesitation before he stepped aside to let them in. "Aaron. Didn't know you'd be joining us."

"Hope it's not a problem," Aaron said, keeping his tone light.

Rob gestured for them to come inside. "Come on in. Let's talk."

Aaron followed Lucas inside, trying to read the older man's mood. Rob's poker face was as good as ever, and Aaron knew this would not be easy. As they stepped into the house, the tension between the three men was palpable. Rob led the way into the living room, where they exchanged terse pleasantries. The air felt thick with unspoken grievances. Lucas fell into his role as the peacemaker, trying to bridge the gap with lighthearted conversation, his voice too casual as he asked Rob about work, the weather, and anything that might ease the tension.

Aaron was less inclined to play along. He moved through the room with deliberate calm, his eyes scanning the familiar space, noting how little had changed—and how much it had all become a tomb of memories he'd rather forget. The walls held the same photos and trinkets, yet they felt foreign to him now. He tuned out the exchange between Lucas and Rob as he made his way into the kitchen, drawn by a sense of dread he couldn't quite shake.

He stopped short when he saw his mother's prized spider plant. It hung by the windowsill, bathed in the dull morning light filtering through the dusty glass. The once vibrant green leaves were now dull and spindly, the edges browned and curled. The plant was dry, neglected—and dying. It was a sad remnant of what once was, much like everything else in this house.

His stomach churned as he stared at it, memories of his mother tending to it flooding his mind. She'd always been so proud of that plant, nurturing it like one of her children. Seeing it in this state, abandoned and forgotten, was like a punch to the gut.

"Mom's spider plant," Aaron said, his voice cutting through Lucas's chatter. He didn't turn to look at Rob, but he could feel the older man's eyes on him. "It's dying."

There was a beat of silence before Rob's voice cut through the air, sharp and dismissive. "Might as well. It's just cluttering up the place."

Aaron turned then, the words striking a nerve. He locked eyes with Rob, and the resentment that had simmered beneath the surface for years boiled over. "Cluttering up the place?" Aaron's voice was low, but the anger in it was unmistakable. "It's the only damn thing in here that still feels like she was here."

The room seemed to shrink around them as the two men squared off, the years of animosity between them coming to a head. Rob's eyes narrowed, his posture stiffening as he stepped closer. He was a man who had never liked Aaron, never accepted him as a son, and he didn't bother hiding it now. "I didn't ask you to come here and tell me how to run my house, Aaron."

Aaron could feel his pulse quicken as he stared back at the man who had caused him and his family so much pain. He could still hear the way Rob's voice cut through the house, and could feel the sting of his hand when it struck. And now, standing in the kitchen of this house, with the ghost of his mother's presence fading from every corner, Aaron's resentment surged to the surface.

"And I didn't come here to watch you let everything she cared about rot." Aaron's anger shot back at his stepfather. "You never gave a damn about her—or any of us. You're just a coward hiding behind this—this bullshit."

Rob's eyes flashed with anger, his fists clenching at his sides. "Watch your mouth, boy. You don't know a damn thing about what went on here."

Aaron took a step closer. "I know enough. I know how you treated her—how you treated us. She drank herself into oblivion, and you didn't lift a finger to stop her or help. You just threatened her and kept her dependent on you. You let her drown, and now you're doing the same to everything she loved."

Rob's face contorted with rage. "You're so high and mighty, aren't you? Moron. You don't know shit, Aaron. You never did."

"And whose fault is that?" Aaron shot back. "You never wanted me to know anything. You just wanted to keep us all in the dark, under your thumb."

The crackling tension hung heavy in the air. Rob's chest heaved as he glared at Aaron. "I don't have to take this shit," Rob spat, his voice low and venomous. He turned and stomped out of the house, slamming the door behind him.

Lucas, who stood to the side, looking torn between the two men, pursued Rob, trying to call him back. "Dad, wait!" he called, his voice desperate. But Rob didn't stop. He jumped into his car, the engine roaring to life as he peeled out of the driveway, leaving a cloud of dust in his wake.

Aaron stood in the kitchen with his chest heaving. The car speeding away echoed in his ears, but all he could see was the dying spider plant, a painful reminder of what he had lost.

Lucas came back inside, looking defeated. The plan to talk had failed immediately, and the distance had only grown wider. Aaron looked at his brother, feeling a pang of guilt for how things had turned out.

"I'm sorry, Lucas," Aaron said.

Lucas shook his head, his shoulders slumping. "Whatever, man. I'm calling Renee." He didn't wait for a response, turning to walk through the front door, and pulling his phone out of his pocket.

Aaron watched him go, a lump settling in his throat. He turned and headed for the bathroom, needing a moment to collect himself before he faced whatever came next.

The bathroom door was right by Rob's office, and Aaron debated his next move. The door was closed but not locked. His hand hesitated on the knob before he turned it and slipped inside.

The room was dim, with only a sliver of light from the hallway seeping in through the crack in the door. Aaron flipped the switch, illuminating the space with a harsh, artificial glow. The desk drawer caught his eye, and he crossed the room to open it, half-expecting to find it still empty, as Marlena had described. But he found a mundane collection of pens, paper clips, and other office minutia. Whatever had been in the drawer before was long gone.

His gaze shifted to the closet that housed the safe. It was always there, no matter which house they had lived in. Rob had never changed that, as if the safe were as much a part of him as his own shadow. Aaron reached for the closet door and opened it, flipping on the light. There it was: the same heavy steel box, just as he remembered.

He paused, a surge of doubt flooding his mind. *Would the code still be the same after all these years? Had Rob changed it, or had he kept it the way it was, assuming no one would ever dare try to open it?* Aaron glanced out the window. Lucas was pacing outside, preoccupied with his conversation on his phone, his back to the house.

Taking a deep breath, Aaron punched in the code: 01-14-1987. *The date Rob always told people they were married.* He half-expected the red light to blink in denial, but it flashed, and the lock clicked open with a mechanical whir.

Aaron froze, the gravity of what he was about to do sinking in. There was no turning back now. He dragged the safe door open.

Inside, the first thing he saw were the guns, lined up on the left side. Handguns, rifles, and ammunition—a small arsenal Rob had always meticulously maintained. But it wasn't the guns Aaron was after. His eyes flicked to the right, where several shelves held a lockbox, a pile of cash, and stacks of folders and papers.

Aaron reached for the folders on the top shelf, rifling through them. He was looking for something specific, but it wasn't there. Frustration flared in him as he moved to the next shelf, sifting through more documents. His breath caught when he spotted a red folder at the bottom of the stack marked "The Red Baron." Just below it was a legal envelope labeled "Kirby/Fresno/Stanley." His heart pounded as he pulled both out, setting them carefully on the bookshelf to his left.

He replaced the stack in the safe, ensuring it looked as it had before. Closing the door, he wiped off the handle, just as his mother had done when she had cracked the code to the safe in 1993. *Like mother, like son.*

Getting the folders out of the house without Lucas seeing them would be tricky. Aaron's mind raced as he scanned the room, looking for something to conceal the documents. There was nothing that Rob wouldn't miss in here. He flipped the light switches off, heading to the kitchen. His eyes landed on a shelf in the kitchen. There it was: his mother's recipe binder, "From the Kitchen of Marlena." It was thick, sturdy, and the perfect place to hide the folders. He snatched it up and shoved the documents inside, tucking them behind the pages of recipes.

He took a deep breath to calm the adrenaline surging through his veins. His mother's spider plant hung by the window, and he couldn't leave it there after what had happened. He lifted the plant from its chain and held it in one hand, the other clutching the recipe binder.

Taking one last look around the kitchen, he walked out onto the porch.

Lucas was still on the phone, but when he saw Aaron, he wrapped up his conversation, sliding the phone back into his pocket. "Everything okay?" Lucas asked, his eyes narrowing as he noticed the binder and the plant.

Aaron didn't give him time to question it. He hurried to the jeep, sliding the folders up under the closed box of ledgers, out of sight. He was flipping through the recipe book when Lucas joined him, trying to look casual as he spoke.

"She had no will," Aaron said, not looking up. "I figured the least she'd want us to have is her recipes. I'll run off copies for everybody."

Lucas nodded, but his gaze lingered on the plant. "And the plant?"

"Yeah," Aaron said, his voice softening as he glanced at the spider plant. "It's not clutter to me."

Lucas didn't press further. He nodded, accepting Aaron's explanation without question. "Alright," he said, his voice resigned. "Let's get out of here."

As they drove away, Aaron couldn't help but glance over his shoulder at the recipe binder on the passenger backseat, tilted to hold his mother's spider plant in place. Treasures, to be sure, though the real prize lay hidden and secure in the trunk, waiting for him to uncover its truths. If luck were with him, perhaps the folders would unlock the secrets Rob had kept buried for so long.

Dinner at Lucas and Renee's house was always cheerful, and

tonight was no exception. The coolness between Aaron and Lucas from the tense encounter with Rob dissipated almost immediately thanks to Renee's warm conversation and the lively atmosphere. When she sent them off to set the dinner table, the brothers fell into their usual rhythm, talking as if nothing had happened.

The house buzzed with energy, as Lucas and Renee's kids had friends over to spend the night. The four children chattered non-stop throughout the meal, their laughter and animated stories filling the room. Aaron couldn't help but smile at the infectious joy of the evening, though he noticed Lucas checking his phone several times during dinner. Renee would nudge him each time, and Lucas would slip the phone back into his pocket with a small, apologetic grin.

Later, while they were washing dishes together, Aaron turned to Lucas, the memory of the earlier confrontation weighing on his mind. "I'm sorry about earlier," he said, keeping his voice low so Renee wouldn't hear from the other room. "I shouldn't have reacted the way I did."

Lucas glanced at him, rinsing a plate before setting it on the drying rack. "It's okay," he said, shaking his head. "I should have known it wouldn't be as easy as an impromptu meeting. Dad's... well, he's Dad."

Aaron nodded, but when Lucas' eyes flickered to his phone again, he couldn't help but ask if everything was okay.

"Yeah, just hoping to hear from Dad," Lucas said. "I'd like to know he got home safely."

Aaron didn't respond, as he had given no thought to Rob's safety. They finished the dishes in silence before moving to the backyard to unwind.

The night air felt chilly, and the stars peeked out from the darkening sky. They sat on the deck in peaceful silence, enjoying the quiet after the whirlwind of the evening. Both their phones chimed together, interrupting the calm. They exchanged a curious glance before reaching for their phones, only to find a message from their sister.

Aaron's eyebrows shot up as he read her text.

3/5/16 9:04 pm
From Elise: Dad's at home safe, but I

don't appreciate you two making him so upset. What were you trying to do?

Lucas sighed, his hand running through his hair as he read the same message. Aaron shrugged, trying to brush off the sting of her words. "First time I hear from her in a year, and she's pissed," he muttered, rolling his eyes in disbelief.

Renee joined them on the deck, having just finished settling the kids for the night. She took one look at the expressions on their faces and knew something was up. "What's going on?"

"Elise," Lucas said, handing her his phone so she could read the message.

Renee sighed, her brow furrowing as she read. She returned the phone, placing a comforting hand on his arm. "Elise has a unique way of dealing with things, you know that," she reminded them. "She's just protective of your dad. Too protective. But she'll come around. You both need to give her some time."

Aaron nodded, still feeling the sting of Elise's anger. "It's just frustrating," he admitted. "I thought maybe... I don't know. After all this time, we could patch things up. But it feels like every time I try, it gets worse."

Lucas didn't respond at first, but after a moment, he reached into his pocket and pulled out a marijuana joint. He lit it, taking a long drag before passing it to Aaron. "She'll come around when she's ready," he said while exhaling smoke. "Until then, let's just not stress about it."

Aaron took the joint, inhaling and letting the warmth spread through him. "Yeah," he agreed. "Maybe you're right."

Renee smiled as the joint came to her. "Family's complicated," she said, taking a small puff before handing it to Lucas. "But we'll figure it out."

The three of them passed the joint around in comfortable silence. The cool night air and the bright stars overhead were comforting, and it was easy to forget the troubles waiting just beyond the horizon.

23

The next morning, laughter filled the house as Aaron joined Lucas and his family around the kitchen table. Aaron smiled as they talked over pancakes, eggs, and bacon. Renee kept the conversation light, asking about Aaron's plans for the rest of the weekend while the kids chatted. It was comforting, despite all the unresolved issues swimming beneath the surface.

As they finished breakfast, Aaron felt a pang of reluctance to leave. He stood from the table and Renee and the kids enveloped him in a series of hugs. Lucas clapped him on the back, his expression lighter than it had been the day before. "Take care of yourself, man," Lucas said, a hint of concern in his voice. "And remember, you don't have to do everything."

Aaron nodded, appreciating the sentiment even if he didn't believe it. "Thanks. I'll be back soon," he promised, meaning it more than he realized.

He waved, the cool morning air biting his skin as he started the jeep's engine. The warmth of Lucas's home faded as he drove away, replaced by a growing sense of unease as his thoughts turned to his next destination. He had one more stop before heading home—a stop he hadn't planned but now felt was necessary.

As he drove through the streets of Lucas's neighborhood, Aaron spotted a grocery store on the corner and pulled in, parking near the entrance. He made a beeline for the floral section, scanning the shelves of bouquets until he found a simple arrangement of sunflowers, daisies, and lavender. They were his mother's favorites, and he knew they were what she would have wanted.

Flowers in hand, Aaron resumed his drive. Suburban neighborhoods gave way to the open countryside. The drive to the cemetery was long, giving him plenty of time to think, though his thoughts were anything but comforting. His mind spun with the past few days—his confrontation with Rob, the strained relationship with Elise, the folders hidden in his trunk. But the memory of his mother tugged at his heart more than anything, pulling him toward where she now rested.

The quiet cemetery was a clear departure from the bustling life he had just left behind. A stiff wind whipped through the bare trees, carrying with it the chill of early spring as Aaron walked down the narrow path that led to his mother's grave. The gravestones stood in neat rows, marking once-robust lives now reduced to names and dates etched in stone.

He stopped in front of the gravestone he had visited only twice this past year, its surface not yet worn by time and weather. Marlena Giorgio Bakker, the stone read, followed by her birth and death dates. Beneath that, the simple inscription: Beloved Mother.

Kneeling, Aaron placed the bouquet at the base of the gravestone, arranging the flowers with care. The cold earth beneath his knees seeped through his jeans; his breath was visible in the frigid air as he exhaled, before speaking. His voice trembled.

"Hey, Mom," he began, feeling a lump in his throat. "I know I should've come sooner. I just... I've been trying to figure things out."

He paused, running his fingers over the carved letters of her name. The cold stone was unyielding, much like the memories that had brought him here. "I'm trying to unravel the mystery," he continued, his voice stronger now. "There was something you never could face about Rob. I want to know why things were the way they were... why you stayed and didn't tell us everything."

His mind flashed to the folders hidden under the box of ledgers in the jeep. He hadn't had the chance to look through them yet, but he knew—deep down—that whatever they contained, it would change everything. "I found something," he admitted, his voice low. "Something I think you would have wanted me to find. But I don't know what to do with it."

The wind rustled the branches above him, the only sound in the silent cemetery. Aaron closed his eyes, trying to picture his mother as she had been—strong and loving, but burdened by secrets she could never bring herself to share. He had always sensed there was more to the story, that there were things she kept hidden to protect them. But now, standing here, he realized those secrets had also been her undoing.

"I'm going to make it right," he said, his voice filled with a quiet resolve. "I don't know how yet, but I'll figure it out."

He stayed there a while, talking to his mother as if she could hear him and her spirit could guide him. It was something he had done before, but today felt different. Today, it felt like he was taking the first steps toward understanding and healing.

When he stood, his legs stiff from the cold, he felt a sense of clarity he hadn't had before. The weight of the past few days was still there, but it was no longer suffocating. He looked at his mother's grave, the flowers he had brought standing out against the gray of the stone, and whispered goodbye.

The wind picked up as he walked to his jeep, sending a chill down his spine. He didn't mind it, though. He needed the reminder that he was still alive and capable of change, of making things right. And as he drove away from the cemetery, leaving the past behind, he knew that whatever came next, he would face it head-on.

For his mother. For the truth. And for himself.

Maybe one more stop, Aaron thought, gripping the steering wheel as he navigated through the quiet, tree-lined streets. The last few days had left him with more questions than answers, and Elise was at the center. If anyone knew what was going on with Rob, it was her.

Elise's house towered ahead as he turned onto her street. It was a large mansion in a fancy neighborhood lined with oak trees—the whole place screamed wealth and privilege. A car was in the driveway, but he paid it no mind as he parked on the street and walked up the sidewalk. It was noon; her husband Tom might be at work, but Aaron hoped his sister was home. He hadn't called or texted first, and he realized now it was for the same reason Lucas hadn't warned Rob that Aaron was with him—he didn't want to give her a chance to refuse. He figured she wouldn't want to see him, especially after the argument with Rob. But he wanted to apologize, if only because it had upset her so much.

He rang the doorbell and waited long minutes. When no one answered, he knocked. Nothing. Aaron was about to turn away when he heard footsteps coming down the stairs. "I'm coming, I'm coming," Elise's impatient voice called out.

The door swung open, and as soon as he saw her face, Aaron knew it was a mistake to have come here. Elise's expression morphed from surprise to anger in a heartbeat. "What the hell are you doing here?" she spat, her voice rising with each word. "Haven't you done enough damage? Are you trying to destroy the entire family?"

Aaron opened his mouth to speak, to defend himself, but Elise was already on the attack, jabbing her finger into his chest as she spoke. "Why do you always have to dig up the past, Aaron? Why can't you leave things alone?"

He backed up, stepping down the front steps out of her reach, trying to create distance. She stood on the top step, glaring down at him, her anger rolling off her in hot waves.

"I came to apologize," Aaron said. "I didn't mean to upset you, Elise. But there's something off about Dad, and I'm trying to figure out what it is. I'm trying to understand what happened."

Elise scoffed, her face a mask of fury. "There's nothing to understand! You're just looking for trouble, as usual. Why can't you let it go?"

"Don't tell me you don't remember how weird Dad and his friends used to be with you?" Aaron shot back, the words escaping before he could stop them. He didn't want to push her, but it was too late.

Elise froze, her eyes wide with shock. For a moment, Aaron thought he saw something else in her expression—fear, perhaps. She tried to hide it; her face hardening into neutrality.

Before Aaron could say anything else, more footsteps thundered down the stairs inside. The door swung open wider, and there stood Patty, their brother. He was furious.

Aaron's confusion deepened. *What the hell is Patty doing here?* The question raced through his mind. Patty was yelling now, joining Elise in her tirade against Aaron, but all Aaron could focus on was the strange scene in front of him—his sister, wearing a lacy nightgown and a silk robe, and his brother, standing there in nothing but gym shorts.

Something clicked in his mind, and he stepped back, his stomach churning with the realization that maybe his private suspicions about Elise and Patty were correct. All those years of wondering, of feeling like something was off between them... it wasn't just in his head. It couldn't be.

He muttered, "I'm sorry," though the words felt hollow.

"You should be," Patty snapped, putting his arm around Elise and guiding her back inside. They disappeared into the house, slamming the door behind them. Aaron stood alone on the sidewalk.

Back in his jeep, Aaron's heart pounded as he gripped the steering wheel, staring at the sleek red Nissan 240SX in the driveway. It was Patty's car. He'd bought it years ago, during his reckless phase. *How did I not notice it before?* The truth of what he'd just seen in Elise's doorway, coupled with the shock of his brother's presence, hit him like a ton of bricks, making it hard to breathe.

He forced himself to take a deep breath, trying to still his trembling hands. *What the hell just happened?* Everything about the situation felt wrong—his sister's rage, her apparent panic when he mentioned their father, and then Patty appearing half-dressed and furious.

He had come to Elise's house with the simple intention of apologizing, trying to mend things after the mess with Rob. It was supposed to be a step toward making things right, toward understanding what had gone wrong in their family. But now, all he could think about was the strange, unsettling scene he had just witnessed, both of his siblings caught in the middle of something they didn't want him to see.

Aaron swallowed hard, the taste of bile rising in his throat. He had always known there was something off about their family, something that had festered in the dark corners of their lives, but this... this was something else. It was a revelation that made his skin crawl, sending shivers down his spine, and making him question everything he thought he knew about his siblings.

He closed his eyes, trying to banish the images from his mind, but they wouldn't go away. It was too much, too fast, and he couldn't figure out what it might mean.

When he opened his eyes again, the Nissan was still there, parked like a glaring reminder of everything that had just transpired. He had to get out of there. He couldn't sit in front of Elise's house any longer, not with the reality of what he had just seen.

With a shaky hand, Aaron started the engine, the familiar rumble a comfort to his turmoil. He glanced at the house, its grand facade now a sinister mask, hiding secrets he wasn't sure he wanted to uncover. He pulled away from the curb and drove off, his mind reeling.

Aaron tried to focus on the road, but his thoughts stayed on the confrontation and how Elise had reacted. His words had touched something deep and raw that she hadn't wanted to be exposed. *Am I overreacting? Is this all just some horrible misunderstanding, or is it exactly what it looks like?* Aaron didn't know, and the uncertainty made him feel more lost and alone than ever before.

But one thing was certain: whatever had just happened had changed everything. The fragile thread that had held their family together was unraveling—Aaron in the middle of it, trying to make sense of a past that refused to stay buried.

As he drove, the miles slipping by unnoticed, Aaron thought of his mother's grave and the promise he had made to her just an hour before. He had vowed to uncover the truth, to make things right, and he couldn't turn back now. Driving further away from Elise's house, the resolve that had brought him there in the first place solidified once again.

He had come this far, and he wouldn't stop now. Not until he knew the full truth—about Rob and his mother, and now about Elise and Patty. No matter how winding the path ahead might be, Aaron was ready to face it head-on, just as he had promised.

With that thought in mind, he pressed down on the gas pedal; the jeep speeding up as he headed back toward the main road. There was still so much he didn't understand, so many pieces of the puzzle that didn't fit. But he was getting closer, inch by inch, to the truth that had eluded him for so long.

And no matter what it cost him, he wouldn't stop until he had all the answers.

July 26, 1996: Marlena

I watch Patty with Elise, and my heart aches with pride. He's a gentle boy, so tender with his little sister, like he's always been. Watching them together, I see how he looks after her, making sure she's okay, holding her hand as they walk across the yard. In these moments, I feel I've done something right.

But something's been off with Elise. My sweet girl, who's always been clingy and sensitive, has been much more so these past few days. She's jumpy, crying at the slightest thing, and it's breaking my heart to see her like this. I can't help but wonder if it has anything to do with that fishing trip she took with Rob and his friends last weekend.

I didn't want her to go. Elise is only six—what sense did it make to take her on a fishing trip without her brothers? She's so little, so fragile. But Rob insisted, said it was "father/daughter" time, that he'd been waiting for her to be old enough to go with him. He was so adamant, so certain that it was the right thing, that I let him take her, even though everything in me screamed not to.

Ever since she came back, she's been different. So quiet and withdrawn. It's like the light in her has dimmed, and I'm not too fond of it. I suspect her behavior is because she misses the weekend with her daddy. She enjoyed being the center of his attention. Now that she's back in the chaos of our loud, busy home, she's feeling the loss of that special time. She is our little princess.

I'm sure it's just a phase, and she'll be her old self soon. She has to be. In the meantime, I'm glad she has her sweet big brother to look after her.

Aaron sat on his front porch, the familiar crackle of the joint between his fingers as he passed it to Alex. The winter air, still sharp but tinged with the promise of spring, filled his lungs with each inhale. He stared out at the yard, trying to make sense of the whirlwind thoughts that plagued him since returning from Virginia.

"What the hell do I do with this, man?" Aaron asked, breaking the silence.

Alex took a drag from the joint, holding it before exhaling. "You've been through a lot. They've been through a lot," Alex said, passing the joint. "But... shit, man. Maybe some wires got crossed more than others."

Aaron cringed at the truth in Alex's words. He had spent hours driving back home, trying to find a rational explanation for what he had assumed when he saw Elise and Patty together, half-dressed. He kept telling himself that they were all damaged goods, all survivors of the same messed-up childhood. But the sight of them together, in that way, was an enigma he couldn't untangle.

"Yeah, but..." Aaron trailed off, unsure how to finish the thought. He didn't even know what he was trying to say.

Alex leaned back in his chair. The seriousness of what Aaron had walked in on weighed on them both. There was no easy way to confront it, no simple way to process what was happening with his siblings.

Jared appeared at the door, breaking the tension. "Alex, someone's on the phone for you," he said, pointing back inside.

Alex sighed, passing the joint back to Aaron. "I'll be back," he muttered, getting up and heading inside.

Aaron watched him go, then turned his gaze back to the yard. The stillness of the night was comforting, a stark contrast to the chaos in his mind. He sat there a few minutes more, letting the cold air numb his thoughts, before he stood up and headed inside. There would be no answers tonight, but at least in the silence, there was some peace.

24

Aaron woke to the soft glow of daylight filtering through his window. His head felt heavy, and a sense of grogginess clung to him as he reached for his phone on the nightstand. A text notification blinked.

> 3/7/16 8:42 am
> From Bethany: Thanks for talking to me last night. It helped a lot.

Aaron frowned, trying to piece together the night before. *Did I talk to Bethany?* His mind was a haze, and the conversation she referred to was nowhere in his memory.

"Shit," he muttered to himself, sitting up and rubbing his temples. The effects of the weed must have clouded his mind more than he realized. It wasn't the first time he'd noticed his memory slipping after a smoke, but forgetting an entire conversation? That was new.

He stared at the text before typing a quick reply.

> 3/7/16 8:57 am
> To Bethany: Glad I could help.

Pushing the blankets aside, Aaron stretched, shaking off the lingering drowsiness. *I need to cut back on the weed. I can't afford to be this out of it. My mind needs to be sharp, not dulled by anything.* He grabbed his phone and dialed into the office, waiting for Nicole to pick up.

"Hey, Aaron," Nicole's voice came through the line, bright as always. "How's it going?"

"Morning, Nicole. Just checking in," he said, trying to shake off the fog in his brain. "How's everything going with Frank and the rest of the crew?"

"Frank's good. He's home, in a sling. The insurance company is insisting on physical therapy before they talk about surgery, which he's not happy about. There's not much we can do about that on our end. As for the rest, Jeff has kept things on track at the park site, and Loren is taking the new crew out to break ground on the parking building by West End. We have no fires to put out today. Not yet, anyway."

"Excellent, that's what I like to hear. I'm going to work from home today. I've got a few things I need to take care of, but I'm right here if you need anything."

"Sure thing, boss," Nicole said, her tone kind and understanding. "And you let me know if you need anything."

"Will do. Thanks, Nicole."

Aaron ended the call and put his phone down, trying to focus on his thoughts. He needed to sort through so many things, and couldn't do it half-asleep. Pulling on clothes, he headed downstairs to the kitchen. He needed to get the ledgers and folders he had left in the trunk. The answers to the mysteries that had plagued his family for years could be in those papers.

Alex sipped coffee at the table.

"Morning," Aaron greeted, heading for his bag to get his keys.

"Morning," Alex replied, glancing up from his phone. "Sleep okay?"

"Not bad I guess. I must have needed the sleep... I can't even remember laying down." He retrieved his keys, pausing before leaving the kitchen. "Hey, who was on the phone last night?"

"Some girl I hooked up with last weekend," Alex said with a smirk, though he didn't elaborate. "Not important."

Aaron raised an eyebrow. "You must have forgotten to mention her."

"Yeah, like I said... not important. Pretty girl at a bar. Wild Turkey shots. It was fun."

Aaron nodded, but his mind was on the ledgers and folders in the jeep. "Later, I want the details. I'm going to head back upstairs. Got some stuff to go through."

Alex nodded, not prying, and Aaron jogged to the driveway to retrieve the documents. He took the pile of papers and headed back to his room. Once there, he sat on the bed and spread out the ledgers and folders on the bedspread. The red folder marked "The Red Baron" and the legal envelope marked "Kirby/Fresno/Stanley" stared back at him. The secrets of Rob's past were waiting to be uncovered.

He took a deep breath, knowing this was the moment he had been preparing for. He would go through each line of each page, and piece together the story that had remained hidden for so long. Whatever was in these documents would bring him one step closer to the truth.

Aaron opened the red folder, his fingers brushing over the worn edges. The first thing that struck him was the sheer volume of pages inside, each covered with neat, handwritten notes. The writing was meticulous, but the content was far from ordinary.

Dozens of pages lay before him, filled with dates, places, and initials, all scrawled in a careful, practiced hand. The arranged dates seemed to record a series of events or transactions. The pattern was unmistakable: "RB meet PA 9/14/86," "KE Kirby C.S. 9/20/86," "RB meet PA 11/12/86," "RH Kirby C.S. 11/20/86." Each notation seemed to mark a meeting or communication, the initials standing out like signposts in a labyrinth of secrets.

A note at the top of one page caught Aaron's eye: "RB/ES Philly 7/8/83." But what drew his attention more was the way a red pen crossed through "RB", followed by the words "FUCK UP" scribbled next to it. The violent correction sent a chill through him. Whoever had written this had been furious enough to mark their frustration in a way that left no doubt. The next line, "RB meet PA 8/4/83" followed by "Leo C.S. 8/10/83", suggested that these men had wasted no time moving forward with their cocaine dealings, even after Big Mike went to prison for murder.

Aaron scanned the dates, noting how they continued through the late 1980s and 2000s. A red pen punctuated various records with words like "DELAYED" or "RESCHED," signaling disruptions in the pattern. But what caught his attention most was the shift in 1990.

On October 30, 1990, a new location: Fresno, California, joined the familiar rhythm of dates and places. "KE Kirby C.S. 11/4/90" followed "RB meet PA 10/30/90" and then "JM Fresno C.S. 11/5/90." Aaron's eyes widened. This was right after his family had moved to Fresno.

His mind raced as he considered the implications. The initials RB could only be Robert Bakker—his stepfather, the owner of this folder, the man who had been the center of so much confusion and pain in Aaron's life. And here was RB, appearing again, making meetings, arranging calls, always present in these cryptic notes. But that first meeting in July 1983 with ES—Eddie Scott—had gone wrong. It was clear from the red-inked outburst that Rob had been involved, just as Big Mike had said, in that "fuck up."

Aaron continued tracing the pattern through the years. RB always handled the contacts. But there were others involved too. RH or KE—two other sets of initials—seemed to run operations on the Kansas end. And then, as the family settled in Fresno, another player entered the scene: JM.

The names and dates swirled in Aaron's mind, pieces of a hidden puzzle. He wasn't sure what it all meant yet, but one thing was clear: Rob Bakker was involved in something criminal that had spanned decades.

Aaron stared at the pages, trying to make sense of it all. His gut told him that this was just the beginning. There was more to uncover, more to piece together. He continued to study the pages, his heart pounding. The shipments of "C.S" had expanded, reaching farther than he had realized.

In late May 1993, Stanley, Alberta, Canada appeared on the list. Valley Glen, just outside Los Angeles, joined in January 1996. These shipments weren't random; they mirrored his family's moves, each coinciding with new plants by Luca Meat Distribution, where Robert Bakker, his stepfather, served as the plant manager.

Aaron's eyes tracked the initials and locations. KE handled transactions in Kirby, Kansas. RH vanished from the records after 1993, only to reappear in June 1996 as the transaction contact again, this time in Valley Glen. JM stayed on as the Fresno contact until the mid-90s, disappearing after another scrawled "FUCK UP". It left a void that made Aaron's skin crawl.

Then, in early 1999, a new location appeared: NC. Greensboro, North Carolina. His stomach lurched as he remembered that move. It happened just in time for his senior year of high school. It had seemed like just another one of Rob's decisions that uprooted the family. In 2002, a new set of initials joined the roster: SC. Looking at the dates and locations, Aaron realized it was all connected, every move tied to the sinister network he was only now beginning to understand.

He sat back, processing all he had read. His family's moves and Rob's job had a darker purpose. The realization hit him like a punch to the gut: Rob had been using the family to cover his tracks, to expand his reach in this illegal operation.

It was all laid out in front of him in black and white. The dates, the names, the places—they told a story of deception, manipulation, and crime that had shaped his entire life without him even knowing it. But as Aaron stared at the pages, a persistent unease settled in his chest. This folder still didn't tell the complete story.

He reached down to the box of ledgers and pulled the one from the top. This ledger began in January 1983 and ended in December 1985. The lines that began with RB started on 8/11/83; the same date as in Rob's list.

Subsequent RB entries in the ledger matched the dates of Rob's meetings and Kirby's shipments from the red folder. In July 1983, Eddie set the cocaine deal in motion, and it persisted long after his death. The trafficking had continued and later expanded: long after Big Mike went away for murder and after Rob moved Aaron's family away from Philadelphia. Rob seemed to have masterminded it, with Big Mike's crew receiving the Philly shipments. If the ledgers and lists were accurate, the Philly end of the cocaine deal had not ended until just a few years ago. He wondered if this was when Rudy had died and left The Red Baron to his son.

A thought struck Aaron: in all these detailed records, there was no mention of international travel beyond Alberta. No Mexico City, no Guatemala. *What were you and your friends doing there?*

He paused with the names echoing in his mind. Rob's friends... Kevin and Roger. *What are your last names? Are you two bastards KE and RH?*

Aaron's breath caught in his throat. He stared at the pages; the connections forming like a spider's web in his mind. *There's more to this than I realized. And if Kevin and Roger were involved, what did that mean for the rest of Rob's network? For my family?*

Aaron felt a cold dread settle over him. The folder in front of him was just a piece that pointed to something even darker lurking beneath the surface. But as overwhelming as the red folder and ledgers were, the legal envelope peeking out from under the mass of papers drew his attention now.

It was much lighter and thinner than the folder was, but something about its sealed, taped-down clasp made Aaron uneasy. He ripped across the top edge and upended the envelope onto the bed.

Dozens of newspaper clippings spilled out, most yellowed with age, some tattered on the edges as though handled more often. The headlines jumped out at Aaron—MISSING. Girl Vanishes. Child Still Missing.

What the hell is this?

His heart pounded as he sifted through the clippings. Each headline seemed to scream at him, the words like echoes of a nightmare. The stories were brief, mere blurbs about missing children, most of them girls, who had vanished without a trace. Some had photos—grainy, black-and-white images of children caught in the middle of a smile or a laugh, or just before they could turn away from the camera.

He flipped through them faster now, his breath catching in his throat. There was no discernible pattern or obvious link between the children. They were from different places, different years. But they were all missing, all lost. He recognized some towns—places his family had lived or passed through.

Aaron's hands trembled as he reached the last clipping. It was newer than the others, the paper crisp. The headline read: MISSING CHILDREN CASE GOES COLD. The date was 2008, eight years ago.

Beneath the headline, in a small, neat hand: "Nothing ever goes cold if you love it enough."

Could missing children be part of the operation too?

He shoved the clippings back into the envelope, his hands shaking. He needed to get out, clear his head, and figure out what to do next. This wasn't just about Rob anymore. It wasn't just about him or his family. This was about something much bigger and he wasn't sure he was ready to face it. But he knew he didn't have a choice.

He left the mess of papers on his bed and got up to stretch, feeling like the oxygen was being sucked from his room. He needed some air. This was too much to process all at once. Wandering downstairs, he hoped Alex or Jared might be around to distract him, but the house was empty and quiet.

As he opened the front door, he noticed the mailman pulling away. The mailman waved, and Aaron returned the gesture, trying to shake off the tension and anger inside him. He collected the mail and dumped it on the foyer table before sinking into the living room armchair. The soft cushions gave way beneath him, but the comfort did nothing to ease his mind.

He pulled his phone from his back pocket, checking his notifications. Nothing important. He scrolled, but his thoughts circled back to the initials that now haunted him: KE and RH.

On a whim, he opened Facebook and tried to navigate to his stepfather's profile page. Nothing. The man's name didn't even appear in the search bar, and Aaron knew he was there, or had been. Rob was a huge fan of posting incendiary political memes and pictures of fast cars, sprinkled with images about how his generation is better than those that followed. Aaron never interacted much with him on social media, save hitting the "like" button on a shiny car or the generic "Merry Christmas, people" that Rob posted every year. Still, at some point, he must have blocked Aaron. Whether this happened yesterday or last year, he did not know.

He thought to search for Kevin and Roger, to see if their last names matched the initials in the files — he felt sure they did — but there was no way to narrow the search to know which profile belonged to these particular men. Kevin and Roger were common names.

"Nicole... maybe you can help me today after all," he whispered.

He dialed his secretary's number, and she answered almost immediately, her familiar voice bringing a small measure of calm to his frayed nerves.

"Hey, Nicole," he said, trying to keep his voice steady. "I need a favor. It's... it's personal."

There was a brief pause on the other end, and then Nicole's voice, always so professional, softened. "Of course, Aaron. What do you need?"

"I'm looking for two guys," he began, the words tumbling out as he explained. "Kevin and Roger. They're old friends of my stepfather, and I need to find them. Could you check my stepdad's social media and see if they're listed there? Maybe narrow down their profiles? I'm not sure how common the names are."

"I'll see what I can do," Nicole responded. "What's your stepdad's name?"

"Robert Bakker," he replied, spelling the last name for her. "He lives in Harrisonburg, Virginia. I'd look myself, but there's been family drama, and... I'd like to find these old family friends if I can. Means a lot to me."

"Say no more, boss. Give me some time, and I'll get back to you with whatever I find."

"Thanks, Nicole. I appreciate it."

As he hung up, the sense of unease settled over him again. Whatever Nicole uncovered might bring him closer to the truth, but he couldn't shake the feeling that this truth was something far darker than he was prepared for. But there was no turning back now. Not with everything he'd already seen.

25

Aaron had already swept the porch three times. His mind wasn't on the task, not with the files upstairs, irritating him like a loose tooth. He couldn't stop worrying. He tried to ignore it, tried to focus on the simple rhythm of sweeping, but the minutes crawled, and soon enough, he found himself halfway up the stairs before he even realized he'd dropped the broom.

The files were where he'd left them, sprawled across the bed like an accusation. The yellowed newspaper clippings seemed to pulse under the light, daring him to look. He sat on the edge of the mattress sifting through the grim pile.

Cherry Hill, NJ: May 1984.

Wyola, PA: October 1985.

Limon, CO: February 1987.

Benton, CA: December 1990.

The names of forgotten towns, the dates of long-cold disappearances, all meaningless on their own. Aaron traced the jagged lines across the map in his mind, and the pieces fell into place, each one another crack in the floor beneath his feet. They weren't random. These places aligned with his family's past, with their moves, road trips, and vacations.

He frowned, thumbing through the clippings until a name stopped him cold.

Axapusco, Mexico: April 9, 1991.

The air left his lungs in a rush. Mexico. He turned the page, flipping through his mother's book, the familiar scrawl filling him with a strange comfort until the words hit him like a punch to the gut: Rob's first business trip abroad. April 6, 1991.

Three days. Just three days before a little girl vanished in Axapusco, Rob and his buddies would have flown into the city less than an hour away. Aaron's stomach lurched, bile rising in his throat as the reality settled in. This wasn't a coincidence.

"What the hell were you doing?" His voice was a ragged whisper, the words burning as they left his mouth.

Hands trembling, he grabbed his phone, the screen glowing as he pulled up Axapusco on the map. There it was, nestled between hills and winding roads, a tiny dot on the landscape that now felt like the center of everything. The proximity sent a chill crawling down his spine. *Did they take her? Or did they know someone who did?* His mind raced, veering toward places too dark to comprehend.

Flores, Guatemala: August 15, 1992.

Another trip with Kevin and Roger.

He slammed the clippings down, heart thudding in his chest. The names, the dates, the places—it was all too perfect, too deliberate. *How many more children? How far did this go?* The list seemed endless, an ongoing drip of dread with each discovery.

Sanford, NC: May 29, 2000.

The room spun as the blood drained from Aaron's face. He remembered this one. A little boy snatched from his front yard. Nine years old. His parents had been everywhere: news channels, posters, pleading for their son's return. Aaron had paid little attention then, caught up in his world, counting down until graduation. And Rob? Gone on another business trip. The sickening familiarity of it hit him all at once.

Stumbling toward the bathroom, he made it to the sink before he retched; the acid burning the back of his throat as he emptied his stomach. The image of that boy's face flashed in his mind, wide-eyed and innocent. It could have been his face as a child, staring back at him from the newspaper. Aaron gripped the edge of the sink, trying to calm himself, but his hands wouldn't stop shaking.

He staggered back to his room, still clutching the clipping, unable to let it go. The boy's picture blurred in his vision as Aaron's pulse pounded in his ears.

Did Rob... did he take him? The thought crossed his mind, and the horror of it took over. Aaron's knees buckled, and he collapsed into the chair by the bed, feeling as though he were suffocating.

And then he saw the next clipping. Norlina, NC: May 24, 2012. The little blonde girl in the photo stared back at him, her bright smile familiar. The girl looked just like Elise, his baby sister. Too much like her. The date of her disappearance—six days after Elise's wedding.

The room closed around him as he sifted through the remaining clippings, each darker than the last. And at the bottom of the pile, there they were—two tiny faces, a brother and sister from Uspantán, Guatemala. They couldn't have been more than toddlers, their innocent smiles contrary to the horror they represented. Icy fear crept up Aaron's spine as he realized the truth.

This wasn't just a puzzle to solve anymore. It was a nightmare—one that had trapped his family and these missing children in a web he never knew existed.

The chime of his phone jolted Aaron from the depths of his thoughts. He picked up the phone to glance at the screen—Nicole's name lit up. He swiped to answer.

"I checked your stepfather's Facebook page," she began. "There's only one Kevin listed: Kevin Earls, living in Kirby, Kansas. There were no Rogers on Robert's list, but Kevin's page had two. Their names are Roger Harris and Roger Hellman. Harris hasn't posted since 2011, and Hellman's in Helena, Montana."

Aaron scribbled the names on a scrap of paper, each word sharp, heavy with implication.

"Thanks, Nicole," he muttered, his voice tight. "I appreciate it."

"Anytime," she replied. "If you need more—"

"I'm good for now," Aaron cut her off, the call ending with a tap as he stared at the names. Silence rushed in as he pulled up Facebook and typed the first name: Kevin Earls.

The moment the profile loaded, Aaron's eyes widened. It was him. KE. The memories slammed into him with brutal clarity—Kevin leaning against the washing machine in their kitchen, that too-wide grin plastered on his face, eyes dark and unreadable. Aaron's stomach churned as the profile picture came into focus: Kevin, now older, balding, standing in a group photo with a Hispanic woman draped under his arm. His hand gripped her shoulder, his smile smug.

Aaron scrolled through the photos: grandchildren, children, and a wedding photo. "June 9, 1994: best day of my life." His eyes locked onto Kevin's wife, Maritza, her compact frame engulfed by a white gown that made her look more like a child playing dress-up than a bride. Kevin towered over her, his suit ill-fitting, his grin wolfish. Aaron's grip on his phone tightened, knuckles white as rage simmered beneath his skin.

She was a kid, Aaron thought, his mind racing. She didn't look happy—she looked lost; her face a mask of quiet resignation, eyes dulled by something far darker than nerves.

Aaron rifled through the newspaper clippings scattered on the bed, searching for the face he now recognized. There—Maria Delgato, the missing girl from Flores, Guatemala. She'd been 14 when she disappeared, walking home from a friend's house in August 1992. Aaron's vision blurred as the pieces snapped into place.

"Bastard," Aaron hissed, his voice shaking with fury. "You stole her and married her?!"

His mind reeled, calculating the years. She was 16. Sixteen when Kevin married her after tearing her away from her home and family. Disgust roiled in his gut.

He slammed the newspaper clipping down, his fingers trembling as he typed in the next name: Roger Harris. The page was barren, just as Nicole had said. No posts, no comments—nothing. Only the profile picture stared back at him, eyes hollow, chin sharp and knobby like a skull. The man's face was a ghost from the files on the bed. It was him. He didn't need more proof.

"I hate both of you," Aaron whispered, his tone venomous. His mind raced through the connections, the web spinning around him.

He checked the last name on his list: Roger Hellman. His page was loud—full of political rants, World War II trivia, fast cars, and Harley-Davidson motorcycles. Aaron skimmed the photos, searching for anything that hinted at a dark past, but there was nothing. His photos were of himself and his wife, no kids.

But it didn't matter.

Aaron's eyes drifted to Kevin's wedding photo. He held the clipping of Maria, her childish face shining with innocence. He compared it with her older self—the mother of Kevin's children.

Aaron could feel anger, hot and uncontrollable, as he stared at the faces of the men who had taken everything from these women and children. His fingers clenched around the edge of the newspaper, the rage simmering in his veins like a fire that would be hard to put out.

March 7, 1998: Marlena

I sat at the kitchen table, staring at the invitation in my hand, and I could feel the frustration building inside me. It was wonderful news—a baptism for Kevin and Maritza's adopted daughter—a celebration. But when I told Rob about it, his reaction was... strange.

"Why would Kevin host a baptism? Why draw attention?" He hadn't even looked at me when he said it, just kept flipping through the TV channels like it was the most normal thing in the world to dismiss his best friend's invitation.

I remember standing there, feeling confusion tighten in my chest. Draw attention? I wanted to scream. Of course, that's the point. It's a baptism, for heaven's sake. It's supposed to be a celebration, a time to gather everyone together and welcome the child into the family. But Rob? He acted like it was something to avoid, like it was some public spectacle he wanted no part of.

I rubbed my temples, trying to ease the tension. This wasn't the first time. I thought back to '96 when they adopted their first daughter—he refused to go to her baptism too. Then the baby shower Maritza threw for their biological daughter the year before that? He made some excuse. And don't even get me started on their wedding in '94. I still remember the sinking feeling in my stomach when he insisted we skip it, saying something vague about not wanting to "get involved." What does that even mean? These are our family friends, aren't they?

I leaned back in my chair, holding the invitation loose, staring at the fancy script without seeing it. I'd always believed Kevin, and Maritza by extension, were like family. It made sense for us to share in these moments—milestones that were supposed to bring families closer. But every time one of these big events came up, Rob shut it down. It made no sense to me.

And yet, he has no problem going on those fishing trips with Kevin, laughing and joking like nothing was wrong. He would come back smelling like bait and beer, telling me stories about their latest catches as if we hadn't just argued about the baptism, or the wedding, or whatever other event he had vetoed.

I got up, restless, and wandered over to the window. The sun was setting. I couldn't shake the feeling that something was off, something deeper than not wanting to go to a baptism. What was the harm in us attending? I thought about Elise—she's only eight, sure, but she would have loved it. She's at that age where she's full of questions about everything, always curious. I pictured her wide eyes, asking about the ceremony.

And Aaron and Patty? They're old enough to watch the younger boys for a weekend. It wouldn't have been a big deal.

But no, Rob wouldn't hear of it. He had shut it down with the same dismissive tone like I was being unreasonable. And I'm left standing here, wondering why. Why is he so resistant to these things? He doesn't want me to get closer to his friends? It's not like he's cutting Kevin out of his life, so what's the deal?

I glanced down at the invitation, now creased from my fidgeting. I don't understand. He's supposed to care about them. Why does he keep pushing them away? Or is it only me that is being kept away from them? Is he hiding something?

Aaron leaned back against the headboard, eyes drifting out of focus, his fingers still clutching the page of Marlena's memory. The words seemed to echo in the quiet room. His chest heaved as everything fell into place, the truth creeping up on him. Rob hadn't wanted Marlena near Maritza, and now Aaron knew why. He swallowed hard. Maritza had been too young—far too young—almost his age back then. *Not old enough to be with a man like Kevin, not old enough to be a mother.*

Aaron blinked, his mouth dry. He pressed his hand to his stomach as if that could settle the icy knot forming there. *How had they managed it? How had they adopted children?* His mind raced, flipping through pieces of the puzzle with frantic speed. Maritza was Maria—the girl snatched from Guatemala—she wouldn't have had documents. *No birth certificate. No social security number. Any adoption agency would've flagged her, seen right through the lies.* His fingers trembled as he rubbed his temples, but his mind wouldn't slow down.

He reached for the newspaper clippings scattered across his bed. His eyes scanned the grainy print with a renewed focus. The little girl in the photo—dark eyes and messy blond hair. His mother's words echoed in his ears: *The little girl they adopted in '96.* Aaron's gaze shot back to the photograph. *Could it be the girl who had vanished from Apple Valley, California? The one no one ever found?* He flipped to another clipping, this one about a child from Tecate, Mexico, who had disappeared just weeks before Kevin and Maritza's second adoption.

His pulse quickened. The horror of it all hit him, a sickening wave crashing against his ribs. *These weren't just adoptions.* These men—Kevin and Rob—had stolen children. Taken them and brought them into their lives, parading them as adopted. The edges of the newspaper crinkled beneath his grip as rage rose like bile in his throat. His teeth clenched so hard his jaw ached.

Aaron stared at the group photo on Kevin's page again. His thumb hovered over the screen, zooming in until the faces blurred. These adopted—stolen—girls had been four years old in 1996 and 1998, so they'd be in their early to mid-30s by now. One woman, a carbon copy of Kevin with her sharp eyes and dark hair, laughed with two others —one blonde, her skin tanned, and the other, her dark curls spilling over her shoulders, standing out with a deep complexion.

A man, maybe 22 or 23 years old, stood next to Maritza, and the resemblance to his mother was undeniable—he had to be their biological son. A teenage girl of around 16 stood to his right, her long dark hair pulled over one warm brown shoulder: Maritza's genes shone in her face. His hand shook as he shifted his focus. Two children, maybe seven and nine years old, stood with Kevin. Their tiny hands clasped in front of them, awkward smiles stretching across their faces. They looked uncomfortable. *Trapped.* The boy wore a shirt too big for him, and the girl's shoes bore scuffs on the toes. Kevin's gnarled fingers held the girl's shoulder, the weight of possession unmistakable.

Aaron's eyes darted between the kids in the photo and the grainy black-and-white images strewn across his bed. The missing brother and sister. Their small, rounded faces from the article stared up at him from five years ago, faded but clear enough to compare.

He shoved the clippings aside and stood, pacing the narrow space. He ran a hand through his hair, fighting the urge to throw his phone across the room. Kevin's face smiled back at him from the screen—a smug expression hinting at a lack of regret for any of the horrible things he had done.

"I'm coming for you," Aaron muttered, the words grinding between his teeth. He sat now, sinking back against the headboard. The room felt smaller, the walls closing in as if they were whispering the truth he had just unearthed. His eyes flitted from the newspaper clippings to the photo on his phone. The image of the two children, their hands intertwined and faces frozen in awkward smiles, burned into his mind.

The resemblance was too strong to ignore. They were the same as the missing Guatemalan siblings from the old article—too similar. His fingers traced the photo as if touching it could pull the truth closer. The stolen girls, now grown, blended into Kevin's family like shadows in daylight, their true pasts buried beneath layers of deceit.

The image of Kevin's smug grin from the Facebook photo seemed to mock him. Aaron could almost hear Rob's voice in his head, spinning tales of righteousness. The thought made him sick.

He struggled to control himself. Realization pressed down on him with relentless force. Kevin, Rob, and Roger had crafted a life of lies so elaborate that it was almost breathtaking. The men's arrogance was like a foul stench seeping through the cracks of their false facades.

The truth felt like a dark stain spreading through Aaron's mind, a suffocating fog that wouldn't lift. He rubbed his temples, trying to clear the haze, and turned back to his phone. His fingers moved with urgency as he scrolled through the online newspaper archives, his eyes darting across the screen. Each click through articles and arrest records felt like sifting through sand—every search for Roger Harris turned up only blank spaces.

The trail went cold in 2011. His frustration grew with every fruitless result. There were no new criminal charges, whispers of his whereabouts, or public records beyond that year. The notations in Rob's red folder ended at the same time. It was like Roger had vanished in a puff of smoke. *Had he died?* The thought lingered like a bitter taste.

Aaron stared at Roger's profile picture, the image of cold, lifeless eyes staring back at him. They mocked him, taunting him with the corresponding absence of any recent activity. His mind raced, trying to piece together the enigma. Roger's past crimes had made headlines—any new offenses should, too. Yet there was nothing. No matter how deeply Aaron dug, Harris remained a ghost.

In a sudden burst of frustration, Aaron slammed his fist against the bed, the impact reverberating through his arm. "Where the hell are you, Roger?" The question echoed in the quiet room, a raw, unanswered cry.

The mystery of Roger's disappearance rankled Aaron's nerves. Kevin's blatant disregard for secrecy made sense—he'd been displaying his crimes in plain sight on social media for years, never bothering to cover his tracks. But Roger? His absence was a puzzle piece that refused to fit. Aaron's thoughts whirled, each unanswered question sharp and jagged, adding to his growing frustration.

He set his phone aside and leaned back, his gaze fixed on the window. The fading daylight painted the room in long, creeping shadows, stretching and curling like dark tendrils. The encroaching dusk seemed to pull at the edges of his memories, wrapping them in a menacing embrace.

Rob had orchestrated the dark symphony of their past, with Kevin as his eager accomplice. Kevin's facade of normalcy masked the warped truth. Their collective sins had built his perfect family. But Roger—Roger had always been different. As a child, Aaron had felt a chill whenever Roger was near. Those cold, unfeeling eyes, his long, groping fingers, always lurking on the perimeter of his childhood, had sent shivers down his spine.

Now, that same darkness from his past loomed ahead, as if daring him to confront it. Aaron's resolve hardened. He had no choice but to delve back into that shadowy world, to confront the man who had always been the most frightening to him.

The mere idea of seeing Rob's face again, now with the weight of these fresh revelations, was too much to handle. The anger simmering beneath his skin was almost unbearable. These men needed to face justice, and Kevin seemed to be the linchpin. Aaron had to unravel the connections, and Kirby was where it all started.

He closed his eyes, picturing the small town. Kirby was not just a place—it was a graveyard of memories, a landscape filled with the echoes of a past that had shaped and scarred him. Shadows of his younger self lined the streets, and the familiar corners whispered of people who had once been central to his world. To face Kevin, Aaron knew he had to step back into that forgotten town, where every street and building held the ghosts of a life he could never escape.

Aaron's thoughts drifted to his mother, Marlena, and the haunting realization of her near brush with the nightmare he had uncovered. The image of her, oblivious to the dark reality, ate away at him. Rob had woven a tight net around her, keeping her away from Kevin and Maritza, stifling any chance she might have had to see through the facade. Marlena would have known, he was sure of it. She would have sensed the falsehoods, the innocence masked by a sinister veil. The ease with which Rob had manipulated her—and everyone else—made Aaron's stomach turn in a way that almost sent him running back to the bathroom.

He rose from his seat, his mind made up. This was no longer a matter of choice—it was an imperative. He couldn't move forward without facing the demons of his past. Rob and Kevin had hidden for too long, and Roger had vanished into the void. But Aaron wasn't about to let them escape justice.

He needed a strategy, a clear path through the maze of his emotions and plans. The enormity of what lay ahead pressed down on him, making him ache for a moment of respite. He stretched, resolving to find Alex and Jared. Maybe a drink, and the comfort of familiar faces, could help quiet the storm within him.

As he approached the door, he glanced back at the bed, littered with clippings and the ominous red folder. His fingers twitched, longing to abandon the puzzle laid out before him. Yet, deep down, he knew he couldn't walk away. The fragments of truth, however unsettling, were crucial. They held the key to understanding, confronting Kevin, and finding Roger Harris.

26

The familiar drumbeat of anger, disgust, and betrayal threatened to overwhelm Aaron. He could feel the tension spreading through his body, a coiled spring tightening in his ribs, making it hard to breathe. His hands shook as he poured a tall glass of whiskey over ice, the clink of the cubes echoing in the empty kitchen, too loud for the silence that had settled over the house. It felt cavernous and cold—like a monument to a life that had slipped through his fingers.

He pushed open the front door and stepped onto the porch, letting the crisp air wash over him, its coolness a minor relief from the pressure inside. The porch swing creaked under his weight as he sat down, the whiskey heavy in his hand. He took a long sip, the burn settling deep in his chest. The early March evening was still. The sky dimmed as the last light of day faded. Across the street, teenage boys played a pick-up game of basketball, their shouts and laughter drifting on the wind. The scene tugged at something in Aaron, pulling him back to another time, another place.

He could almost feel the leathery texture of the basketball under his hands, and see the chain-link fence of the elementary school court in Valley Glen. He had been four days past his 15th birthday. The sun was setting behind him in a blaze of colors while dark clouds gathered in the distance. The court had been theirs, a ragtag group of neighborhood kids, coming together for one of their regular games. He had been unstoppable that day, dunking from the free-throw line in a move that left everyone cheering, both teams caught in the sheer thrill of the moment.

The bruises on his wrists from slamming them against the hoop had been badges of honor, proof of his invincibility. When he couldn't jump the fence afterward, his friends cut it open. The memory had always been a strange mix of triumph and pain, but it felt like a lifeline tonight, one of the few enjoyable moments he could cling to. He wondered if his mother had ever thought of it, or if she remembered her relief when he made it home that night, long after his dinner was cold.

He blinked against the sting of unshed tears threatening to spill over and took another sip of whiskey. The warmth dulled the edge of the emotions welling up. It was funny, he thought, how a single memory—so distant, so small in the grand scheme of things—could hold so much weight now. He had been a kid then, feeling like he could take on the world, and in those days, the basketball in his hands had felt like the only safe place in the world. Never since had he come close to that feeling.

He stared down at the crocuses just beginning to poke through the dirt along the front walk. Rachel had planted them almost eleven years ago, their fragile green leaves breaking through the earth at the first hint of spring every year since. The sight of them, so delicate, made his heart ache. They were one of the many things she had left behind, small pieces of her woven into the fabric of the home they had built together.

When only a few drops of whiskey remained in his glass, Aaron stood and went inside. The house was still silent, empty of the life that had once filled it. He rinsed the glass in the kitchen sink, the sound of the water a quiet echo, and returned it to its place in the oak sideboard that Rachel's father had made for them as a wedding gift. His hand lingered on the polished wood for a moment before he let it fall to his side, his mind already retreating into the shadows that had been waiting for him.

He was alone, with only the memories to keep him company.

Aaron knew he needed to sleep, to put the dark revelations of the day to rest, at least for a few hours. Tomorrow, he would make plans —actual plans—to go to Kirby and figure out how to unravel the terrible things his stepfather and those men had been part of for so long. But for tonight, he wanted to hold on to something good, something pure, before the weight of the world crushed him.

Upstairs, the house felt even quieter than before. The silence pressed in on him from all sides. He moved with weariness, stacking the newspaper clippings and articles before sliding them back into the legal envelope. Each piece of paper felt tainted, heavy with the evil they represented, as if the crimes they documented might seep into his skin if he wasn't careful. With a shudder, he shoved Rob's notated records into the red folder and placed them and the ledgers back into the cardboard box from Big Mike's garage.

He hesitated. His fingers hovered over the edge of the box, unwilling to let the day close just yet. Aaron reached for his mother's book, pulling it toward him as if it held some answer or clue that could make sense of it all. He knew it wouldn't. He flipped through the familiar pages; his eyes scanned the neat handwriting.

He found that summer day from his memory, buried in the middle of the entries. His mother had written about it—of course, she had. Aaron smiled.

His mother had remembered. She had held onto that moment, just as he had. He clung to that small piece of her now, wishing he could go to those simpler days when basketball and teenage rebellion were the only things that mattered.

But there was no going back. Not now. Not after everything he'd uncovered today.

He closed the book and placed it in the box with Rob's dark records. He would deal with it all tomorrow. Tonight, he needed to hold on to that memory, the one bright spot in the darkness that threatened to consume him. With a sigh, he turned off the light before pulling his covers over his head, hoping sleep would come and the nightmares would keep their distance—for just one night.

June 16, 1997: Marlena

Most of the day was like any other: laundry, dishes, a quick trip to get the Mercedes' oil changed. Nico went to the dentist this morning. He has a referral for braces. I'm not convinced he needs them, but Rob keeps saying Nico will thank us when he's older. I suppose he's right.

Lucas is spending the night at his friend's house down the street, and he begged me for money for the arcade before he left. Those boys would drain our bank account if I let them, with how often they go there. And Patty—I dropped him off at his buddy's a few hours ago, and now that summer's here, I won't see him for a day or two.

Elise is away at dance camp until Friday, and though I miss her, I'm a little relieved for the break. She's our little princess, and sometimes she thinks the world revolves around her. Rob doesn't help—he jumps through hoops for that girl and spoils her like she's a queen. Sometimes I wonder if he loves her more than he ever loved me. I feel ashamed just thinking about it, but deep down, I can't shake the feeling that it's true.

Aaron won a basketball game today. He was glowing, soaked to the bone from the rain, but grinning like he'd just conquered the world. His wrists were all bruised up from the basketball hoop, but he didn't seem to care. I was ready to be furious with him for staying out past dark, especially with that storm rolling in, but the second I saw his face, all that anger just melted away. How could I stay mad at him when he was so proud, so happy? My sweet, handsome boy.

I've never seen him play. Rob won't let him try out for the high school team. He says it'll mess with his grades. I can't say I agree, but there's no point in fighting Rob on it. But tonight, listening to Aaron tell me about that game while I reheated his dinner, I felt like I was there, watching him make that winning shot. The way his eyes lit up, the excitement in his voice—he relived the moment with every word. My boy's growing up so fast. Too fast, sometimes. But in moments like that, when he's full of joy, it's like he's still my little boy, even if only for a minute.

Wednesday morning slipped by faster than Aaron expected. He'd spent an hour in the office, making sure everything was in order before heading out. The suitcase sat packed and ready in his trunk, and his travel agent had gotten him a flight out of Philly at 5:20 this evening. He had a nonstop flight to Denver with a rental car waiting for him at the airport. If everything went well, he would drive into the ghost town of his childhood by midnight.

His mind wasn't there yet, though. After leaving the office, he did his usual rounds in town: first at the park building site, then a couple of hours at the new parking structure downtown. His foremen had things under control, but he wanted to ensure they and Nicole knew he was just a phone call away. Pulling away from the construction site, he glanced at his watch—noon. He'd need to be on the road by 2:30 to beat the traffic and get to the airport in plenty of time.

Frank's place was his last stop. Modest, a brick duplex near the elementary school. Aaron parked and tried not to scan the lot for Rachel's minivan. It wasn't important today.

Inside, his injured crewman lounged in his living room, his left arm strapped to his side in a sling, a bottle of beer balancing on the arm of his recliner. He was driving like a maniac through Mexico on Forza Horizon 5, his car swerving and bouncing off dirt roads.

"Shouldn't you be working on that recovery instead of wrecking cars?" Aaron said, stepping into the room.

Frank gave a lopsided grin without looking away from the screen. "Gotta keep the reflexes sharp, boss. And besides, it's therapeutic."

Aaron chuckled, eyeing the empty beer bottles on the coffee table. "What's the therapy plan? Drive a hundred miles an hour and knock back a six-pack?"

Frank laughed, pausing the game. "Something like that. You want a beer?"

Aaron nodded. "Yeah, why not." He pulled a grocery store gift card from his back pocket, holding it out. "Here, for you and the fam."

Frank waved it off. "Ah, you didn't have to do that, boss. I'm good."

"Take it," Aaron insisted, tossing it onto the table. "The least I can do after what happened on-site. Besides, I'm about to crush you in a couple of races. You owe me a beer for that."

Frank laughed again, grabbing a cold one from the fridge. "Oh, you think so, huh?"

They played for a bit, Frank watching as Aaron wove through the digital streets, and it felt good to unwind for a while, even if the gnawing anxiety of his trip still lingered in the back of his mind.

When Aaron stood to leave, it was already two in the afternoon. He drained the last of his bottle, clapped Frank on the good shoulder, and said, "Take it easy, alright?"

Frank nodded, his smile fading a bit. "Hey, seriously, thanks for stopping by, boss. And, you know… for everything else."

Aaron waved him off, grabbing his keys. "Anytime."

In the car, the time on his dashboard flashed 2:05. Just enough time, he thought as he pulled onto the main road and started toward the highway. He dialed Alex on speaker.

"Yo," Alex answered, his voice casual. "Let me guess… you're going to see Bethany again?"

Aaron laughed, shaking his head. "Not this time, man."

"Sure, sure. You can't fool me. That girl's got you hooked." Alex was teasing, but then his tone shifted. "Wait, if you're not heading to Philly for her, then where?"

"Kansas," Aaron said, his voice tense as he turned onto the highway ramp.

There was a pause. "Kansas?" Alex asked, his voice now serious. "You sure you're good alone, man?"

"I'll be fine. I need to figure this out." Aaron kept his eyes on the road, trying to push down the unease in his chest.

"Alright," Alex sighed, sounding uncertain. "But if you need anything, you know I'm always right here, right?"

Aaron smiled. "Yeah, I know. Thanks, man."

"Just… don't be a hero, okay?" Alex added, his voice warning.

Aaron shook his head, laughing. "No hero here, Alex. I'll be alright."

After they hung up, the silence of the car was thick. The highway stretched out, and with every mile, he felt himself getting closer to the truth.

27

Aaron arrived at the airport with time to spare. The traffic had been light, and he wondered why he'd been so nervous. It wasn't often that he flew—the last time had been five years ago. LAX was a hell of an airport to land in—once he passed through that chaos, he rented a green Mustang 5.0. He'd taken it up the Pacific Coast Highway, winding through cliffs and ocean views, ending at Morro Bay, one of his favorite places. It had been a last-ditch attempt at a vacation, a couple of years after Rachel left. It had been a favorite spot for the family to camp when he was a child: one of the few places they all went together.

The memory lingered as he passed through security, feet shuffling on autopilot. He found his gate, scanning for a place to sit before spotting an empty bench. Settling in, Aaron pulled out his phone, thinking about Bethany. He thumbed out a quick message.

> 3/9/16 4:55 pm
> To Bethany: I'll be in Philly in a few days. Dinner?

He pocketed the phone, glancing around the terminal, trying to focus on the people instead of his thoughts. A minute passed, and then his phone buzzed in his pocket.

3/9/16 4:56 pm
From Bethany: Couldn't stay away? I'd love to have dinner with you. What day?

3/9/16 4:58 pm
To Bethany: Not sure yet, I'm about to catch a flight, but I'll let you know. I'm looking forward to it.

3/9/16 4:59 pm
From Bethany: Flight? Where are you headed?

3/9/16 5:01 pm
To Bethany: Fill you in over dinner. I hope your week is great!

Powering off the phone, he leaned back against the bench. He tried to push everything out of his mind, but the images from yesterday crept in. The old, grainy photos of missing children, the scrawled notes in Rob's files, and the horror he felt piecing it all together. Squeezing his eyes shut, he focused on the sound of the bustling terminal, the low hum of announcements over the PA system, and the memory of that long-ago basketball game, his mom's concerned but proud face when he'd come home, wrists bruised from that dunk.

Soon enough, the boarding call came, and Aaron stood, slipping his phone back into his jacket. The seat by him remained empty as people filed into the plane, but he wasn't concerned. Once the aisle cleared, he reached up, unzipped the suitcase in the overhead bin, and pulled out his mother's book. It felt heavy in his hands, a bridge to the past that he wasn't sure he wanted to cross again—but knew he needed to.

Settling into his narrow seat, Aaron opened the tome and let himself sink into the comfort of his mother's handwriting, a quiet refuge from the storm that waited for him in Kansas.

* * *

May 17, 1993: Marlena

Most of the day was a blur, just trying to keep it all together. The moving van came early, hauling off the last of our furniture. By then, the cars were long gone—sold off earlier this week. Rob promised he'd buy me a new one once we got to Stanley, but I couldn't help but feel like it was all such a waste. He never worried about money, never showed even a flicker of concern. It's like he's got some secret line to the bank account that I'm not part of. Maybe he does.

Rob pulled into the driveway in that rented van and the kids were so worked up, clamoring to get inside and claim their seats. Aaron hopped up front, always eager to sit close. I watched Rob's face harden as he glanced over, and I knew what was coming before he opened his mouth.

"Back row, Aaron. With the dog. The front row's for my kids."

I winced, feeling that deep pang of guilt that's become too familiar. Aaron's face fell, but he slunk back to the last row without arguing, Alf beside him. I gave him a soft look to let him know I cared, but Rob saw. He leaned over, buckling me in and planting a hard kiss on my cheek. His voice was low, but I felt the edge in every word.

"Don't start, Marlena. The boy is fine. Don't ruin the whole damn day."

I wanted to scream. But I swallowed it down, as usual.

The airport felt like chaos from the moment we walked in. So many people, so many signs I couldn't make sense of. Escalators went in every direction, and long hallways stretched out in front of us like mazes. Rob was striding ahead, leaving me to wrangle the kids. Aaron had the dog's leash, doing his best to keep Alf under control while Patty, Nico, Lucas, and little Elise trailed behind, like ducklings trying not to fall too far behind the pack.

When we caught up to Rob at the check-in counter, he yanked the leash out of Aaron's hand without a word and passed the dog off to some airport clerk. Aaron's face crumpled.

"Where's Alf going?" he asked, his voice cracking. "Why can't he ride with us?"

Rob didn't even look at him. "Grow the hell up, Aaron. Get your shit together."

Aaron's eyes darted to me, searching for comfort, an explanation, something, but I didn't have it in me. Not today. I just kept walking.

The crowd at the boarding area was making my skin crawl. People jostled past, and every stranger was a potential threat in my mind. I couldn't shake the terror that one of my kids would get pulled away, snatched up in the blink of an eye. Rob saw me fidgeting and looking around like a hawk.

"Don't be stupid," he said under his breath. "Things like that don't happen with people like us."

But it didn't stop the pit in my stomach from growing. I couldn't help it. The boys were hanging over the fountain, their arms stretched out, fingers brushing the coins at the bottom, and all I could see was them falling in, disappearing into some abyss.

When we boarded the plane, I felt like I couldn't breathe. I settled Aaron, Patty, and Lucas into their row. They were excited, all with wide eyes and nervous energy. Rob had Nico and Elise with him in the row just ahead of theirs.

"Sorry, babe," he called out with a smirk, already buckled in. "You could always swap with Aaron."

Swap? Seat a ten-year-old on his first flight alone? That would not happen. My seat was two rows up, alone in the aisle. I gripped the armrests as the plane moved; the ground slipping away beneath us. My heart was pounding and nausea rolled through me.

It was only a short flight to Denver. From there we would fly to Stanley: The Great White North. I should be excited, right? New beginnings and all that. But all I felt was dread.

Aaron squinted at the phone screen as the alert flashed: *Winter Storm Warning for Eastern Colorado and Western Kansas*. He swiped it away, trying not to feel concerned. It wasn't the first storm he'd driven through by far, but the idea of a snow-covered road stretching before him in the dark was not appealing. He stuffed the phone into his pocket, focusing instead on the task ahead.

The memory of Alf tugged at him, a familiar ache rising in his chest. The dog had been his only real friend for so long, always there with a wagging tail and a head to nuzzle into when everything else felt unbearable. Aaron remembered summer afternoons in Fresno with the heat radiating from the pavement. His laughter echoed through the yard as Alf chased after the Frisbee. But everything else about that time — about the move, about Stanley—was distant, like it belonged to someone else's life.

He couldn't even remember what happened to Alf. One day, the dog was there, and the next... gone. No goodbyes. No answers. It was another piece of his childhood snatched away, leaving only jagged edges in its place.

At the rental counter, Aaron's eyes scanned the airport while he waited. It was quiet now, the rush of earlier flights dying down. The fluorescent lights buzzed above, reflecting off the sterile floors. He shifted his weight from one foot to the other, trying to shake off the uneasy feeling crawling up his spine.

The attendant handed over the keys, and soon he was weaving his way out of the terminal, the frigid Denver air hitting him as he stepped outside. He climbed into the rental car: a Ford Escape that could handle the slick roads. The seats were cold, the air inside heavy with that new-car smell, but at least it felt like his space for the moment.

> 3/9/16 5:05 pm, received 8:10 pm
> From Bethany: Be safe, Aaron.

Bethany's last text echoed in his mind as he powered up the GPS, charting his route toward Kirby. He hadn't told her anything about his quest for the truth of his past. He had told no one the full truth about why he was making this trip. Something about Bethany made him feel like he could share that burden with someone. For now, though, the silence suited him just fine.

Snow was already falling by the time he merged onto I-70, fat flakes swirling in the beams of the headlights. The road stretched out, an endless ribbon of black and white, and with each mile, the city lights faded further behind him. The memories, though, stayed close. Closer than ever.

28

The windshield wipers thumped hard to keep up with the endless snowfall blanketing the highway. Aaron's knuckles were tight around the steering wheel, tension crawling up his arms as the odometer ticked upward. Two and a half hours—85 miles at most. It felt like an eternity. The road ahead was empty except for the occasional flicker of headlights in the distance, swallowed by the storm almost as quickly as they appeared.

Snowflakes danced in the headlights before turning to freezing rain that slapped against the glass. It would last only a few minutes before the snow reclaimed its dominance, transforming the road into a white blur. He squinted at an upcoming sign, green and faded under the layers of snow. The letters came into focus as he passed: Limon, CO.

Limon. In his mind, the blurry image of a little girl floated up, unbidden. Blond ponytail, big blue eyes—just a kid. The newspaper clipping had shown her with a bright smile, playing in the snow with her brother before she vanished from the park. He could almost see her laugh echoing through the cold air, the snowball fight cut short by the unimaginable.

"Things like that don't happen with people like us," Rob's voice reverberated in his skull, a memory he couldn't shake. It was Marlena's memory, but it felt real to him now, his teeth grinding at the thought of Rob's dismissive tone. "Nah, you bastard," he muttered under his breath. "People like you do that to others."

Frustration boiled over, and he slammed his fist against the steering wheel, the dull pain spreading from his knuckles down his arm. The same hand had taken a beating against Big Mike's garage last week, and it still hurt, a constant reminder of how much he'd been through. He rubbed it against his thigh, trying to shake off the sting. He wasn't stopping here, not in Limon.

Hours later, the snow had eased into a soft drizzle of rain, the road now slick and reflective under his headlights. Darkness had shifted into the early morning light, a faint glow edging over the horizon. Aaron's body sagged with relief when he spotted the sign welcoming him to Kirby, Kansas. The haze of rain blurred the letters, but he could make out the tall shock of wheat on the town's emblem.

The clock on the dashboard read 3:22 AM. He felt hollow, drained in every sense of the word. Rain drummed on the roof as he saw the neon glow of a hotel up ahead. Its bright letters offered a respite from the long, grueling drive. The sight was like a lifeline—he almost wanted to cry at the thought of being able to rest. His body ached for sleep, and his mind could not focus anymore.

He guided the car into the parking lot; the gravel crunching under the tires. The rain was now a steady drizzle. He shut off the engine, staring at nothing. His muscles unwound, his exhaustion heavier than ever. He needed sleep. *God, I need to sleep.*

Aaron had slept harder than he had in weeks, maybe months, waking only when the sunlight peeked through the edges of the heavy hotel curtains. 10:15. He blinked at the clock on the nightstand, shocked at how late it was. His body still felt like he could sleep another week, but he forced himself out of bed, stretching stiff muscles as he pulled on yesterday's jeans and headed downstairs.

By the time he got to the breakfast bar, the hostess was already sweeping away the last trays of food. He grabbed a plate in time, piling it high with bacon, scrambled eggs, toast, and a blueberry muffin—comfort food. Balancing the plate and a steaming mug of coffee, he found a round table by the window and sat down, letting his eyes wander outside.

Kirby, Kansas. He did not know what to expect from this place anymore. The view from the hotel window wasn't much to look at — old brick buildings and the sleepy, flat roads of a small Midwestern town. A few cars rolled by, kicking up rainwater from last night's storm. His mind drifted back to the drive and the endless stretch of highway, the newspaper clippings, and the girl with the ponytail. But he pushed them aside, focusing instead on the plate before him.

He didn't have a solid plan for today. *Maybe it's better that way.* Aaron thought he'd start by driving around town, seeing what might come back to him, if anything at all. *Get a feel for the place.* Maybe somewhere in these streets was the key to figuring out what had happened all those years ago. He bit into the toast, his gaze still fixed on the town outside, waiting for something to stir a memory.

An hour later, Aaron slid into the driver's seat of the rented SUV, his breath fogging the air as he exhaled into his cupped hands. His fingers, stiff from the cold, tingled as they warmed against his palms. The heater kicked in after a few moments, filling the car with a low hum and pushing out heat that thawed his body. He tapped his fingers on the wheel, waiting for the windows to clear.

He made a right turn, heading toward the center of Kirby, his eyes scanning the streets. The town was bigger and busier, with more buildings crammed into places that had once been wide open. New storefronts lined the roads, and a few chain restaurants broke up the rows of local diners and shops. It wasn't the sleepy place he remembered as a kid. Rob had grumbled about Kirby's lack of options, complaining about the "two bars in the whole goddamn place." Things had changed. Aaron's search had pulled up 14 bars, eight new within the past decade.

As he drove, he ran through the list in his head. Four of the bars were downtown, in the part of town he could still recognize, and he started with the one that looked the oldest in the tiny images online. An older establishment was his best chance at finding someone who had known Roger Harris, or any of the men his stepfather had called friends. Rob, Roger, Kevin — they'd spent years together in this place, hiding in plain sight.

Aaron could still picture Rob sitting in one of those bars, half-drunk and spinning some exaggerated story, a cigar clamped between his fingers as he laughed with his cronies. Roger would be there too, leaning back in his chair, eyes always too sharp, like he knew everyone's secrets.

The thought made Aaron's stomach turn. He gripped the wheel tighter, forcing his focus back to the road. He slowed as he approached another intersection, scanning for the sign he'd seen in the photos —"The Rusty Nail." The bar looked like it had been here for decades, worn down by time, with a faded wooden sign swinging in the wind.

Perfect, this is a place where the past might hide in the corners.

He hoped someone inside would recognize the name Roger Harris, or at least recognize the man who loomed so large in his mind. If they did, Aaron was ready.

No luck at the first bar. "Established 1973" was painted in bold letters over the door, but it turned out to be more of a personal statement than a marker of the bar's history. The bartender explained with a grin that 1973 was the year the owner was born. "Born to drink!" he shouted, and a few hipsters playing pool in the back let out a collective cheer.

Aaron fought the urge to roll his eyes, keeping his expression neutral. He leaned in and asked if the guy had heard of Roger Harris or Kevin Earls. At the mention of the names, the bartender lit up, his man bun bobbing as he got excited. "Oh, are they in *The Wheat and Rye*? The folk band from up north in McCook? They play here sometimes."

Aaron blinked, shaking his head. "No, not a band. These guys would be older, in their seventies by now."

The bartender threw his head back and laughed like Aaron had told him a joke. "Nah, man, does this look like a place where old dudes hang?"

Aaron glanced around at the dim lights and worn wooden tables, the sort of place he'd bet on for that crowd. It seemed like it had the potential to attract an older set. Instead, plaid shirts, ironic hats, and craft beer cans filled the room. He smiled, thanked the guy for his time, and headed for the door.

Outside, the cold air hit his face and cleared his thoughts. *One bar down, thirteen to go.*

After three hours, Aaron was on the verge of abandoning the bar angle. Every place he walked into had the same vibe—young, loud, and as far from the late 80s as it could get. The old, smoky dives he'd pictured seemed to have vanished. Each bartender had either shrugged at the names or given him a blank look, one even saying, "Dude, we're all about IPAs and vinyl nights here."

He had pinned his hopes on one woman behind the bar of a spot that looked older, with its sagging ceiling tiles and worn stools. She was in her forties, wiping down glasses, and had squinted at him when he mentioned the names. Aaron's heart had lifted, thinking maybe this was it. But then she'd shaken her head and said, "The only place I can think of was Bob's Bar. My old man used to go there. It closed back in 2010 when Bob died."

Aaron asked if there was another older bar in town, but she only shrugged. "There was another, but I can't remember the name. It's closed too. Sorry, buddy."

Aaron nodded, thanked her, and pushed open the exit door. Defeat crept into his chest as he stepped into the street. All his leads seemed to be dead ends.

The orange gas light blinked on with a faint click, cutting through the quiet hum of the rented SUV. Aaron sighed, muttering, "Of course," under his breath as the light at the intersection lingered red. He leaned back, staring at the sky. The clouds were moving fast, swirling and shifting in a way that made him feel dizzy.

Two blocks later, a sign jolted him out of his thoughts: Pump N Dash. He almost couldn't believe his eyes. It was still there, looking almost exactly as it had when he was a kid. The same faded red and white sign hung over the lot like this small corner of Kirby had refused to change, frozen in the amber of 1988.

He swung the SUV into the station, pulling up to a pump. As he unbuckled his seatbelt, he noticed the new digital pumps; the sleek screens were out of place against the old brick walls of the store. The familiar hum of the modern pump sounded too clean, too efficient. He could almost picture the old ones, the mechanical clatter of numbers flipping as he filled his mother's car—bright, hot Kansas summer days when the smell of gasoline and fresh-cut grass filled the air.

Aaron stood there holding the nozzle, the distant memory of his mother's quiet voice reminding him to fill it only halfway. He filled the tank to the brim, ignoring his mother's old advice as he shoved the nozzle back into place. The rhythmic click of the pump's handle echoed in the cool air. He turned toward the gas station, the glass door creaking as he pushed it open. Inside, the clerk waved at him with a halfhearted smile, but Aaron didn't stop. His destination was the bathroom, tucked into the far corner, just like it had been decades ago.

The harsh glow of fluorescent light buzzed above him in the cramped space. Everything felt too familiar—the faded wall dispenser of "Genie's Delites" offering the same tacky, outdated, intimate items as it had when he was a boy. The neon description promised "four vivid colors and four pleasing scents". Back then, Aaron had understood none of it. The shiny knobs and the cryptic language had fascinated him.

He let the sink water run, splashing his face with a handful of lukewarm water. The mirror, dented and scratched beyond recognition, reflected a tired man staring back at him. His eyes were dull, the surrounding lines deeper than he remembered. He grabbed a rough paper towel, rubbing his face dry before tossing it into the overflowing trash bin.

"Not much better," he muttered, wiping his hands on his jeans as he left the bathroom. He headed for the counter, grabbing bottled water, but something pulled at his memory. The clerk was talking to an old woman, his words full of the same worn-out cheeriness Aaron remembered from years ago. The man's voice felt like a familiar song—one he hadn't thought about in years but could suddenly hum perfectly.

Aaron shifted in line, pretending not to be too interested as the old woman finished her transaction and shuffled toward the door with her grandson in tow. He set his bottle on the counter, studying the man across from him. The years had added heft to the clerk's frame and thinned out his hair, but there was no mistaking the face.

"How's your dad these days?" the man asked, ringing up the bottled water as if they were picking up right where they'd left off.

Aaron's brow furrowed, unsure of what he'd just heard. "What?"

The man's eyebrows lifted in recognition, a smile across his face. "Rob Bakker, right? Your dad? You look the same as you ever did, kid."

Aaron froze. His throat tensed as the past crept up like a rising tide, threatening to pull him under. "Oscar, right? I can't believe you recognize me, man. I haven't been back here since the end of 1990 when I was eight."

Oscar chuckled, leaning on the counter. "You and your brother were always after those Cow Tales." He shook his head with a grin.

"Cow Tales and strawberry milk. Every day after school."

Aaron couldn't help but smile. "Damn, man. That memory of yours is A-1. I'm impressed."

Oscar shrugged. "This town got bigger, but I still see the same faces for years. You see people enough, you remember them. Your dad was always in for coffee, gas, beer, bait, and cigarettes. Every single day for years, and even sometimes after you moved away. How is the old man?"

Aaron paused. The mention of Rob always brought up feelings he couldn't quite handle. "Oh, he's good, I think. My mom passed last year, though, so that's been rough..." His voice trailed off.

Oscar's face softened. "I'm sorry to hear that, bud. She was a wonderful lady. Everybody loved Mrs. Bakker around here. She didn't come by as much as your dad, but still. And your dad... expanding the plant like he did, giving people jobs. I'm surprised they didn't put up a statue of the man. He was such a good guy—always friendly, always smiling. Just a likable dude, your dad."

Aaron felt his stomach drop. *Likable? Friendly?* He did not know who this version of Rob was, but it wasn't the man he'd grown up with. The Rob he knew had never smiled without a reason. Aaron forced a nod, unsure how to respond. He didn't have to. Oscar must've picked up on his discomfort because he switched gears.

"So, what brings you back to this hole in the wall after all this time?"

Aaron blinked, searching for the right words. "It's related to my mom. I'm looking for some old friends of my parents—folks who might have pictures of her. Something for my brothers and sister, you know? Thought I'd track them down."

Oscar raised an eyebrow, then laughed, turning to ring up the next customer. "They don't have phones where you live?"

"It's a surprise for my dad," Aaron lied, hoping it sounded convincing. "Maybe you know them?"

"Probably do. Who are you looking for?"

Aaron's pulse quickened. "Uh, one is Kevin Earls, and the other is Roger Harris."

Oscar nodded. "Oh, yeah. Those guys were always with your dad, like his bodyguards or something. Kevin, he's still around. Got a farm out east toward Gem. But Roger..." He scratched his chin, eyes drifting for a moment. "I haven't seen Roger in years. Almost as long as you've been gone."

Aaron's heart thudded in his chest. He was about to ask more when Oscar raised a finger, signaling him to wait. "Hey, Ed!" Oscar called out to an old man shuffling near the beer coolers. "You remember Roger Harris, right? Worked out at Luca with Rob Bakker?"

The old man nodded as he approached the counter with two 40-ounce bottles of malt liquor. He wiped his mouth, looking up at Aaron before answering. "That dirty old man? Yeah, he died a few years back. He moved away to California for a bit but came back when his mama got sick. He died himself around... 2010 or 11, I think. Buried over there with her. Never married, that one."

Roger was dead.

Aaron stood there, a flood of disappointment surging through his mind. And yet, within it, the realization that he would never have to face the man. There would be no confrontation or answers.

The two men were still deep in conversation, their voices a low hum in the background as Aaron stared into the distant corners of the store, his thoughts tangled. He only tuned in when the old man said something about an auction, "...supposed to be at the auction with four of his prize cattle tomorrow."

Aaron blinked. "Who?" he asked, his voice cutting into the old man's sentence.

The man glanced at him, squinting as if trying to place Aaron's earlier question. "Earls. The one you were asking about. Ain't that him?"

Aaron nodded, his brain catching up. Kevin Earls: the name landed with a sense of urgency, like a door creaking open in some long-abandoned room in his mind. "The auction... when and where?"

The old man scratched his head, looking out the window. "Fridays at 11. Every other week. Next one's tomorrow, down the road a piece, past the interstate."

He gestured toward the window; the vague directions doing little to clarify things, but Aaron nodded anyway, knowing he could track the place down on the internet.

Oscar and the old man drifted back into their conversation, and Aaron, taking the cue, grabbed his water and raised a hand in a silent goodbye. He reached for the door handle, his mind racing ahead, when Oscar's voice called after him.

"Hey, kid!"

Aaron turned, catching sight of something flying toward him. He snatched it out of reflex—his hand closing around a familiar, soft package of Cow Tales.

Oscar grinned. "I'll see you next time I see you, kid!"

Aaron chuckled and the sweetness of the gesture lingered as he pushed open the door and stepped out into the brisk air. *Some things don't change.*

Once in his SUV, Aaron turned back onto the road. The wheels crunching over bits of gravel as he eased out of the gas station lot. The thought of the cattle auction filled his mind, a vague sense of dread gnawing at him. Kevin Earls. He would face him tomorrow, and Kevin, unaware of what Aaron knew, might even be glad to see him. The thought soured in his gut. *What should I say? How will I ask the right questions without tipping my hand?* He tapped his fingers on the wheel, the slow churn of his thoughts pulling him into the unknowns of tomorrow.

He flipped on his blinker, spotting a shady patch of curb up ahead. The sun had dipped lower in the sky, casting a soft light over the street, and he rolled to a stop beside the sidewalk. He typed "cattle auction" into the GPS, the glow illuminating his face as the search results popped up. One location. Right where the old man had said —"down the road a piece, past the interstate." Aaron huffed, leaning back in his seat. *Tomorrow.* There was nothing to be done until then.

He stared ahead, the steering wheel solid beneath his grip and his mind blank. "What now?" he muttered, the words hanging in the stale air of the car. His eyes drifted over the surrounding blocks, buildings, and signs blending into the backdrop—until something caught his attention. Across the street, on a diagonal corner, an iron fence rose from the ground, black and imposing. Behind it, a scattering of tombstones.

The cemetery.

Aaron's pulse quickened. The name, Roger Harris, echoed through his brain, begging for closure. The man was dead, buried out there somewhere behind that fence. He couldn't talk or answer for the things he'd done. But Aaron could.

"Maybe I'll chat with you anyway," he muttered, his voice low. His eyes locked on the cemetery gate. The dirty old man might not speak any more—but Aaron had a few things to say to his ghost.

29

"Third cemetery in two weeks," Aaron muttered under his breath as he pulled into the small parking lot in front of the building marked OFFICE. He shut off the engine and sat there, staring at the structure. "Some hobby I've picked up," he added, shaking his head. He slid out of the SUV and made his way inside.

It didn't take long. The clerk, somber and uninterested, had directed him to Section D, assuring him that while there were no printed maps, the Harris plot was hard to miss. The man was right. As Aaron rounded the corner of the winding perimeter road, the black marble mausoleum stood by the humble gravestones like a monument to wealth and arrogance. His lips curled in distaste as he parked and stepped out.

The mausoleum loomed before him, its polished surface reflecting the fading light of the late afternoon. The chiseled name of HARRIS sported glinting gold leaf in the engraving. Two low steps led up to a wrought-iron gate with black flower pots on either side. Perennial ivy filled the pots and draped over the stone.

He stepped onto the top step and leaned forward, peering through the bars. Two marble crypts lay inside, cold and silent. The crypt on the left read "DORIS", with her birth and death dates. And across from her, the man who had haunted Aaron's nightmares for years: ROGER 1951-2011.

Aaron's jaw clenched. He gripped the iron gate, the cold metal digging into his palms, and leaned closer. "Remember me, you piece of shit?" he seethed through the bars, his voice low but brimming with rage. The crypt stood silent, unfeeling, but the weight of what it represented pressed down on him, thick and suffocating. The man inside could no longer hurt anyone—but the pain he left behind still clawed at Aaron like it was fresh.

The rage had lived in him for so long it had carved out its own space in his soul, and he wanted to scream and let it all out. He could see Roger: the wolfish smile, the too-rough hands, always around him, always trapping him, just like those horrible fishing trips. He wanted to beat the man who had promised to teach him how to fish but had instead molested him, raped him, and covered the trauma by convincing Aaron's mother that the boy had fallen on the slippery dock.

The memories played in his mind like scenes from a nightmare, clear as day but distorted with time and trauma. He wished Roger was alive just so he could kill him, to pay him back for every time his groping fingers had jerked him or Patty onto his lap in their living room and rubbed his knobby chin on the top of their heads while his hands roamed inside their clothes.

His anger bubbled over and he had nowhere to direct it except this cold, immovable tomb. He slammed his fist against the gate in a fury, metal echoing in the stillness. His fists throbbed from the relentless pounding on the gate, his knuckles raw and bleeding. The pain somehow felt right.

"You bastard," he spat, hitting the gate harder. It rattled but didn't give an inch, standing there like Roger had stood in his life—unshakable, cruel, and always just out of reach.

A voice from behind jolted him out of his violent haze. He spun around, stumbling on the step. "You okay there, sir?" A man stood a few feet away, wearing the worn green uniform of a groundskeeper. He was older than Aaron, but not by much. His eyes were sharp, taking in the scene with no judgment, just quiet observation.

Aaron breathed hard, trying to calm himself. "Friend of yours?" the man asked, gesturing toward the crypt.

"No!" The word tore out of him like a growl before he realized he was yelling. He dropped his voice. "No. He's no friend of mine. Piece of shit."

The groundskeeper just nodded, his expression unchanged. "Yeah. Roger's had a few visitors like you over the years," the man said, his voice gravelly with a hint of something more. "Came out here to yell at it myself a time or two, before I got the job. Now I just ignore it, as best I can. He was no good." His eyes softened, and Aaron felt a wave of understanding between them.

"He... messed with you?" he asked.

The man looked down, kicking at the dirt with the toe of his boot. "Ain't no good reliving the past," he said, voice thick with years of buried pain. "But it's no surprise to me he's behind bars in death, just like he should've been his whole life. No good at all, that one." He glanced up, his face hardening, but not toward Aaron. It was a hardness that came from surviving.

Aaron glanced at the mausoleum, the garish black marble, the gold-embossed name. It made him sick. "Who paid for this fancy crypt?"

The man gave a short, humorless laugh. "Oh, this tacky piece of shit? Roger paid for that when his mama died and left a spot for himself. He had his name put on it, and everything. The only thing they had to do when he blew his brains out was chuck him in the box and slap on the death date. Now wasn't that thoughtful of him?"

Aaron's head snapped toward the groundskeeper, shock flickering across his face. "He killed himself?"

The man nodded, staring at the crypt with disdain. "Yeah. He took the easy way out, as they say. He blew his brains out in his kitchen, right after his mama passed. I guess he couldn't handle being alone. Shame," the man said, the words drenched in sarcasm. "But at least he saved us the trouble of dealing with him."

Aaron flexed his right hand, the skin tight and bleeding from the force of his punches. The groundskeeper's gaze flicked down to his hand, wincing in sympathy. "You're gonna wanna doctor that up," he mumbled. "Make sure it ain't broken."

Aaron tried to move his fingers, but pain shot through them, sharp and unforgiving. "It'll be okay," he muttered, his voice flat. "It was worth it."

The man shook his head, doubt clouding his expression. "Put this man behind you," he advised. "He's gone and can't hurt nobody anymore." He took a step closer and gestured to the iron bars. "I'll make sure he never gets out of these bars."

The man extended his right hand, and Aaron reached out, but the moment his battered knuckles brushed against the other man's palm, a sharp, searing pain shot through his hand. He winced, dropping it with an apologetic smile. "Let's try that again," the man chuckled, switching to his left hand. Aaron hesitated for a second, then offered his awkward left hand. The brief gesture carried more weight than Aaron expected—a silent understanding between two people who had both suffered under Roger's shadow.

As Aaron turned back to the SUV, the pounding in his knuckles faded into the background, replaced by the heavy realization settling deep in his chest. Roger was gone. But the anger? That was still there, simmering, refusing to be buried with the man who had ruined so much.

He glanced back at the mausoleum, its black marble gleaming in the waning light. The groundskeeper was already returning to work, pulling at the weeds along the fence line. On impulse, Aaron called out, "Hey, man, you ever met a guy named Kevin Earls?"

The groundskeeper straightened, tipping his head back to squint at Aaron through the distance between them. He wiped his brow with the back of his hand. "Nah, it doesn't ring a bell. Someone I should know?"

He shook his head, feeling relief that this man hadn't also been one of Kevin's victims. "No. Just wondered. Thanks, man."

The groundskeeper gave a slight nod before returning to his task, while Aaron turned away, buckling his seatbelt and putting the car into gear using only his left hand. His knuckles throbbed with each movement, the pain unrelenting. Now, he thought, he needed to find a drugstore.

Pulling out of the cemetery, he scanned the streets ahead, searching for a sign of a corner pharmacy. His swollen and aching right hand rested on his lap. He sighed, focusing on the road, determined to patch himself up before tomorrow's confrontation with Kevin Earls.

He spotted an urgent care as he entered the stretch of road near his hotel and sighed. His hand throbbed with every movement. Urgent care seemed like a necessary step. He reached across the steering wheel with his left hand to click on the right turn signal; his right hand was too painful for even that small motion.

The clinic's lobby was bright and almost empty on this Thursday evening. Aaron hadn't sat in the uncomfortable beige plastic chair long enough to watch a full commercial on the enormous overhead TV before his name was called. The red-headed nurse took his vital signs and examined his swollen right hand. She palpated the swelling tissues with her vibrant purple nails until his groan of pain made her step back. "Let me get the doctor," she said.

The doctor, a middle-aged man with a no-nonsense demeanor, examined Aaron's hand and pronounced it broken. He sent Aaron down the hall for X-ray confirmation of his diagnosis. The tech, looking nervous, stretched Aaron's fingers on the X-ray table as if he might get punched at any moment. Aaron grimaced through the discomfort, trying to stay still. The nurse returned afterward to clean the wounds with care.

After a brief wait, during which Aaron stared at anatomical posters detailing the delicate bones of the hand, the doctor returned with the news: a complete fracture of the 4th and 5th metacarpals, with the 4th displaced. "Shit. Displaced? That means..." Aaron's voice trailed off, his tone resigned.

The doctor interjected, "It means we need to realign the bone before applying the cast. Fortunately, it's not too far off, so we can handle it here."

Aaron let out a loud, exasperated sigh. "Well damn, I screwed up, didn't I?"

"And how did you say this happened?" The doctor peered at him from behind his clipboard.

Aaron lied, "Helping my buddy move. He has these boxes—put all the heavy books in one of them. I tripped, fell, slammed my hand against the doorway on the way down."

"Uh-huh," the doctor said, unfazed. "We call this a boxer's fracture. It often happens during a fight."

"Nah, no fight. Just that heavy box and the damn doorway." Aaron's voice wavered, lacking conviction.

The doctor let the subject drop. While he made notes, the nurse rejoined them with a tray of surgical supplies and a cup containing two white oval pills. "Vicodin, because this will not be comfy," she said with a smile.

She wasn't lying. By the end of the hour, Aaron's right hand had been pulled, manipulated, reduced, iced, and coaxed into a plaster cast extending from the tips of his pinky and ring fingers to halfway up his forearm. The Vicodin provided slight relief, but his hand still throbbed inside its plaster prison.

The nurse returned with a discharge form, care instructions, prescriptions, and a single bottle of pills. "5 mg Vicodin, take one to two every six hours as needed. There are only 16 pills in there, so use them only when you need them. We don't want you getting addicted." Her expression was serious, but her tone was almost flirtatious. She pointed to the two pieces of paper. "There's also a prescription for 500 mg Tylenol—start alternating with the Vicodin every six hours starting tomorrow. And Cephalexin for those cuts—take one every eight hours until they're gone. Don't stop until you're finished. You don't want an infection under that cast." She gestured to his cast with a stern look.

He followed her to the front desk and fumbled for his wallet in his right back pocket, out of reach with his good hand. The receptionist helped him retrieve it, and he slid his credit card into the machine. He was starving, staring out the window at the Arby's across the street when the receptionist handed him his card back. The redheaded nurse appeared again. "You're not driving, are you? No one can pick you up?"

He shook his head. "I'm not from here. My hotel is right there," he gestured out the front window at the hotel looming over the Arby's. "It's a 60-second drive, I promise."

"Well, okay. No side trips," she warned. "Not with pain medicine on board."

"Yes ma'am. Straight there and straight to sleep. I appreciate everything."

She held the glass door open for him, her hand grazing his shoulder as he passed her, then held out a folded piece of paper between two polished fingers. "You let me know if you need anything, Mr. Callahan. Dinner maybe? I'll be off work in a couple of hours." She winked at him.

"Well, Miss..." He trailed off, flattered but confused at her suggestion. He looked for her name tag.

"Annie," she breathed out in a husky voice. "I'm Annie."

"I'm pretty sure I'll be asleep long before then, Miss Annie," he smiled down at her, "but I appreciate the offer." He nodded at her and walked to his SUV, fumbling in his left coat pocket for his keys.

"Let me know if you change your mind," she called after him.

"Will do, ma'am," he smiled again and waved before closing his door and wrestling his keys into the ignition. "What a pain in the ass this day has been," he muttered to the cold interior.

The drive to the hotel was less than 60 seconds away if one didn't have an immobilized right hand and forearm. Driving was easy, but getting the vehicle into and out of gear would take some practice. He parked in front of the hotel and walked to the Arby's for some sustenance—the drive-thru line was above his current ability level. Carrying a sandwich, fries, and a drink back to his room was probably above his level, too. He'd eat there and then head to his room to sleep. He still needed to figure out a strategy for tomorrow's auction day.

June 4, 2006: Marlena

I don't know what's gotten into Elise today. Kevin flew into town Friday evening; Rob picked him up at the airport. They disappeared on their fishing pilgrimage—another lake to conquer. They've got this obsession with fishing every lake they can find. I wish Kevin had brought Maritza. I could use some adult conversation, but she's knee-deep in kids. Maybe more than we have at this point.

I made steak and baked potatoes, Rob's favorite, hoping for a quiet night. The men retreated to the den, their laughter and clinking glasses mingling with the smell of brandy and cognac. I took my vodka to the bedroom, curling up under the covers. The bottle warms my insides. Elise's voice drifted in when she came home, but she didn't come to talk to me. At almost sixteen, she's more into her friends and her looks than she is into talking to her old mom. It's just how things are now, I suppose.

Rob stumbled in late. I felt the mattress shift as he settled behind me. The vodka lulls me to sleep, though sometimes it drags me deeper than I want to go. It's better than lying awake, tangled in thoughts that circle forever.

The next morning, I woke alone. The men had already left—off in search of another lake. I folded up the sofa bed Kevin had used and tackled the usual chores. Dishes clattered as I washed them, and laundry spun in the machine. Patty texted a photo of baby Drew. We exchanged a few messages. Elise was out, so I texted asking when she'd be home. No response.

I sank onto the couch, my vodka and soda water in hand, flipping channels without watching. The men stormed in after one in the morning, their voices loud and their clothes reeking of fish. I said hi and retreated to the bedroom, too drunk to do anything else.

This morning, I made breakfast and Rob took Kevin to the airport. I knocked on Elise's door, and when I opened it, she sat perched at her vanity, staring at her reflection with a vacant look. I gathered her dirty clothes and asked when she'd come home last night.

"What do you care?" Her voice was flat and dismissive.

"I'm your mom. I care. Now, what time was it?" I wasn't asking to be nosy—I'm sick of these late nights and uncertainty. What's she up to? Sex, drugs, who even knows?

She sighed, a long, dramatic exhale. "Mom…"

"Yes, Mom. What time did you get home?" I'm never in the mood for her games anymore. I'm tired of her playing loose with my rules.

"Kevin came in here last night and… did things to me. And then Dad…" Her voice cracked, and she hid her face in her hands, sobbing.

I was stunned, a cold anger burning in my chest. "Okay, Elise. So you were out all night with your boyfriend, ignoring my rules, and now you're telling me this? Is this some excuse?"

"Mom!" Her voice escalated, sharp and screeching. "Listen to me! It wasn't my boyfriend, it was Kevin! And Dad just—"

"Just what? What did your dad do? I can't even believe you, Elise! Kevin? Your dad's best friend? One of our oldest family friends? You expect me to believe that?"

"You never listen to me!" she wailed, her tears muffled by her hands. She's so dramatic, so theatrical.

"I'm listening. But you're not answering my question. What time did you get home? And you're grounded for a week, next time you're out past 11. Take some responsibility. Don't go throwing around these wild accusations!" I seethed with anger and frustration. Kevin? He's been so respectful to me all these years, even though he had about a million opportunities to flirt with me, or even more. Never anything but a gentleman, that man. This is absurd.

"I hate you," she screamed, her voice trailing down the hallway as I slammed her door and carried her laundry downstairs.

"Yeah, you're not my favorite either, princess," I muttered. I leaned against the washing machine, my body sagging with exhaustion. I needed a drink. And now that I've had a few… I'm so tired, so worn out. So sick of it all.

Aaron couldn't sleep much, his hand throbbing under the cast. The awkward bulk of it made every shift in bed uncomfortable. During the night, he hit himself in the face with the cast while tossing around, and the sudden streak of pain shot through his hand and jolted him awake. Only with another Vicodin did he close his eyes again, though it wasn't for long.

He woke for good when the sky was still dark, a faint pink and orange beginning to edge over the horizon. He stood at the window, staring out at the early morning light, mind racing as he tried to figure out how to handle seeing Kevin later today. The cattle auction didn't start until 11, so he still had hours to kill. An idea was forming—half a plan, anyway. He wasn't sure if it was good, but it was better than nothing.

He headed to the shower, tying the clear plastic bag meant for the hotel ice bucket over his cast, doing his best to wash with only his non-dominant hand. Drying off and dressing was a battle, especially buttoning his jeans with one hand and the thumb of the other. By the time he managed it, his hand was aching, and he reached for another pill. Frustration gnawed at him—he was furious at himself for letting his emotions take over yesterday at Roger's tomb.

Dressed and ready, he headed downstairs to the breakfast buffet. Even something as simple as grabbing a bagel and coffee required planning now. Balancing the coffee cup on the hood of his SUV, he used his thumb and cast to hold the bagel in place while unlocking the door, moving one item at a time into the car before closing the door behind him. "Total pain in the ass," he muttered. "You're an idiot, Aaron Callahan."

He wasn't sure if he meant breaking his hand or everything that had led to this moment. *Maybe both.*

The GPS pointed him to a nearby Walmart. He had been standing in the pharmacy waiting for his prescriptions to be filled when the other half of his plan hit him. By the time he left the store, his mind had settled on it—no backing down now.

He arrived at the auction grounds just before 10:30 a.m. The place was already buzzing: cattle trailers and pickup trucks packed in as far as the eye could see. The long, squat metal barns toward the back had their front doors flung wide open, a flood of people pouring in. Aaron found a parking spot and took a deep breath.

"You got this, Aaron, c'mon." His voice sounded hollow, lacking the confidence he needed. But the anger he felt, the deep simmering rage beneath the surface, was enough to pull him out of the SUV and into the crowd.

30

The pungent, earthy scent of animals hit Aaron before he even stepped inside. He moved through the entrance, engulfed by the cacophony of the auction. The space reminded him of a state fair: pens lining the walls, animals shifting and stomping. The sound was overwhelming—layered with the chatter of farmers and families, some laughing, some negotiating deals.

Aaron was in the sheep barn, though he paid little attention to the animals. The press of bodies made it hard to move, each step slow and deliberate. People brushed past him without thought, and he was glad he'd had the foresight to grab a sling for his broken hand. The cast rested inside it; the strap digging into his shoulder, but at least it kept his arm somewhat shielded from the jostling crowd.

He wove his way through, keeping to the far right side, eyes scanning for the exit to the next building. His pulse drummed in his ears as he navigated the crowd, the noise fading to hum in his mind as anticipation built inside him. Each step forward felt heavier.

The stench hit Aaron when he stepped into the next shed—the thick, gamey, and unmistakable odor of goats. The layout was similar: pens packed with animals, but here, large metal signs hung over sections labeled Meat, Dairy, and Fiber.

Aaron felt a sudden tug at his pants leg and looked down to see a brown and white goat tugging at the fold of his jeans through the fence. Its curious eyes locked onto his, and Aaron bent down, scratching its head around the short, stumpy horns.

"That there's a Kiko," a voice drawled behind him. Aaron straightened to see the goat's owner, a stocky man with a wide grin, perched on a stool. "Best meat goat breed you'll ever taste. That's a buck, too—a perfect addition to your herd. You buyin'?"

Aaron gave a quick smile, shaking his head. "Not today, no thanks," he said, his eyes shifting to the thinning crowd ahead. The way had cleared enough for him to slip through.

Beyond the next set of double doors, a large sign hung overhead: Cattle. The heavy thrum of hooves and lowing reached his ears, and the tension in his chest coiled tighter.

The cattle barn was larger than the other two, its sheer size intimidating. Aaron sighed. *How the hell am I supposed to find Kevin in this mess?* He wove through the mass of people, navigating the perimeter for an eternity. Forty minutes later, he was almost back to the door he had entered through, with no sign of Kevin.

Desperation creeping in, he stopped near a farmer standing beside one of the biggest cows he'd ever seen. The animal towered over his owner, a mountain of muscle and hide. "Excuse me, sir," Aaron called out.

The man looked up. "Yes, sir? Do you want to know how much she weighs? Well... let me just—"

"No," Aaron cut him off, waving a hand. "I mean... she's amazing, but I wanted to ask if you might know where I can find someone."

The farmer raised an eyebrow, annoyed. "Well, she's 2,375 pounds, since you're asking. Who are you looking for?"

Aaron forced a polite smile, feeling the heat rise in his face. "That's... an impressive weight. I'm looking for a man named Kevin Earls. You wouldn't know where I could find him?"

The man glanced around as though Kevin might materialize from thin air. "Don't see him. Why don't you check the other cattle barns?"

Aaron blinked. "There's more than one cattle barn?"

"There's three," the farmer said with a chuckle. "Or you can check with registration and see where they stuck him."

"Right. Thanks," Aaron mumbled, stepping away. Feeling the need to make up for his awkwardness, he turned back. "And your cow... she's something."

The farmer's face softened a little. "She's a heifer, but thanks."

Aaron shook his head, retreating into the crowd. *Two more barns... Jesus.*

He was halfway around the second cattle barn, searching for the registration desk or Kevin when he heard his name. Aaron's pulse quickened, his body tensing as he spun to his left. Kevin Earls stood there—red-faced and broad, his presence as commanding as ever. The man had wrecked lives, and here he was, grinning like they were old friends.

"What in the Sam Hill are you doing out here, boy?" Kevin's voice boomed. "Is your daddy here too?" He craned his neck, scanning the crowd, those beady eyes as piercing as Aaron remembered.

"Nah, it's just me," Aaron said, forcing an amiable tone. "Had some time off work, thought I'd check things out. Haven't been here since I was a kid, you know?"

Kevin's eyes zeroed in on Aaron's sling across his chest. "What'd you do to your hand?" he asked, suspicion lurking behind the question.

Aaron fell back on the lie he'd told the doctor. "Helping a friend move. Had a minor accident with a heavy box. Stupid."

Kevin leaned in close as if they were sharing some secret. "Accidents happen," he said with a conspiratorial grin. "That's why they call them... accidents." He erupted in a loud belly laugh, as if he had just delivered the punchline of the century.

Aaron clenched his teeth and chuckled. "Yeah, that's right," he agreed, hoping he sounded more sincere than he felt.

"Well, you're here now! Come meet my family!" Kevin's thick arm clapped Aaron on the back, pushing him forward. Aaron's stomach turned, but he swallowed the feeling. Meeting Kevin's family was what he wanted.

Kevin's hand clamped down on Aaron's shoulder. His laughter still echoing as he steered them through the crowd. The barn seemed to shrink around them. The noise of cattle and chattering voices dulled to a hum. Aaron's focus narrowed on the man beside him. The urge to turn and bolt grew stronger, but he forced himself to keep moving.

This was part of the plan, no matter how much his stomach protested.

Kevin talked a mile a minute, and Aaron listened to every word, hoping for useful information. They stopped in front of a pen. Kevin's chest puffed out with pride as he gestured toward a small cluster of people gathered around a few cows. "Here we are!" he declared, like a king showing off his kingdom. "This here is my flock."

A petite woman rose from her crouch by the pen, five feet tall, her dark hair pulled back into a messy ponytail. Sweat-dampened strands curled over her bronze forehead, framing high cheekbones and full lips. She stepped forward, offering Aaron a hand.

"This is my wife, Maritza," Kevin said, his arm still draped heavily over Aaron's shoulder. He swung his other arm toward two children playing in the straw by the cows. "And these are my hellraisers—Eli and Casey." Kevin's grin stretched wide as if he were presenting a grand prize.

Aaron swallowed, his mouth dry, and forced a smile. "Nice to meet you all."

Maritza nodded, her smile tight and distant. The kids, as bronzed as their mother, glanced up from their play. "Jackson and Malachi went to pick up Maggie," she mumbled, her voice almost lost in the barn's din.

Kevin squeezed Aaron's shoulder a little too hard. "Oh, good! You'll get to meet the rest of the flock. You might as well be one of my kids, Aaron. I've known your family for so long. Aaron is Rob's boy, Mari. His family lived out here, over by the park near…"

Kevin's voice faded into the background as Aaron's mind churned. This was Kevin's world—his wife and kids, living the life he'd built for them. Aaron's eyes swept over the scene, taking in every detail. This family, torn from their pasts, was Kevin's idea of normal. They stood before him like exhibits in a twisted museum.

The realization lit a fire inside Aaron. He had needed to see this: Kevin was smug and secure in the life he'd crafted. Aaron forced himself to keep his breath even as he inhaled the thick air of the barn. His eyes darted around, searching for any opening, any way to turn this day into the reckoning it needed to be.

The PA system's piercing screech cut through the barn's noise. It silenced the room for a moment. Then, a man with a thick Midwestern drawl spoke. "Cattle auctions for Shed 2 beginning in 20 minutes. Shed

2, Numbers 1-40, please move your animals to the staging area."

Kevin's head swiveled toward the boy, his gaze narrowing. "What number are we, Eli?"

"Number 44," Eli muttered, eyes darting between his father and Aaron.

Kevin's eyes were cold steel. "Number 44, what?"

Eli hesitated. The question pulled his gaze down. He answered, "Number 44, sir."

Kevin nodded, satisfied, but his voice carried an edge. "That's right. Sir. Don't make me remind you again." His gaze shifted to Aaron, a smirk curling at the corner of his lips. "Got to train them right, or they'll grow up wild. No respect. I'm sure you remember that, Aaron. Your daddy sure knew how to teach respect. I learned everything I know about parenting from Rob. Yes, I did."

Aaron could feel his pulse hammering against his temples. Kevin's words stung, twisting the knife deeper. He forced a step forward, shrugging off Kevin's heavy arm. His jaw clenched, his voice tight as he asked, "Kevin, you think we could get a few minutes alone? Talk about a couple of things?"

Kevin studied him for a moment. His eyes glinted with something unreadable. Then a slow smile spread across his face. "Of course, of course. Not right now, though. I've got my heifers to sell soon, but afterward? Absolutely! What are your plans for the day?"

"I'll be around," Aaron said, his words short, holding back the storm inside.

The old man's grin stretched wider as he spotted the approaching couple, sidestepping Aaron with an eager wave. His voice boomed with cheer as he hugged two dark-haired men. Then, he turned to a curly-haired young girl of around 11. He pulled her into an exaggerated embrace. "This is my oldest boy, Jackson. Pride and joy, that one. This is Malachi— he's a genius with numbers and figures. And here," he said, squeezing the girl's waist, "this is Daddy's little cup of sugar, Maggie." He waved a hand toward Aaron, all teeth and showmanship. "Aaron here is my old friend Robert's son!"

Aaron extended his hand, correcting Kevin with a tight smile. "Stepson, but yes, nice to meet you both." He shook their hands.

Kevin waved off the correction as if it were irrelevant. "Stepson, son—what's the difference? Family's family, right? Maritza and I have four adopted kids ourselves! Can you believe that? People call us crazy, but I say there are too many kids who don't know what it means to be loved. And if we can give them that—" He spread his arms in a grand, theatrical gesture, like a politician soaking in applause. "Well, by God, I want to give it to them. Right, kids?"

"Yes, sir," Eli and Casey chimed, their voices devoid of emotion. The words rolled off their tongues like a reflex.

"Four adopted kids, Kevin?" Aaron forced a casual tone, wondering if this might be the moment he had been searching for, his chance to confront the man.

Kevin's chest puffed with pride. "Yep! Let me tell you. Lindsey, she's married now. She adopted a little girl of her own with her husband, Mark, a couple of years ago, and then they recently had a baby. Then there's Josephine, the poor thing, orphaned in Mexico. Her parents abandoned her. She's working at the hospital now, doing some office work or something like that. Eli and Casey, well, their parents died in some gang violence down south. Those countries below the border are dangerous." His fingers ticked off each name as he spoke, his voice dripping with self-congratulation.

"And of course, I've got the three I made myself." Kevin's hand landed on Jackson's back. "Jackson here, Maggie, and Malachi. All by myself," he added, winking and pulling Maggie tighter against him. Her smile never wavered, though her posture was rigid, her body almost stiff under his arm. "Well, I guess your mama helped a little, didn't she?" He threw his head back with a familiar belly laugh, loud and boastful, basking in the attention as if he were the hero in his own story.

Aaron could feel the weight of Maggie's fixed smile, the way Jackson's eyes darted to the floor whenever his father spoke. The act Kevin had perfected was fraying at the edges, and Aaron's pulse quickened.

Kevin's face lit up, his grin widening further as he clapped Aaron on the shoulder with a resounding smack. "So Aaron, if you're free tonight, come for dinner. Maritza makes a meatloaf that's the talk of four counties! You don't want to miss it."

The PA system crackled to life again, a sharp burst of feedback cutting through the murmur of conversation. "Cattle auctions for Shed 2 beginning in 20 minutes. Shed 2, Numbers 41-80, please move your animals to the staging area."

Kevin's attention snapped to the cattle. He turned to his kids with a flourish. "That's us, folks! Time to get moving." He waved Aaron along as he headed toward the pen. "What do you say, Aaron? Dinner with my flock—can't beat that, right, kids?"

The four kids chimed in as one, their voices robotic in their enthusiasm. "Yes, sir!"

Aaron forced his smile wider, feeling the strain in his cheeks. "Sure, I'd be glad to join you for dinner." The hustle and noise of the auction felt like a distant thunder now. Meeting Kevin at home would give Aaron the privacy he needed to follow his plan.

31

The family led their cattle through the crowd. Kevin's public persona was a show of unrestrained affection and praise. He doted on his animals with exaggerated compliments. His praise seemed to flow as freely as his hand when it rested on a cow's flank, or when he boasted about his children to anyone who would listen. As Aaron watched, he noticed the shift when Kevin thought no one was looking.

When Eli faltered with the cow, Kevin's gaze hardened. His beady eyes narrowed, and his fingers dug into the boy's arm with a grip that made Aaron's stomach turn. Eli flinched under the pressure, his face flushed with embarrassment and pain.

When Malachi asked his mother to skip the family dinner to go out with his girlfriend. Kevin reacted in an instant. His voice boomed across the staging area, all sweetness and forced cheer. But as soon as Malachi's back turned, Kevin's demeanor shifted. He followed him with a swift, angry stride, his hand closing around his arm in a vice-like grip. "Don't ask again. You can do much better than that—" His harsh whisper cut off as he caught Aaron's gaze. His tone softened. "That young lady isn't good enough for you, son," he said. He patted Malachi's back in a show of fatherly affection. Then, he returned to his place at the front of his cattle.

Malachi shot Aaron a quick, defiant look. "My girlfriend is black," he said, his voice sharp. "That's why he doesn't approve." He rolled his eyes and turned away, sinking onto a bench alone. His lonely posture stood out against the bustling auction.

Aaron watched as Kevin stepped up to the auction block, his face a mask of practiced enthusiasm. Aaron's resolve solidified. When this confrontation happened, it would do so where he could see all the cracks behind the facade.

After the new owners took all the family's cows, Kevin engaged Aaron in a passionate lesson about heifers and cows. "You see, Aaron, an unbred heifer is a better investment than a cow who has already calved. Economically, it makes more sense."

He paused for a moment, glancing at Aaron with a self-satisfied grin. "Maybe it's just me, but there's something about getting a fresh heifer, untouched and unspoiled. You get to pick the bull that'll make the perfect match. It gives you better control over your herd, don't you think?"

Aaron nodded, though his mind was far from Kevin's economic arguments. The comparison struck him as unsettling. Kevin's hand clamped around little Casey's, his grip firm and possessive as he steered the girl along. The tightness of his fingers holding the child close felt eerily reminiscent of how Kevin discussed his views on heifers.

As they reached the pens, Aaron focused on staying composed and preparing for the evening ahead. He had to see this through.

The drive to the Earls' farm was uncomfortable. Each bump in the road sent a sharp pain through Aaron's throbbing hand. Gritting his teeth, he swallowed some Tylenol at a red light, hoping it would dull the pain. He followed Jackson's sporty red Toyota Tacoma, while Kevin's black Ford F-350, towing a long silver cattle trailer, led the way.

As they turned onto the winding driveway, the farm sprawled before them like a testament to Kevin's success. The sheer scale of it was imposing: three expansive barns stood in the distance, their metal roofs gleaming in the afternoon sun. Endless fields of neat rows surrounded them: tilled, ready for corn and wheat to be planted in the coming weeks. Pastures filled with cattle, a silent sea of grazing animals, lay beyond. The nearby tractors and farm equipment were immaculate. Their polished surfaces reflected the sunlight.

Kevin guided them up to a sprawling two-story farmhouse—the centerpiece of his empire. He parked beside the barn, his broad frame blocking the sun as he gestured for Aaron to join him. He expounded on the "details and intricacies" of his operation in an animated voice, as if it were the most fascinating topic in the world. Aaron tried to focus, but Kevin's chatter was distracting. He saw Maritza and the younger children retreating toward the house. They seemed relieved, as if escaping a gilded cage.

The sun was dipping low when Kevin's tour wound down. Aaron had said only a few words—Kevin dominated the conversation. The man's voice had become white noise to Aaron, his mind wandering between strategies and his growing exhaustion.

Entering the house, Aaron's nerves felt raw, his smile a thin shield that had been in place far too long. He marveled at how Kevin's family could bear this charade, maintaining the veneer of perfect contentment. Maritza, her face expressionless, was pulling a meatloaf from the oven. She had arranged the dining table like it was Thanksgiving. It was a forced formality, with cloth napkins and placemats—more fitting for a holiday than a typical Friday night.

"Oh good, Lindsey's here!" Kevin's booming voice filled the living room as they entered. Aaron's pulse quickened, though he kept his face neutral. The blonde woman who stood to greet him was unmistakable —he'd seen her face before, in a grainy black-and-white photo. *Apple Valley, CA: March 1996*, the voice in his head whispered, sending a chill down his spine.

Lindsey smiled as she extended her hand. "Nice to meet you," she said, her voice warm but detached, as though this were just another introduction in her orchestrated life. A tall blond man stood beside her, a squirming toddler on his hip. "I'm Mark," he said, shaking Aaron's hand. "And this little one is Sophia. The baby is Lily, but she's sleeping, right Sophia?" The child, wide-eyed and restless, had skin as dark as Maritza's and nothing like her adoptive parents.

Aaron's gaze lingered on the girl for a moment before returning to Lindsey and Mark, the façade of familial bliss clear to him now. He nodded, every muscle in his body coiled tight, waiting for the right moment to strike.

Dinner was a strange, uncomfortable affair. Kevin spoke louder than anyone, fixated on Mark's work as a plumber. He kept insisting that Aaron and Mark had the same job. Aaron corrected him many times, explaining he was a contractor and didn't do plumbing. Kevin kept circling back to the same point. It was as if Kevin needed to fit Aaron into some preordained box, paying no mind to the details.

As the meal wound down, Lindsey stood to excuse herself. "Time for the baby to eat," she whispered, cradling the now-fussy Lily.

Kevin's booming voice cut across the table. "Sit down, girl. Feed her here. This is the dinner table."

Lindsey froze, a flush creeping up her neck. "Daddy, I'm breastfeeding Lily."

"And? It's a natural thing. You don't need to hide in the living room," Kevin replied, his tone leaving no room for debate.

Lindsey hesitated, uncomfortable. "But—"

"Feed the baby, Lindsey," Kevin commanded with finality. His words landed heavily on the table, casting an oppressive silence.

Lindsey glanced at her husband, but Mark just chuckled, flashing a nonchalant grin at Aaron, as if the whole thing were a joke. Resigned, Lindsey lifted Lily into her lap, adjusting her shirt to nurse the baby. The scene should have been normal, but Kevin's lingering gaze made Aaron's skin crawl. Kevin watched his daughter like a man starving for something more than affection.

Aaron shifted uncomfortably in his seat as Maritza moved silently behind him, clearing away dishes. She shook her head when he offered to help clean up, silently whisking the dirty plates away. Cherry cobbler replaced the remnants of dinner. Its sweet smell filled the room. Kevin focused on the small amount of Lindsey's breast visible as she fed the baby. His eyes locked there with a hungry glint.

"Maritza, grab me a beer," Kevin barked without moving his eyes. She nodded and disappeared into the kitchen, returning with a cold bottle.

Aaron took a slow, measured breath, the moment building inside him. He needed to disrupt this disturbing scene. "Maritza," he asked, his voice calm but pointed, "how old are you?"

Maritza's eyes widened, darting to Kevin for approval. Kevin tore his gaze from Lindsey and turned his full attention to Aaron. "She's 40. Why do you ask?" His voice was low, warning.

Aaron held his gaze, unblinking. "That's funny. I'd have guessed she was closer to 38." Maritza froze, her hands holding a dessert bowl inches above the place in front of Aaron. "How'd you land such a young wife, Kevin?"

For a moment, a tense silence stretched between them. Then, Kevin's face split into a wide, toothy grin, and he let out another of his booming laughs. "Just got lucky, I guess! I'm a charmer, you know. She saw a good thing in me and grabbed it."

Aaron forced a smile, but inside, the disgust churned hotter. Kevin's response might have seemed lighthearted, but the truth felt darker than the room's pleasant warmth.

Aaron took a slow bite of the cherry cobbler. It was tart, the sweetness sharp on his tongue. "And the little kids, Kevin?" he asked, setting his fork down. "Why choose to adopt such young kids at your age?"

The atmosphere shifted. Kevin's fork clattered into his bowl, the sound cutting through the room like a warning bell. His jovial expression dimmed, his eyes hardening. "Time for bed, kids," he barked. "Eli, Casey, upstairs. Wash up and get into your pajamas. Your mama will be up to tuck you in. No arguments."

The two children slipped from the table without a word, their small frames moving toward the stairs.

Kevin's attention then snapped to Malachi and Maggie. "You two, upstairs. And no..." His thick finger rose like a judge delivering a sentence. "Not a word. Bed. Now."

Malachi's lips pressed into a tight line, his face contorted with anger, but he obeyed, rising from the table and walking out with a stiff, defiant gait. His silence was louder than anything he could have said.

The room stilled after they left. Kevin's beady eyes fixed on Aaron, and his voice carried a low, simmering edge. "Why the questions, Aaron?"

Aaron didn't flinch, keeping his tone calm and measured, though inside, his nerves buzzed. "I just want to understand, that's all. You're what, 65? Maybe 6? You've got a 4o-year-old wife and plenty of kids. Yet you decide to adopt little ones now. Start over, in a sense. I wonder why."

The room seemed to hold its breath. Kevin's grin was long gone, replaced by a cold, calculating look. Aaron stared back, ignoring the electrical tension surrounding them.

Kevin took a slow bite of his dessert. "Well, I'll tell you, Aaron. Kids are special. Kids are... well, kids are everything. They're the best of people, I think. I love children. Why not have as many as I can?" His tongue reached out to lick the cherry remaining on his fork, and Aaron suppressed a shudder.

Around the table, Jackson ate without a sound, and Lindsey's eyes remained glued to her baby. Mark was the only one who didn't seem to listen, caught up in feeding dessert to his three-year-old daughter.

Kevin continued, "So I guess that's my answer: because I love children, Aaron."

"Oh, I know you do," Aaron's voice came out harsher than he intended.

Kevin's eyes flickered, his fork hovering mid-air. He smiled, but it didn't reach his eyes. "What's that supposed to mean?" His voice remained calm, but there was a dangerous undertone beneath the words.

Aaron held his gaze, refusing to back down. "It means," Aaron said, leaning forward, his voice low and controlled, "you have a real... affection for children. Seems like you'd go to great lengths to surround yourself with them. To keep them close."

Kevin's smile faltered, but only for a second. "Children need love, Aaron. Guidance. They need someone to show them the way." His eyes narrowed, but his tone remained as smooth as ever. "And I give them that."

Aaron's knuckles whitened as he gripped the table, every muscle in his body tense. "I'm sure you do," he replied, the words sharp, like shards of glass. He seized the moment, no longer filtering the words spilling out. "Hey, Maritza?"

She froze mid-scrub at the sink, her hands submerged in the soapy water, glancing over Kevin's shoulder, her eyes cautious. "Yes?"

"It's funny," Aaron began, his voice casual but his heart racing. "I was going through some old files from my dad's place. I found a newspaper clipping. The girl in the picture... she looked just like you." He leaned forward, meeting her gaze. "Her name was Maria, though. Maria Delgato, from Guatemala."

The clink of dishes stopped, and her shoulders stiffened. Her eyes, wide and unblinking, locked onto Aaron's. He pressed on as the tension in the room thickened. "There were kids too. A brother and a sister." He glanced toward the hallway where Eli and Casey had disappeared moments ago. "They looked just like your two."

Kevin's chair scraping across the floor made a sound that cut through the air as he stood abruptly. His hands, heavy and meaty, gripped the white tablecloth. His gaze bore into Aaron, nostrils flaring.

Aaron didn't blink. "And a girl..." He turned his attention to the blond woman. "Lindsey, you could've been that little girl's twin. The one from one of those articles. Kidnapped, along with the others."

Silence swallowed the room. Lindsey's hand stilled on her baby, her face draining of color. Even Mark, who had seemed indifferent all night, paused mid-spoonful, his gaze flicking between Aaron and Kevin.

Kevin's face darkened, his skin blotchy with rage. His voice, low and tight, broke the silence like a threat. "It's time for you to leave, boy."

Aaron didn't move. He'd already come too far to back down. His heart raced, but his voice was steady as he held Kevin's furious gaze. "You see, that's the thing, Kevin. I don't think I'm ready to leave just yet."

Maritza's hands remained in the soapy water, trembling as her wide eyes darted between Aaron and her husband. Lindsey shifted in her chair, clutching her baby closer to her chest, her face pale and lips tight. Mark, who had caught up to the tension in the room, straightened up in his seat, his eyes confused but wary.

Kevin's face turned an alarming shade of red, the veins in his neck bulging as he moved to walk around the table. "I said it's time for you to go, boy," he growled, his voice low and dangerous, all pretense of joviality gone.

Aaron pushed his chair back. He stood but made no move toward the door. "You think this is over, Kevin? Do you think you can throw me out, and it all disappears? What about them?" He nodded toward Lindsey and Maritza. "Do they even know the truth?"

Kevin took a step closer, looming over the table, his massive frame casting a shadow over everyone. "I said get out. Now." His voice had dropped to a menacing whisper, but the threat in his tone was unmistakable.

Aaron glanced at Maritza, her face pale as she seemed to shrink at her husband's anger, her eyes pleading. He looked at Lindsey, who avoided his eyes.

He took a deep breath, keeping his eyes on Kevin. "You'd have to make me."

Kevin stepped even closer, his chest heaving with his rage, eyes blazing. "Boy," he growled, "you do not know what you're stepping into." With a sudden motion, he whirled around, his boots pounding against the wide heartwood planks of the floor. The front door slam echoed through the room, making Mark jump. Sophia, startled, let out a piercing wail, her toddler body shaking as she dissolved into tears.

Outside, Kevin kicked the storm door open, the sound of it banging against the wall rattling through the house. His voice, booming and furious, roared from outside. "If you want to talk to me, you'll do it outside my house!"

32

A heavy silence hung in the air. Aaron glanced around the table. The wide-eyed, terrified faces told him everything he needed to know. Lindsey sat frozen, clutching her baby. Jackson's hand gripped his spoon, his eyes fixed on the cobbler's remnants. Mark seemed paralyzed, one arm still halfway raised toward his crying toddler.

The only one who met Aaron's gaze was Maritza. Her lips parted, poised to speak, before snapping shut. Her eyes showed what she couldn't say: fear, resignation, and a plea for change.

Aaron spoke, his voice soft but even as he broke the silence. "I'm sorry, guys. Everything I said is true." He paused, looking between Lindsey and Maritza. "But you already knew it, I'm sure." Turning, Aaron moved toward the door. The cool night air hit him as he stepped outside into the darkness. Kevin was pacing in the gravel driveway. His massive frame cut an ominous silhouette against the dim porch light.

"You want to talk?" Kevin growled, his eyes narrowed, fists clenched. "Then let's talk." His face contorted. His skin was blotchy and red. Veins pulsed beneath the surface, ready to explode. "I invited you to my house, to eat at my table, and this is what I get?" His voice cracked, and the surrounding air seemed to vibrate with rage. He stepped forward, the force of his words pushing the air between them. "This is how you repay me? With lies and accusations? Pulled from where? Tell me!" His breath came in short bursts, his eyes wild as he glared at Aaron.

"Shut up," Aaron spat, stepping to the edge of the porch. The rawness in his voice sliced through Kevin's tirade like a knife. "How dare you stand there and pretend you're an innocent man? Like you haven't ruined every life you've touched. You don't remember me, huh? I was there. I know who you are."

Kevin blinked, a split second of confusion crossing his face before he erupted again. "You're out of your damn mind! Just as thick in the head as your old man said you were. Do you think you can throw accusations at me? Don't you know who I am?" His voice rose, almost hysterical, as he jabbed a finger into his chest. "I'm a big deal! People respect me, boy! You think you can walk onto my farm, into my house, and disrespect me?"

Aaron didn't flinch, his eyes locked on Kevin. His pulse was pounding, but he wouldn't let Kevin see that. "How did you pay for this farm, Kev? Is the meat-packing business that good? Or maybe it's the cocaine." Aaron's voice dropped, but the words hit like a hammer. "You think no one knows what you and your buddies were up to?"

Kevin stopped in his tracks, his whole body stiffening. For the first time, Aaron saw it—panic. A flicker of fear flashed across Kevin's eyes, masked by fury. The truth landed. Kevin knew it. He stepped forward, his breath coming in short, angry puffs. "So that's what this is? Digging up buried things? You're treading dangerous ground, boy. You don't know what you're talking about."

Aaron stood tall, still on the porch, looking down at Kevin. "I know enough," he said, his voice calm but sharp. "Enough to know you don't deserve any of this. Not this farm. Not that family. And not anyone's respect. You think you've scared everyone into silence, but people know, Kevin. You can't erase what you've done."

Kevin let out a sharp, humorless laugh, shaking his head. "You think you're a hero now? Like anyone's going to believe you after all these years? You're nothing, Aaron. A nobody with a chip on your shoulder. Just like your real father."

Aaron stepped onto the first step of the porch. His voice was low, but each word cut deep. "Maybe I'm nobody. But I know who you are. And so does everyone else, even if they're too afraid to say it. Including her." He tilted his head at the house. Maritza's silhouette was behind the curtain, witnessing the exchange.

Kevin's nostrils flared. His hands trembled. He wanted to swing. His breath came in rapid, shallow bursts, the anger pouring out of him like steam. "You've made a big mistake coming here tonight," he hissed. "And it's the last one you'll ever make."

Aaron didn't waver. "The only mistake I made was not coming sooner." His words hung in the air, heavy and unshakable.

Kevin's face contorted into something ugly and familiar, the veins in his neck bulging as he sneered. "You're like your mother. So self-righteous: always judging, always bitching. I know where you get this from."

Aaron didn't flinch. He let the words wash over him, stepping forward instead of retreating. He spoke in a cold, calm voice. "Limon, Colorado: February '87." He took another step down from the porch.

Kevin's smirk wavered, but he held his ground.

"Alamosa, Colorado: June '88."

He took another step. The old man's eyes flickered with something —fear. His body shifted back, just a fraction.

"Benton, California: December 1990."

Aaron's feet hit the dirt, standing inches from Kevin now. Each name and date hit like a hammer, cracking Kevin's armor.

"Axapusco, Mexico: April 1991."

Kevin took a step back, his eyes wide, wild. "You don't know what you're talking about," he muttered, but his voice had lost its edge.

Aaron looked the old man up and down with disgust. "What happened with that one, Kev?" His voice dripped with venom. "I don't see her in your little flock. Did you boys sell her after you used her up? Or did she put up too much of a fight and end up in a shallow grave?"

Kevin's breath hitched, his eyes darting away for the briefest moment. His bluster was gone, replaced by something darker—fear, guilt, maybe both. But Aaron didn't stop. He leaned in, his voice a whisper.

"What did you do with her, Kevin?" The old man spun on his heel, fury in every movement as he stormed toward the barn, his boots kicking up dust. "You're just making shit up now, boy! You've got nothing!" His voice rang out in the night, desperate, a cornered animal fighting to hold on to control.

Aaron followed him, his steps measured and his voice calm.

"Flores, Guatemala: August 1992." He paused. "Your lovely wife, Maritza. I'm sorry, Maria. She's only 38, you know, Kev. You took her when she was 14. Married her at 16."

Kevin's shoulders stiffened, but he kept walking, his fists clenched at his sides.

Aaron didn't stop. "Where was I? Shelby, Montana: April 1994."

That's when Kevin whipped around, his face panicked. "Stop!" he screamed, his voice cracking. "Where are you getting those dates?"

Aaron moved closer. It took all his effort to hold back the rage pulsing through him. "I can keep going all night, Kevin," he breathed, his words cutting through the air like a knife. "And I wouldn't run out of those dates, you sick bastard."

Kevin's face blanched; his chest heaved with every breath.

"All those fishing trips… guess they weren't always about using up Rob's kids, were they?" Aaron stopped a couple of feet from the old man, towering over him. "Sometimes they were about fishing for other people's kids to claim as your own."

Kevin's rage faltered. His face drained of color, and fear crept into his eyes. Aaron's words hung between them. The truth was too powerful to deny.

"Disgusting," Aaron finished, his voice a low growl.

Kevin began pacing again. He clenched his fists until his knuckles turned bone white. His meaty hands twitched as if he were seconds away from trying to strangle Aaron. "You don't know shit, boy!" he spat, shooting Aaron a look of pure malice. His eyes glinted with cruel satisfaction as he circled him like a predator.

"You wanna stand there like some righteous prick, huh?" Kevin sneered, his tone dripping with hatred. "Like you're better than me? Do you know anything about your family? Hell, Rob hated you. He hated everything about you. You were a disappointment to him: weak and always complaining. He wouldn't have kept you around if he had an actual option. If your damn mother hadn't had something to say about it."

Aaron's anger simmered beneath the surface, but he didn't move.

Kevin laughed, a low, evil sound. "Oh yeah, your mother was always a bitch. She kept Rob from tossing you out like he should've. I always told him—get rid of her too, get yourself a younger one.

Someone who'd do as she's told without flapping her damn mouth all the time. Like your sister. The best thing that ever came out of your mother."

Aaron's face turned red, but he stayed frozen, his fist trembling.

Kevin's lips curled into a sickening grin, eyes dark with purpose. "Elise... now there's a girl who knows her place. Sweet, obedient, and willing." He savored his lips, eyes fixed on Aaron. "She knows how to make a man happy, Aaron. Real happy."

Aaron's breath came in sharp, shallow bursts, his body rigid with fury. Every word from Kevin was like a blade, twisting deeper into him. His body shook with the effort of holding back his rage. "I'll end you, you disgusting old man."

Kevin's cruel grin widened, unrepentant. "Give it your best shot, you little worm. Your big brother made threats, too. He thought he could shutter our business and said he'd bring the cops."

Aaron's eyes flashed with confusion. *Harrison? What?* He hadn't thought of him in days, focusing only on Kansas. Kevin's next words drove the point home even harder.

"Be a shame if you ended up with a heroin problem like he did."

Aaron's breath hitched. "What did you do to Harrison?"

Kevin lifted his shoulders in a casual gesture. "Oh, was that his name? I never learned it. That wasn't me. That was all Rob. Rob was in charge, the real puppet master. He was the smartest man in any room. You know, Roger tried to get smart like you once, too. He thought he could blackmail us. He was a sick man." Kevin's eyes narrowed, full of satisfaction.

"And you're not?"

Kevin's laughter erupted, harsh and mocking. "I'm a connoisseur of young ladies, that's all. Roger? That pervert liked little boys. I'm sure you remember. He sure did like your little ass, didn't he? Liked your brother Patty too, and he played better than you did." A cruel, mocking laugh accompanied his taunt.

Aaron's gaze was unflinching. "He was your friend. You were there too."

Kevin's laughter became a sneer. "He was my friend until he was no good to me. The idiot got caught and thrown in the pen, and then everybody knew what he was. Rob gave him another chance out in

Cali, but Roger fucked that up. He got greedy and wanted all the coke, all the rewards. Had to remind him who was in charge." He paused, a dark look in his eyes. "You know they found him with his brains splashed across his kitchen floor?"

Aaron's voice was a tight, cold accusation. "You did it."

Kevin's cruel grin widened. "Naw, that wasn't me. Didn't you hear me? I wasn't in charge and never wanted to be. My job was to meet the shipments. I was a good soldier and was well-rewarded for my service." His eyes flicked over to his wife, standing on the porch now. "Don't you think so? Look at my pretty wife. She's getting old, but hey, that's why I got Maggie and Casey now. And you know what? There's not a goddamn thing you can do about it, you fucking joke!"

Aaron's gaze hardened, his tone sharp as he cut through the pretense. "I have a question, Kev... that grandbaby in there. The little Hispanic one. Did you pick her out for future use?"

Kevin lunged forward, closing the space between them. "Get off my property, Aaron. You have nothing on me!"

Aaron's shoulders tensed as he turned to leave, his mission complete. "See you, Kev. Enjoy your flock while you can."

Kevin's voice cracked with frantic anger as he shouted after him. "You have nothing on me!" The sound of his laughter, wild and unhinged, followed Aaron as he walked away.

Aaron slid into the driver's seat of his SUV, slamming the door behind him. With a grim expression, he reached into his shirt pocket and pulled out a small digital recorder. He dropped it into the center console; the device making a soft clink against the plastic. He turned the key and the engine erupted into a deafening din. The SUV's engine started with a low growl, drowning out the fading echoes of Kevin's maniacal laughter.

The drive to the hotel felt eternal. He kept hearing Kevin's words: the taunts, the sickening laughter. The rush of satisfaction faded, replaced by nausea. Kevin was right about one thing—he held power in this town. He had been untouchable for years. *How much did that mean now, though?*

Harrison's face flashed in Aaron's mind, the brother he never knew, lying cold from a heroin overdose at 23. *A life stolen before he could even live it.* And Roger, dead on his kitchen floor with his brains splattered by the very people he trusted. Aaron felt a spike of dread in his gut. Kevin's threats felt larger than before. A*re they empty words, or a promise? Is he on the phone with Rob, demanding to know where my information came from? Rob will know. He will open his safe and know I took his red folder.*

He wondered what had happened when Kevin stormed back inside his house. *Did chaos erupt? Did everything snap back into position without a hitch?* He pictured Lindsey, Jackson, and Mark at the dining table. *Were they still sipping beer and cutting into their cobbler? Did they continue to force smiles while Maritza washed the dishes?* He shuddered at the thought of them ignoring the horrors beneath their roof.

Denial was a powerful beast. Aaron knew this all too well. It slithered through lives, suffocating reality until lies felt like home. If he ever doubted its reach, all he had to do was flip through his mother's book. It was a scrapbook of the selective truths Marlena had believed. It was a chronological betrayal of the reality behind the masks.

She survived by rewriting the past. She papered over the abuse, neglect, and all the things Aaron could never forget. He wondered if Maritza had started a book of her own yet. Whatever chaos Kevin stirred behind him, Aaron didn't care. Kirby had given him only ghosts and scars. He felt them all as he gritted his teeth against the pain in his hand. He pulled into the hotel parking lot and turned off his engine before his body caught up with his thoughts. *One more night*, he told himself. *Numb the pain. Sleep. Leave in the morning.*

But when he stepped out of the SUV, his senses sharpened. Two men loitered by the Arby's across the lot. One was tall; the other was shorter but thick, like a boulder. The squat man fiddled with a piece of wood, dragging lazy circles in the dirt, but the taller one locked eyes with Aaron.

"Hey man… got a cigarette?" The tall one moved toward him.

Aaron's gut clenched, a shot of fear rooting him for a beat too long. His instincts kicked in. He sidestepped, keeping his distance from the man.

"Hey! I'm talking to you!" The man's voice hardened, but Aaron only managed, "I don't smoke." His feet were already carrying him toward the hotel entrance.

He shoved through the glass doors. Relief washed over him as the lobby's fluorescent lights cast everything in sterile clarity. The space felt too quiet for 10 p.m. Aaron noticed the clerk emerging from the back office to give Aaron a nod. He returned the gesture, but quickened his pace toward the elevator. Something about the exchange felt off. The clerk shuffled papers. He glanced at the elevator where Aaron waited. The desk phone rang, and after a brief exchange, the man hung up, his eyes settling on Aaron again.

He stabbed at the elevator button, nerves firing. The light flashed, and he stepped in, his chest heaving as the doors thudded shut. His reflection in the elevator mirror stared back at him, drawn and exhausted. His hand throbbed, syncing with the memory of Kevin's sickening grin and his threats. He clenched his jaw, fighting back the nausea rising in his chest. *Get to the room. Numb the pain. Leave tomorrow.*

The elevator dinged. The doors slid open, revealing a dim, empty hallway. Aaron stepped out, his eyes scanning the corridor. No sound, no movement.

He let out a sudden breath, fingers scrambling to find the key card as he rushed to his room. Inside, his gaze darted around, scanning every corner, noting that housekeeping had cleaned his room. Nothing was out of place. He clicked the top lock with a sharp snap, then rushed to his suitcase. The red folder and his mother's book lay untouched where he had stashed them. A wave of relief washed over him—but it didn't last long.

A knock at the door sent his pulse racing. Glancing through the peephole, he spotted a man in a hotel uniform holding a covered silver tray. *Room service?* Aaron's brow furrowed. He had ordered nothing. Flipping the latch, he cracked the door open.

"Room service for you, sir?" The man stepped forward, nudging the door with his shoulder.

"No," Aaron snapped. "Wrong room."

"Are you sure? I could've sworn it was this room." The man bent, lowering the tray to the carpet. His free hand dipped into his pocket.

Aaron's stomach dropped. "It's not mine," he barked, slamming the door shut and locking it tight.

He pressed his ear against the door, muscles tense, breath shallow. Silence. After several minutes, he heard the faint sound of footsteps retreating down the hallway.

Aaron's forehead pressed hard against the door. He squeezed his eyelids closed. His breath came in short, uneven bursts. He strained to hear anything, but the faint shuffle of footsteps had long since faded. His muscles stayed tense. *Something is off.*

That knock—it had been too normal. A uniform, a silver tray, polite words. But the push against the door, the hand in the man's pocket—that sent his instincts screaming. *Get out.*

He took shallow breaths, trying to breathe. He backed away from the door, sinking onto the edge of the bed, cradling his broken hand against his chest. The pain throbbed, but it wasn't enough to ground him. Every noise in the hall, every shift in the building, crawled under his skin. It all seemed louder and sharper. He seized his phone from the nightstand, scanning for notifications to distract himself.

Nothing.

Shouts exploded in the hallway, piercing the air with sudden force. His pulse quickened. An arguing couple stopped right outside his door. Aaron froze, waiting, breath held. After a long minute, the voices shifted, moving into the room next to his. A door slammed, rattling the walls. The vibrations sent a shiver through him. His mind raced, picturing that man again. The deliberate nudge at the door. The hand, almost hidden, hanging at his side. *It wasn't a simple encounter. It was a setup.*

Aaron drew a shaky breath, trying to calm the panic clawing at him, but it was pointless. His gut screamed the truth: he couldn't stay.

Not here.

He had to leave. *Now.*

Within seconds, Aaron had zipped his suitcase and slung it off the bed. He tugged the curtain aside to scan the parking lot below. The two vagrants had shifted closer to the front entrance. Swinging a stick like a lightsaber, the stocky one slashed the air with exaggerated motions. The taller man leaned against a trash can, arms crossed, legs folded at the ankles. Aaron's breath caught. The way he lounged there was the same stance Kevin had taken, leaning against his mother's washing machine all those years ago. The memory flashed across his mind, quick and unsettling.

He forced it away and unlocked the door, taking care to be silent. The hallway stretched out before him, quiet and empty. With the suitcase dragging behind him, its wheels muffled by the thick carpet, he crept past the elevators. *No way am I going that way.* He needed to stay unseen, unheard. At the far end, the glowing red "EXIT" sign beckoned.

He pushed the door open with his shoulder, gripping the suitcase as it thudded down the stairs. Each bump echoed in the enclosed stairwell, his heart jumping with every thud. *Too loud,* his mind hissed, but there was no turning back. He reached the ground floor, the exit now a glass door leading into the dark. Beyond it, the night stretched out in stillness, broken only by the dim parking lot lights casting long, jagged shadows.

Stepping into the cold air, Aaron fixed his eyes on the parking lot. The breeze shifted, and with it, every shadow seemed to move. He yanked the suitcase behind him to start, but the clatter of wheels on asphalt echoed. He stopped, gripping the handle tighter. *They'll hear you. They'll see you.* He glanced toward the front of the building. The two men hadn't noticed him yet. One leaned with his head down, lost in thought or sleep, while the other paced, scanning the far side of the lot.

Aaron's pulse hammered. He'd have to make his move soon. His SUV sat halfway down the side of the building, just out of sight. If he could keep quiet, he'd have a chance. *Go,* his instincts screamed. *Now.*

33

Aaron sucked in a sharp breath, the cold air biting his lungs. He lifted the suitcase with his left hand and broke into a run. Each step felt too loud: his feet slapping against the pavement as he neared his SUV. He dropped the suitcase, fumbling for the keys. The wheels scraped against the ground, echoing in the stillness. *Too loud.*

The tall man straightened, his eyes locking on Aaron. "Hey, man!" His voice cut through the night as he started toward him, quick strides closing the gap.

Aaron's pulse spiked. He yanked open the SUV door, tossing the suitcase into the passenger seat. His keys slipped in his sweaty fingers as he tried to shove them into the ignition. The tall figure moved faster now, his shadow stretching across the hood. With the key jammed in the ignition, Aaron's shaking left hand struggled to get the right angle. *Come on, come on.* He gritted his teeth, twisting the key. The engine roared to life as the man slapped a dirty palm against the window.

"You got a cigarette, man?" The man's breath fogged the glass, fingers smearing across the window as he pressed his face close.

Aaron didn't answer. His heart pounded in his ears, every muscle tense as he shifted into reverse. He slammed his foot onto the gas without a second thought. The SUV lurched backward; the tires squealed as he peeled out of the parking space. He looked away from the blur of shadows in the mirror.

As Aaron turned onto the road, panic gripped him. *The voice recorder!* His heart raced. He plunged his hand into the center console, fingers fumbling against the armrest. *It should be right there.*

The top tray was empty, and the void hit him like a punch to the gut. His breath came in ragged gasps. The lights from the street blurred into streaks. Sweat beaded on his forehead. *Where is it?* His cast made it impossible to reach the bottom.

Desperation clawed at him. He tried to calm his breathing, focusing on each shallow inhale. He glanced in the rearview, half-expecting to see the two men chasing him with that stick. *What if the room service guy had something more dangerous in his pocket — a gun or a needle? He was coming after me! Get it together, man.* He thumbed the button to roll his window down just a crack. The rush of cold air hit his face, clearing his head.

He pulled into the parking lot of the urgent care clinic. His eyes darted to the hotel in the distance. He eased into a spot facing the building, the gears clicking into place as he shifted to "park."

He turned in his seat, peering down into the center console. There, wedged in the bottom corner, lay the voice recorder. The bumpy road must have jostled it from the top tray. Relief washed over him. *Thank God.*

Aaron leaned against the headrest — his eyes shut tight, forcing his breathing to slow. He inhaled through his nose and exhaled through his mouth, trying to calm the tremors in his chest.

A sudden, sharp tap on the window yanked him out of his trance. His eyes flew open to see a pale face framed by a halo of bright red hair. Purple nails drummed an impatient rhythm on the glass.

He flicked the window down another inch, just enough to hear her voice. "Well hey there, Mr. Callahan. Did you decide you needed something after all?"

The nurse's long lashes fluttered as she winked with one big blue eye. "I can hop right in. I just got off work."

He blinked, confused and wary. *Was she part of some trap?* His instincts bristled. "No," he said, more sharply than he intended. "I have to go."

Her expression was the picture of disappointment: her bottom lip jutting out in a pout. "Oh, well... okay."

He shifted into reverse, his gaze still locked on her. "I'm sorry... Annie. I have to go now."

He maneuvered the vehicle into a right turn toward the interstate, glancing in the mirror. Annie remained on the curb, her forlorn figure shrinking into the distance.

Aaron sped down I-70 West, the surrounding night a wall of darkness. Music pounded through the speakers, the bass thudding in time with the dull ache in his cast. He was bone-tired, but fear kept his foot on the gas. When he crossed into Colorado, a slight weight lifted off his chest. *Don't get comfortable, Aaron. Complacent men die on kitchen floors.*

The thought sent a chill through him, sharper than the stiff wind rocking his SUV. By 12:30 a.m. His body screamed for a break. The pain, the exhaustion—it was all catching up to him. *I need to walk around. Grab some caffeine.* His eyes scanned the highway signs.

He took the next exit, pulling into a small gas station with a handwritten sign in the window that read, "Closes at 1." He stepped out, stretching his stiff legs. A heavyset woman with a hairnet sat behind the counter, staring ahead.

Aaron grabbed a soda and an energy drink, eyeing the clock. "Let me get one of those energy shots too," he said, pointing to the display behind her. "It's way past my bedtime." He forced a chuckle, hoping for a response.

The woman didn't look amused. She rang up his items without a word; her face set in a scowl. Aaron swallowed his disappointment and paid with cash. He downed three Tylenol and chugged half the soda. He needed to keep moving, but the miles dragged on, his eyelids growing heavier with each one.

Thirty minutes later, the caffeine wasn't cutting it. His head sagged, and he knew he had to stop. He took another exit: the road was dark and empty. A gas station with no lights on sat just off the highway. He pulled into a spot on the side, away from the street.

After double-checking the door locks, he pulled his jacket hood up and cranked the heat a notch. Warmth wrapped around him. As soon as his head hit the seat, sleep claimed him.

A sharp knock jolted Aaron awake, his heart pounding in his chest. Fear gripped him, Rob's face flashing in his mind. He blinked, disoriented, shaking the thought away as the knock came again, sharper this time. A man stood outside, broom in hand, his expression apologetic. Aaron cracked the window, just an inch.

"Sir, you can't sleep here. You gotta move along, or I'll have to call the cops."

Aaron gave a tight nod. "Yeah, understood. I'm going."

Goddamnit.

He shoved his hood back, fingers running through his tangled hair. The dashboard clock glowed with the time: 1:45 a.m. He muttered a curse, shifting into reverse. As he pulled away, the man with the broom gave a small wave, his smile awkward and apologetic. Aaron raised his hand.

He'd been hoping for more than a 45-minute nap, but the rude wake-up did the job. He felt more alert now, his mind sharpening again. The GPS flickered on, showing 114 miles to the airport. If he kept his speed, he could be out of the Midwest before the storm hit. *Just keep moving.*

At 3:36 a.m., Aaron crested the hill and the looming figure of Blucifer, the eerie blue horse outside Denver International Airport, came into view. He followed the signs to the rental car office. Tossing his trash into a nearby bin, he yanked his suitcase from the passenger seat. He slipped the voice recorder into the inner pocket of his coat, safe and close.

The line to return the rented vehicle was short. He didn't argue about the fee for the empty gas tank; stopping for gas had been out of the question. Suitcase in tow, he hurried through the terminal to the flashing boards showing flights.

Philadelphia wasn't an option. Kevin had called his stepfather by now, and even though the old man wouldn't drive to the airport in the middle of the night, the sun would rise soon. Aaron needed to stay ahead and keep his distance. His tired eyes darted over the board, crossing off cities one by one. *Dallas is too close. Same for Missouri or Iowa. Chicago? Charlotte? Rob had friends in those places—bad friends.*

Atlanta glowed at the top of the screen, and Aaron thought of Harrison. *No. That can wait. The priority is to get away from the Midwest and anyone connected to Rob.*

He stepped up to the United Airlines counter. "I need a seat on the next flight to Baltimore, Washington, DC, or New York," he said.

The young woman behind the desk raised an eyebrow. "Which one? Or all three?"

"Whichever leaves first. I saw a flight to Baltimore at 5:20?"

She glanced at the clock behind him. "It's 4:03 a.m., sir. You won't make that flight. We recommend two hours for security this time of morning."

Aaron exhaled hard. "What's the next flight I can make?"

She typed, her nails clicking against the keyboard. "There's a 6:30 to Washington, DC. The only seats left are First Class. That okay?"

"Yeah, that works."

With his boarding pass in hand, he rode the elevator up and joined the security line. He felt light-headed as he dropped his phone and the voice recorder into the plastic bin. He watched them disappear into the X-ray machine, his pulse racing until the recorder was in his coat pocket. *Safe again. For now.*

Once through security, Aaron grabbed a coffee and downed it in one gulp. The bitter liquid burned his throat, but he didn't care. Forty-eight hours without proper sleep: just bits of rest before the auction and a quick nap in the car. Exhaustion clung to him like a weight. But he couldn't afford to sleep yet. His phone buzzed in his hand: 6:04 a.m. Boarding would start soon.

He opened his messages and typed out a text to his secretary.

> 3/12/16 6:06 am
> To Nicole: I need a favor. The box of ledgers in my bedroom—hide it. You have keys. My mom's spider plant is on the kitchen table. Take it too.

3/12/16 6:08 am
From Nicole: Should I ask why?

> 3/12/16 6:09 am
> To Nicole: Please don't. Just take it to your house, not the office. It's important.

3/12/16 6:10 am
From Nicole: Consider it done, boss.

When they called first-class passengers, Aaron found his window seat. He squeezed his suitcase between his legs and moved the voice recorder to his pants pocket. Two chilled bottles of water rested in the cup holders, and he twisted one open, swallowing a Vicodin to numb the pain pulsing from his hand.

As the plane taxied, he pulled the thin airline blanket over his lap and leaned against the cool window. The horizon glowed, the first hints of sunrise casting light over the distant mountains. His eyes flickered closed, but he forced them open, watching the world come alive outside.

34

Aaron slept through the entire three hours and 14 minutes of the flight. When the plane touched down at Dulles International, he felt better able to focus. He grabbed his suitcase and headed straight for the rental car desk. A Subaru Forester with heated seats—perfect for the cold but milder DC weather—was soon his. He devoured the breakfast biscuit he'd grabbed at the airport and downed a cup of coffee with his morning Tylenol. The caffeine cut through the lingering fog.

Settling into the driver's seat, he pulled up the GPS, considering his next move. A quick text to Nicole confirmed she had hidden the ledgers as he'd asked. He punched in the address for Pottstown, where Nicole and her family lived. Rob would want his files, and Aaron knew his house wasn't safe. Rob would come for them and find the ledgers there, too. He might already be on his way.

Aaron sent Bethany a quick text before leaving the airport parking lot.

>3/12/16 10:15 am
>
>To Bethany: Sorry I've been out of touch — I'll be in Philly this evening. Hoping you're still down for dinner.

3/12/16 10:16 am

From Bethany: I was wondering when I'd hear from you. Def still interested! Know what time?

3/12/16 10:18 am
To Bethany: Aiming for 6:30 — same restaurant? I can pick you up.

3/12/16 10:19 am
From Bethany: Let's try new things! We'll decide when you pick me up. See you at 6:30!

Along with her message, she sent her street address. Aaron smiled. After everything this week had thrown at him, the thought of seeing her lifted his spirits. He tossed his phone onto the passenger seat and pulled out of the lot. The drive to Pottstown was three hours, but the Beltway was clear, and he cruised through downtown Baltimore, making better time than he expected.

Traffic slowed through the McHenry Tunnel but cleared on the other side. Aaron pulled into Nicole's driveway at 4:30 in the afternoon. She stepped out onto the porch, eyebrows shooting up at the sight of his cast.

"What did you do to yourself, boss?!"

He shrugged. "Got into a fight with a gate... it's a long story." He didn't want to lie to Nicole—after nine years of working together, they didn't do that to each other—but he wasn't ready to unpack it either.

She shook her head, amused. "I'm sure the gate had it coming. Care to elaborate?"

"Not today. But soon, okay?"

"Does it have something to do with that box you had me grab?" She held the door open for him, gesturing inside.

Aaron stepped into the warmth, glancing at her teenage son, Theo. The boy was playing Call of Duty. "Something to do with it, yeah. Yo, Theo, think you can help me with something?"

Without turning, Theo sighed. "Yeah, just a sec. I'm in a round."

Nicole rolled her eyes and waved Aaron toward the kitchen.

"Come on, boss. You look like you could use lunch."

"I'll take you up on that," he said, perching on a stool.

She got to work, and within minutes, a fresh club sandwich on rye, topped with sour cream and onion chips, sat in front of him. He dug in, devouring it. She set a glass of root beer next to his plate.

"You missed your calling as a chef," he said, wiping his mouth.

She laughed, but studied him with concern. "Are you okay? You don't look good."

Aaron chewed his last bite before responding. "I don't know. But I will be. Don't worry, you can keep things running. I'll be back in a few days."

Her smile faltered. "So you won't be in on Monday?"

"Nope. Got to finish what I'm working on. It can't wait."

Nicole's brow furrowed. "I wish you'd let me help."

He reached across the counter, squeezing her hand. "You always help. But I have to handle this alone. Won't be long, promise."

She nodded, her eyes concerned.

He finished his root beer and stood, turning toward the living room. "Hey, Theo! Did you finish yet?"

Theo's voice drifted out. "Yeah, yeah. What's up?"

"It's back here," Nicole called, leading them into the laundry room. "This box. Can you carry it to Uncle Aaron's car?"

The boy sighed but hoisted the box and followed Aaron to the car, setting it in the trunk before retreating to his video game.

"You sure you won't stay and rest, boss?" Nicole asked.

Aaron smiled. "Don't worry so much. I'm good." He gave her a quick hug and winked. "Besides, I've got a date tonight."

Her face lit up. "A date? That's fantastic! Is she a keeper?"

He hopped into his car and lowered the passenger window, grinning at her. "She might be. There's something special about her."

"Well, good luck!" Nicole waved, beaming.

"I'll be in touch," he promised, pulling away from the house and heading back on the road. On the drive to Philadelphia, Aaron called Alex, giving him a heads-up. "Might be best to steer clear of the house for a bit," he warned.

"No worries," Alex replied, accepting Aaron's vague explanation about Rob being angry without hesitation. "I've got a honey I can crash with for a few days. I'll let Jared know too."

With that settled, Aaron turned the music up, letting Imagine Dragons blast through the speakers. He sang along; the tension loosening from his shoulders. Just as he hit a high note, his phone chimed. He pressed the button on his steering wheel, waiting for the robotic voice to read the message.

3/12/16 5:47 pm
From Rob: We need to talk.

Aaron's stomach dropped. He cut the music and let the silence stretch, every mile filled with the pounding of his thoughts. *What the hell am I going to do? He's going to kill me.* He gripped the steering wheel tighter; jaw clenched as he sped toward Philly.

When he reached downtown, it was 6:20. He hit a red light and punched Bethany's address into the GPS. It wasn't far from the restaurant where they had first met, but it felt like a different world now. He glimpsed himself in the rearview mirror—tired eyes, rumpled clothes, days of stress, and no sleep written all over him. He wished he'd had time to shower, to change, but the past 72 hours had been a blur of caffeinated chaos. There had been no time for something as simple as that.

Bethany's neighborhood was much nicer than the one Aaron had grown up in. Gentrification had crept in, replacing the decay with pristine rowhomes and bright accents. Her home was brick, the front door painted a bold lime, and a wreath of bells jingled in the evening breeze. A planter with forget-me-nots and primrose sat on the small porch, adding a delicate touch. Aaron straightened his hair, adjusting what little he could. *It'll have to do.* He took a deep breath and knocked.

Bethany opened the door on the second knock, and for a moment, the stress of the past few days melted away. She looked stunning—her strawberry-blonde curls pulled back, framing a face that radiated warmth. Her blue eyes sparkled as she smiled.

"You're here!" she said, her excitement contagious.

"I'm here," he replied, grinning back. He hesitated for a second before leaning in for a light kiss, but she pulled him in closer, her hands finding his neck and jaw, deepening the kiss. Her touch lingered on his arms until she bumped into the cast.

"Oh, my God! What happened?"

Aaron shrugged it off. "Let's talk about it over dinner."

She nodded, glancing up the stairs. "Okay, give me one second to grab my purse." She motioned for him to come inside before jogging upstairs.

Aaron admired the soft, calming decor of her living room. It felt simple, yet elegant, like everything about her. He felt a pang in his chest—a dangerous liking. *Terrible timing.* He knew all too well how fast this could unravel.

Bethany descended the stairs, looking beautiful in tight blue jeans, winter boots, and an oversized cream sweater that slipped off one shoulder, exposing her collarbone. He couldn't hold it in. "Gorgeous," he muttered, still a little awestruck.

She beamed. "Well, thank you, sir. You look pretty gorgeous yourself."

He laughed, not believing it, dressed in the same dark jeans and flannel overshirt he'd been wearing for two days. But her compliment made him feel lighter. He took her arm, escorting her to the passenger side of his rental car, ready for a night that felt like a brief escape from everything spiraling around him.

"Where to?" Aaron asked, fiddling with the heat and adjusting the mirror. The nerves were creeping in. He hadn't been on a proper date in ages. He felt like a schoolboy, unsure of himself.

Bethany tapped her finger against her chin, her eyes playful as she considered the options. "Hmm... we could do Tony Luke's or Reading Terminal Market, but if you want to talk, maybe somewhere like The Cheesecake Factory. Your call."

"The Cheesecake Factory it is," he smiled, feeling more at ease. "I owe you a few explanations."

She reached over, touching the free fingers of his injured hand. "You owe me nothing," she breathed. "But I'll listen to you, regardless."

Her touch made his stomach twist in a way he hadn't expected. It was a reminder that despite the chaos swirling around him, someone cared.

The hum of conversation filled the air of the packed restaurant as they waited over 45 minutes for a table. Bethany updated him on her week, her light stories distracting him for a while before she turned her focus to his cast, brushing her fingers across it.

"What happened to your hand, Aaron?"

He hesitated, taking a deep breath. "It's a long story. I... well, I—"

"Callahan, party of two," a server called, saving him from the answer. They followed her through the maze of tables to a cozy booth.

After ordering their drinks—a whiskey ginger for him and a Georgia peach vodka for her—Bethany asked again. "So, your hand?"

He felt the heat rise in his face. "It's embarrassing. I punched a gate. An iron gate." He paused. "I... my mom died last year. Her name was Marlena. She was incredible. I miss her a lot."

Bethany listened, her face soft with empathy. "I'm so sorry, Aaron."

He nodded, swallowing hard. "She left me a book. It's kind of like a diary of all of her memories. There's a lot of good in it," he said, sipping the drink the server placed by him. "Mm, speaking of good."

Bethany smiled as she sipped hers. "Mine too. They make great drinks here."

The server interrupted again, asking if they were ready to order. They hadn't even glanced at the menus. "Give us a few more minutes, please," Aaron said. He looked at Bethany. "Let's figure out food, then I'll continue."

They flipped through the massive menu, debating options. Aaron settled on the bang-bang chicken and shrimp.

"So, you're in the mood for spicy tonight?" Bethany teased, a playful glint in her eyes.

Aaron grinned. "What can I say? It's been that kind of week."

She laughed. "Well, I guess I'll have to match your mood." She ordered the Cajun jambalaya pasta with a side salad.

Aaron grinned. "Good idea. Let me get one of those salads too," he added, smiling at the server.

The server took their menus and disappeared into the sea of tables, leaving them in the cozy bubble of their booth. Aaron exhaled, feeling the moment catch up with him. "So, where was I?"

Bethany leaned in, her eyes focused on him. "Your mom's book... the memories."

Aaron traced the rim of his drink with his fingers, eyes distant.

"All of her memories are in this book she left. It's like she's talking to me, even though she's gone." His voice dropped. "But it's not all good. Some of it... some of it's dark. Stuff I remembered, and things I didn't. Stuff I wish I hadn't."

Bethany's gaze stayed on him, her fingers playing with the condensation on her glass, silent but steadfast.

"I needed to know if it was all real," he said, voice rough. "I had to prove it to myself. And, well..." He lifted his cast, a simple answer to his unfinished sentence. "Now, it's more complicated."

He slumped back in his chair. "I thought I'd find peace, you know? But all it's done is drag up old ghosts, things I buried long ago."

Bethany reached across the table, her hand resting on his cast. "You don't have to do this alone, Aaron."

He looked at her hand, then met her eyes. "It's hard to know who to trust right now," he admitted. "But I'm trying."

She gave his hand a gentle squeeze. "One step at a time. You don't have to figure it all out tonight." Her smile was reassuring.

Aaron exhaled, nodding. "Yeah. One step at a time."

As they lingered over their meal, the conversation flowed. When the server returned, asking if they wanted dessert, Bethany shook her head with a grin. "No way. I have no room for dessert."

Aaron chuckled at her, pausing for a moment before smirking. "Yes. We'll take a whole red velvet cheesecake to go."

Bethany's eyes widened in mock horror. "What are you doing?"

"You'll thank me later. There's nothing like a late-night cheesecake," he said with a grin, then added to the server, "And the check too, please."

When they stepped out into the chilly night air, Bethany slipped her hand into his. "This was fun, Aaron. Thanks."

He bent to kiss her, and she leaned in, her lips brushing his as she whispered, "You were right. I am looking forward to dessert."

His heart quickened as they walked back to the car. By the time they pulled up to her rowhome, her hand had drifted to his right thigh, and any fatigue he had felt earlier vanished.

Opening her door, he helped her out, and she rewarded him with another kiss. Once they stepped through her front door, she took two steps up the stairs, pulling off her sweater in one motion. Turning back, she beckoned him with one long finger. "Come have dessert?"

He did not need to be asked twice.

"Have I mentioned how much I like you?" Bethany laughed as she slid from atop him, settling into the crook of his arm. She tossed a lean leg over him, nuzzling her head into his chest.

"Nah, I don't think I caught that part," Aaron teased, wrapping his arm around her and giving her side a playful tickle. She giggled, retaliating with her own tickling as they tumbled together, skin against skin until he pinned her body beneath him.

His hand cradled her jaw as they kissed, mouths hungry, breath mingling. When he pulled back, he searched her eyes, smiling. "You want some cheesecake?"

She laughed again, her voice like warm honey. "Of course I do!"

Aaron hopped out of bed, taking the stairs two at a time to grab the cheesecake he'd abandoned on the foyer table in his hurry to get upstairs. Bethany's voice floated from the bedroom, light and teasing. "Forks are in the second drawer by the fridge."

He returned moments later, sliding back under the covers and cracking open the container. She didn't wait, stabbing her fork into the cake and offering him a bite with a sly grin.

"Mm, almost as good as you," he teased.

Bethany chuckled. "Almost?" Aaron scooped up a piece for her, leaning closer to guide it to her lips. "Okay, you're right. This is almost as good as me."

Her laughter rang through the room, bright and carefree. They took a few more bites, but soon set the dessert aside, finding warmth in each other's arms. Aaron glanced at the clock—11:36 p.m.—and felt the week's exhaustion settle over him. The stress that had plagued him seemed to fade, if only for the moment.

"I'm so tired," he whispered against Bethany's neck, his eyes growing heavy.

She curled into him, fingers stroking his hair, her lips brushing his. "Then let's sleep," she whispered, her tongue just grazing his lips in a soft kiss.

Aaron smiled, closing his eyes as Bethany's warmth surrounded him. He listened to the soft rhythm of her breathing against him. With a last kiss, he let himself drift, feeling safe and content for the first time in weeks. Her presence felt like a quiet promise beside him.

35

Aaron cracked a smile as the sunlight nudged him awake, spilling through the crack in the curtains. The cozy bed made him want to sink back into sleep, but the dull ache in his hand wouldn't allow that. He shifted, feeling the sheets tangled around his legs. The house was quiet as he surveyed Bethany's room.

A sound from downstairs caught his attention, and he sat up, spotting his jeans on the floor. He'd just finished buttoning them when Bethany appeared, balancing a brown bag and a tray that filled the room with the smell of coffee and breakfast.

"Already dressed?" she teased, setting the food on the nightstand. "You were sleeping so hard, I didn't want to wake you."

He stepped behind her, spinning her around to kiss her. "You're wonderful, you know that?" The sincerity in his voice made her smile.

"I'm so glad you're here, Aaron," she whispered, her voice filled with affection.

Bethany busied herself pulling biscuits and hashbrowns from the bag and arranging them on napkins across the bed. Aaron grabbed his phone, but the screen was dark. "Damn," he muttered under his breath.

"What's wrong?" Bethany's tone shifted, suddenly concerned.

"Phone's dead," he said, holding it up as proof.

"No problem, I've got a charger." She reached out, taking the phone from him and plugging it in on her dresser. "Now, come eat."

They ate and talked. Aaron shared surface details about his family—the six siblings, two he'd never met, the four nieces and nephews scattered across different homes, the constant moving in his childhood. Bethany listened, adding in bits of her life between bites.

Mid-breakfast, their eyes locked, and the spark ignited again. The food lay forgotten as they gravitated toward each other, making love in the quiet warmth of the morning. Later, they showered together. Bethany wrapped his cast in a plastic bag, then washed his hair and face. When the water hit his face, Aaron flinched, anxiety surging through him as he stepped forward. She understood without a word, guiding him back and directing the water away from his face. He kissed her then, pinning her against the cold tile, claiming her once more.

Aaron sighed as they dried off. "All my clean clothes are in the car," he said. He pulled his jeans on and started down the stairs. "Be right back," he called over his shoulder.

Bethany's voice followed with a teasing laugh. "You need a shirt! It's March, Aaron!"

He waved her off. "I'll be fine. Big tough man."

The moment he opened the door, cold air smacked him in the face, biting his bare skin. It was below 40 degrees, and he regretted his decision instantly. Barefoot and freezing, he sprinted across the sidewalk to his Subaru, grabbed his suitcase, and hurried back inside, shivering.

"Told ya!" Bethany teased, tousling her damp hair with a fluffy towel. "Need me to warm you up again, big tough man?" She pressed her hands against his chilled chest.

Aaron chuckled, kissing the tip of her nose. "At this rate, I'll never get dressed." He fumbled through his suitcase, fishing out a clean change of clothes. As he undressed, he remembered the voice recorder in his pants pocket, slipping it into the front compartment of his bag.

Bethany caught the motion. "What's that?"

"Nothing, just a recorder. Don't want to lose it." He unbuttoned his flannel shirt, struggling with the sleeve to fit his cast through.

Without a word, Bethany jumped up to help. Her fingers guided the fabric over his hand, folding the sleeve back over his forearm where the cast ended. She bent down, kissing the cast. "Your poor hand."

Aaron touched her chin, lifting her gaze to meet his. "Where did you come from? I wasn't looking for you… but here you are. Beautiful, sweet, and…" He trailed off, words failing him, as she rose on her toes to kiss him.

"You have a way with words, Aaron Callahan," she murmured against his lips. "I'll bet you'd be a wonderful storyteller."

He sat back on the bed, smiling. "What kind of story do you want to hear?"

She settled beside him, her eyes curious. "Tell me more about your mother's book. It sounds fascinating."

Aaron smiled, adjusting the sleeve of his flannel shirt as he sat beside her. "The book is… kind of like a diary, but more than that. It's a record of my mom's life. Memories, thoughts, things she never said out loud. I've been reading through it, trying to piece together things I never knew or didn't understand when I was younger."

Her eyes widened with interest. "That sounds incredible. What's in it?"

He ran his fingers through his hair, a little hesitant. "It's got everything. The good stuff, the hard stuff… things I didn't even realize happened. Some parts are heavy. But… some are normal moments, everyday stuff. The kind you don't appreciate until later."

She smiled, resting her hand on his. "I'd love to see it if you're okay with that."

"Yeah, of course." He bent down, unzipping his suitcase and pulling the book from beneath a few layers of clothes. He flipped through the pages, pausing here and there to show her small passages. "This one's about a summer road trip when I was a kid. I didn't even remember the trip until I read this. Funny how much you forget." He turned another page, skimming the lines before moving on.

Bethany leaned in closer, her curiosity piqued. "Do you want to read something to me?"

Aaron paused, thoughtful. "Yeah, I do. But I want to make sure it's… light. Not too much." He leafed through the pages, searching for the right memory without too much emotion. Finally, he found it—a small entry, simple and unburdened. He smiled softly and looked at her. "I think I've got one."

* * *

August 27, 1997: Marlena

I stood on the balcony, gazing at the empty spot where Rob had parked his car. He'd left after breakfast, saying something about running an errand. Now, with the kids down at the beach, the room felt too quiet. I had hoped for this trip to be a chance for the two of us to reconnect. Instead, we were sharing a room with Elise, and Rob was nowhere to be found. I sighed, grabbed my towel, and decided I had waited long enough.

The salty breeze hit me as I walked across the sand. Seeing my kids all playing together eased my earlier frustration. Aaron, so tall and lean at fifteen, balanced at the far end of the jetty, squinting into the water. Patty, a year younger but almost as tall, pointed out a spot in the tide pools, his dark hair plastered to his forehead. His tanned skin glowed under the sun.

Nico and Lucas huddled over a sandcastle, digging trenches around it to create a wide moat. Elise, just a few feet away, buried her feet in the wet sand, squealing as the waves rushed over her toes.

Everything else faded away. The missed connection with Rob and the disappointment of another day slipping by didn't matter. Watching the kids laugh and play, with the sun casting a golden light over the water; it felt like time had stopped. These moments remind me why we come back to Morro Bay year after year.

Next week, we'll be shopping for school clothes. Aaron starts high school, and though he won't admit it, I can see he's nervous. But he'll be fine—he's so charismatic, even more than Patty, and he's such a charmer.

I wish Rob was here. It's been hours since he left, and I had hoped for some time alone with him today. We haven't had a moment to ourselves in weeks, maybe months. I wonder where he went. I wonder why he disappears when I need him.

Aaron finished reading the passage and looked at Bethany. She had been watching him, her eyes lighting up with a smile. "It's beautiful. I can almost see it. She wrote that?" She leaned in to study the page.

"Not exactly," Aaron said, his voice hesitant. "She paid for a procedure that extracts all your memories. They implant a chip—it outputs everything, even stuff you might not think you remember. After her death, they sent it to me."

"That's crazy cool. I've heard of it but never seen it. Mind if I flip through?" She reached for the book, but Aaron closed it, setting it on his suitcase.

"Uh... I don't know. There's more bad than good, I think... maybe..."

Bethany pulled back. "Another time, maybe. I just got excited, sorry."

"No, don't apologize. I'm just—"

His phone interrupted, buzzing as it powered on, and the screen lit up with a cascade of notifications. *What the hell?*

"Well, someone sure is popular," Bethany said, glancing at the phone.

Aaron crossed the room, staring at the dozen messages blinking at him.

> 3/12/16 11:12 pm
> From Rob: We need to talk, Aaron.
>
> 3/13/16 1:56 am
> From Rob: Answer the phone.
>
> 3/13/16 4:33 am
> From Rob: I'm coming there to talk.
>
> 3/13/16 5:18 am
> From Rob: Are you at home?
>
> 3/13/16 8:34 am
> From Rob: You started this. Let's talk about it.

3/13/16 10:04 am
From Rob: We need to talk.

3/13/16 12:16 pm
From Rob: I'm knocking. Open the door.

3/13/16 12:23 pm
From Elise: Aaron, Dad drove there to see you. He's on your front porch, calling me worried about you. Where are you?

3/13/16 12:27 pm
From Rob: Answer the door, Aaron.

He checked the time: 12:40 pm. Rob was standing on his porch right now. The pit of anxiety in his chest grew, and everything else in the room seemed to shrink. He struggled to focus, his thoughts muddled by the rush of blood in his head. Bethany's voice was a distant murmur.

His phone chimed again.

3/13/16 12:41 pm
From Rob: Aaron, no more bullshit. I need my property now.

Bethany touched his arm. "You okay, Aaron?" Her eyes shone with concern.

He shook his head, pushing the anxiety aside. A new feeling took its place: resolve. No more running or hiding. It was time to face what he'd been avoiding. He looked at Bethany's face, apologizing with a small smile. "Everything's okay, but I need to go. Family business. It can't wait."

He gathered his mother's book, placing it back in his suitcase atop the Red Baron and Kirby files. He slipped into clean socks and laced up his boots. As he headed for the door, he stopped and turned to Bethany.

"I'm sorry to leave like this," he said.

Her smile was smaller now, tinged with sadness. "Will I see you again?"

He dropped the suitcase handle and walked to her. Cradling her face with one hand and the fingers of his injured hand, he gave her a deep, passionate kiss, holding her close. "I will be back if you'll have me." She nodded, and he gave her a small smile. "I promise, Bethany Lombard. I will be back."

He stepped back, grabbed his suitcase, and started down the stairs. From the top of the flight, Bethany called out. "You better be back, Aaron Callahan."

He turned, flashing a wide grin. "Of course. We haven't finished that cheesecake yet."

Outside, he set his suitcase in the trunk, flipping open the cardboard box to confirm that all the ledgers were there. Satisfied, he slammed the trunk shut and climbed into the car. He pulled away, still uncertain of his exact destination, but by the time he hit the interstate, a simple goal had formed in his mind: Doylestown.

Rob's texts kept coming every few minutes. Aaron ignored them, focusing on the road. He turned up the radio and pressed the gas pedal, speeding down the interstate.

> 3/13/16 12:51 pm
> From Rob: Where are you? Stop fucking around and come back.

> 3/13/16 1:02 pm
> From Rob: You do not know what you're messing with. Get back here now.

> 3/13/16 1:16 pm
> From Rob: This is your last chance, Aaron. Don't make me come find you.

3/13/16 1:23 pm
From Rob: If you think you can avoid this, you're wrong. I'm done waiting.

3/13/16 1:35 pm
From Rob: You're in deep shit. Answer the phone.

3/13/16 1:43 pm
From Rob: Aaron, please, just talk to me. I don't want to escalate this. Just come home.

3/13/16 1:51 pm
From Rob: I'm serious. This isn't a game. You need to face this.

3/13/16 1:58 pm
From Rob: I'm calling you now. Answer the phone.

He turned into the gravel driveway an hour and a half after leaving Bethany's house. Duke, the hound dog, lunged at his tires. Big Mike Callahan appeared from the garage, wiping his hands on a dirty rag. He squinted across at Aaron, then shouted, "Well, what the hell are you doing here again, kid?"

Aaron cut the engine and climbed out of the car. He strode across the gravel and grass to his father. "I, uh, I need to talk," he said. "It's important." Big Mike raised an eyebrow, crossing his arms. "What's going on?"

Aaron shifted his weight, feeling the gravel crunch under his boots. He ran a hand through his hair, then looked up at his father's weathered face.

"I've… got a situation," Aaron started. He pulled in a slow breath to keep his nerves in check. "It's about Rob."

Big Mike's eyes narrowed, and he tossed the rag onto a nearby workbench. "What kind of situation?"

Aaron hesitated, rubbing his injured hand. "Well, at the moment, he's bombarding me with messages and threats. I think he's at my house in Boyertown."

Big Mike unfolded his arms and stepped closer, his expression hardening. "What's he after?"

"Something I have. Something he thinks belongs to him," Aaron muttered, feeling the pull of everything he'd been avoiding.

Big Mike didn't blink. He stared at Aaron for a long moment before turning toward the road. "Sounds like you kicked over a hornet's nest."

Aaron nodded, exhaling as the pressure in his chest eased. "Yeah. I need to figure this out before it gets worse."

Big Mike clapped a hand on Aaron's shoulder, giving it a firm squeeze. "You came to the right place, kid. Let's talk inside." Inside the garage, the old man yanked a metal folding chair from behind a stack of boxes and pointed. "Sit."

Aaron dropped into the chair, his fingers fidgeting with the edge of his cast. Anger and nerves tangled inside him, and he couldn't tell which was winning.

"So, you left here... then what? Fill me in." Mike pulled a fat blunt from his shirt pocket, lit it, took a long drag, then held it out. Aaron shook his head, but Mike waved it closer. "Boy, listen to your old man. Hit the blunt, pass it back, and talk."

Aaron took the blunt, hesitating before bringing it to his lips. He inhaled, the smoke scratching his throat. The burn gave him a momentary calm. *Maybe this was what I needed right now.*

"I left here," he began, still holding the blunt. "Went home and dug through the ledgers. They didn't make much sense. Then I read part of Mom's book: something about a file on The Red Baron in Rob's stuff. She never figured out what it was, but... I had to know." He paused and took another drag. "Went to Rob's, pissed him off. When he left, I took the file from his safe."

Mike chuckled, holding out his hand. "Don't forget to pass that back." After a drag, he walked a few steps, shaking his head with a grin. "So, you broke into your stepfather's safe and stole his secret file?" Aaron nodded and Mike laughed louder, slapping his knee.

"Goddamn, boy. You've got my blood in you for sure."

Aaron continued, "There's a folder, too. Labeled with all the places we lived when I was a kid. I took that too. The file is like the ledgers—details of the coke business. It was big, cross-country, decades-long. Not just some neighborhood gang shit."

Mike's face flexed. "Neighborhood gang shit? Watch your mouth, boy. We were badass—"

"It's not an insult, Pops," Aaron cut in, his voice sharp. "It's the truth. Rob's operation was from coast to coast, even stretched into Canada. But that's not the worst part." He paused, holding out his hand. "Who's hogging that blunt now?"

Mike, still frowning, handed it over. "What's the worst part?"

Aaron took a deep drag on the blunt, holding it until his lungs burned. He coughed, then handed it back to Mike. "The worst part is the folder. Missing kids. Kidnapped kids. It was Rob and his crew."

Mike's eyes narrowed. "The folder says that?"

"Yeah. The missing kids' locations match the places we lived, same dates, all of it."

"That son of a bitch."

"I went to Kansas to check it out. I looked for his two buddies—the ones who used to come around and mess with…" Aaron stopped, not meeting Mike's eyes.

Mike prompted, "Go on."

"I found them. One's dead. Buried behind an iron gate," Aaron said, nodding toward his cast. "That's how I got this."

Mike shook his head. "And the other?"

"Kevin Earls." Aaron took a breath. "I found him. He has some kids with him."

"Still? What do you mean?" Mike looked puzzled.

"He married one of them when she was 16. She's 38 now. They have three kids together, and he stole four more. He calls it adoption. Nobody in that town questions him." Aaron took another drag. "He admitted it. I called him out at his dinner table, and he admitted to all of it." He handed the blunt back. "I recorded it."

Mike's eyes widened. "You recorded it?"

Aaron nodded with a grim smile on his face. "Recorded every word that scum said—about taking those kids, being 'rewarded' for his 'service' and handling coke shipments, having sex with the stolen girls, about my sister…" He trailed off, his voice dropping. "And about Rob killing their other friend and my brother Harrison."

"Holy hell, Aaron!" Mike leaned back, scrubbing through his hair with his large hand. "You have proof of all that? And now Rob's at your house, sending threats?" He laughed. "Yeah, you've got a situation, all right. So, what's your next move? Get to him first and take out the piece of shit?"

Mike paced, running a hand along the old Camaro with its engine exposed. "Take them out like the rats they are, bury them somewhere no one will find them. Or maybe where anyone could find them. Why hide it? Let the people they hurt have some goddamn peace."

Aaron cleared his throat. "I was thinking more like going to the police. I've got proof—initials, dates, notes, pictures, and the recording. They deserve to rot behind bars."

Mike's face hardened. "No, boy. They don't deserve prison. They deserve a hole in the ground. To be dead as a door-nail, pushing up daisies, sleeping with the fishes—whatever you want to call it. Three hots and a cot? That's too good for them."

"No, I'm not killing anyone, Mike." Aaron stood, shaking his head. "I'm not a criminal. I'm a victim. Those kids are victims. My brother and sister were victims. My mom was a victim. I want justice for all of us."

"You don't have to be a victim if you take charge," Mike said, his voice low and intense. "Erasing scumbags—now that'll set you free."

36

"No!" Aaron's voice rose, his anger bubbling over as he paced beside the Camaro, staying opposite Big Mike. "That's not how I want it! Nothing is that black and white!" He stopped at the back of the garage, leaning his forearms against the wall. "If I did that, I'd be just as bad as them."

Big Mike stepped closer, clearing his throat. "Listen now. A: You'll never be as bad as them—they did sick shit to kids. B: I didn't say you had to kill anyone. I said someone should. I know people. You got me?"

"I don't want that, Pops." Aaron's voice softened, but his resolve didn't. "They need to pay for what they've done. I want people to read about it. Those kids deserve to go home. Kevin and Rob haven't earned a quiet death. People will turn them into martyrs, and I can't stand the idea of that."

"I hear you. But when I picture him putting his hands on you…" Mike's voice trailed off, and he spat on the concrete floor, grinding it out with his boot. "I'm no saint. Hell, I'm the villain in a lot of stories. But what they did—it's disgusting. Scumbags."

Aaron rubbed his hand through his hair, the weed calming his mind, though his broken hand throbbed in sharp waves. He needed a Vicodin. He needed a plan. "Can I crash here, Pops? Or should I find a hotel? My place isn't safe, and I don't want Bethany involved."

"Bethany, huh?" Mike raised an eyebrow. "You've got a girl now?"

"Yeah, it's new. So can I stay?"

"Well, that's not my call," Mike chuckled. "You'll have to ask the boss."

"Loretta?" Aaron smirked, knowing how Big Mike had ruled the house when he was young.

"Yep, gotta run it by her first. I'm sure it's fine, but I don't offer invites without checking in." Mike grinned. "I run this garage. She runs everything else. Let's talk to her."

He closed the garage door, and they walked across the yard and up the porch steps. The hound dog followed behind. Inside, the house smelled of apples and cinnamon.

"Damn, woman, what you cooking in here?" Mike slid behind his wife, giving her a playful squeeze. She turned and swatted him with a towel.

"Apple fritters. And no, you can't have any. They're for after dinner." Mike grabbed a piece of apple anyway, ducking her towel as she tried to hit him again, laughing.

Loretta spotted Aaron by the door and grinned. "Well hey there, Aaron. I didn't know you came back."

"Got things to handle," Aaron began, but Mike interrupted.

"He's kicked a hornet's nest and needs to lie low for a while. Can he do that here, babe?"

She gave them both a long look. "Kicked over a hornet's nest, huh? Sounds like some Callahan shit." She sighed, throwing her hands up. "Guess that's fine. Mike, you can clear your junk off that guest bed. You like chicken pot pie, Aaron?"

"Yes ma'am, that sounds delicious." Aaron's stomach rumbled — he hadn't finished his breakfast that morning.

"What's this 'ma'am' business?" Loretta teased, giving him a light swat with the towel. "Do I look old to you? Call me Loretta."

He nodded, a smile pulling at the corners of his mouth. He hadn't expected this kind of warmth in Big Mike's home. *I never would've guessed.*

Mike led him down a narrow hallway to a bedroom cluttered with magazines, boxes of ammo, and a couple of rifles and a shotgun leaning against the wall. Stacks of old LP records covered the bed.

"Been organizing," Mike said, gathering up the records. "Alphabetizing. Figured I'd build a bigger shelf in the living room." He talked about his plans as he moved the records aside, stacking them by the closet. "I'll clear these out and grab you some clean sheets." He turned to the door.

"Hey, Pops," Aaron said.

Mike turned back, raising an eyebrow.

"Thanks."

Mike chuckled, shaking his head. "No need for that. Least I could do, considering I wasn't Father of the Year, right?" He laughed as he walked out.

Aaron made two trips out to the car. The first was for his suitcase, the second was for the cardboard box of ledgers. When he finished, Loretta was in the guest room making the bed.

"You didn't have to do that," he said.

"Oh no, I don't mind, and you've got that cast," she replied, glancing at his arm. "What happened, anyway? Did the hornets you kicked kick back?" She raised an eyebrow, waiting for his answer.

"Nah, nothing like that," Aaron said, shaking his head. "I just reacted without thinking. Didn't realize my hand wasn't stronger than actual iron."

"Callahans, I tell you," Loretta teased with a smirk before heading to the kitchen.

Aaron powered his phone back on, having turned it off when he left the car. The screen lit up with 16 new text notifications—every single one from Rob. He carried the phone into the living room, holding it up for Big Mike to see.

"Holy shit," Mike muttered, glancing at the flood of messages. "That guy doesn't know if he's coming or going, right?" He shook his head and returned to rolling a blunt, more amused than concerned. "Why don't you just block him?"

"I was considering talking to him. Maybe." Aaron sank onto the couch, unsure.

"If you want to talk to him, you unblock him. Simple, right? In the meantime…" Aaron's phone chimed again.

> 3/13/16 5:18 pm
> From Rob: Your mother would be ashamed of you, behaving like this!

Mike glanced up, shaking his head. "In the meantime, you don't have to put up with shit like that."

Aaron nodded. "You're right." He clicked the button to block his stepfather's number, feeling a weight lift as soon as he did. "It's done."

"Good. Now let's spark this up before Loretta calls us to dinner."

Right on cue, she poked her head around the doorway. "I heard you. You have 20 minutes, big man, so get it smoked and get your butt in here. I'm not letting this pot pie go cold waiting on you."

Mike gave her a mock salute, sparking the lighter with his other hand and taking a long drag. As he exhaled, he grinned. "Yes, ma'am."

Loretta's voice echoed from the kitchen. "I heard that."

Both men chuckled.

The meal was delicious, and the apple fritters even better—each bite warm and sweet, melting in his mouth. Lying in bed now, Aaron's thoughts drifted to Bethany. He wondered if she could cook, though the idea seemed distant. *Doesn't matter.* After years of fending for himself, the thought of coming home to a girlfriend or wife felt foreign.

The two pills he'd taken with sweet tea at dinner, along with the weed, had him relaxing. *Does Bethany cook? How old is Bethany? Did you even ask?* Alex's voice chimed in his head, always with the big questions. He smiled to himself. The house was quiet and warm. Safe, even. Strange, feeling that here, under Big Mike's roof. *If nothing else, Rob fears him.* Now Jared's voice echoed in his head, as if his friends were beside him. His mind swirled; the weight of the pills was heavy in his body.

Maybe I shouldn't have taken two.

He closed his eyes and sleep swallowed him.

June 11, 1998: Marlena

I was making dinner. Rob had called at lunch, his voice sharp with that familiar edge—angry about some deal falling through at work. He didn't even say hello, just barked, "Make a pot roast tonight. Vegetables too."

I could already hear the kids groaning in my head. They hated how I made pot roast, but it wasn't for them. Rob liked it overcooked, dry enough to chew like leather. It tasted better juicy, but I knew today wasn't the day to push back. I could tell he'd be in one of his moods when he got home.

I stood at the counter, peeling potatoes and thinking about how I used to love cooking for them—before it felt like a chore... before it became another thing I could get wrong. The kids were playing in the living room, their laughter filtering in. I didn't want it to stop. I didn't want them to notice the tension creeping into the house.

But it always did.

I heard the front door slam shut; the vibrations rattling through the walls. "Rob?" I called, forcing cheer into my voice. No response. The kids' laughter, which had filled the house moments earlier, had fallen silent. Something was wrong.

The strange thunking noise followed, over and over, accompanied by the unmistakable sound of Elise crying. My heart jumped into my throat. I dropped the knife, its clatter forgotten as I bolted down the hall.

Lucas and Nico stood frozen in the living room. They had paused their game of Super Mario 64, and both of them stared at the back hallway. Their faces were pale, wide-eyed with fear. Elise stood in the doorway, sobbing.

Then I heard it again—the sickening thunk—and a groan of pain, deep and guttural. My feet felt like lead as I ran toward the boys' bedroom, but nothing could've prepared me for what I saw.

Rob hunched over Aaron's bed, his knee pressing into the mattress. In his hand was one of the heavy dumbbells the boys got for Christmas. Aaron lay curled on the bed, his face buried in the pillow, arms cradling his sides as if he could shield himself from the blows. Rob brought the weight down again, smashing it into Aaron's ribs. The sound—bone against metal—made me nauseous.

"What the hell are you doing, Rob?!" I screamed, rushing forward, panic fueling my every step. He paused only long enough to shoot me a look so filled with hatred it chilled me. Then he raised the weight again and slammed it into Aaron's legs.

"Mind your goddamn business, woman," Rob snarled, standing up and letting the dumbbell drop to the floor with a heavy thud.

My breath caught as I spotted Patty in the corner of his bunk bed, curled into himself, his body trembling. He hadn't seen what happened, but I knew he'd heard everything. Rob straightened and turned toward him, his voice cold, cutting through the air. "That'll teach him a lesson, won't it, Patty?"

Patty didn't respond, his terrified eyes on his stepfather.

"Won't it, Patty?" Rob's voice boomed, harsher, and Patty nodded, his face ashen.

Rob shoved past me, stopping to grip Elise's arm hard enough to make her wince. "Big girls don't cry, Elise. Stop crying or I'll give you something to cry about." Her tears stopped as if on command, her small body trembling as she tried to hold it all in.

I hurried to Aaron's side. His cheeks were wet, but his jaw was a defiant, tight line. I touched his side, and despite his efforts, he let out a low groan. "What happened?" I whispered, brushing the sweaty strands of hair from his forehead. He shook his head, refusing to speak. His silence told me more than words ever could.

I turned toward Patty, who was still curled in the corner. "What happened, Patty?" I asked him.

He shrugged. "Dad said he needed a lesson."

"A lesson in what?" I pressed.

Patty just shrugged again, eyes downcast. I could see Aaron's back now, already bruising, the skin around the angry red welts turning an ugly purple and blue.

I stormed down the hall to our bedroom. Rob sat on the bed, peeling off his shoes like nothing had happened. His face showed no emotions—that was more infuriating than his rage.

"What did Aaron do?" I demanded.

He didn't even glance at me as he continued to undress, his movements slow and deliberate. I asked again, louder this time. He turned to look at me, eyes cold. "When I left for work this morning, he didn't say goodbye. The ungrateful little prick needs to learn some respect. You won't do your job and teach him, so I have to. This is your fault, Marlena. You can thank yourself for this."

He grabbed his belt, snapping it in the air. "Now, finish dinner, or

I can teach you too."

I left. I forced my shaking hands to finish cutting the potatoes, each slice releasing a little of the anger that simmered just below the surface. When I was done, I grabbed an ice pack and some Tylenol and brought them to Aaron. He was half-asleep, his body twitching in pain.

When I woke him, he grimaced, the bruises already deepening into dark splotches. I handed him the ice pack and asked, "Were you awake when Rob left this morning?"

He shook his head, his eyes half-lidded with exhaustion. "No."

I knew it. None of us had been. Rob left at 5:15 every morning, long before the family was awake. I served the dry pot roast to my husband and our four silent children. Aaron wasn't at the table. He was unconscious when I checked on him next, and I had to feel his chest to make sure he was still breathing. The rest of us sat in tense silence, the gravity of what had happened still thick in the air.

"The boy isn't coming to dinner?" Rob asked like it was any other day.

"No. He's not. He's..." I hesitated, glancing at the younger ones, not wanting to scare them. "He's asleep. I should call a doctor."

Rob raised an eyebrow. "No, you will not. You want all the kids taken from you because you didn't do as you should? You forget what that's like, Marlena?"

"How dare you!" I thought, and I almost said the words but caught myself. All I said was, "I'm sure he'll be fine. I'll take him a plate later when he wakes up."

Rob opened his mouth to argue, but then let it drop. After dinner, he flipped on the news, sprawling out on the couch like he owned the room, monopolizing the living room like always. I took the kids into the kitchen to clean up, hoping to avoid the inevitable questions.

It didn't take long. Lucas, ever the sensitive one, was the first to speak up. "Mom, why did Aaron get into trouble?"

I turned to meet his eyes, brushing his hair back as I tried to find the right words. "Your dad was just angry at him, buddy."

Lucas frowned. "But... what if he gets angry at me? Or somebody takes me away, like Dad said?"

I hugged him, whispering reassurance. "No one will get angry at you or take you anywhere, sweetheart. Don't worry."

Patty, drying dishes at the sink, chimed in with a voice reminiscent of Rob. "Dad gets mad at Aaron 'cause he looks like our real dad. You don't look like that loser, so you're safe, Luke. You too, Nico."

My instinct kicked in. I wanted to defend him, to say out loud that Mike wasn't a loser, but I bit back the words. The kids don't need to hear any of my thoughts on that. It's not their burden to carry. But Patty's words stung, even more so because I knew there was a twisted truth in them.

Aaron can't help that he looks like his father. And Rob... Rob had no right to punish him for it. But what can I do? If I try to stop him, he'll beat me the same way he beats Aaron.

I saw that look in his eyes today, that wild, dangerous look, and for a moment I felt like I'd made the same mistake twice. Maybe I should've waited for Big Mike. But it's too late for that now. It's too late for a lot of things.

Aaron woke up from a nightmare about Rob beating him unconscious. Reaching for his mother's book, he found the page he was looking for: the day before his 16th birthday. Rob had beaten him so badly that he had trouble moving. He had not gone to the dining room to enjoy his birthday cake. He had spent the following week at his friend Benji's house, watching the NBA Finals. Benji's dad had made popcorn, and they all cheered for the Bulls. Aaron remembered wishing his own dad could be like Benji's—a normal dad who watched games and made snacks, instead of someone who inflicted pain.

Aaron climbed out of bed, feeling anger and sadness. Blocking Rob's texts and calls seemed like the easy way out. *Killing him?* Even that felt too simple, despite the dark thought creeping in. *Confronting him is the only option. Not face-to-face, though.*

That would be suicide. Rob had erased people before—Roger, Harrison, and maybe others—when they became threats, and they hadn't even had the leverage Aaron did. He was sure Rob would end him if given the chance. *He's been trying since you were a kid.*

A meeting in person was off the table. *A phone call, maybe? Or should I go to the police first?* He sat there, head spinning. He had no clear path forward.

Aaron pulled on his clothes and headed for the bathroom. When he came out, the smell of bacon, coffee, and marijuana filled the hallway. In the kitchen, Mike sat smoking a blunt, muttering complaints about the newspaper. He greeted Aaron with a grunt and held out the blunt. "Sleep okay?"

Aaron nodded, taking a drag. "Slept like the dead. Nightmares, but that's not unusual." He passed it back to Mike as Loretta handed him a glass of orange juice and set a plate of bacon and eggs on the table in front of him.

"Damn, Loretta, you're the best hostess I've ever known," he said with a grateful grin.

She chuckled. "Of course I am. Why do you think your father keeps me around?"

Mike nodded, feigning agreement, before cutting to the chase. "So, you decide what you want to do?"

Aaron paused for a second, then decided. "I'll call the FBI and see if I can set up a meeting—show them what I've got. I have a life and a business. Running from these guys forever is not part of my plan."

"Calling the feds…" Big Mike shook his head, drawing in another deep drag from the blunt. "Ain't something I've ever been keen on. I steer clear of those old boys." He chuckled, the sound like gravel in his throat. "But if you're set against killing the man, that's your only move left."

Aaron gave a small nod, turning the idea over in his mind. "I'm sure there's a field office somewhere nearby."

"Probably back in Philly," Mike added, eyes narrowing in thought. "Doubt the G-Men have much business out here in the boonies."

Aaron continued eating as Mike buried his nose in the paper again. His thoughts spun like a wheel out of control—flashes of Rob and the dumbbell, the welts, the dry pot roast, Benji's dad, and the breakfast he'd shared with Bethany yesterday. It all felt like a tangled mess: one wrong move and the whole thing might come crashing down.

37

The FBI field office in Fort Washington was a short drive from Big Mike's place. Aaron settled into the waiting room with his cardboard box of ledgers and files. After about forty minutes, a burly man with a crew cut and a solid handshake called his name.

"Special Agent Eric Dawson," the man said, offering his hand. "And you must be Aaron Callahan. Follow me."

Agent Dawson led Aaron down a long, carpeted hallway, swiping his key card to open several doors. When they reached a boardroom-like space, Dawson gestured to a chair. "Make yourself comfortable, Mr. Callahan. Can I get you anything—coffee, soda, water?"

"I'm fine, thanks. Just Aaron is good," Aaron replied, picking a blue padded rolling chair and placing his box on the table to his right.

A few minutes later, Dawson returned. "I'll record this conversation if you don't mind."

Aaron nodded. Dawson set up the recorder and signaled for Aaron to start. He began his account, starting with his mother's death and the book of her memories. He described the ledgers his father had given him and how he had learned of Rob's folder, detailing his cocaine trafficking. When he reached the folder full of newspaper clippings of missing children and dead associates, Dawson's posture stiffened, his gaze locked on Aaron even as he sipped his water.

Aaron continued, recounting his trip to Kansas and meeting with Kevin Earls. Clearing his throat, he spoke of his childhood abuse and his suspicions about the abuse of his siblings. He pointed out the corroborating evidence from his mother's book and Kevin's outburst. He finished by showing Dawson the threatening texts from Rob on his phone.

Dawson cleared his throat. "That's quite a story, Aaron. Can I see what's in the box?"

Aaron opened the box, laying out the ledgers. He stacked the file folders and placed the voice recorder at the top of the pile.

The agent examined the ledgers and files with a practiced eye. He flipped through the ledgers, his brow furrowing as he absorbed the details. He scrutinized the newspaper clippings, each one receiving a thorough inspection.

Once Dawson had reviewed the materials, he looked up, his expression a mix of concentration and concern. "These documents are significant. We'll analyze them further, but this is encouraging information."

He gestured to a stack of folders. "I'll have our forensic accountants and analysts go through these ledgers. They'll verify the information and cross-check it."

Dawson returned the evidence to the box and glanced at Aaron. "In the meantime, can you provide a written statement of what you've told me today? It'll help us organize our investigation."

Aaron nodded. "Sure, I don't mind doing that, but I can't write with this thing on." He gestured to the cast. "Can I dictate to someone and then sign that? Or type it up?"

The man smiled. "Of course. Let me see what I can do about that." He left the room, carrying the box full of evidence, and returned with a young intern in a suit and tie.

"This is Isaac. He'll take down everything you tell him. Start from the beginning, and when he's done, you can review and sign it if it's accurate."

Aaron agreed. "I can do that. But… how long do you think it'll be before something happens with Rob or Kevin? Kevin's holding those kids, and Rob—"

Dawson cut him off. "I can't give you a timeline, Aaron. These investigations take time. I assure you, we're already looking into the files. We have ongoing investigations related to Luca Meat Distribution. That's all I can say for now."

"You were already looking into Rob?"

Dawson hesitated before clarifying, "No, not just Robert Bakker. Luca Meat Distribution. But let's keep that between us for now. Focus on working with Isaac to get that statement sorted, and I'll keep you updated as best I can."

Aaron nodded, trying to absorb the information. Dawson's reassuring smile was a minor comfort. "You did the right thing coming here," Dawson said as he left the room. "Thank you, Aaron."

He spent the next two hours with Isaac, recounting every detail of the saga that had spanned decades. Isaac wrote in precise handwriting. When he finished, he tapped the papers together and stapled them before handing the stack to Aaron.

"Read through this, and if it's accurate, sign and date it at the bottom," Isaac said, pointing to where his neat print read "Aaron Michael Callahan," and the date: March 14, 2016.

Aaron skimmed the document and signed it. A few minutes later, Special Agent Dawson returned.

"Aaron, I've just been on the phone with our offices in Virginia and Kansas. My team is excited about what you've brought in," Dawson said, looking like a man on a mission. "Now, Robert Bakker is desperate to reach you. Our best shot at a full admission from him is a recorded phone call. But we can't do that here—Pennsylvania's wiretapping laws require both parties to be informed."

Aaron nodded as if he knew all about recording laws.

"In Virginia," Dawson continued, "only one party needs to consent. That can be you. We'll send you to our Roanoke office to make the call tomorrow. Does that work for you?"

Aaron felt his insides churn. "Roanoke? That's... close to where Rob lives. He's looking for me. I don't know..."

Dawson's voice stayed calm. "We can send an officer with you if you feel unsafe. But we need to get his admission on record."

Aaron stared at the agent for a moment. "You think Rob will confess? Over the phone?"

"People like Robert think they're untouchable," Dawson said, leaning forward. "If you keep him talking about the business, he might slip. We don't need him to confess everything. Just enough to lock this case down."

Aaron ran his fingers along his cast, the thought of confronting Rob—even over the phone—twisting his insides. But he knew this was his only chance to stop running and seek justice for himself and the other victims.

"I'll do it," Aaron said, his voice even but low. "I'll go to Roanoke and make the call."

Dawson's expression softened. "Good man. We'll have someone with you the whole time—you won't be alone."

Aaron nodded, but the knot in his stomach refused to loosen. Tomorrow, he'd be one step closer to Rob—and to whatever chaos followed.

The drive back to Big Mike's felt endless. Traffic ground to a halt at every intersection. Aaron had nothing but time to think, his mind circling the same dark thoughts. *A recorded phone call with Rob—how will I pull this off?* He tried to joke with himself. *No pressure, right?* But the humor didn't stick. *What if Rob admitted to nothing? Worse, what if Rob figures out I'm working with law enforcement?*

Roanoke wasn't far from Harrisonburg. Aaron swallowed hard, imagining Rob's fury and the lengths he might go to. The sinking sun cast shadows over the road, pulling his mind deeper into those fears. A sharp honk behind him jolted him back to the present. The light had turned green.

Aaron turned the front doorknob at Big Mike and Loretta's house, and the smell of garlic and simmering tomato sauce hit him. Dinner was already on the table—spaghetti piled high with juicy meatballs and a thick slab of buttery garlic bread that made his stomach growl.

Big Mike motioned for Aaron to join. "How'd it go with the FBI?" he asked, his tone casual but his eyes sharp with interest.

Aaron slid into his seat and took a breath. "Went fine," he said, keeping it brief. "Told them everything, handed over the files."

"That's it? What's the next step?"

"They're sending me to Roanoke tomorrow. They want me to make a recorded phone call to Rob," Aaron explained.

The old man nodded, jabbing his fork into a meatball. "Well, you did well. Followed your gut, and no one can say otherwise. I guess they didn't suggest you track down some old gangster and have the bastard taken care of, huh?" He chuckled, a low rumble in his chest.

Aaron forced a grin, trying to match the light tone. "Nah, no one brought that up."

Big Mike turned to Loretta, flexing his arm. "I should've been a fed, huh? I'd look sharp in one of those G-Man suits, don't you think?"

Loretta laughed, leaning in to kiss him on the cheek. "Agent Michael Callahan. Has a nice ring to it, doesn't it?"

Aaron jumped in with a grin. "Special Agent Callahan. Don't forget the special part."

Laughter filled the room as the three of them enjoyed the moment, but the brief happiness faded as tomorrow crept back into Aaron's thoughts. "I should leave for Roanoke soon," he said.

Big Mike's irritation was immediate. "What? Why? It's Roanoke, not fucking Jupiter! Why would you need to leave tonight? Go in the morning."

Aaron blinked, taken aback by the intensity in his father's voice. He couldn't figure out why it mattered so much. "If I wait until morning, I won't get there until noon, maybe later with traffic. I won't meet with an agent until after lunch, then they'll have to set up the call… it pushes everything back. I want this done."

His voice grew more certain as he explained, but Big Mike stared at him, his expression unreadable. Finally, he stood up from the table. "I'm going to roll a blunt. Come smoke with me, son."

Aaron hesitated, looking over at Loretta. She gave him a small, understanding smile as she dried the last dishes. "Don't let him get to you. He didn't think he'd ever see you or your brother again, and he's trying hard not to mess it up. I know he was bad, Aaron. He's trying now."

Aaron nodded in understanding. He retreated to the guest room to pack up his suitcase. The wheels echoed as he rolled it into the living room, parking it by the door. Then he sat on the couch across from Big Mike, watching him roll a fat blunt with a practiced hand.

"I've got something I want to read to you, Pops."

June 10, 1986: Marlena

I thought I would live in Philadelphia forever. I grew up here and had my first kiss at the park around the corner from the house where I've lived since I was born. Thirty-three years of my life have been on this dirty block, and I believed I'd stay here until I died. I considered nothing outside this place—until now.

Robert is a good man, and I trust him. He's a businessman with money and savings; he wants to take care of me and the boys. I love him, though it's not the same as how I felt about Harrison and Lydia's father when I was young and naïve. Back then, I didn't understand what love was. And it's not the same as my love for Mike. God, I loved Mike—still do, in a way. I hate him, too. Or I say I do, but no one has ever looked at me like Michael Callahan did. I never would have believed anyone who said he'd go so far off the rails, with drinking, drugs, and violence. I have to force myself to remember the truth.

It's easier to think about the good times. When I told Mike I was pregnant with Aaron, it was December and snow was beginning to fall. I met him at his auto shop at lunch, and I told him, "You're going to be a daddy." His smile was so wide, his eyes crinkled and sparkling. He kissed me like I'd given him the best news in the world. That night, he came home with a gift: a Betty Boop for my collection. Her pink evening gown sparkled like a new diamond, her arms raised in excitement. She's one of my most prized possessions, a reminder of happier days, even after Mike's descent into drugs and crime.

I don't love Robert the way I loved Mike, but he's safer. I have to focus on the boys now, not just on my desires. Who cares how much you love kissing a man, or how he makes you feel, if he's just going to hurt your children or end up in prison? Rob is the better choice.

I'll keep telling myself that with every box I pack until the move is done. I thought I'd live in Philadelphia forever, but now I know there are better places to go. And Rob will take me there. Me and Betty Boop.

Aaron closed the book and set it on the couch beside him, taking a deep breath. Big Mike, elbows resting on his knees, ran his fingers through his silver hair. The room was silent for several minutes until

Mike cleared his throat. His eyes were red-rimmed and watery when he looked up at Aaron. "Thank you, son," he said, his voice thick with emotion. He coughed, wiped his eyes with the back of his hand, then lit the end of the rolled blunt. He inhaled, closed his eyes, and exhaled before passing it to Aaron.

"I loved her, you know," Mike whispered. "I love Loretta like crazy—wouldn't trade her for anything, and she knows it. But back then, my whole heart belonged to your mama. I just… couldn't get it right."

"Couldn't get what right?" Aaron asked.

Mike took another drag, his voice growing heavy. "I couldn't get any of it. I needed money. I had a wife, a baby on the way, then two babies. The shop was losing money, and I could never make ends meet. So we started dealing—small-time gang shit, just like you said." He held up a hand to dismiss Aaron's unspoken apology. "It helped. It put food on the table, let us hire another mechanic, made Christmas happen. But it still wasn't enough. The deals got bigger, and the stress grew. And before long, I was drinking and snorting coke like it was the only thing that mattered. It was like… I didn't have little boys at home who needed their daddy." He threw his fist in the air, his frustration evident. "Like I didn't have a beautiful wife who just wanted me to love her."

"Is that why you tried to kill me?" Aaron asked, his voice trembling.

Mike's face contorted with pain. "I don't know, Aaron. I was high. It's a lousy excuse, but it's all I've got. Maybe I had a rough day. A deal fell through. Maybe it was the day Rudy raised his fees and threatened to foreclose on the shop. I don't fucking know. I dream about it sometimes… you know? Nightmares?" His pained expression made Aaron almost feel pity.

"Yeah, I have nightmares about it too, Pops," Aaron replied. They passed the blunt back and forth until it was nothing but ash.

"I gotta go, Pops," Aaron said, rising from his seat. "Thanks for letting me stay here."

"Thank Loretta," Mike said, his voice thick. "She's the—"

"The boss. I know." Aaron paused at the back of the couch, turning to face his father. "Thanks for changing, Mike. Thanks for not being a piece of shit anymore. I wish I'd known sooner."

Mike swallowed hard, his gaze darting away from Aaron. "Yep. I wish that too." He stood, avoiding Aaron's eyes. "Thanks for reading what Marlena wrote. It means a lot."

Aaron found Loretta in the kitchen and wrapped her in a grateful hug. "Thank you for your hospitality and the amazing cooking," he said sincerely.

Loretta smiled and patted his back. "Don't be a stranger now, Aaron. You're not that far away."

"Yes ma'am—Loretta," he corrected with a chuckle.

She laughed and swatted him with a dish towel. "That's better. Take care now."

The older couple walked him to the door and out onto the porch. Mike bent to scratch Duke behind his floppy ear while Loretta watched Aaron lift his suitcase into the trunk of his car.

As he settled into the driver's seat, she nudged Mike's shoulder, prompting him to speak. Mike shouted, "When you're done in Roanoke, you can come here and help me alphabetize those records."

Aaron laughed, the sound echoing in the cool evening air. "I got your number from Loretta. I'll be in touch. Thanks for everything, you two." Backing out of the driveway, a bittersweet feeling settled over him. As he headed to the main road, he glanced in the rearview mirror, catching a last glimpse of the house and the people who had offered him solace in the most unlikely place.

He flipped on the radio and cued up the best song he could think of to fight off the anxiety and face the hard things ahead. The beat of "X Gon' Give It To Ya" by DMX blasted through the speakers. He rapped every word, his voice rising and falling with the rhythm as if he were on stage. With each verse, he felt a surge of adrenaline, the music pushing him forward as he sped down the highway. The night sky stretched out before him.

38

The clock on the beige wall read 10:38 a.m. the next morning—Special Agent Mark Collins sat down to brief Aaron on the upcoming phone call with his stepfather. Collins leaned forward, his gaze intense.

"Robert's most likely furious," Collins began, adjusting his glasses. "He's been trying to reach you for days and wants that file back. Expect threats and demands—ignore them. Don't engage or provoke him. Keep your cool."

"Our goal is to get him talking about the cocaine trafficking, especially how it ties to Luca Meat Distribution. That's our primary focus. If he mentions the kidnapped kids or any abuse, that's a bonus, but right now, we need detailed information about his company's involvement in the drug trade."

He straightened his tie and gave Aaron a firm nod. "Remember, stay calm and focused, and let him do the talking. We need his own words to build a stronger case."

Another agent knocked before opening the door. "We're ready, Collins," he announced.

The agent turned to Aaron, his expression encouraging. "You ready?"

Aaron nodded, trying to suppress the nervous flutter in his stomach. He knew it was time to face what he'd been dreading.

"Then let's go," Collins said, leading the way.

They stepped into a mid-sized room, where laptops and recording devices covered desks that lined the walls. A few agents and techs moved between stations, making final adjustments. Collins approached a woman in a navy suit stationed at one desk. "Legal's ready?" he asked.

She nodded with confidence. "One hundred percent. I'll be monitoring."

Collins gestured toward a chair in the center of the room. "You'll sit here and use this phone," he explained. "It will show as your number on Robert's end, so he'll think you're on your cell. Just act natural. Keep him talking, especially about any link between his company and the drugs."

He flashed a thumbs-up and took the seat next to Aaron. "You got this, man."

Aaron swallowed hard, his nerves buzzing, but he nodded. It was time.

He lifted the receiver in front of him and waited as a tech counted down from ten. As soon as the countdown hit one, the phone started ringing. Once, twice, three times. Just as he wondered if Rob would answer, the fourth ring cut off, and the angry wave of his stepfather's voice flooded out.

"Aaron! Where the hell have you been, boy?"

"I've had some things to think about, Dad," Aaron replied.

"You went to Kansas thinking about them, I hear. Just what the hell are you playing at? Where's my file folders, Aaron?" He could sense the thin thread of Rob's control barely holding.

"Why don't you explain what's in these files, Dad? Tell me about all these dates, these names, these places where we used to live. Is this the work you did for Luca Meat—"

"Listen to you! Explain to you? Are you fucking kidding me, Aaron? I'm not explaining a fucking thing to you. Moron, you're a moron. You've stolen from me, boy, and I know you can remember what happens to morons who break the rules."

"I'm not a child anymore, Dad," Aaron said through clenched teeth. "I know about the drugs and the kids. The missing kids at Kevin's place. His wife… he couldn't tell me what happened to that first one you took from Mexico, though. Couldn't seem to recall if she ended up dead or—"

"Enough! You stop right now! Oh, you're in so much trouble, boy. If your mother could see you now… after I tried to teach you, tried to straighten you up… wasted time. You're no better than your father."

"My father didn't give me, and my brother and sister, to his friends to pass around, so there's that."

Agent Collins, seated beside him, slid a note across the desk: *Stay on target. Stay calm.*

Aaron took a breath, composing himself. "Tell me about the drugs, Dad. Tell me about all the money you made for your company. Meetings in Philly and Kansas and L.A. Sending your lackeys to meet shipments of cocaine."

Rob fell silent for a few seconds, his heavy breathing audible on the line, before hissing. "You think you're so smart, don't you? Talking big now, aren't you? Let me tell you something, you ungrateful punk— you do not know what you're messing with."

Aaron pressed on. "I know what I'm messing with. Luca Meat Distribution isn't about the meat, but the coke you're moving."

Rob let out a sharp, bitter laugh. "And what do you plan to do with that knowledge? Run to the cops? You don't know the half, Aaron. Luca Meat's been running this game for decades, and people far more powerful than you or me are involved. You can't stop this thing, so don't even try. I'd hate for you to end up dead."

"You mean like my brother Harrison?" The words slipped out before Aaron could stop them, cold and sharp in the air.

Rob chuckled. "You didn't even know that boy. Why do you care? The kid wanted in, and I said no. He wasn't family anymore, wasn't ever my family. He was a nobody who got pushy, so he got pushed back. Simple as that."

Aaron glanced at Collins, who gave him a nod to keep going. He pressed forward. "I know who KE is. Kevin Earls. RH—Roger Harris. Did you pull the trigger, or did you make him do it?"

Rob's laugh turned darker. "Oh, now you're trying to piece it all together, huh? What else you got?"

Aaron forced himself to stay calm. "JM. Jeanette Masterson… carjacked, right? Convenient. But SC… who's SC, Dad?"

The moment the initials left his lips, it clicked. *SC. Sean Callahan. Patty.* His blood ran cold. *Patty's coke habit. His sports cars.* Pieces he hadn't wanted to fit together were snapping into place, and the realization was like a punch to the gut. His stomach churned at the thought.

"I can hear the wheels turning in your empty brain," Rob sneered. "Why don't you take a deep breath and let it out? We'll get together. You bring my property, and we'll get you set up. Why bust your ass at that useless little company of yours,"—he spat the words out like poison—"when you could take a plane ride every few months, meet some of my associates, and call it a good day's work?"

Aaron's jaw clenched. His pulse pounded in his ears, but he kept himself calm. "Is that what you have Patty doing? Running for you?" His voice cracked as he spoke his brother's name.

Rob's voice on the other end was low and condescending. "Patty knows how to play the game. He always did, ever since he was a kid. Toe the line and do what's asked: don't get beaten. Maybe you should take a page from his book, Aaron. Stop wasting your life."

"What about the kids?" Aaron's voice trembled. "Is Patty—?"

"Patty's not involved with the kids. That ended a long time ago. Besides, I haven't—"

A loud knock interrupted Rob mid-sentence. "Now who the hell is that?" Rob's irritation crackled through the phone. "Aaron, is that you? You planning to show up while we're on the line, like some surprise birthday-gram?"

Aaron shot a confused look at Agent Collins. "It's not me, Dad."

"Then who the fuck is it? I'll call you back later." There was a brief pause before he added, "And Aaron, I need those files. That part is not negotiable. The rest? We can work something out."

The line went dead.

He lowered the phone, his heart thudding in his chest. *We can work something out.* Rob's words were hollow in his mind. Aaron had heard something else in his voice—fear.

Agent Collins leaned in. "He gave us much more than we expected. You did well."

Aaron wasn't listening. His stepfather's mention of Patty had left him reeling. *How deep is my brother caught in this?* As his anxiety from the call faded, Aaron realized it was almost lunchtime. His stomach churned, this time from hunger.

Agent Collins stood up, stretching his arms. "You've been great so far, Aaron. We're not done yet, though. Rob's still holding back a lot. We need to hear the rest of it—and most importantly, we need to know where he is right now. So I'd like you to stick around. We'll try to call him again in a little while."

Aaron nodded, though his head felt heavy. He couldn't shake the lingering thoughts of Patty and what else his stepfather might reveal.

Collins gave a glance at the clock. "You hungry? I can bring you some lunch. What do you want?"

"Yeah, I could eat." Aaron hadn't realized how drained he felt. "Whatever is fine. Sandwich, maybe?"

Collins smiled. "I'll get you something. Sit tight."

As Collins turned to leave, another agent approached Aaron, his hands tucked into his vest pockets. "Listen, Rob might try to call you back. You should unblock his number, in case he reaches out."

Aaron nodded again, taking out his phone. His finger hovered over the block settings, then he unblocked Rob's number. As soon as he did, the flood of missed texts poured in. Aaron blinked, scrolling through them—messages from Rob over the last two days, some calm, some furious, and one or two that sent a chill up his spine.

At 2 pm, Aaron received instructions to make another phone call to Rob. The line rang and rang—no answer. The same thing happened at 3 pm, 4 pm, and again at 4:40 pm.

"Try texting him," Agent Collins suggested.

Aaron tapped out the message.

> 3/15/16 4:42 pm
> To Rob: You said we would talk later. It's later. Let me know when it's a good time.

Collins glanced at the message, nodding. "We want you to sit tight for a while longer. We've got officers executing search warrants, and you're safer here until that part is over." He reached out and took Aaron's phone from him. "I'll hold on to this if you don't mind." He set it on the desk of the woman in the navy suit. "Don't worry, we're not keeping it."

Aaron's hand throbbed, the familiar ache pulsing with each heartbeat. Hours had passed since he last took his painkillers, and he had left them in his car. "Can I get some Tylenol or something? My hand…"

"Of course. I'll be right back," Collins said. A few minutes later, he returned with a small cup containing two Tylenol pills and a cold water.

Aaron heard his phone chime an hour later and sat upright, watching the woman at the desk check his messages. "From Elise," she read aloud. Officers have carried out the search and arrest warrants. She's unhappy about it and wants to know if you know what's going on."

Aaron sank back into his chair, then sat up again, his heart racing. "Arrest warrants? Did they arrest Rob?"

"No," the woman replied, adjusting her skirt. "We don't know the current whereabouts of Robert Bakker. They brought Sean Callahan in for questioning, though."

The police arrested Patty. Fuck. This was not how Aaron had expected his day to go. Rob was out there, doing who knows what, and now his brother was in custody. The air in the room felt too heavy for him to breathe.

He turned again to the woman at the desk, frustration clear in his voice. "When can I leave? I'm tired and I've been here for hours. I want to go to bed."

"Soon, Mr. Callahan. Give us a little time."

Aaron tried to focus on the minor comforts of his situation—like the cold water Collins had brought him—but his thoughts kept circling back to his brother and his stepfather. He felt trapped in a web of uncertainty and dread.

Agent Collins returned after a short while with a serious expression. "We've just received word that a couple more search warrants are being executed. We need you to stay until we get more information."

Aaron sighed, rubbing his tired eyes. "I just need to know what's going on. Can you at least tell me if there's any news about Rob or my brother?"

The agent nodded, his demeanor less stiff now. "I understand it's frustrating. We're doing everything possible to locate Rob and figure out the situation with your brother. I'll keep you updated as soon as we hear anything."

Aaron glanced at his phone across the room, hoping for a call or text from Bethany. He hadn't spoken to her since Sunday, and the silence was unsettling. He took another deep breath, knowing there was little he could do but wait.

As the minutes ticked by, he stared at the desk, lost in thought, and tried to push away the gnawing worry. The clock on the wall read 8:47 pm when Agent Collins returned. "Alright, here's the plan. We're going to move you to a local hotel. You'll have a detail assigned to you, rotating around the clock until further notice. Sound good?"

Aaron, exhausted, rubbed his eyes. "I already have a hotel. My stuff is there."

Collins nodded. "Give this agent the details of your hotel. We'll check it out. If it's secure enough, we'll stick with that room. If not, we'll bring your belongings to a new place. Sound good? Good."

Aaron sighed, frustration edging his voice. "Can I get my phone back, Collins?"

He hesitated, then shook his head. "Not right now. It might be a bit before we can return it. There are moving parts with your stepfather and brother involved... give us some time, okay?" He attempted a sympathetic look. "For now, let's get you settled. Give this agent your hotel information, please."

After another wait, the agents decided that Aaron's choice of hotel was "sufficient" and agreed to let him drive his rental car back. He appreciated the gesture—it gave him time to retrieve his bottle of remaining Vicodin. *Tonight would be a good night to numb my head and my hand.*

Not like there was much else to do, he thought. No phone: he couldn't reach Big Mike, Nicole, Lucas, or Bethany. The agent checked his room as thoroughly as if he were a presidential candidate with a target on his back, and once it was determined "clear," Aaron could be alone again. He took a shower, but it did little to clear his tired mind. Popping two of the pain pills, he swallowed them with a swig of water and lay down, hoping for some escape in sleep.

* * *

September 17, 1991: Marlena

I got married today for the second time. The first was to Big Mike, but today was quieter, simpler. It's funny. Rob's been telling people we've been married for years. He says he didn't want folks thinking the kids were bastards. I guess it's fine if they're born out of wedlock, as long as no one knows.

Vegas is… overwhelming. The lights, the noise, the people—it's a lot. We're staying at The Bellagio, and I have to admit, it's beautiful. There's a massive fountain out front with synchronized water jets that dance in time with the music. I stood there watching for what felt like forever, mesmerized by it all. But Rob was in a hurry to "get on with it."

The chapel he chose wasn't one of those tacky places with Elvis officiants—although part of me found that idea amusing. It was small, quaint, but still cute. I bought my wedding dress this morning, just something simple—a white sundress with a satin bow under the bust. Rob wore one of his business suits. I have to admit that we looked good together.

Afterward, Rob wanted to hit the casino floor. He took $500, saying he'd be back when he hit zero. That was over four hours ago. I'm tempted to find him, but he always says he's luckier alone, and I don't want to upset him tonight of all nights.

The hotel room is more extravagant than I expected. There's a king-sized bed with soft linens. There are marble accents in the bathroom. The view from our window is breathtaking—the city lights stretch out as far as I can see. I changed into the silk nightgown I'd packed for tonight, hoping to surprise him. It's delicate, something you save for a special occasion like tonight.

I ordered champagne, thinking we'd toast to our new married status together. The bottle arrived a while ago, but he's still not back. It's getting late. I popped the cork myself and poured a glass. I'm sitting here, sipping, waiting.

* * *

Aaron had been awake for hours, unable to shake the heaviness settling in his chest. He flipped through the television channels, but nothing held his attention. He gave up and reached for his mother's book, buried in the bottom of his suitcase. It brought him a strange comfort: flipping through the pages and peeking into parts of her life he hadn't known existed.

He started from the beginning, tracing her early life with her mother, father, and sisters. She remembered the house in Philly with great detail. Her memories showed the closeness of the family, but also the ever-present tension. Marlena walked a fine line between responsibility and longing for something bigger. Aaron read through her pain, how losing her father shattered her at thirteen. The rawness of that grief echoed on every page.

He skimmed forward, stopping on her wedding day with Rob in Vegas. He studied her words, describing the simplicity of it all—her sundress, his business suit, the rushed vows. There was no romance, just a sense of obligation.

"You were always a shit, weren't you, Rob?" Aaron muttered to himself, shaking his head. The memory of his stepfather, towering over everyone with that smugness, made his skin crawl. He stood up from the armchair, stretching his sore limbs, feeling coiled up like a thick rope on a ship's salty deck—tense, bound, and ready to snap.

Aaron opened the door, thinking maybe a walk down the hall would clear his head. He could grab a soda from the vending machine to break up the hours of sitting and thinking. When he stepped out, a federal agent was there to his left, hand raised like a crossing guard.

"Sir, I need you to stay inside the hotel room," the agent said, his voice flat but firm.

Aaron sighed, already feeling the tension creeping back in. "I was just grabbing a soda or something, man. I'll be right here," he pointed up and down the hall, hoping to make his case for a little freedom, just enough to stretch his legs.

The agent didn't budge. "No, sir, that's not an option. Please stay inside your hotel room."

Without another word, Aaron stepped back inside, closing the door with a soft click. The confinement was getting to him—every minute felt like it dragged on forever. He stared at the TV, the muted channels flashing images of shows he had no interest in.

"Back to the TV then, I guess," he muttered, collapsing onto the bed again. But the tension in his chest wouldn't let up.

Several hours later, Aaron sprawled out on the bed, paying little attention to the third consecutive episode of NCIS New Orleans playing on the muted TV. He shifted the cold, half-empty soda can the agent had brought him earlier. He was about to zone out again when a sharp knock rattled the hotel door.

With a sigh, he got up and opened it. Agent Collins stood in the doorway, looking like he had stepped out of an old detective flick. "Need to talk to you, Aaron."

Collins walked to the window, staring at the distant freeway before speaking. "We found your stepfather this morning."

Aaron felt a surge of relief—an end to all this. He closed the door and sank into the armchair. "Good. Maybe I can get out of this room. Where did you find him?"

"Aaron, they found him dead," Collins said, his face somber, his eyes locking onto Aaron's. "Someone beat him and shot him twice in the chest. Left him in a field. Some workers at a nearby cafe found him early this morning."

"Rob's... dead?" Aaron repeated, the words feeling unreal as they left his mouth. The air in the room seemed humid—the air felt too thick to breathe. "Who?"

Collins shook his head. "We don't know yet. But based on the preliminary findings, it seems like someone beat him for hours, maybe most of the night. My guess? Whoever knocked on his door yesterday during your phone call led him to his death."

Aaron's mind spun, everything feeling out of focus. He could almost hear Big Mike's voice in his head, that low gravelly tone: "Erasing scumbags—now that'll set you free."

Collins was still talking, but Aaron couldn't concentrate. His thoughts kept circling back to Rob and the violence of his death.

"Since this is a federal case, we're having the body transported to our Roanoke medical examiner's office." Collins continued, his tone grim. "It may take a couple of hours, but I need you to come in and identify the body, if you can, Aaron."

"Identify the... so it might not be Rob?" Aaron felt a surge in his gut—he wasn't sure if it was hope or dread.

Collins shook his head. "He had a wallet with ID and credit cards. A cell phone and an engraved watch. We believe this is Robert Bakker," he stated. "But the procedure is for a family member to make a positive ID."

Aaron nodded. "Yeah, okay," he mumbled, though the idea of looking at Rob's dead body made him sick.

The agent's gaze sharpened, and he leaned forward. "I need to ask you, Aaron. Who else did you discuss this case with?"

Aaron hesitated, his mind racing. He had been careful. "My father," he said. "My actual father, Big Mike."

"Big Mike?" Collins raised an eyebrow, jotting something down.

"Michael Callahan. He lives in Doylestown. But... he's old, like in his late 60s. He didn't do this." Even as he spoke, Aaron wasn't sure he believed himself. He felt like he was lying to the agent, even though the image of Big Mike brutalizing anyone seemed absurd at this point.

"How close are you with him?" Collins asked, his pen still poised.

Aaron rubbed his temples. "We... talk, I guess. We're not super tight. But he's been there for me when I needed someone to talk to. He's... protective... but he wouldn't beat a man to death." *Not anymore.*

"Anyone else? Wife, girlfriend, business partner, best friend?" Collins kept his eyes on him.

Aaron shook his head. "No wife. My girlfriend, if you could call her that, knows nothing about this. I haven't talked to anyone else. It's all happened in the last three weeks—since I got the book, the file, and remembered all this stuff from my childhood." He started pacing, running his fingers through his hair until it stood straight up. "Kevin's kids know. I called him out at their dinner table, in front of all of them."

"Their names?" Collins asked, writing.

"Jackson Earls, Lindsey, and her husband Mark—don't know their last name. Malachi Earls, but he's just a teenager. The kids... and Josephine, but she wasn't there that night."

"What about Kevin Earls?" Collins waited for Aaron's response.

Aaron threw his hand up in a half-shrug. "I doubt it. He acted like Rob called all the shots, and he was following orders. You heard him on the recording."

"I did," Collins said, snapping his notepad shut. "Just wanted your take."

He walked to the door, hand on the knob. "We'll take you to the medical examiner when it's time for the ID. Shouldn't be too long now."

"Where was he found, Collins? Boyertown?"

"No. Honesdale, a couple of hours north of here," Collins replied, flipping through his notes again. "Found in a field across from the Betty Boop Cafe. Does the name ring any bells?"

Aaron kept his face still, but inside, everything crashed together. *Betty Boop. Mom's favorite.* "Never heard of it," he said.

Collins nodded, tucking away his notepad. "Sit tight, Aaron. You'll be out of here soon." He left, the door closing with a soft click.

Aaron sat back, staring at the wall. "Found in a field across from the Betty Boop Cafe." His stomach dropped, and he ran to the bathroom to vomit.

39

At three o'clock, Aaron walked into the medical examiner's office in Roanoke, flanked by two federal agents. The sterile hallway stretched ahead, long and cold, leading to a set of double doors. A man in scrubs met him with a firm handshake, explaining the process in a low voice. Aaron nodded, wanting it over as soon as possible.

They entered a small, chilled room. In the center, a metal table waited with a green drape covering the shape of a body. The man in scrubs walked to the opposite side, gripping the drape. With a careful motion, he folded it back to the shoulders.

Robert Bakker lay beneath it.

Aaron's breath hitched. Rob's face was almost unrecognizable, swollen and bruised beyond anything he had seen. His skin had turned dark, mottled like overripe fruit, with distorted features from the violent death. Blood still clung to his silver hair, even though someone had tried to clean him up.

Aaron stared without blinking. The feelings came all at once—anger, relief, guilt. He gripped the edge of the metal table, knuckles white.

"Sir? Do you need a minute?" The tech's voice broke the silence, stepping toward him and glancing at the agents behind Aaron.

"No. It's him." Aaron forced the words out. "It's Rob."

The tech nodded, covering Rob again. The bruised face disappeared, but Aaron's eyes stayed on the spot where it had been, frozen in disbelief.

"The decedent is Robert James Bakker of Harrisonburg, Virginia?"

The tech held out a clipboard. Aaron took the pen and signed his name, unable to focus. The man mentioned belongings—a wallet, and an engraved watch—but Aaron could not process it. He signed the papers, eager to leave the cold room and the harsh reminder of what Rob had become.

At the exit of the medical examiner's office, Agent Collins stood waiting, arms crossed, trench coat still draped over his broad shoulders. He straightened when Aaron stepped out.

"You're all done, Aaron, for now." Collins' tone was professional, but not without a hint of sympathy. "The investigation is far from over. Robert was a piece of a much larger operation. The documents you gave us have been a goldmine for our forensic accountants. We'll need you to testify later, but that's down the road."

He reached into his coat and pulled out Aaron's phone, holding it out. "This is yours. You're free to go."

Aaron took the phone, shoving it into his pocket, then hesitated before shaking Collins' hand. It felt awkward and formal—this was just business to the agent.

"My brother?" Aaron asked, his voice quiet but tense.

"Still in custody, I'm afraid. He's more concerned with your sister than he is with sharing useful information."

Aaron clenched his jaw, feeling the walls closing on him—the death, the secrets, and now, the uncertainty about his brother. Collins gave him a nod, a wordless promise of more updates to come, but it did little to ease the tension gripping Aaron.

"Can you give me a ride back to my hotel to get my car?" Aaron asked.

"Of course, of course," the agent replied.

The ride was quick, and neither of them spoke. It was as though they both knew words wouldn't help. When they reached the hotel, the agent gave a quick nod. "Take care, Aaron," he said before driving off.

He stood on the sidewalk, staring after the car. Numb and shaken, he felt like the world had tipped sideways. He wasn't sure how to stand upright again.

Hours later, Aaron parked at the end of Big Mike's driveway, the engine's hum fading into the quiet of Doylestown. As soon as he stepped out, the porch light flicked on. Loretta peeked through the storm door, her bathrobe pulled tight against the cool air.

"Oh, it's you, Aaron! I wasn't expecting you so late. It's almost midnight. Have you eaten?" she asked, concern creasing her brow.

"Hey, Loretta. Sorry for the time." He stopped at the bottom of the steps. "Where's my Pops?"

Loretta pointed, her eyes searching his face for answers. "He's in the garage. He's been out there most of the last two days. Is everything okay?"

Aaron crossed the yard, waving a dismissive hand. His mind swirled with thoughts of the long drive, his argument with Big Mike, and Rob's brutalized face.

The lights in the garage glared, forcing Aaron to blink. Big Mike sat on a low stool, buffing the Camaro's fender, his focus only breaking when the door slid shut behind Aaron.

"Hey there, Aaron. How was your drive?"

Aaron crossed the room, his voice tight. "What did you do, Mike?"

Big Mike glanced up, his hands still busy. "Got the engine lowered in. Not hooked up yet, but she will purr like—"

"What did you do to Rob?" Aaron's voice cracked, raw with emotion.

Mike paused, his hands slowing. "Now you sound like that G-man who came by earlier, all worked up." He gestured toward the camera in the top corner of the garage, its red light blinking. "I told him the same thing I'll tell you—I've been right here. If you want to watch hours of boring footage like he did, be my guest. Didn't do a damn thing, Aaron. I'm an old man."

Aaron stood still, his anger unraveling into something heavier. "I know it was you, Mike. They found Rob in a field across from the Betty Boop Cafe." He searched his father's face, hoping to find the truth. "Her collection... the figure you gave her. I read it to you the other night." His voice cracked as exhaustion seeped into him. "It was you... it has to be." These last words came out as a whisper, carrying all his suspicion and pain.

"It wasn't me." Big Mike lit a blunt, taking a deep, deliberate drag.

His eyes remained fixed on Aaron, as if challenging him to read between the lines. "Rob had a lot of enemies. He did a lot of bad things. If someone knew where to find him, where to leave him, and how to make it hurt…" He exhaled a thick cloud of smoke. "Why would you assume it was me?"

Aaron bent at the waist, his head hanging low, hand covering his face. "Pops, goddamnit. I wanted this taken care of through legal channels. They're investigating Rob's entire company. The files, the ledgers from Beans… they could use all of it. They could've put him behind bars, where he belongs, for good."

Big Mike snorted, a humorless chuckle escaping him. "He's where he belongs, son. If I had to guess, he didn't go down easy. He had nothing but vile nonsense spilling out of his mouth until he took that golf club to the face for the last time."

"Golf club?" Aaron looked up, confused.

"Speculation and rumors," Mike said, taking another drag from the blunt. "That's all I've got these days."

Aaron straightened, meeting his father's gaze. The old man offered him the half-smoked blunt, but Aaron shook his head. "If it wasn't you, who was it?"

"Could've been anybody, I guess. Someone he hurt when they were little. Or the parent of someone he hurt. Or a business associate of that parent. The list could be very long." Another drag of the blunt.

Aaron regarded him for a long moment, his eyes searching for any hint of truth. "Okay, Mike." He exhaled, trying to keep his emotions in check. "I'm going home. I'll talk to you later."

"Are you sure you don't want to stay the night? You don't want to disappoint Loretta."

The rumble of the garage door closing was Aaron's only response.

He backed out of his father's driveway for the fifth time in two weeks and sped toward the interstate, the familiar rhythm of tires on the pavement a backdrop to his thoughts. "Spent most of two days in the garage… got the engine lowered in… golf club to the face." He muttered to himself, trying to make sense of it all. "What's so special about that car, anyway?"

Then, a passage from earlier that day flashed in his mind, a fragment of the book he had read alone in the hotel room. "The car is for her."

A sudden realization struck him. "Goddamn, Pops. It was all for her, wasn't it?" The highway unrolled before him like a ribbon that led to home. The fog in his mind was beginning to lift.

January 1, 1983: Marlena

We started the New Year at our favorite diner, just me, Mike, and little Aaron. I remember the warm smell of pancakes and bacon, the clatter of plates, and the murmur of other families chatting around us. Aaron cooed from his highchair, and Mike ordered his usual—the "Big Mike Special," as he called it—two eggs over easy, sausage, and extra crispy hash browns. I couldn't help but smile at the familiarity of it all.

After breakfast, we bundled Aaron up in his little blue jacket, and Mike took him from my arms as we made our way to the bus stop. "Here, I got him," Mike said, cradling him close like it was second nature. Watching the two of them together filled my heart. I climbed onto the bus, and Mike followed, Aaron resting on his chest. He held him the entire ride; his hands cradling our baby boy.

When we got off the bus, the crowd buzzed with excitement. The parade hadn't started yet, but you could feel it in the air. Mike led the way, nudging through people to find us a spot near the front. I could hear the distant sound of drums and trumpets as the first float rolled into view.

The colors! I've been to the Mummer's Parade every year since I was a kid, but it still took my breath away. The bright costumes, the shimmer of sequins, and the crowd's laughter made the wintry day feel alive. "Look at this," I said, bouncing on my toes like a little kid. Mike smiled at me, his arm wrapped around my shoulders, and gave Aaron a soft squeeze. "Nice spot, huh?"

"Oh, perfect," I replied, clapping as the string band played. The music had this pulse like it was running through you. I swayed to the beat, Aaron wide-eyed at the sight of all the colors and movement. "He's mesmerized," I laughed, pointing at our little boy, trying to follow the action.

After a couple of hours, I could see Aaron's little nose turning pink. "We should head back," Mike said, glancing at me. "It's getting cold for him." I nodded, even though I could've stayed all day.

Walking back to the bus stop, I saw a sleek, red sports car rumbling down the street, its engine powerful. "Mike, look at that!" I pointed, my eyes wide with admiration.

"That's a 1967 Camaro," he said, a little awe in his voice. "Classic street racer." We both stared as it rolled by, the deep purr of the engine fading as it disappeared down the street.

"You like it?" Mike asked, turning to me with a grin.

I smiled back. "It's beautiful."

He leaned down and kissed me, then pressed his lips to Aaron's head. "I'll buy you one someday, pretty lady," he said, his voice soft and full of promise.

I laughed, shaking my head. "What would we even do with a sports car, Mike?"

"Doesn't matter," he said, smiling at me in a way that made me believe him. "It'll be ours."

And right there, at that moment, with our baby boy tucked between us and the sound of the parade still ringing in the distance, I felt like anything was possible.

At two in the morning, Aaron's car crept into the driveway, his home dark and silent after eight days away. The house's wide windows seemed to glare at him, their emptiness stark. He dragged his suitcase inside and let it thud onto the foyer floor, scanning the shadows. Everything was as he'd left it. Flipping on the living room light, he glanced at the mound of unopened mail on the side table.

He poured a glass of whiskey; the liquid sloshed as he walked to the front porch. The swing creaked under his weight. *Where is everyone?*

The screen door banged open, and Alex emerged, a blunt dangling from his fingers like a prop from a noir film. "Hiya, mate. Fancy a bit of Mary Jane?" Alex's simple grin was a welcome sight.

Alex called back inside without turning. "Yo, Jared… you in the mood for some premium ganja on the veranda?"

Jared stepped into the light, heading for the swing. "Depends. Are you lighting it up or just talking about it?"

"Oh, aren't you the pushy one? You're so cute when you're like this," Alex teased, his voice dripping with mock affection. He flicked his lighter, igniting the blunt, and passed it to Aaron. Settling onto the porch, he stretched his long legs across the floorboards. "So... hell of a week, right?"

"A hell of a week," Aaron agreed, flexing his fingers and wincing. "Fucking hand hurts like a bitch."

"Yep, yep. At least you showed that old gate who the boss is, right?" Jared chuckled while Alex mimed a series of exaggerated punches at an invisible gate.

Aaron chuckled, but his eyes remained shadowed. "Easy to laugh now, but I was so fucking mad at that bastard. Still not healed enough to find much humor in it."

"And then the red-headed nurse," Jared nudged Aaron with his elbow, "She was into you, man. Should've pulled out the old Callahan moves."

"I wasn't thinking about nailing anything but that son of a bitch, Kevin, at that point. Piece of shit." Aaron took a deep sip of whiskey, then set his glass down and grabbed the blunt from Alex. "I got him too."

"Sure did." Alex's laughter was subdued. "I'll bet he shit his pants when you told his wife she looked just like that missing girl. Awful fucking man."

"Rob's dead." Aaron's voice was flat, stripped of emotion. "I'm glad he's dead."

His friends nodded. "Yep, he deserved everything he got," Alex said, and Jared bobbed his head in agreement.

"Where have you guys been, anyway?" Aaron asked, taking another drag from the blunt.

Jared and Alex exchanged looks before Jared replied, "We've been around, man. You just... you haven't needed us. You were handling all of it fine."

Alex nodded, taking the blunt from Jared with an outstretched hand. "Proud of you, Aaron. You got through this like a fucking champ." He inhaled, then continued. "Like a right fucking champ."

Aaron stared out at the dark street. "I guess. Just felt like everything was collapsing around me."

Jared gave a sympathetic nod. "Yeah, but you handled it, even when it felt like no one was there."

Alex exhaled slowly, smoke curling around him like a fog. "Exactly. You faced down the shitstorm and came out on top. That's something."

Aaron took another drag from the blunt, feeling the warmth spread through him. "Thanks, guys. It means a lot to hear that."

Jared grinned. "Anytime. We're here for you, even if you don't always see us."

Aaron passed the blunt back to Alex. "To being a champ."

Alex tipped his head and smiled. "To whatever comes next."

After they smoked, Aaron climbed the steps to his bedroom. It felt like his head had barely touched the pillow when Aaron's phone buzzed to life, lighting up with a flood of notifications. He groaned, rolling over to grab it from the nightstand, squinting at the screen through bleary eyes. *Lucas. Elise. Nico. Bethany. Nicole.* His stomach clenched.

Agent Collins had returned the phone yesterday, but Aaron hadn't plugged it in until he fell into bed four hours ago. He could already tell that the decision had been a mistake.

Stretching, he perched on the edge of the bed. He scratched his head, then rubbed his face, feeling the scruff of a beard that had gone untended for days. It was rough beneath his fingers: another thing he needed to take care of. He stared at the phone again, debating whether to dive into the chaos waiting inside those messages.

He sighed, staring at the phone. *It's time to deal with the chaos.* His brothers and sister had lost their father. While he didn't feel the grief himself, he knew they would. As the oldest, he had to step up, no matter how distant his emotions felt. With a deep breath, he dialed Lucas' number first.

It rang twice before his brother picked up, voice shaky on the other end. "Aaron?"

"Yeah, it's me," Aaron said. "How are you holding up?"

"Not good, bro. Not good. How did this happen?" Lucas' voice shook, and he let out a loud exhale and a sniffle.

Aaron ran a hand through his hair, bracing himself. "It's… complicated, Lucas. Dad had… problems. It seems like all that caught up with him."

"It makes no sense," Lucas mumbled. "He wasn't perfect, but…" His voice cracked.

"I know," Aaron said, closing his eyes. "I wish I could explain it better, but… focus on yourself and the others right now. They need you too. Have you talked to Elise or Nico?"

"Elise, yeah. She's the one who told me about Dad," Lucas said. "Between him and Patty getting arrested, she's distraught. I left a message for Nico, but he hasn't called back yet. I don't even know why the cops arrested Patty… it was before Dad died, I think. So I don't think it's that." His voice trailed off, shrinking as though the idea that Patty could be involved in their father's death was too horrible to finish.

Aaron took a deep breath. "He didn't hurt Dad. Dad was… involved in some bad stuff. Cocaine trafficking. Child trafficking." He cleared his throat, choosing his words. "The company he worked for was involved. He got Patty mixed up in it. I don't know how deep, though. The federal agent couldn't say."

"Federal agent?" Lucas sounded shocked. "You talked to a federal agent?"

"Yeah." Aaron's voice was level, trying to downplay the admission. "He's the one who told me about Dad. And Patty." He kept it simple, not wanting to overload Lucas with too much too soon.

"So it's federal charges, then," Lucas muttered, the reality sinking in. "Damn. Cocaine? And child trafficking, for God's sake? This is… it's too much, Aaron. We just saw Dad… and he was so pissed. We hadn't spoken again, hadn't made up…" The words gave way to muffled sobs, though Lucas tried hard to hide it.

"I know, man," Aaron whispered. "We'll get through it."

"We have to have a funeral," Lucas said, louder this time. "I'll bet Elise is already planning it."

"She might be, yeah," Aaron agreed. "Elise is good at that kind of thing."

"She was always Dad's favorite," Lucas whispered, the sadness tangible.

Aaron fought off a shiver at the thought that crept into his mind: *Daddy's little princess.*

After a few more minutes of conversation, the brothers hung up. Aaron took a deep breath and dialed Nico's number in Maryland. The phone rang several times before the voicemail clicked on: "Hello, you've reached Nicolaus, Andy, and Julian. We're unavailable right now, but leave a message and we'll call you back as soon as possible."

The beep sounded in his ear, and Aaron blurted out, "Hey Nico, it's Aaron. I'm sure you've heard the news by now. I saw you tried to call yesterday. My phone was off. I'd like to hear from you. Please, bro. I love you. Call me back." He ended the call and sat still, staring at the screen.

Leaning forward with his elbows on his knees, he rubbed his face, his mind replaying Nico's voicemail. The cheerful tone in the message felt out of place with everything happening now. He wished Nico would call back soon. They had spoken little since Nico moved to Maryland, and Aaron missed his brother.

Outside, the pale morning light filtered through the curtains. The world continued as if nothing had changed. But inside, Aaron felt the hurricane circling, threatening to turn his direction—his shattered family, the unknowns ahead, the responsibilities thrust upon him.

He sighed, slipping his phone into his pocket. There were more calls to make, more pieces to gather, but he needed a moment.

40

He took a quick shower—as fast as his bulky cast would allow—and shaved his days-old beard, feeling more human afterward. Heading downstairs, he buttoned the cuff on his clean shirt with difficulty; the cast made for a slow process. Sunlight streamed through the windows, brightening the kitchen and hinting at the start of a beautiful early spring day.

Aaron poured a glass of orange juice and sat at the table with a bowl of Fruity Pebbles, opting for something simple, since cooking with one hand was out of the question. The sugary cereal crunched in his mouth, but it did little to distract him from what he had to do next. Taking a deep breath, he steadied himself and dialed Elise's number. Of all the calls, this one was going to be the hardest.

Her voice was hoarse when she answered. She sounded like she'd been sobbing for hours. "How could this happen, Aaron? Patty…" Her breath caught, breaking into shallow gasps. "They arrested him like he was some criminal. Face down on the hallway floor, Aaron, right here. I'm looking at the spot where they pressed his face into the ground." Her voice trembled, rising in pitch. "Why would they do that, Aaron? Why?"

The sob that followed was a painful, guttural wail, and Aaron could almost see her coming apart at the seams.

"Elise, Patty will be okay…" he began, trying to sound reassuring, but she snapped, cutting him off.

"How do you know?" Her voice cracked with desperation. "Nobody will tell me anything! Nobody seems to know anything! It's like they kidnapped him and just took him away. I need to know where he is. Aaron, I need to see him today!" Her breath was ragged, as if she was on the edge of hyperventilating.

"Hey, kiddo, calm down for a second," Aaron said. "I'll make some calls, okay? I'll try to find out what I can about Patty."

She quieted a little, her sobs subsiding into sniffles. He could hear her wiping her nose, trying to pull herself together.

"They arrested him at your house? Where's Patty's son now? Do you know?"

"He and Drew were both here," she said, "when they came barging through my door like they thought this was a cop movie. They had guns and helmets… oh my God, Aaron, it was so scary."

"Where's Drew now?" Aaron asked, his concern for his nephew rising. Drew was only ten years old, still a little kid.

"He's here… well, he went to school. He insisted on going, but I'll pick him up after school. They stay over a lot with me, especially when Tom is out of town," she explained, her voice softening.

Uh-huh. Half-dressed sleepovers. The thought flashed through Aaron's mind, and he remembered walking in on the two of them less than two weeks ago.

"I get so scared, Aaron." Elise's voice trembled through the phone. "My anxiety gets so bad. I have panic attacks and nightmares, and I can't be here alone. If Tom knew how bad it gets, he'd take my kids from me. Patty helps me feel calm. He always has, ever since everything happened when we were little." She paused, trying to compose herself. "He's the only one who listens to me. And they took him! I need him, Aaron. I need him."

Aaron's heart ached at her distress, and he wondered if he'd been wrong about the relationship between his brother and sister. "Elise… are you and Patty… involved?"

"Involved?" Her voice rose, almost deafening him. "You shouldn't ask questions like that, Aaron. Patty's our brother. He's my… he's my best friend. I can't sleep now, thinking about what they're doing to him. Did they haul him off to some hole in the desert to interrogate him and pull out his fingernails? Is he even alive!?" She was on the edge, breaking down.

"He's not a war criminal, Elise. Nobody's torturing him. Dad and his company were into some shady stuff—drugs, kidnapped kids, abuse. Like what happened with…"

She cut him off again, her voice cracking. "I don't care about that or what he did. I just need him, Aaron!"

He took a deep breath. "I know you need him, Elise. Let me find out what's going on with Patty. You're not alone in this. I've got you." He paused, then continued, "We also need to figure out a funeral for Dad."

It took her a few minutes, but she calmed herself enough to say, "I know. I'll figure it out. I have an… event planner. She can organize everything."

"It doesn't need to be an event, Elise," Aaron said, his voice soft but firm. "Just a basic funeral. I do not know how many would even want to come."

"Dad was a popular man, Aaron. He had friends, business associates, people who will want to come." She insisted. "It is an event."

Aaron glanced at the headline on the side of the Boyertown News: *Virginia Man Dead, Drug & Child Trafficking Ring Uncovered.*

"There might not be as many people as you think, especially after they read the news," he mumbled.

When Aaron hung up with Elise, she seemed calm enough to handle calling the funeral home and her event planner. He sighed and glanced at his text messages.

> 3/17/16 9:03 am
> From Nico: Hey bud, I heard the news. I can't say I'm torn up about Dad, but maybe it will hit later. And Patty… well, a hell of a way to celebrate St. Patty's Day, eh?

> 3/17/16 9:06 am
> To Nico: Too soon, bro, but still made me lol. Talk?

3/17/16 9:09 am

> From Nico: At work, but I'll call after, okay?

Aaron smiled as he tapped out his agreement. Next on his to-do list was Nicole. He had been an absent business owner all week, and he paced the kitchen as the phone rang.

His secretary answered with a bright note in her voice. "Boss! Are you back?"

He returned the smile he could hear in her tone. "I'm at home now, heading to the office. I assume the place hasn't burned down in my absence?"

"Almost," she laughed. "No, of course not. Jim and I have held down the fort. We've had a couple of requests for meetings on new projects… that shopping mall they've been talking about putting down my way? They want to meet with you about taking the whole contract!" Her excitement was infectious.

"Damn, that's amazing! You're serious?" Aaron felt pride swelling in his chest. It was a huge, lucrative contract, and the idea of landing it was thrilling. "They want us?"

"They want you, boss," Nicole clarified.

"How's my mom's spider plant doing?" he asked, ignoring the blush creeping up his cheeks.

"Oh, she's good! Turns out she wasn't dead at all, just neglected. I've been giving her some TLC, and she's perked right up!"

"That's great, Nicole, thank you." He smiled as he drained the last of his orange juice. "I'll be there in a bit, okay?"

"Be safe, boss." The line disconnected.

Nicole must not have seen the news today. Just as well—he'd rather tell her about his stepfather and brother in person. He had one more phone call to make, though.

He sent a text message first, hoping he wouldn't interrupt her at work.

> 3/17/16 9:31 am
> To Bethany: Are you busy? Can I call?

Her response came quickly, as his phone rang, and her name lit up his screen.

"Aaron! How are you? No, wait… I have some bad news first."

His stomach tensed, bracing for more trouble. "Bad news?"

"I ate the rest of the cheesecake. I'm sorry!"

He laughed, and her laughter joined him, a welcome distraction from the week's chaos. "Guess we'll have to get another one."

"Yes, but let's make it chocolate this time!"

He hesitated, then surprised himself with his next question. "What about tonight?"

"Tonight?" she echoed. "You'll be in Philly?"

"I need to return this rental car," he explained. "I've had it for five days. It's costing me a fortune. I was wondering if… if it's not too much trouble…"

"Aaron," she interrupted gently, "wondering if what?"

"I was hoping you could give me a ride back home after I drop off the rental," he said, taking a deep breath. "And maybe stay the night?" He would save his bad news for later, during dinner, or after… but later.

"Oh," she breathed. "Well… yes, I'd love to. I can take tomorrow off. I never use my time off. Yes, Aaron, I'd love to."

He smiled at his empty glass of orange juice. "I'll text you when I'm on the way after work."

"You better, Aaron Callahan," she teased, and they ended the call with a laugh.

He headed into the office with a smile on his face. Peeking into Jim's office, he tipped his head to the man. "Thanks for handling everything this week."

His accountant grinned. "Anytime, Aaron."

He then approached Nicole's desk. "Any news about Frank's surgery?"

She sifted through her papers, her fingers finding the details. "Yes, the insurance company called after lunch. They've scheduled rotator cuff surgery for next Thursday at 7 a.m. Frank will be out for a few months—healing and physical therapy. Hopefully, he'll be back by the end of summer."

"Good to know," Aaron said, relieved. He had a stack of papers to sign and documents to review, but it felt good to be at his desk. It had been more than a month since his mother's book of memories had arrived, upending his life like a trauma-filled snow globe. At five in the afternoon, he closed his laptop, satisfied with the day's work. He grabbed his coat and baseball cap, heading toward the door.

"I'm going to drop off the rental in Philly. I'll be back home tonight or tomorrow, then gone again for the weekend. It depends on the funeral arrangements. Still waiting to hear about that." His voice carried a flat tone, hinting at his detachment.

Nicole's face softened. "I'm so sorry about your stepfather and brother."

Aaron waved a hand. "It's okay. Rob wasn't a good man, and Patty... well, I don't know him anymore. I'll be fine." He forced a smile. "You take care of Mom's plant, alright?"

"Sure thing, boss," Nicole replied, already picking up the phone. "Drive safe. I'll get that appointment set for your hand."

"Thanks, Nicole. I wasn't about to fly all the back to Kansas for that follow-up," Aaron said as he stepped out. The mention of Kansas made his stomach drop, but he chuckled to cover it. "See you soon."

He unlocked the rented Subaru Forester and slid into the driver's seat. Flipping on the radio, he caught the opening notes of "Levitating" by Dua Lipa. He rolled down the windows, letting the fresh air mix with the music. Pulling out into the street, he set the city of Philadelphia in his sights, with the prospect of seeing Bethany—and her healing smile—on his mind.

They arrived at The Cheesecake Factory and even though it was a holiday, the wait was shorter this time. Bethany was in high spirits, her eyes bright as they browsed the menu. The hum of conversation around them and the clinking of silverware felt cozy after the week he'd had.

"I'm starving," Aaron said, setting his menu down. "Think I'll go with the barbecue chicken burger."

Bethany nodded, studying the options. "I'm getting the white chicken chili. I've been craving something warm all day."

He smiled, appreciating the easy way she made decisions. When the server came, they placed their orders, then leaned back, enjoying the relaxed atmosphere.

"You know, we could take the rental back in the morning," he suggested, trying to buy some time.

She tilted her head, her lips curving into a mischievous grin. "You're just stalling. I'm excited to see where you live, Aaron. I want to get the rental done tonight."

Her enthusiasm was contagious, and he nodded. "All right, after dinner it is."

Their plates arrived, steam rising off the food. Aaron dug into his burger, savoring the tangy barbecue sauce mixed with the crisp bite of onion rings. Across the table, Bethany spooned up her chili—the rich aroma of slow-cooked chicken and spices filled the air.

"So," she said between bites, "tell me about Boyertown. What's it like?"

He wiped his mouth, thinking. "Quiet. Slower pace. Good people. It's not Philly, but it has its charm. I think you'll like it."

Bethany gave a light laugh. "I'm looking forward to it. We should grab a cheesecake to take with us."

Dinner flowed, though it turned serious when Aaron shared the news of his stepfather's death and his brother's arrest. "If you've seen the news today," he said, pushing his fork through his burger, "he's the 'Virginia man' on the front page with the federal charges."

Bethany reached across the table, resting her hand on his. "I'm so sorry, Aaron. Is there anything I can do?"

He looked at her, a weary smile tugging at his lips. "Honestly? Just come home with me. Let me forget about the mess that is my family, even if it's only for tonight."

She nodded, smiling. "There's nothing I'd like more."

Before long, they were back in their cars, heading to the airport to return the rental. The cool night breeze brushed Aaron's face as they stood in the parking lot after handing over the keys. Bethany's car smelled of lavender as they settled in. The city lights faded, replaced by long stretches of quiet highway. Boyertown came into view as night settled around them.

With Aaron's directions, Bethany coasted through the quiet streets and pulled into his driveway. Her eyes widened as she took in the house, the soft glow of porch lights highlighting the details on the windows and roof.

"Your house is so big," she said, admiring the intricate touches around the edges that Aaron had always loved but rarely heard others mention.

His grin widened. Without a word, he wrapped her in his arms and kissed her, leaving them both breathless.

"What's that for?" she teased, her eyes sparkling.

"I'm just glad you're here," he whispered. "I haven't brought a woman to this house in… I don't even know, seven years maybe? My secretary watches the place when I'm gone, gets my mail and all, but she's…" He shrugged with a laugh, his hands rising in an awkward gesture. "She's my secretary."

Bethany smiled, leaning into him, her hand resting on his chest. "Well, I'm glad I'm here too. Show me the inside?"

"Of course, my lady," Aaron said with a grin, unlocking the front door and guiding her in. They walked through the cozy first floor. Bethany's fingers brushed the smooth wood of the oak sideboard that doubled as his liquor cabinet while Aaron poured her a vodka tonic, then grabbed a whiskey for himself.

"Your home is lovely, Aaron," she said, settling onto his old floral couch. She eyed it for a moment, smirking. "But this couch could use a little update."

He laughed. "Yeah, I got that thing when I rented my first apartment in Virginia. Secondhand then, and somehow it followed me here. I'll replace it one day."

She raised an eyebrow. "What's upstairs?"

He smirked, teasing her. "Come on, I'll show you the bedroom since you can't wait." He led her toward the stairs, his hand slipping into hers as they climbed.

"The bed's not from my college days… it's pretty comfortable," Aaron said with a grin, wrapping his hands around her waist. He turned her, bringing her close until his lips captured hers. The kiss started slow and tender, igniting into something deeper. As their bodies pressed together, he backed her until the bed hit the back of her legs. "Want to test it out?"

Bethany flashed a mischievous smile and, in one swift motion, whipped around, pushing him onto the mattress. She crawled up his body, straddling him with a teasing grin. Reaching up, she unclipped her curls, letting them fall around her face. She pulled her shirt over her head and tossed it toward the foot of the bed.

"I thought you'd never ask, Aaron Callahan."

They had worn each other out before collapsing into a warm, sated sleep. The dark sky outside mirrored Aaron's emptiness when he woke up to find the bed beside him cold. He pulled on his pajama pants and stepped into the hallway. His pulse quickened when he saw the open door at the end of the hall. A sense of dread settled in his chest. *Not tonight. I'm not ready.*

He moved toward the open door, his heart pounding.

Inside, Bethany sat in an old rocking chair, her eyes full of quiet questions. She looked up as he entered, the room heavy with a past he had long avoided.

"Aaron... what is this?" she whispered, her voice weaving a subtle melody through the stillness.

He stood frozen, his eyes drawn to the wooden crib in the corner. He had built it with love, but it would never hold a baby.

Rachel's mural was still vivid on the wall: rainbows, butterflies, sunshine, and hot air balloons. It was a bright future that had faded before it could begin. Dust coated the rug and furniture. Everything froze in time. Unopened diapers sat on the changing table. The dresser overflowed with unworn baby clothes. The shelves held board books, untouched and waiting.

He cleared his throat; his voice was as rough as the memories he'd buried for over a decade. His voice cracked as he spoke. Memories surfaced like wreckage. "I was married once. We had a baby. He died... before he ever took a breath." Tears spilled down his cheeks, unchecked, his body sagging against the door frame. "Full-term. She went into labor. We were so excited." His breath hitched as the flood of emotions surged. "The doctor said there was no heartbeat."

Bethany shifted, about to rise, but Aaron caught her gaze and shook his head. She understood, sinking back into the chair, allowing him space to release the pain.

"We moved here after he died… after Oliver died," he continued, his voice a ragged whisper. "Rachel—my ex-wife—wanted to have another baby. She painted the walls herself. I spent weeks putting everything together." He gestured toward the crib, his gaze distant, lost in the past. "It wasn't the right time. I wanted to build up the business, have more money, be more ready… get everything right that time. And then… it was just gone. Oliver was gone. And then Rachel was gone."

His chest heaved as he tried to compose himself, the raw grief that he had buried for years now cracking through his composure. "I haven't touched a thing in this room since that day. I couldn't face it. Every time I thought about moving the crib or packing up the clothes… I'd break."

Bethany's eyes softened. She didn't speak, didn't fill the silence. She let him feel, let him share the wound he had carried for so long in isolation. The dusty reminder of a lost life hung between them. It was fragile, heavy with unspeakable sorrow.

Aaron wiped his face with the back of his hand. "I don't know why I'm telling you all of this," he said, "but I guess… I needed to say it out loud. To someone."

"I'm sorry you went through that, Aaron," she whispered. "No one should have to carry that kind of pain alone."

He let out a shaky breath, feeling lighter but still raw. "I thought I could… bury it. Move on. But it's always there, you know? A part of me that never healed."

She stood up and moved toward him, stopping before they touched. "You don't have to deal with it alone anymore. I'm here now, and I'm not going anywhere. But you don't have to rush to make peace with it either."

Aaron blinked, his vision still blurred with tears, but he felt a surge of warmth in his chest. He hadn't expected her compassion.

Bethany reached out, taking his hand in hers. "Come on, let's go back to bed. You've been through enough for one night."

He nodded, not trusting his voice, and followed her back into the hallway. They didn't speak on the way back to the bedroom. But, as they settled into the sheets, Aaron felt a shift inside him. For the first time in years, he wasn't carrying his grief alone.

As they lay side by side, Bethany wrapped her arm around him, her touch grounding him in the present. Aaron closed his eyes, his body relaxing as he took in the quiet comfort of her presence. The pain was still there, but so was she—unwavering.

He didn't know what tomorrow would bring. But, for the first time in a long while, he knew he could face it.

41

The shrill chime of the phone woke Aaron. He threw his arm out, silencing it with a touch and squinting at the Caller ID. *Elise?* He answered in a low voice, careful not to wake Bethany. "Hello?"

His sister's voice came through, frantic and breathless. "Aaron? Hey, I've got the funeral details all sorted out."

Aaron groaned. "What time is it, Elise?"

"It's 7:30. What, you're not up yet? Anyway, listen. The funeral home is picking Dad up today. There's a viewing tomorrow at 5 p.m., then the funeral is on Sunday at 2 p.m."

"Five tomorrow, two Sunday, I've got it." He jotted the times down on a scratch pad. "Did you talk to the others?"

"I called you first, but I will. I don't know if Nico's coming. Tom's back tonight… I wish I could talk to Patty. Every time I call, they give me the runaround. I want him there, Aaron. He should be there." She continued rambling about flowers and arrangements.

Bethany stirred beside him. She gave him a questioning look. Aaron raised a finger to signal that he would be off soon.

"Elise," he interrupted, "I'll see if I can reach someone about Patty. Maybe they can bring him, bond him out… I'll figure it out."

When they hung up, Aaron let out a long sigh, rubbing his eyes. "Yeah, it's fine," he said, answering Bethany's unspoken question. "Just… funeral details." He sat up, letting the sheet fall as he swung his legs over the edge of the bed. "Viewing tomorrow, service on Sunday."

Bethany watched him, concern in her eyes. "And how are you holding up with all this?"

He ran a hand through his hair, searching for the right words. "I don't know. Elise is trying to get everything together, but she's fragile. She wants Patty there. I don't even know if that's possible." He shook his head, releasing a slow breath. "It's a lot."

Bethany reached out, her hand resting on his back. "You don't have to fix everything, Aaron."

He gave her a small smile. "I know, but it's hard not to try."

She wrapped her arms around his shoulders. "I'm here for whatever you need. Even if it's only sitting with you while you make some calls."

He leaned into her embrace, letting her warmth soothe his tension. "Thanks," he whispered, closing his eyes for a moment. "I'll make some coffee… and call Collins with the FBI. See if they'll even talk to me about Patty."

Bethany kissed his shoulder. "Okay. I'll be right here."

Aaron nodded, pulling himself together as he stood. Downstairs, he paced the kitchen, the weight of the conversation pressing on him as Agent Collins spoke. "Aaron. How are you, sir?" The agent's voice was friendly.

"I'm fine," Aaron said, not wanting to get into details. "I'm wondering if there are any updates on my brother or Kevin Earls?"

"Kevin Earls is in federal custody. Officers served warrants at his property. He resisted, as did his eldest son. Both are now in custody in Wichita, Kansas."

Aaron's mind raced. "And the kids?"

"The minor children are with Child Protective Services. Their families are being notified and they will go home within the next several days."

Aaron sighed with relief, still feeling uneasy. "And the adults? His wife, Maritza?" His voice had an edge of impatience. He wanted justice, closure—anything that felt like resolution.

Collins's tone changed. "That's a bit more complicated. The adults will have the choice of reconnecting with their families, of course. After so many years, they may stay where they are. It depends on the individuals."

Aaron clenched his jaw. "I get it. I wish it was easier."

"So do I," Collins admitted. "But it's a delicate process."

Aaron shifted, leaning against the counter. "And Patty? We're having a viewing and a funeral for Rob… it's important to Elise that he be there. Is that even possible?"

There was a pause on the other end. "I can't answer that right now, Aaron. Text me the details of both the viewing and the funeral, and I'll see what I can do. No promises."

"I can't bond or bail him out?" Aaron asked, desperation seeping into his voice.

"This is a federal case, Aaron. We're not local law enforcement. Patty's a key witness, and he's the only one we have right now, aside from your documents. He's an important asset." Collins's tone was firm but not unkind.

Aaron nodded, though Collins couldn't see him. "I understand. I'll send the details." He ended the call.

"Is everything okay?"

Aaron met Bethany's gaze, unsure how to answer. "Not yet."

"Didn't you tell me you have roommates?" Bethany asked, opening a cabinet to pull out two coffee mugs. "Where are they today?"

"Uh yeah. Alex and Jared… I don't know what they're up to."

"Where do they sleep, anyway? You have more secret rooms around here that I didn't see?" Her tone was light as she busied herself pouring the coffee and spooning sugar and creamer.

Aaron stared at the coffee mugs, his mind spinning. *Where do they sleep?* The question shouldn't have been hard, but it was. He had never thought about the presence or absence of Alex and Jared like that—or even the logistics of where they went when he wasn't with them.

"Uh," he began, but his voice faltered. He didn't know.

Bethany turned, handing him a steaming cup. "You okay?" she asked, noticing the distant look in his eyes.

Aaron forced a smile, trying to shake off the unease. "Yeah… it's funny. I've never really thought about that." He chuckled, though it felt hollow. "They're… around, you know?"

"Aaron, that's a little weird, don't you think?" She was joking, but her curiosity was real.

He shrugged, trying to brush it off. "Yeah, I guess so." He took a slow sip, but the warmth of the coffee did nothing to ease the chill creeping into his thoughts.

Alex and Jared. They're always here. But where?

The thought gnawed at him as he watched Bethany scan the refrigerator's shelves.

"Are you hungry?"

He shook off his thoughts and tried to focus on her. "I could eat. I have a lot of cereal these days."

"Well, you've got bacon, a little sausage, and about a half-dozen eggs." She moved to the pantry, glancing over the shelves. "And a bell pepper… we should use the poor thing or toss it." She tossed it in the air, catching it with a grin. "Feel like an omelet?"

"Yeah, I do. That sounds delicious." Aaron sat at the table, watching her gather pans and utensils. She cracked the eggs, chopped the bell pepper and a clove of garlic like she was competing on a cooking show, then slid it all into a bowl with the edge of her knife.

"You like to cook?" he asked, wanting to know everything about her.

"I do. I love it. We grew up poor, and my mama could turn the most random ingredients into something delicious. Everything I know, I learned from her, since I was a little kid." The pan sizzled as she added the sausage, her hands moving, never pausing in her rhythm.

Aaron watched her, hesitating for a moment before speaking again. "I was thinking… maybe it's too soon, or a weird question…"

Bethany laughed, flipping the sausage. "What's too soon? The omelet?"

He chuckled, shaking his head. "No… I wondered if you'd want to go with me this weekend."

"To the viewing of your stepfather?"

"And the funeral, yeah." He felt awkward, unsure if he was crossing a line.

She paused, considering, as she flipped the sausage in the pan. "I'd like that. I have nothing to wear, though. Didn't pack for something like that."

"Oh, well, don't worry about it then…"

Bethany turned, her eyes affectionate. "You misunderstand me. My place is an hour away. I can grab some clothes. I don't mind."

"You're sure? I don't want you to feel you have to."

She smiled now, her voice soft but sure. "I don't feel like I have to. And yes, I'm sure."

His smile grew, this time reaching his eyes. "Good."

After a few quick minutes, Bethany handed Aaron a plate piled with a steaming spicy sausage and pepper omelet alongside crispy bacon strips. Without hesitation, he dug in, even though it was too hot. "Holy hell, Bethany. This is amazing!"

She beamed, her eyes lighting up as she sat beside him. "Thank you." She cut into her omelet, savoring the moment.

When they had washed and dried the dishes, they headed upstairs. Their shower, meant to be quick, stretched on much longer than necessary, distracted by the feel of each other's bodies, which led them back to the bedroom.

Two hours passed before they dressed, the morning slipping away in a mix of passion and warmth. Bethany laced up her boots, twisting her curls into a bun at the back of her head. "I'll run home and grab some things, then be back. Unless you want to ride along?"

Aaron shook his head. "I'm going to stay if that's okay... get in touch with Alex and Jared, maybe figure out where they're staying these days, you know?" He hesitated, his earlier uncertainty resurfacing. Her question about his roommates had planted a nagging thought in his mind.

Why don't I know where they are or where they sleep?

Bethany smiled, not pressing the issue. "Okay, I'll be back then." She kissed him and left, leaving Aaron alone with his growing unease.

May 17, 2012: Marlena

I was helping clear the last of the plates at Elise and Tom's rehearsal dinner. The steakhouse was lit only by dim candlelight, and the laughter and chatter warmed the place. Aaron came up beside me, his hands reaching for the same plate I was stacking.

"Need some help, Mom?"

I smiled, grateful for the company. "Sure, but I think I've got it under control." The plates and glasses clinked together as we moved through the task. He worked with efficiency, but I could feel his attention on me.

"You okay?" Aaron asked, a softness in his voice. He's good at reading me, that boy.

I forced a smile. "I'm fine, sweetie. Wasn't it a beautiful dinner?"

He nodded, glancing around at the guests still milling about, the low hum of conversation filling the air. "Yeah, it was nice."

As I wiped the table, I asked what had been on my mind all night. "So, when will you find someone to settle down with?"

He went quiet, his face closing off like it does when I've touched something sore. He didn't look at me, just stared at the empty table. "I'm not ready for that, Mom, not after Rachel."

The weight of her name hung between us, and I sighed. "It's been three years, Aaron. Maybe it's time to get ready. You can't stay alone in that big house forever."

His jaw flexed, and he looked at me, his eyes distant. "I'm not alone, Mom. I have Alex and Jared."

My heart squeezed. I wanted to tell him that Alex and Jared weren't real, that he deserved more than this… loneliness. But I'd never say that. Not to Aaron. He's been through too much already—too much loss, too much grief. I'd never be the one to pile more weight on him. So, instead, I reached out, placing my hand on his arm, feeling the sadness rise inside me. "I know, sweet boy, but it's not the same."

He only nodded, his face still unreadable, and went back to clearing the table. The space between us felt heavier, as though the mention of Rachel always brought an unspoken burden with it. It's as if she still held a piece of him, something he couldn't—or wouldn't—let go of. And I wonder if he'll ever be ready to move on from that shadow.

Aaron closed the book hard on the couch next to him, the confusion swirling in his mind. *What the hell?*

"Hey…" A voice startled him, and he turned toward the kitchen doorway to see Alex leaning on the door frame, peeling an apple. "Dude, what? We're real. What the hell?"

Jared padded in from the hallway, his features similar to Aaron's—so much so that Aaron wondered how he'd never noticed the likeness before. "Not real? Okay, Mom. We're standing here, aren't we?"

Alex looked annoyed. "More real than her sham marriage was. More real than those fucking 'fishing trips' were. We've been here for you when no one else was."

Aaron struggled to process what he was hearing. "Where do you guys sleep?"

"We sleep here, same as you. Like, duh." Jared rolled his eyes, dropping into an armchair.

"Where do you go when you're not here?" Aaron pressed, his unease growing.

"We're never not here, man. I mean, we're not here when you're not here... not usually, though there have been times." Jared was casual, like they were discussing weekend plans instead of his entire reality.

"I don't understand." Aaron stood up, running a hand through his hair, his mind spinning.

"We showed up because you needed us, Aaron," Jared explained. "First Alex... then me. And now? We need you as much as you need us."

"Are you... in my head? Am I crazy?" Aaron's voice cracked as he paced the room, the pressure in his chest building.

"You're not crazy, man." Jared exchanged a glance with Alex. "You're who you're meant to be. We all are. You survived... we survived together."

Alex poured a glass of whiskey, handing it to Aaron with a knowing look. "Just go with it, man. We've got a good thing going here."

Aaron took the whiskey with a shaky hand, the liquid burning down his throat as he swallowed. "And Mom always knew... she knew about you guys?"

Alex's expression softened, his voice quieter now. "Mom knew us very well. She always did. We were her favorite... maybe because of everything we endured. She couldn't do much to protect us, but she saw we figured out how to protect ourselves."

Aaron sank onto the couch, his mind a tangled mess of emotions. "So, Mom… she knew I wasn't alone?"

"She knew something was off," Alex said, crossing his arms. "But she never pushed. She just wanted you to be okay. She didn't care how you got there."

Aaron rubbed his face. "So what now? I just… live like this? You guys are my backup in case everything falls apart again?"

Jared smiled, walking over and resting a hand on Aaron's shoulder. "We're always here. You don't have to understand it. Just accept it."

Aaron stared at both of them, feeling torn between relief and madness. It wasn't how he pictured his life—living with people who only existed because he needed them. But somehow, their presence felt real. Maybe that was enough.

Alex fished a blunt from his pocket, flashing a grin as he held it up. "Anyone down for a smoke?"

Aaron exhaled, trying to keep his irritation in check. "Does this seem like the time for that?"

Jared, sprawled in the armchair, chuckled. "Yeah. Feels like the perfect time. Come on, man."

Aaron ran a hand through his hair, shaking his head. "We're talking about my entire reality here, and you guys want to get high?"

Ignoring him, Alex sparked the blunt, taking a long drag before blowing out a lazy stream of smoke. "That's why you need to chill, Aaron. None of this has to make sense right now. It just… is."

"Take it outside, damn it. Use your brain." Aaron stood up, exasperated.

Alex grinned, exhaling smoke. "I use your brain all the time. More than you do, I'll bet."

Aaron shot him a look that could cut steel. Jared, still lounging, laughed as he got up and headed to the porch, Alex following suit. They settled into their usual spots, with Jared sinking into the swing. He took a drag, holding out the blunt to Aaron without a word.

"You overthink everything, man. This isn't about figuring it out. It's about surviving." Jared's voice was calm but direct.

Aaron hesitated. His mind screamed for an escape. He sighed, reaching for the blunt. "Fine. Give it here."

Alex smirked from where he sat on the floor. "That's a good boy."

"Bite me," Aaron muttered, struggling to hold in the smoke as they both burst out laughing. The familiar warmth spread through his chest, and for a moment, the noise in his mind quieted. *Maybe they're right. Maybe sometimes survival means not asking for answers.*

They passed the blunt in comfortable silence, the usual banter slipping back in, familiar and soothing. When it was done, Aaron flicked the stub into the yard, leaning back to watch the teenagers across the street playing basketball. He didn't need to listen to Alex and Jared's chatter—he let the peace sink in, a rare feeling these days.

When Bethany's car pulled into the driveway, it snapped him out of his daze. He stood, ready to greet her, and turned to call Alex and Jared over. The porch was empty.

Aaron blinked. *They were just here.*

Bethany stepped out of the car, catching his distracted look. "Hey," she called, her voice light but curious. "Everything okay?"

He hesitated, his eyes scanning the empty porch again before he forced a smile. "Yeah, I'm fine. Just... spaced out for a second."

She reached for his hand, her warmth grounding him. "You sure?"

"Yeah," he nodded, though his thoughts spun in circles. As they walked inside, he glanced back one last time at the porch, half-expecting Alex and Jared to materialize, leaning in the doorway or making another sarcastic comment. But there was nothing except the sounds of the kids across the street and the thud of the basketball on the asphalt.

Even as Aaron followed Bethany into the house, a part of him lingered on the empty porch and the absence of his friends. He didn't know what it meant yet, but something had irrevocably changed.

42

Nothing had changed since Aaron was last at the funeral home ten months ago. The same low lighting, the same heavy scent of lilies. *Ten months without you, Mom.* He squeezed Bethany's hand, more for his steadiness than hers, and stepped forward into the center of the room.

Rob's casket sat against the far wall—polished mahogany with gunmetal gray satin lining. Tall sprays of yellow gladioli and white carnations framed the casket like sentinels. A cascade of white roses and lilies covered the closed half. The flowers gave the scene a forced elegance, but the weight of loss made the room feel hollow.

Aaron's eyes caught Lucas first. He was standing with Renee and a couple Aaron didn't recognize. He guided Bethany toward them. When the couple moved on, Aaron introduced her. Renee and Lucas greeted her with warmth, shaking her hand, but there was a tension beneath their smiles. When Renee turned to Bethany, Lucas tugged Aaron to the side.

"This is surreal, Aaron," Lucas said, his voice cracking. "We were just here… you know? Just here. It hasn't even been a year." His eyes glistened, and Aaron could see the effort it took for his brother to hold back tears.

"I know," Aaron whispered, his throat tight with grief. The weight of standing here again, another loss in so little time, felt impossible. He forced a breath, trying to focus. "I've got something for you, bro." Reaching into his suit coat pocket, he pulled out a silver watch and Rob's leather wallet. The watch gleamed under the dim lights, the back engraved with Rob's initials: RJB.

Aaron placed the watch in Lucas' hand. He ran his thumb over the smooth crystal face, then turned it over, tracing the engraved letters with his finger. His breath hitched. "Thanks, man. I'm honored to have it." He unclasped the band, struggling as he threaded it onto his wrist. Once it clicked, he turned his wrist, admiring how it caught the light against his shirt cuff.

Aaron handed over the wallet next, worn leather bulging. Lucas whistled low. "It's stuffed full! Holy shit, Dad... how much cash is in it?" Aaron shrugged.

"You didn't look?" Lucas asked, raising an eyebrow as he opened the wallet. His eyes widened as he pulled out a thick wad of cash. "There's like... four thousand bucks in here. What the hell, Dad, why?" He split the pile in two without a second thought, holding half out to Aaron. "Take it."

"No, it's yours, Luke," Aaron said, pushing his hand back. "Use it for whatever."

But Lucas wouldn't hear it. "Take half, Aaron. I'm serious." The determined look on his face made it clear that arguing was pointless. Aaron hesitated, then accepted the bills, folding them and sliding them into his pocket.

For a moment, they stood there in the quiet. The absence of their father hung between them like a thick fog that neither could escape.

Nico and Andy arrived with the next group, and Aaron waved them over and hugged both men. Nico excused himself, walking to the casket to stand with his back to the room. "He's got some things to get off his chest," Andy explained. Aaron and Lucas exchanged knowing looks, understanding what he meant.

Scanning the room, Aaron spotted Bethany holding a glass of red wine, talking to Renee and a cousin from North Carolina whose name escaped him. Elise stood nearby, looking polished but worn, the strain clear on her face. Her husband, Tom, sat behind her, staring at his phone and ignoring the surrounding scene.

Nico rejoined them, wiping tears from his cheeks. "I said what I needed to say. First time he's never argued with me. Can't say I hate it," he half-joked, prompting chuckles from the group.

"Guess that makes it my turn," Aaron sighed, feeling the finality of the moment settling over him. He made his way across the room, shaking hands and accepting condolences. When he reached the casket, he froze. The man who had loomed so large over his childhood, ruling with cruelty and control, lay lifeless before him. The funeral home had done its job well—Rob looked peaceful, almost as if he were asleep. A far cry from the bruised and battered body Aaron had last seen in Roanoke.

Taking a deep breath, Aaron leaned down toward his stepfather's body, close enough to catch the faint chemical scent of formaldehyde.

In a low whisper, he said, "I'm glad you're dead."

Straightening up, Aaron gave Rob one last glance. He turned and walked away, passing two men in black suits by the door. A flicker of recognition hit him—the one on the left had been the guard stationed outside his hotel room in Roanoke.

"Hey, what are you doing here?" Aaron asked, his voice tinged with suspicion.

The man gestured toward the entrance. Aaron's heart raced as he followed the man's thumb. There stood Agent Collins, engaged in a serious conversation with Patty. Elise spotted them then and hurried over in her elegant heels, throwing her arms around Patty. He enveloped her in a hug, their embrace suggesting a reunion long overdue, although it had only been days.

Patty leaned in to whisper something in Elise's ear. Aaron watched, perplexed, as Tom appeared, seizing Elise's arm and pulling her away. "Stay away from my wife, criminal!" he snarled.

Patty's laughter cut through the tension, his voice filling the room. He extended his hand to Elise, who stepped back towards him. "She's my sister, asshole."

Tom yanked Elise's arm again, his face contorted in anger. "You don't belong here!" he hissed.

Agent Collins intervened, placing himself between Tom and the siblings. "Sir, I need you to calm down. Sean is here to pay his respects to his stepfather. Please refrain from causing a scene."

Tom's voice rose to a snarl. "They're fucking, you know." Across the room, conversations fell silent, the collective gasp echoing through the space. "These two. The criminal and the princess." He spun as if to leave but lunged past Collins, landing a punch on Patty's jaw.

Patty stumbled backward, regaining his balance and firing back with a punch that connected with Tom's upper cheek. Tom doubled over, clutching his bleeding face. He tried to lunge forward again, but federal agents closed in, escorting him away.

"We never should have brought you in, Patty! You fucked up!" Tom's shouts were a jumbled mess, but they had no visible effect on Patty. Patty stood with his arm around Elise, his other hand pressed against his bruised jaw. His son Drew stood behind him, his small jaw set as though ready to defend his father.

"Keep running your mouth and digging your grave, Tom," Patty said. "I don't have to bury you; you're doing it yourself."

Tom darted toward the far side door, his face contorted in anger. One agent followed and stayed by the exit, while the other returned to where Patty and Agent Collins were, both men looking on with confusion and concern.

As Aaron approached, Collins turned to Patty, his expression stern. "What was that about?"

Patty, still holding his sister close, shook his head. "Can we talk about it later, Collins? I'd like to see my family first." He walked away with Elise, heading towards Aaron and the casket. The crowd's murmur resumed, though all eyes lingered on the couple moving across the room.

Aaron tried to catch Patty's attention, but his brother raised a dismissive hand. "You've done enough, don't you think?"

Aaron opened his mouth to reply, but Patty cut him off. "Leave it, Aaron, unless you want the entire crowd to know all your business, too. This is supposed to be about Dad, not our drama."

"Trauma, I think you mean," Aaron muttered, but Patty, Elise, and Drew were already weaving through the crowd toward Lucas and Nico.

Agent Collins stepped up beside Aaron. "He can't stay long. I told him thirty minutes, and that was before the fistfight." Collins' gaze fixated on Patty and Elise. "Any idea what that was about between Tom and Sean?"

Aaron shook his head. "No clue. Tom's always been calm around me. He and Rob were close friends, so maybe... I don't know."

Collins looked thoughtful. "Thanks, Aaron. Just another tangle in the web." He followed Patty, but Aaron touched his arm to stop him.

"Thanks for bringing him tonight, Collins. He won't talk to me, but my sister was desperate to see him. They're..." He glanced over to see Elise smiling at Patty, who returned the grin. The couple looked like they were at a celebration, not the viewing of their dead father. "They're close."

Collins followed Aaron's gaze. "Yes, they are. You're welcome, Aaron. I'll be in touch."

Aaron spotted Bethany and made his way over. She was talking with one of Rob and Marlena's former neighbors, but excused herself when she saw him approach. "Sorry to abandon you like that," he said as she handed him a glass of wine.

"It's okay," she replied, taking the glass. "I met your other siblings. Nico and I had a pleasant talk. Elise and Patty were pretty wrapped up, though. They're quite the pair."

They both turned to watch Elise and Patty at Rob's casket. Elise was crying, her face buried against Patty's shoulder. Patty had one arm around her, and with his free hand, he wiped her tears.

Bethany glanced at Aaron. "Do you think what her husband said is true?"

"It's possible," Aaron said, finishing his wine and setting the glass on a nearby table. "We had a tough childhood. We all faced abuse in different ways, but Elise... I'm surprised she even has tears for Rob. Patty's been an immense support for her. How? My guess is as good as yours." He shrugged, a mixture of frustration and resignation in his gesture.

When Agent Collins tapped Patty on the shoulder to signal that it was time to leave, Elise crumpled into tears, dissolving like sugar in a sudden downpour. "Please don't take him. I need him," she begged, her voice breaking.

"Mrs. Littleton, let's not make a scene," Collins said, his tone polite but firm.

Lucas stepped forward, enveloping Elise in his arms as the agents escorted Patty out of the room. Elise sobbed, her cries piercing the air. "Will he be there tomorrow? Patty, will you be there tomorrow?"

Lucas shushed Elise, soothing her like a distressed child as he guided her through the remaining crowd. He brought her to Renee, who offered her a tissue and attempted to calm her tears. Turning to Aaron and Bethany, Lucas said, "We're taking her and Drew to our house. Her kids are there and I don't think she should be alone tonight. Who knows where Tom is?"

"Let me know if you need anything," Aaron said, and Lucas nodded in acknowledgment.

"See you tomorrow for the… the funeral," Lucas added. Both men looked toward the casket, where the funeral home director was now closing the wooden lid, preparing to roll Rob into cold storage until the next day.

November 14, 2014: Marlena

My second child is dead. Lydia Walker. Well, he was married, so she's Lydia Bryant. Her father called this morning, his voice crackling through the receiver. Lydia is gone. Liver failure, Roy said. He sounded so frail, so much older than I remembered. I could almost picture him, huddled in his old armchair, cradling that sad news.

Thirty-eight years since he left with my babies. It's like time has folded in on itself. Harrison, gone sixteen years now, and Lydia, taken from the world last night. How long would they have lived if I'd been there with them? The thought haunts me.

I imagine that all of my children are here with me now. Harrison: he would be over forty, and Lydia with her children—Roy said they're eighteen and twenty. Aaron, my handsome boy. Patty with his wife and their baby. Nico might come with his boyfriend. Lucas and his little family, and Elise, all full of attitude, at sixteen. She would have Lydia's girls to hang out with. It could be… something wonderful.

I can't go to Lydia's funeral. Roy gave me the details, but Rob will never allow it. Rob's view on funerals grates on me. He doesn't get it— the finality and need for closure. "Time is money?" None of that matters when someone you love is gone forever. But I know him too well. When it's his time, I doubt he'll be so dismissive. It's always "one rule for me, another for everyone else" with him. It makes me wonder how he'll handle his mortality when his time runs out.

Fort Worth feels like a world away anyway, though. It's too

costly, and her family... her husband and kids... they don't know me. What they know isn't kind. I am the mother who walked away. That's what I was and will always be to them now. No amount of regret can mend the rift I created.

Aaron lay against the pillows as Bethany propped herself on one elbow beside him. "So, you have an older sister and brother that you never met?" she asked, her voice soft.

"Yep. Harrison died... the story is that it was a heroin overdose, but Kevin and Rob both made it sound like Rob killed him for threatening their business. Lydia was younger than him, but not by much... I didn't know she was dead until I found this memory." He sighed, staring past the pages of the book in his lap. "Mom never told me they existed. I never knew them."

"I'm sure she had her reasons," Bethany whispered. "It sounds like your stepfather had her under his thumb pretty hardcore."

"He did. He had us all under his thumb." Aaron reached for the glass of water by the bed, took a sip, and handed it to her. "I used to think my real father was the Boogeyman in my life story... and he was awful, don't get me wrong. But, I feel like he learned his lesson in prison, maybe. He seems so much different now. I wish Mom could have known that."

He trailed off; the words settling in the quiet between them. "I wish Mom could have known that Mike had changed," he repeated. "But Rob... he overshadowed everything. She traded one nightmare for another when she got with him."

Bethany handed the glass back after taking a sip. "It makes sense, though. After everything she went through with your dad, maybe Rob seemed safer, at least back then. But holding that kind of control over someone..." She shook her head. "No wonder she couldn't tell you about Harrison and Lydia."

"Yeah, I get that," Aaron said, though the understanding came with a sting. "But it's still hard, you know? It's like a whole life I never knew existed, and now... it's too late to know them. The chance is gone." He exhaled. "I think about what it would've been like to grow up with them. But it's just all questions now."

She took his hand, her thumb brushing over his knuckles. "You can still remember them in your way, even if you never met them. It doesn't mean they didn't exist in your life. Maybe it's not too late for that."

Aaron nodded, though the feelings lingered. "Maybe. But it's hard to remember something you never had."

They were dressing for the funeral the following afternoon when Aaron's phone buzzed. He glanced at the screen, then answered, his voice low and clipped. After a brief exchange, he hung up, his face unreadable.

Bethany, who had been adjusting her dress in the mirror, turned to him, concern etched across her brow. "Aaron... are you okay?"

He stood there, processing what he'd just heard, before responding. "That was Collins. Patty, Elise... and their kids won't be at the funeral."

"What? Why not?" Bethany took a step toward him.

"They're being moved. Collins says it's for their safety—something about the federal trial with Luca Meat Distribution." Aaron paused, rubbing the back of his neck. "They've got additional evidence. Tom... they think he's involved in the cocaine trafficking, maybe even the child trafficking."

Bethany's eyes widened in disbelief. "Tom? Elise's husband?"

Aaron nodded. "Yeah, it's looking bad. Collins said they are moving them all to a safe location until the trial's over. They're not taking any chances. Patty, Elise, Drew, Elise's kids—they're all going into hiding. They won't be anywhere near here."

Bethany was quiet for a moment, taking in the situation. "So... they're not coming to the funeral at all?"

"No." Aaron's voice was heavy, his shoulders sagging with the news. "None of them will be there. I have to tell Nico and Lucas."

43

White chairs lined up in neat rows, facing the casket that hovered over Robert Bakker's dark grave. A green cloth draped the mound of dirt to the side as if the rawness of death needed softening. A cascade of white roses and lilies crowned the middle of the mahogany box, with the sprays of gladioli and carnations from the viewing standing sentry, overseeing the burial of a man who had cast a long shadow over Aaron's life.

In the front row sat Lucas and Renee, their children Elisabeth and Samuel beside them. Nico, Andy, and Julian occupied the seats next to them. Behind them, in the second row, a thin woman dressed in black sat alone, her face hidden by a veil. She wore black gloves and dabbed at her eyes with a tissue as the funeral director delivered his eulogy.

Aaron sat with Bethany, his hand clasped around hers, trying to mimic the somber expressions around him. But inside, he felt no grief or relief—only a vast emptiness. Rob's people were there too, filling the rest of the chairs: men and women from his years at Luca Meat Distribution. Sprinkled among them were federal agents—Aaron could feel their presence, even if they blended in. The gravity of it all pressed down on him, yet he remained motionless, empty, observing.

"We gather today to remember Robert James Bakker, a man with a complex life. While there were challenges, it's important to reflect on the moments that revealed his humanity. To those who knew him, Robert was a hard-working man with a fierce dedication to his work.

His strong leadership spanned across multiple locations in the U.S. and Canada. He guided teams with the same determination that won decades of career success."

"Beyond work, Robert enjoyed fishing and playing tennis, approaching both with his no-nonsense attitude. He shared these passions with his sons, Nicolaus and Lucas. Moments like these show the man beneath the toughness. He could be generous, as when he organized a charity dinner after the passing of his friend and colleague, Jeanette Masterson. These are the memories we hold on to today."

"Robert was a loving husband and father, and only last year, his wife of 29 years, Marlena Bakker, preceded him in death. Grief is never simple. Today, our hearts—and those of his five children and six grandchildren—are heavy. But even in the pain, we gather to honor the parts of Robert's life that brought light and connection."

"There were difficult times in Robert's life, but today is not for judgment. It is for remembering the man we knew, supporting one another through loss, and focusing on healing. In times like these, we must turn to each other for strength and seek the peace that comes from understanding and forgiveness. May we find comfort in our shared memories and move forward with love and compassion."

As the funeral director concluded his speech, the cemetery workers began the somber task of lowering the casket into the ground. An eerie silence marked the scene, broken only by the occasional rustle of the wind. Renee dabbed at her eyes, her shoulders trembling, while Lucas stood beside her, weeping, his arm wrapped around his daughter.

The director stepped forward to take a shovelful of dirt from the mound beside the grave and cast it into the hole. He then invited those present to follow suit, to partake in the last act of farewell.

Lucas was the first to step forward. Tears streaked his face as he approached the grave. With a heavy heart, he looked down into the open space where his father would rest. "I love you, Dad," he whispered. With a shaking hand, he took a spadeful of dirt and let it fall into the grave.

Renee moved forward next, her hands trembling as she took a spadeful of dirt and scattered it into the grave. Her children, Elisabeth and Samuel, followed, each one placing their small contribution of earth onto the casket.

Nico approached after them, his face contorted with a grief so profound it overwhelmed Aaron. He stood at the edge of the grave, struggling with his emotions. Andy, ever supportive, guided him closer to the hole. With Julian at his side, Nico took a spadeful of dirt and let it fall, his movements slow. Despite the years of estrangement and the disapproval he faced, Nico and Andy stood together, honoring a complicated relationship with their quiet goodbye.

The director's gaze fell on Aaron, waiting for him to rise. But Aaron remained seated, his expression stoic. He wasn't ready to reconcile with his stepfather, and the path to peace seemed uncertain, if not impossible. The director turned his attention to the next row of mourners. They approached the grave in a line, their hushed voices blending into a soft murmur as they offered their last goodbyes to Robert Bakker.

As the crowd thinned and the chairs emptied, only Aaron, Bethany, and the woman in the black veil remained. The woman stood up and made as if to leave, but then hesitated. She turned and walked back toward the gaping hole in the frozen ground. Her movements were deliberate, her steps slow, as if drawn back by a force she couldn't quite name.

Bethany gave Aaron a puzzled look, but he could only shrug in response. He didn't recognize the woman, and her presence was a mystery. Rising from his seat, he moved toward her as she spoke. Her voice, though shaky, had an angry edge that cut through the somber atmosphere.

"You had eight children, you bastard," she said, her words bitter. "You hurt us. Then you left us, and we never heard from you again. There are not six grandchildren; there are twelve. I loved you, and you didn't deserve it, and I wish I'd never met you. I don't know where you're going, but I'm sure it's hotter than here."

With a final, vehement shove, she dropped the spadeful of dirt into the grave, the clump landing with a heavy thud.

She turned to leave, her gaze meeting Aaron's. Her eyes were sharp with anger and sadness, her face lined with years of hardship. "I'm sorry you had to hear that. I've been waiting to say it for almost 30 years."

"It's okay," Aaron said, extending his left hand. "What's your name?"

"Carmelina Moretti," she replied, taking his hand with a firm squeeze. "I am the former Mrs. Bakker. We were married for ten disastrous years, a long time ago. We had three children."

"I'm sorry," Aaron said. "Rob was... not a good man."

"He was a monster," Carmelina said in a flat tone. "You're better off without him in your life." She nodded at him, then at Bethany, before turning and walking toward a black Lincoln Town Car parked along the curb.

Aaron looked at Bethany, who was watching Carmelina leave. "Damn," she whispered, "quite the legacy he left behind."

"Ain't that the truth?" Aaron replied, bending to lift the shovel. He scooped up a mound of dirt and held it out. "This is the last thing you ever get out of me, Rob. Time is money, after all."

He let the dirt fall onto the still-exposed mahogany casket, each clump settling with a finality that echoed like a heavy, unshakable truth.

June 15, 1996: Marlena

As I reflect on today, I can't help but smile. It was a rare gem of a day, filled with simple, genuine joy. We spent the entire happy day at Knott's Berry Farm.

Aaron and Patty rode the Boomerang roller coaster until their cheeks were pink with exhilaration. They would have kept going if we'd let them, but we dragged them away. The younger kids were in heaven at Camp Snoopy. The petting zoo was a massive hit, even with the older boys. They all had a blast feeding and petting the animals. And the log flume? That was the highlight for everyone.

Rob smiled on the Timber Mountain Log Ride—something I don't see too much. We all got soaked, of course, but it didn't matter one bit. We ate a hearty meal at the Ghost Town Grille, and everyone was so full and content, but we somehow saved room for those delicious funnel cakes.

By the time we were leaving, Elise couldn't walk anymore. She'd run and played her little heart out, and Rob had to carry her to the car. She was out like a light before we even made it out of the park.

Today was a perfect escape from our usual worries, a day where we enjoyed being together and had fun. These moments with my beautiful children are precious. My heart feels full when I look at every one of them.

Aaron finished reading and set the book on the table, his gaze sweeping over the familiar faces of the people he loved most. The Blue Ridge Diner was empty, a quiet haven for their family, cleared out by the FBI agents to give the Callahan-Bakker family one last meal together.

Patty, his arm draped around Elise's shoulders, grinned. "I remember that! The Boomerang — hell yeah, buddy! We kept betting each other on who'd tap out first, but neither of us wanted to give in, so we kept riding and riding until Mom made us quit." He laughed, the memory still bringing him joy. "You guys wanted to ride too, but you were too little. And Nico, man, you were so mad about it."

"Was not!" Nico chuckled. "Besides, I got to ride the Twister, and you guys were too big for that one — you missed out! Right, Luke?"

Lucas raised an eyebrow, recalling. "Was that the little coaster that went right by the petting zoo?"

Nico nodded, enthusiasm in his eyes. "Yep, Mom took Elise down there, and she kept waving at every car, thinking we were in them all."

Elise joined in the laughter, her face lighting up with a playful grin as she mimed waving at the imaginary rollercoasters. "I was FIVE, guys. Five years old. Besides, I got to pet the pigs and goats without you stinky boys." She wafted her nose, adding to the humor.

"Oh c'mon now, you don't mind stinky boys so much anymore, do you?" Renee teased with a wink, and Lucas jumped in, "Right, you got Patty right next to you, and whoo boy, did he stink when he was a teenager? Damn, sharing a room with him and Aaron was something!"

Patty interjected, "You've got a lot of room to talk, Mister Track and Field Preteen. You could give life to a dead man with what you had going on in those armpits. I hope he's learned to wash better, for your sake, Renee."

"He does alright. I don't mind a little man stink," Renee grinned at Lucas and the entire group laughed.

"How's Aaron doing in the stank department these days, Bethany?" Andy asked with a grin, prompting a sarcastic side-eye from Bethany.

"Oh, he's the cleanest man I've ever had the pleasure of..." Bethany began, but Lucas cut her off with a loud laugh.

"Of lying about! Come on, girl, you don't have to bullshit us. We remember ol' Aaron's pits. He'd come in from playing basketball all day in the blazing sun, and we'd know he was coming before he even turned onto the block."

Nico chimed in, laughing, "He's over there like, 'I scored this many points,' and Luke and I would hide under our blankets like, 'Yeah, boy, that's cool, go shower.'"

The room erupted in laughter again, the playful teasing bringing everyone closer together in the shared memory.

"The one who suffered the most was Mom," Patty said, drawing everyone's attention to him. He cracked a grin. "She had to do our stank-ass laundry. Four boys in the house, plus the ten fluid pounds of Juicy Couture Elise poured onto her body every day of the 2000s. Bet she had stock in laundry detergent... someone check the files, see if we're all about to be 'Tide rich'!"

Laughter erupted around the table once more, as everyone imagined Marlena juggling the endless laundry.

"She never complained either," Nico said, his voice tinged with nostalgia. "All the crap we pulled, all the crap Dad pulled... she took it all on the chin and kept going."

"Remember those stuffed bell peppers she made?" Renee reminisced, a smile on her face. "And I don't even like bell peppers!"

"Or that dry pot roast," Patty added with a chuckle. "You know she could have made the best pot roast in the world, but Dad liked it a certain way. The man had broken taste buds."

The siblings groaned in unison, recalling the memory.

"But her macaroni and cheese casserole?" Elise said with

excitement. "Oh my God, it was the best thing ever! And the meatloaf!"

"Don't forget that trail mix she'd make every Christmas," Lucas added. "She'd hand it out to the neighbors, and I was always like, no, keep it all, we'll eat it. Don't give it away!"

Aaron lifted his glass of wine high. "To Mom... she was the best mom, the smartest mom, the wisest mom, politics notwithstanding," he laughed, his gaze warm.

Nico raised his glass to join in. "Amen! She was the most accepting mom, never judged me, even when she didn't understand why I was different."

"Best grandma too," Elisabeth chimed in from the kids' table, lifting her Sprite and waving her hand for the other kids to join. "And she had the coolest Christmas decorations!"

"Grandma had the big fork and spoon," John, Elise's little boy, called out, holding his cup high in memory of the giant decorative utensils Marlena had hung on her kitchen wall.

"Best big fork and spoon," Drew said. "I asked her once if I could eat from them. She said no, that they belonged to a giant who gave them to her to take care of, and he might be upset if she let a little boy use them. It made sense to me; I never asked again."

"She told me the same," Elizabeth said. "I always wondered why the giant didn't come for them."

The adults laughed, standing to clink their glasses.

"To Marlena Giorgio Callahan Bakker," Aaron said, smiling at his family. "You weren't always perfect, but you were perfect for us."

"To Mom!" everyone called out in unison.

"To Grandma!" the kids echoed, their voices ringing.

They settled back into their seats, the laughter and chatter resuming as they finished their meals and dug into dessert. A warm, communal atmosphere filled the room; a rare sense of normalcy after years of emotional rollercoasters.

When Agent Collins appeared in the doorway to get Patty's attention, the room fell quiet, the lighthearted mood shifting to sober understanding.

"Party's not over, folks," Patty said, a broad smile lighting up his face. "We won't be gone forever—just until this case wraps up. And hey Aaron," he continued, addressing his brother in front of everyone, "I'm not mad at you. It was stupid to buy into what Dad was selling. I had no clue about all the shit he was involved in." He shrugged. "I wanted the money, you know? The cocaine was a bonus," he chuckled. "Forget I said that, kids. Drugs are bad."

Patty's gaze softened as he turned back to Aaron. "You saved our family, man. You put that bastard Kevin in prison... he's looking down the barrel of multiple life sentences without parole. Praise the justice system. We'll get through this. We'll be back together again—bigger, stronger, and more functional than before."

Aaron nodded, his eyes reflecting a mix of gratitude and affection. "I love you too, Patty."

Patty tipped his head in acknowledgment. "I love all of you."

Agent Collins approached. His presence was a reminder of the impending departure. "Elise, Sean... we need to get going."

Patty stood and pulled Elise up by the hand. "C'mon, sis. Let's blow this popsicle stand."

The others stood as well, hugging one another and exchanging heartfelt goodbyes. Elise gathered her children, handing baby Lily to Drew. She then took Patty's hand, ready to walk with the agent toward the door.

They turned back one last time, giving their family a wave before stepping through the door into the uncertainty of their future.

44

Two months after the family dinner, Aaron's cast came off, and after another three weeks of physical therapy, his hand was as good as new —though it still ached in rainy or cold weather.

Four months later, Kevin Earls went on trial. The proceedings for his multiple federal offenses had been intense. A jury sentenced him to eight life sentences without the possibility of parole. Aaron felt the sentence wasn't long enough.

Tom Littleton had been on the run for seven months after his dramatic exit from Robert Bakker's service. A jury sentenced him to four consecutive life sentences for his extensive criminal activities. Justice had been served, but the scars of the past remained.

Patty and Elise remained with Witness Protection Services to ensure their safety. More trials were coming for the executives of Luca Meat Distribution. The fallout from the cases was significant—it was unclear what the future held for the company.

In October, Aaron had closed on a block of eight rowhomes in north Philadelphia. At the head of the street sat the rowhome where he and his mother, Marlena, had grown up. The properties were in rough shape. Winter had slowed progress, but by summer, interior renovations were underway.

The crew completed the first rowhome—Aaron's new home—in late June. He had driven down to see the finished product and the progress on the rest of the block. He swung by to pick up Bethany before heading to the site. They walked through the front door of the corner rowhome, the smell of fresh paint in the air.

"It looks incredible," Bethany said, her eyes wide with delight as she traced her fingers over the sleek quartz countertops in the kitchen. "The paint colors we picked look even better than I imagined."

"Yeah, it's amazing," Aaron agreed, taking in the transformation. "It's nothing like how I remember it from my childhood. Give me a second. Let me call Jeff and see how the rest of the block is coming."

He pulled out his phone, dialing his foreman, while Bethany admired the fresh paint and new fixtures with obvious excitement. After a few rings, Jeff answered, his voice cheerful.

"Hey, boss! How's it going?"

"Hey, Jeff. The first one is perfect, man. Looks amazing!"

"Thanks, boss. We busted ass on that one—the boss' place has to be perfect, you know?" He chuckled. "I'm glad you like it."

"Love it! I wanted to check on the other houses. How are things going?" Aaron asked, glancing around at the pristine drywall and refinished wooden stairs leading to the second floor.

"Things are looking good," Jeff said. "We're wrapping up the main floor renovations on the next three rowhomes. The drywall's up, and we've started the painting. The kitchen cabinet installation will be next week."

"That's great news," Aaron said, nodding in approval. "How are we on the plumbing and electrical work?"

"Plumbing's all set—had a few minor issues, but nothing we couldn't handle. Electrical's moving along too," Jeff replied. "We hit a bit of a snag with the roofing. It's behind on the far end of the block, but we'll catch up next week."

Aaron looked over at Bethany, who was inspecting the new fixtures. "Okay, so we're still on track for the end of summer, right?"

"Yes, sir," Jeff assured him. "We're aiming to have everything ready by mid-September. I'll send over the updated timeline later today so you can see how things are shaping up."

"Perfect. Thanks, Jeff," Aaron said, feeling a weight lift off his shoulders. "I appreciate the update. Not sure of the moving timeline, but I'll swing by next week to check on things again."

"Sounds good. I'll talk to you soon," Jeff said before ending the call.

Aaron pocketed his phone and turned to Bethany. "He says everything's moving along well. The main floors of the next three are almost done, and they're working on the kitchen and bedrooms next."

She smiled, pleased. "That's fantastic. It's feeling real now."

They continued their walk through the house, Aaron pointing out the new installations. "We refinished the wooden floors here and restored the old porcelain claw-foot tub. I don't know about you, but I can't wait to try it out."

Bethany ran her hand over the live-edge mantel of the fireplace in the main bedroom, framed on either side by built-in bookcases. "It's all so beautiful. I don't even know what to say."

Aaron grinned, feeling a mix of relief and anticipation. "I have something for you." He held out a glittering green glass figurine of a cat peeking from a boot. It was the one he had spotted over a year ago in Doylestown, and he had waited all this time for the right moment. "I thought of you when I saw it... it seemed to call out your name."

She took the figurine, turning it over, one hand covering her mouth. "It's Fenton, right? My mother has some of these. They come in... like a zillion colors. It's gorgeous, Aaron."

"These bookshelves... I'll have my mother's Betty Boop collection on one side, but I thought. Well, I thought you could start a new collection."

She kissed him then, and the lack of a bed or mattress in the main bedroom did nothing to slow their passion. After their tour of the rowhome, Aaron and Bethany strolled down the sidewalk, hand in hand. The sun shone on their faces, and the hum of summer filled the air.

At the end of the block, an artist friend of Bethany's was hard at work painting a vibrant mural on the outer wall of the last rowhome. The mural was a swirling blend of colors and abstract shapes that danced across the wall in a burst of energy and creativity.

Aaron and Bethany stopped to admire the mural, captivated by how it transformed the once drab wall into a lively piece of art. The artist, a man in his early thirties with paint splattered on his clothes, glanced up and gave them a friendly nod.

"Hey, that's looking amazing!" Bethany called out, her eyes shining with appreciation.

"Thanks! I'm glad you think so," the artist replied, stepping back to survey his work. "I wanted to add some color and life to this block. It's been great seeing the neighborhood come together."

Aaron looked around, noticing how the mural brightened up the entire street. "It makes a difference. It's like a breath of fresh air for the block."

Bethany squeezed Aaron's hand, beaming. "I'm so happy you like it. It feels like we're starting a new chapter."

Aaron nodded, feeling the same sense of optimism. "Yeah, it does. I can't wait to see what's next for this place."

They lingered for a few more moments, soaking in the creative energy of the mural before continuing their walk down the street, their hearts light with the promise of what lay ahead.

Turning the corner, they heard the rhythmic thud of leather on asphalt. A group of teenagers played a game of basketball; their movements were swift and fluid, like a choreographed dance. The ball zipped between players with the grace and precision of a well-oiled machine. Each dribble and pass added to the electric atmosphere of the game.

Aaron and Bethany stopped to watch, their faces lit with amusement as the teenagers showcased their skills. During a brief break, one player waved his arm, inviting them to join. Aaron laughed, shaking his head, but then hesitated. He hadn't played basketball in ages, but the sight of the game ignited a spark of nostalgia within him.

He turned to Bethany, his eyes twinkling with excitement. "You want to play?"

She grinned and nodded, and they jogged over to the court. The summer heat warmed their faces and the sound of the game buzzed around them. As they approached, the teenagers welcomed them with cheers and playful taunts.

They dropped into the rhythm of the match. The basketball court was a patchwork of worn asphalt and vibrant graffiti, the summer sun casting long shadows as the game intensified. Bethany's curls were damp with sweat, sticking to her forehead and framing her face in a wild halo. She laughed as she darted around the court, her movements agile.

The teenagers, eager for fresh competition, passed the ball between them with impressive speed. Aaron grinned, the familiar thrill of the game flooding back as he dashed up and down the court, his legs pumping in time with the dribbles and shouts around him. Bethany was a natural. She maneuvered around defenders with a surprising grace, her sweat-slicked curls bouncing with every move.

At one point, a kid with a bright red headband caught Aaron's eye. He made a swift pass, sending the ball hurtling towards Aaron from the edge of the key. Aaron grabbed it, then glanced around, assessing the defense. He took a deep breath and stepped back to the free-throw line.

He released the ball with a smooth, practiced motion, watching it arc through the air. It swished through the hoop, the satisfying sound of the netting confirming his shot. The court erupted in cheers and high-fives, and Aaron turned to Bethany. Her face beamed with exhilaration.

She leaned in and kissed him, their laughter mingling as they moved out of the way to embrace on the side of the court. The heat of the game and the warmth of their closeness felt perfect, and Aaron nuzzled his face against her sweaty neck, inhaling the faint scent of summer and exertion.

Over her shoulder, he saw Alex and Jared standing off to the side. Alex leaned against the chain-link fence, his legs crossed at the ankles, while Jared stood beside him, one foot propped up on a bench. They both had amused expressions on their faces.

Alex, grinning, hollered, "You gonna ask her or what, chicken?"

Jared chimed in with a playful yell, "Do it, man!"

Aaron chuckled, his heart pounding with excitement and nerves. He reached into the pocket of his cargo shorts and pulled out a small velvet ring box. Dropping to one knee, he opened the box to reveal a sparkling engagement ring; the diamond catching the light.

Bethany's eyes widened in surprise, her breath catching in her throat. Aaron looked up at her, his eyes filled with love and anticipation. "Bethany, will you marry me?" he asked, his voice sure despite the whirlwind of emotions.

The court fell silent, and the cheers from the game faded into a background hum as Bethany's face lit up with joy. She nodded, tears of happiness welling up in her eyes. "I thought you'd never ask, Aaron Callahan," she whispered, her voice choked with emotion. He slipped the ring onto her finger, and the crowd erupted in applause and cheers, celebrating the moment with them.

This neighborhood had been a place of painful memories and unfinished dreams. Now it was a canvas for new beginnings. With their fresh paint and bustling energy, the old rowhomes transformed into a symbol of hope and renewal.

Aaron glanced around, seeing the streets and sidewalks of his childhood from a new perspective. He could sense his mother's presence, a comforting whisper in the summer breeze, reminding him she would be proud of the man he had become. The ghosts of his past seemed to dissolve into the background, replaced by the promise of a brighter future.

With a contented sigh, Aaron turned to Bethany, his heart full of love and gratitude. He cupped her face and kissed her, savoring the moment. Then, with a smile, he took her hand, squeezing it in a silent promise of the life they would build together.

"Let's get back to the game," he said, his eyes sparkling.

Hand in hand, they jogged back to the court, joining the game with renewed enthusiasm. The sun dipped lower in the sky, casting a warm, golden glow over the neighborhood. As they played, Aaron felt a profound sense of belonging and fulfillment. The past had shaped him, but the future was his to embrace, and with Bethany by his side, he knew it would be a beautiful journey.

Thank you for reading Book of Life: Marlena!

If you enjoyed the book, please consider leaving a positive review on Amazon, Goodreads, or your social media! Make sure to tag me on social media: my user name is @heather.obrien.author on all platforms! Reviews are so so important to independent authors, so your review is much appreciated!

If you did not enjoy the book, or have constructive criticism to offer, or even if you just want to talk about the book, please feel free to reach out: heatherobrienauthor@gmail.com.

Thank you for your support!

Heather

Book of Life: The Series
By Heather O'Brien

In a world where memories can be immortalized in a "Book of Life," created using advanced neural chip technology, the past is never truly forgotten. Upon a person's death, these books are sent to a chosen recipient, revealing secrets, truths, and hidden histories that might otherwise have been lost forever.

The 12-book series follows Aaron Callahan and the generations of his family, whose lives are forever altered by the revelations within these books. From uncovering long-buried family secrets to confronting painful truths, each installment unravels the complex tapestry of their shared pasts—leading to discoveries that challenge everything they thought they knew about themselves and each other.

Book 1:
Book of Life: Marlena
https://a.co/d/6p4oFZf

When a mysterious book arrives on his doorstep a year after his mother's death, Aaron finds himself drawn into a past he thought he'd left behind. Within its pages, his mother's hidden memories surface—revealing long-buried secrets and painful truths about his family. As he delves deeper, Aaron uncovers shocking details about his estranged father's past, including a crime his mother witnessed when he was just a child.

Driven by a need for answers, Aaron embarks on a journey to confront the man he once called his dad. But what begins as a search for understanding forces him to confront dark connections that threaten to unravel everything he thought he knew. With each revelation, Aaron edges closer to the truth—but it may come at a cost he never anticipated.

* * *

Book 2:
Book of Life: Lydia
Coming Dec. 2024!
Https://a.co/d/7IyRosd

Aaron never knew his older siblings, Harrison and Lydia, but their secrets are about to change his life. As he plans his wedding, a search for answers about his family's past pulls him deep into the rural South, where long-buried truths are hidden in plain sight. A journal left behind by Lydia reveals a history of betrayal, addiction, and loss, drawing Aaron into a dangerous mystery.

Struggling with his mental health, Aaron's journey unravels disturbing connections between his siblings' past and his future. As the pieces come together, he must decide how far he's willing to go to uncover the secrets that could shatter everything.

Author Profile

Heather O'Brien is a passionate storyteller who loves literary fiction, contemporary fiction, and mysteries. Growing up in Greenville, South Carolina, Heather found solace and adventure in the world of books, which later sparked a desire to create worlds of her own.

After spending 20 years as a stay-at-home mom to three, she began her writing journey, focusing on family, grief, and identity issues.

Heather's stories often tackle family drama, generational trauma, childhood memories, and the complexities of interpersonal relationships. Her published works reflect a unique blend of literary fiction, drawing readers into thought-provoking and emotional narratives.

Currently, Heather is working on her Book of Life series. When not writing, she enjoys reading and traveling to exciting places.

Amazon	https://www.amazon.com/author/heather-obrien
Threads	https://www.threads.net/@heather.obrien.author
Patreon	https://www.patreon.com/heatherobrien
Website	https://heatherlakinobrien.wordpress.com
Listen to Aaron's Playlist on Spotify!	https://open.spotify.com/playlist/5GOrODLaV8TjW4Rn8xzhZ2?si=71669644a3da4128

Acknowledgments

My partner, George: thank you for being my sounding board for the three years this story has been rumbling around in my head. Without you to bounce ideas off, I could not have developed my passing ideas into this amazing book. You are my motivation and my favorite person to read to.

My kids: Owyn, Addah, and Katie, I love you each dearly and I would not be half the person I am today without you. I am infinitely proud to be your mother.

David: Thank you for being my most excellent support system for over three decades. Who even was I before you awkwardly flirted with me in 1993? You've been my friend for so long that I can't imagine life without you (and I don't want to).

My editor: Wolfgang Barrowe, you are an invaluable source of help. I don't know how many "just, like, very, barely, sort of" bloat words had to be cut from my first draft, but you hung in there and got the job done. You're the master of comma splices and sentence variance and you've made me a better writer. Thank you for spotting my plot holes!

To my friends: Tore, Daniel, Melissa, Nicole, Badass Vivian, and the Segundo family—you have been there for me along the different paths of my life's journey, and you all hold a special place in my heart.

Content Warning

This book contains adult themes that may be difficult for some readers. Reader's discretion is advised.

- Profanity
- Child Abuse
- Domestic Violence
- Childhood Sexual Abuse (vague, not explicit)
- Mental Health Issues
- Infant Loss
- Loss of Parent
- Violence & Murder
- Drug & Alcohol Use

While I have done my best to handle these subjects with care, I understand if you are uncomfortable reading these themes. Reading should be fun, and I do not wish to cause harm to anyone with my book.

If you or someone you know struggles with these issues, resources are available for you. Here are some places you can go for help.

Crisis Text Line (For All Issues)

Text HELP to 741741

Learn more about the Crisis Text Line or apply to volunteer at www.crisistextline.org

RAINN (Rape, Abuse, and Incest National Network)

(800) 656-4673 Website/Live Chat

Childhelp National Child Abuse Hotline

(800) 422-4453 (Call or Text) Website/Live Chat

National Domestic Abuse Hotline

(800) 799-7233 Website/Live Chat

Milton Keynes UK
Ingram Content Group UK Ltd.
UKHW020154291024
450401UK00008B/164